THE CORPS

BOOK I
SEMPER FI

by

W.E.B. GRIFFIN

JOVE BOOKS, NEW YORK

THE BERKLEY PUBLISHING GROUP
Published by the Penguin Group
Penguin Group (USA) LLC
375 Hudson Street, New York, New York 10014

USA • Canada • UK • Ireland • Australia • New Zealand • India • South Africa • China

penguin.com

A Penguin Random House Company

SEMPER FI

A Jove Book / published by arrangement with the author

Jove Books are published by The Berkley Publishing Group.
JOVE® is a registered trademark of Penguin Group (USA) LLC.
The "J" design is a trademark of Penguin Group (USA) LLC.

For information, address: The Berkley Publishing Group,
a division of Penguin Group (USA) LLC,
375 Hudson Street, New York, New York 10014.

ISBN: 978-0-515-08749-9

PUBLISHING HISTORY
Jove mass-market edition / November 1986

PRINTED IN THE UNITED STATES OF AMERICA

60 59 58 57 56 55 54 53 52 51

THE CORPS *is respectfully dedicated to the memory of*
Second Lieutenant Drew James Barrett, III, USMC
Company K, 3rd Battalion, 26th Marines.
Born Denver, Colorado, 3 January 1945,
Died Quang Nam Province,
Republic of Vietnam, 27 February 1969
and
Major Alfred Lee Butler, III, USMC
Headquarters 22nd Marine Amphibious Unit.
Born Washington, D.C., 4 September 1950,
Died Beirut, Lebanon, 8 February 1984

"Semper Fi!"

PREFACE

In 1900, with the approval of the Dowager Empress of China, a Chinese militia, the I Ho Chuan, (or "Righteous Harmony Fists," hence "Boxer") began, under the motto "Protect the country, destroy the foreigner!" to kill both Westerners and Chinese Christians. The German ambassador in Peking was murdered, as were thousands of Chinese Christians throughout China, and the Boxers laid siege to the Legation Quarter at Peking.

The ninety-day siege of Peking was relieved on August 14, 1900, by an international force made up of Russian, French, Italian, German, English, and American troops.

The Imperial Court fled to Sian. Although war had not been declared against China, the "Foreign Powers" nevertheless demanded a formal settlement. The Protocol of 1901 provided, among other things, for the punishment of those responsible for the Boxer Rebellion; the fortification of the Legation Quarter at Peking, to be manned by "Powers" troops; and the maintenance by foreign troops of communication between Peking and the sea.

As far as the Americans were concerned, this initially meant the stationing of U.S. Army troops and U.S. Marines in Shanghai, Peking, and elsewhere; and the formation of the U.S. Navy Yangtze River Patrol. The Navy acquired shallow draft steamers, armed them, designated them "Gun Boats," and ran them up and down the Yangtze River.

The Russians, following their resounding defeat in the Russian–Japanese War of 1905, had for all practical purposes turned over their interests in China to Japan. Furthermore, the Versailles Treaty, which had set the terms of the peace between the Western Allies and the Germans and Austro-

1

Hungarians at the end of The World War of 1914–1918, had also given the Japanese rights over the Shantung Province of China.

The reality of the situation in China in 1941 was that the lines had already been drawn for World War II. It was no secret that Japan's ultimate ambition was to take as much of China as it could, into the "Greater Japanese Co-Prosperity Sphere." It was also no secret that they intended to expel the British, the French, and the Americans when the time was ripe. And they most likely wanted the Italians out, too, although the Italians and the Japanese were on much better terms than either was with the French, the English, or the Americans.

The official hypocrisy was that all were still allies, in very much the same way they had been since the Boxer Rebellion in 1900.

It had been agreed then, when the international military force was formed to relieve Peking, that they were not waging war upon China, but rather simply suppressing the Boxers and protecting their own nationals from the savagery of the Chinese.

Thus the Japanese view in 1941, which no one challenged, was that their actions in China were nothing but extensions of what the "allies" started in 1900. The Japanese were prepared to protect all foreigners from Chinese savagery, and they expected the French, the Italians and the Americans to do likewise.

But because the Imperial Japanese Army's tanks and artillery were doing nothing more than protecting their own, and other foreign nationals, they could logically raise no objection to the Americans or others protecting their nationals with token military forces.

The Japanese carefully restrained themselves, with several notable exceptions, from becoming involved in incidents involving an exchange of gunfire between themselves and troops of the neutral powers. They still paid lip service to international convention, because international convention condoned their occupation of Shantung Province. If an incident came before the League of Nations, it was likely to go off at a tangent into such things as the behavior of the Imperial Japanese Army.

Everyone understood that the Japanese prefer not to openly tell the League of Nations to go to hell. If necessary, of course, they would. But as long as they could avoid doing so, they would.

In January 1941, the American military presence in China consisted of the U.S. Navy Yangtze River Patrol; the U.S. Navy Submarine Force, China and the 4th Regiment USMC (both based in Shanghai); and the U.S. Marine Detachment, Peking.

I

PFC Kenneth J. McCoy, USMC, stood with his hands on his hips staring at the footlocker at the end of his bed. He'd been that way for quite some time; he was trying to make up his mind. McCoy was twenty-one years old, five feet ten and one-half inches tall, and he weighed 156 pounds. He was well built, but lithe rather than muscular. He had even features and fair skin and wore his light brown hair in a crew cut. His eyes were hazel, and bright; and when he was thinking hard, as he was now, one eyebrow lifted and his lip curled as if the problem he faced amused him. He had once been an altar boy at Saint Rose of Lima Church in Norristown, Pennsylvania, and there were traces of that still in him: There was now, as then, a suggestion that just beneath the clean-cut, innocent surface, was an alter ego with horns itching for the chance to jump out and do something forbidden.

It was the day after New Year's, and PFC McCoy had liberty. And it was two days after payday, and he had his "new gambling money" in his pocket. So he wanted to go try his luck. But what he couldn't quite make up his mind about was whether or not he should leave the compound armed, and if so, how.

What had happened was that on Christmas Eve at a dance hall called the "Little Club," there had been a not entirely unexpected altercation between United States Marines and marines assigned to the International Military Force in Shanghai by His Majesty, Victor Emmanuel III, King of the Italians.

4

It wasn't the first time the Americans and the Italians had gotten into it, but this time it had gotten out of hand.

McCoy had heard that as many as eighteen Italians were dead, and there were eight Marines in sick bay, two of them in very serious condition. Rumor had it—and McCoy tended to believe it—that there were bands of Italian marines roaming town looking for U.S. Marines. The officers certainly didn't doubt it. They'd granted permission for Marines to wear cartridge belts (with first-aid pouches) and bayonets. A sheathed bayonet made a pretty good club; a drawn bayonet was an even better personal defense weapon. But sending the men out with bayonets, sheathed or unsheathed, was far short of sending them out with rifles, loaded or otherwise.

McCoy had not been at the Little Club on Christmas Eve, partly because a Marine who wanted to celebrate Christmas Eve by getting drunk had offered him three dollars (McCoy had negotiated the offer upward to five) to take the duty. But even without the offer, McCoy wouldn't have gone to the Little Club on Christmas Eve. He had known from experience that the place would either be depressing as hell, and/or that there would be a fight between the Marines and the Italians. Or between the Marines and the Seaforth Highlanders. Or between the Marines and the French Foreign Legion.

Getting into a brawl on Christmas Eve was not McCoy's idea of good clean fun. And getting into any kind of a brawl right now was worse than a bad idea.

McCoy's blue Marine blouse had two new adornments, the single chevron of a private first class and a diagonal stripe above the cuff signifying the completion of four years' honorable service. He had just shipped over for another four years, with the understanding that once he had shipped over he would be promoted to PFC. With the promotion came the right to take the examination for corporal.

It had also been understood, unofficially, that he would get a high rating when he went before the promotion board for the oral examination. They were willing to give him that, he knew, because no one thought he would stand a chance, first time out, of getting a score on the written exam that would be anywhere close to the kind of score needed to actually get promoted.

Well, they were wrong about that. He wanted to be a

corporal very much, and he had prepared for the examination. The tough part of it was "military engineering," which mostly meant math questions. He had a flair for math, and he thought it was likely that he hadn't missed a single question. But McCoy had more going for him. When the promotion board sat down at Marine Barracks in Washington to establish the corporal's promotion list, they paid special attention to something called "additional qualifications."

McCoy had found out, by carefully reading the regulations, that there was more to this than the sort of skills you might expect, skills like making Expert with the .45 and the Springfield. You got points for that, of course, and he would get them, because he was a pretty good shot.

But you also got points if you could type sixty words per minute or better. When he took the test, he had been rated at seventy-five words a minute. He had kept that ability a secret before reenlisting, because he hadn't joined the Marine Corps to be a clerk. But even that wasn't his real ace in the hole. What that was, was "foreign language skills."

"Foreign language skills," he was convinced, was going to make him a corporal long before anyone else in the 4th Marines thought he had a chance. His mother had been French, and he'd learned that from her as a baby. Then he'd taken Latin at Saint Rose of Lima High School because they made him, and French because he thought that would be easy.

When he'd come to Shanghai, he had not been surprised that he could talk French with the French Foreign Legionnaires, but he *had* been surprised that he could also make himself understood in Italian, and that he could read Italian documents and even newspapers. And that still wasn't all of it.

Like every other Marine who came to the 4th, he had soon found himself exchanging half his pay for a small apartment and a Chinese girl to share the bed, do the laundry, and otherwise make herself useful. Mai Sing could also read and write, which wasn't always the case with Chinese girls. Before he had decided that he really didn't want a wife just yet—not even a temporary one—and sent Mai Sing back wherever the hell she had come from with two hundred dollars to buy herself a husband, she had taught him not only to speak the Shanghai version of Cantonese, but how to read and write a fair amount of the ideograms as well.

There was a standard U.S. Government language exam, and he'd gone to the U.S. Consulate and taken it. So far as the U.S. Government was concerned, he was "completely fluent" in spoken and written French, which was as high a rating as they gave; "nearly fluent" in spoken and written Italian; "nearly fluent" in spoken Cantonese; and had a 75/55 grade in written Cantonese, which meant that he could read seventy-five percent of the ideograms on the exam, and could come up with the ideogram for a specific word more than half the time.

The guy at the consulate had been so impressed with McCoy's Chinese that he tried to talk him into taking a job with the Marine guard detachment. He could get him transferred, the guy said, and he wouldn't have to pull guard once he got to the consulate. They always needed clerks who could read and write Chinese.

McCoy had turned that down, too. He hadn't joined the Corps to be a clerk in a consulate, either.

The promotion list would be out any day now. He was sure that his name was going to be near the top of it, and he didn't want anything to fuck that up. Like getting in a brawl with a bunch of Italian marines would fuck it up.

They wouldn't make him a corporal if he was dead, either, and the way this brawl was going, getting meaner and meaner by the day, that was a real possibility.

There were two things wrong with going out wearing a cartridge belt and bayonet, he decided in the end. For one thing, he would look pretty silly walking into the poker game at the Cathay Mansions Hotel with that shit. And if he did run into some Italian marines, they would take his possession of a bayonet as a sure sign he was looking for a fight.

McCoy finally bent over the footlocker and took his "Baby Fairbairn" from beneath a stack of neatly folded skivvy shirts. He had won it from a Shanghai Municipal cop after a poker game. He'd bet a hundred yuan against it, one cut of the deck.

There was an officer named Bruce Fairbairn on the Shanghai Municipal Police, and he had invented a really terrific knife, sort of a dagger, and was trying to get everybody to buy them. He had made quite a sales pitch to General Smedley Butler, who commanded all the Marines in China. And Butler, so the story went, had wanted to buy enough to issue them, but the Marine Corps wouldn't give him the money.

McCoy's knife was made exactly like the original Fairbairn, except that it wasn't quite as long, or quite as big. It was just long enough to be concealed in the sleeve, with the tip of the scabbard up against the joint of the elbow, and the handle just inside the cuff.

McCoy took off his blouse, strapped the Baby Fairbairn to his left arm, put the blouse back on over it, looked at himself in the full-length mirror mounted on the door, and left his room.

Their billets had once been two-story brick civilian houses that the 4th Marines had bought when they came to China way back in 1927—blocks of them, enough houses to hold a battalion. Cyclone fences had been erected around these blocks. And the fences were topped with coils of barbed wire, called concertina. At the gate was a sandbagged guardhouse, manned around the clock by a two-man guard detail.

As McCoy walked through, the PFC on guard told him he had heard that the Wops had ganged up on some Marines and put another two guys in the hospital. If he were McCoy, he went on, he would go back and get his bayonet.

"I'm not going anywhere near the Little Club," McCoy said. "And I'm not looking for a fight."

The faster of two rickshaw boys near the gate trotted up and lowered the poles.

"Take me to the Cathay Mansions Hotel," McCoy ordered in Chinese as he climbed onto the rickshaw.

The guard understood "Cathay Mansions Hotel."

"What the fuck are you going to do there, McCoy?" he asked.

"They're having a tea dance," McCoy said, as the rickshaw boy picked up the poles and started to trot down Ferry Road in the direction of the Bund.

As they approached the hotel, McCoy called out to the rickshaw boy to pull to the curb at the corner. He paid him and then walked down the sidewalk past the marquee, and then into an alley, which led to the rear of the building. He went down a flight of stairs to a steel basement door and knocked on it.

A small window opened in the door, and Chinese eyes became visible. McCoy was examined, and then the door opened. He walked down a long corridor, ducking his head from time to time to miss water and sewer pipes, until he came to another steel door, this one identified as "Store Room B-6." He knocked, and it opened for him.

United States Marines were not welcome upstairs in the deeply carpeted, finely paneled lobby and corridors of the Cathay Mansions Hotel. The often-expressed gratitude of the Europeans of the International Settlement for the protection offered by the United States Marines against both the Japanese and Chiang Kai-shek's Kuomintang did not go quite as far as accepting enlisted Marines as social equals.

PFC Ken McCoy was welcome here, however, in a basement storeroom that had been taken over with the tacit permission of Sir Victor Sassoon, owner of the hotel, by its doorman, a six-foot-six White Russian. The storeroom was equipped with an octagonal, green baize-covered table and chairs. A rather ornate light fixture had been carefully hung so as to bathe the table in a light that made the cards and the hands that manipulated them fully visible without causing undue glare.

McCoy was welcome because he always brought to the table fifty dollars American—sometimes a good deal more— which he was prepared to lose with a certain grace and without whining.

In the nearly four years that he had been in China, McCoy had evolved a gambling system that had resulted in a balance of nearly two thousand dollars at Barclays Bank. He thought of this as his retirement program.

He began each month's gambling with fifty dollars, twenty-five of which came from his pay (by the time they had made the deductions, this now came to about forty-nine dollars) and twenty-five of which came from the retirement fund in Barclays Bank.

He played until he either went broke or felt like quitting. If he was ahead of his original fifty dollars when he quit, he put exactly half of the excess over fifty dollars away, to be deposited to his account at Barclays. The rest was his stash for the next game.

Almost always, he went broke sometime during the month, and he never played again until after the next payday. But again, he had almost always put a lot more into Barclays Bank during the month than the twenty-five dollars he would take out after the next payday. And sometimes—not often—the cards went well, and post-game deposits were sixty, seventy dollars. Once there had been a post-game deposit of $140.90.

As he approached the group, the bright light illuminating the table made everything but the lower arms and hands of the players seem to disappear for a moment into the darkness, but gradually his eyes became adjusted, and he could see faces to go with the hands.

The White Russian, who claimed to have been a colonel of cavalry in his Imperial Majesty's 7th Petrograd Cavalry, was at the table. Piotr Petrovich Muller (he had a German surname, he once told McCoy, because he was a descendant of the Viennese who had been imported into Moscow to build the Kremlin) was a very large man with a very closely shaven face.

He bowed his head solemnly when he saw McCoy and then gestured for him to take an empty chair.

There was another Russian who had found post-revolution employment with the French Foreign Legion, and a Sikh, a uniformed sergeant of the Shanghai Municipal Police. There was also Detective Sergeant Lester Chatworth of the Shanghai Municipal Police, who looked up at McCoy and spoke.

"I thought you'd be out bashing Eye-talians."

Except for a thick, perfectly trimmed mustache, Chatworth looked not unlike McCoy, but he spoke with the flat, nasal accent of Liverpool.

"I thought I'd rather come here and take your money," McCoy said.

"Why not? Everybody else is," Detective Sergeant Chatworth said, grinning.

The men at the table had nothing at all in common except that they met Piotr Muller's rigid standard of a decent poker player: Each could play the game well enough and each, at one time or another, had lost a good deal of money gracefully. PFC Kenneth McCoy was younger than any of them by at least a decade, and a quarter of a century younger than Muller. Neither he nor any of the others associated when they were not playing cards, nor were they friendly with any of the perhaps forty other more or less temporary residents of Shanghai who were welcome at Muller's table in the basement of the Cathay Mansions.

There were no raised eyebrows when McCoy took off his blue blouse and revealed the Baby Fairbairn strapped to his arm. It was prudent, if technically illegal, to arm oneself when going out for a night on the town in Shanghai.

McCoy hung his blouse on the back of his chair, unstrapped the knife and tucked it in a pocket of the blouse, then sat down and laid his gambling money on the table. Fifty dollars American that month had converted to just over four hundred yuan. He had before him four one-hundred-yuan notes, which were printed lavender and white in England and were each the size of a British five-pound banknote. He also had some change, including an American dollar bill.

He made himself comfortable in the chair, and then watched as the hand in play was completed. When it was over, Muller nodded at him, and he reached for a fresh deck of cards, broke the seal, and went through them, finding and discarding the extra jokers. He then spread the cards out for the others to examine.

Afterward, he gathered the cards together, shuffled, announced, "Straight poker," and dealt.

Three hours later, there were twenty-odd lavender-and-white one-hundred-yuan notes in front of McCoy; the Sikh and the Foreign Legionnaire had gone bust; and it was between McCoy, Piotr Petrovich Muller, and Detective Sergeant Chatworth. A half hour after that, Muller examined the two cards he had drawn, threw his hand on the table, and pushed himself away from it.

That left only McCoy and Detective Sergeant Chatworth.

"I don't play two-handed poker," McCoy announced.

"I'm willing to quit," Chatworth said, and tossed the just-collected deck into the wastebasket, where it joined a dozen other decks of cards.

Stiff from three hours of little movement, McCoy stood up and stretched his arms over his head. He then strapped the

Baby Fairbairn to his left arm, put his blouse on, and followed the others out of the storeroom.

When he was back out on the street, McCoy considered having his ashes hauled. It had been about a week, and it was time to take care of the urge. But he decided against it. For one thing, he had too much money with him. He hadn't counted it out to the last yuan, but he'd won a bunch—say at twelve dollars to the hundred-yuan note, a little better than $250. That was too much money to have in your pocket when visiting a whorehouse.

Even if the Italian marines weren't on the warpath.

The smart thing to do was go back to the billet. He put his hand up and flagged a rickshaw, and told the driver to take him down Ferry Road.

Three blocks from the compound, he saw the Italian marines, hiding in an alley. There were four of them, in uniform. The uniforms were a mixture of army and navy—army breeches and navy middie blouses.

I am minding my own business, McCoy told himself, *and I am not carrying a bayonet, and I was not at the Little Club when this whole business started. With a little bit of luck, they will let me pass.*

They didn't say anything to him as the rickshaw pulled past the alley and there could no longer be any question that the rickshaw passenger was a Marine. So for a moment he thought they'd decided to wait for Marines who were looking for a fight.

And then the rickshaw was turned over on its side. The rickshaw boy started to howl with fear and rage even before McCoy hit the ground, striking the elbow of his blouse on the filth of the street.

McCoy sat up and looked around to see if there was someplace he could run. But the Italian marines had picked their spot well. There was no place to run to.

Maybe I can talk to them, McCoy thought, *tell them the fucking truth, I wasn't at the Little Club, I have no quarrel with them.*

Then he saw the Italian marine advancing on him with a length of bicycle chain swinging in his hand. McCoy felt a little faint, and then tasted something foul in the back of his mouth.

"I don't know who you're looking for," he said in Italian. "But it isn't me."

The Italian marine replied that his mother fucked pigs and that he was going to mash his balls.

The bicycle chain missed McCoy's leg, but before it struck the pavement with a frightening whistle, it came close enough to catch his trouser's leg and leave the imprint of the chain there. McCoy quickly slid sideward, taking the Baby Fairbairn from his sleeve as he got to his feet.

The Italian marine told him his sister sucked Greek cocks and that he was going to take the knife away and stick it up his ass.

McCoy sensed, rather than saw, that two other Italian marines were making their way behind him.

The idea was that the two would grab him and hold him while the other one used the bicycle chain. The thing to do was to get past the Italian marine with the bicycle chain.

He made a feinting motion with the knife, and the Italian marine backed up.

It looked like it might work. And there was nothing else to do.

He made another feinting move, a savage leap accompanied by as ferocious a roar as he could muster, at the exact moment that the Italian marine lunged at where McCoy's Baby Fairbairn had been.

The tip of the Baby Fairbairn punctured the Italian marine's chest at the lower extremity of the ribs. McCoy felt it grate over a bone, and then immediately sink to the handguard. The knife was snatched from his hand as the Italian marine continued his plunge.

The man grunted, fell, dropped the bicycle chain, rolled over, sat up, and started to pull the Baby Fairbairn from his abdomen. He gave it a hearty tug and it came out. A moment later, a stream of bright red blood as thick as the handle of a baseball bat erupted from his mouth. The Italian marine looked puzzled for a moment, and then fell to one side.

Jesus Christ, I killed him!

One of the three remaining Italian marines crossed himself and ran away. The other two advanced on McCoy, one of them frantically trying to work the action of a tiny automatic pistol.

I can't run from that!

McCoy picked up the Baby Fairbairn and advanced on the two Italian marines.

He made it to the one with the gun and started to try to take it away from him, or at least to knock it out of his hand. The other one tried to help his friend. McCoy lashed out with the Baby Fairbairn again. The blade slashed the Italian's face, but that didn't discourage him. He got his arms around McCoy's arms and held him in a bear hug.

The other one managed to work the action of his tiny pistol.

McCoy remembered hearing that a .22 or a .25 will kill you just as dead as a .45, it just takes a little longer—say a week—to do it.

With a strength that surprised him, he got his right arm free and swung it backward at the man who had been holding him. He felt it cut and strike something, something not anywhere as hard as the ribcage, but something. And it went in far enough so that he couldn't hang on to it when the man fell down.

Then, free, he jumped at the man with the pistol. The pistol went off with a sharp crack, and he felt something strike his leg hard, like a kick from a very hard boot. And then he knocked the pistol from the Italian marine's hand and, when it clattered onto the cobblestones, dived after it.

He picked it up and aimed it at the Italian marine. Then he followed his eyes. What he had done when he had swung his knife hand backward was stick it in the man's groin. The man was now holding his groin with both hands. The handle of the Baby Fairbairn was sticking out between his fingers. The man was whimpering, and tears were on his face.

Down the street, McCoy could hear the growl of the hand-cranked siren at the compound.

This is going to fuck up my promotion, he thought. *God-damn these Italians.*

(Two)

Captain Edward J. Banning, USMC, was S-2, the staff Intelligence Officer, of the 4th Marines. He was thirty-six years old, tall, thin, and starting to bald. And he had been a Marine since his graduation from the Citadel, the Military

College of South Carolina: a second lieutenant for three years, a first lieutenant for eight years, and he'd worn the twin silver railroad tracks of a captain for four years.

There were four staff officers. The S-1 (Personnel) and S-4 (Supply) were majors. The S-3 (Plans and Training) was a lieutenant colonel. As a captain, Banning was the junior staff officer. But he was a staff officer, and as such normally excused from most of the duties assigned to non-staff officers.

He took his turn, of course, as Officer of the Day, but that was about it. He was, for instance, never assigned as Inventory Officer to audit the accounts of the Officers' or NCO clubs or as Investigating Officer when there was an allegation of misbehavior involving the possibility of a court-martial of one of the enlisted men. Or any other detail of that sort. He was the S-2, and the colonel was very much aware that taking him from that duty to do something else did not make very good sense.

So Banning had been surprised at first when he was summoned by the colonel and told that he would serve as Defense Counsel in the case of the United States of America versus PFC Kenneth J. McCoy, USMC. But he was a Marine officer, and when Marine officers are given an assignment, they say "aye, aye, sir" and set about doing what they have been ordered to do.

"This one can't be swept under the table, Banning," the colonel said. "It's gone too far for that. It has to go by the book, with every 't' crossed and every 'i' dotted."

"I understand, sir."

"Major DeLaney will prosecute. I have ordered him to do his best to secure a conviction. I am now ordering you to do your best to secure an acquittal. The Italian Consul General has told us that he and Colonel Maggiani of the Italian marines will attend the court-martial. Do you get the picture?"

"Yes, sir."

The picture Banning got was that he was going to have to spend Christ alone knew how many hours preparing for this court-martial, participating in the court-martial itself, and then Christ alone knew how many hours after the trial, going through the appeal process.

About half of the total would have to come from the time

Banning would have normally spent with his hobby. His hobby was Ludmilla Zhivkov, whom he called 'Milla.'

Milla was twenty-seven, raven-haired, long-legged and a White Russian. And he had recently begun to consider the possibility that he was in love with her.

Banning was a Marine officer—even worse, a Marine intelligence officer—and Marine intelligence officers were not supposed to become emotionally involved with White Russian women. It had not been his intention to become emotionally involved with her. He had met her, more or less, on duty. There had been an advertisement in the *Shanghai Post*: "Russian Lady Offers Instruction in Russian Conversation.'' It had coincided with an unexpected bonus in his operating funds: two hundred dollars for Foreign Language Training.

There were supposed to be fifteen thousand White Russian refugee women in Shanghai. They made their living as best they could, some successfully and some reduced to making it on their backs. He had somewhat cynically suspected that the Russian Lady offering Russian Conversation was doing so only because she was too old, or too ugly, to make it on her back.

Milla had surprised him. She was a real beauty, and she was the first White Russian he'd met who was not at least a duchess. She was also devoutly religious, which meant that she was not going to become a whore unless it got down to that. Milla told him her father had operated, of all things, the Victor Phonograph store in St. Petersburg. They had come from Russia in 1921 with some American dollars, and it had been enough, with what jobs he had been able to find, to keep them while they waited for their names to work their way up the immigration waiting list for the United States.

And then he had died, and she hadn't been able to make as much money as she had hoped, even working as a billing clerk in the Cathay Mansions Hotel and teaching Russian conversation. When he met her she was down to living in one room. The next step was to become somebody's mistress. After that she'd have to turn into a whore. Becoming a whore would keep her from going to the States.

The first thing Banning had done was pay her the whole two hundred dollars up front. Then one thing had led to another, and they had gone to bed. Soon he had helped her get a larger place to live.

But the ground rules established between them were clear: It was a friendly business relationship and never could be anything more. When he went home, that would be the end of it. She understood that. She had lived up to her end of the bargain. And she would, he believed, stick to it.

Her powerful character, he sometimes thought, was one of the reasons he was afraid he was in love with her. And sometimes he wondered if she wasn't playing him like a fish (she was also the most intelligent woman he had ever known) and nobly living up to her end of the bargain because she had figured that was the one way to get *him* to break it.

But what he nevertheless knew for sure was that if he married her, he could kiss his Marine career good-bye; and that he could not imagine life outside the Corps; and that he could not imagine life without Milla.

For the first time in his life, Ed Banning did not know what the hell to do.

Banning went by the orderly room of "D" Company, First Battalion and read through PFC Kenneth J. McCoy's records slowly and thoroughly. He talked to his company commander, his platoon leader, his platoon sergeant, his section leader and his bunk mate.

The picture they painted of McCoy was the one reflected by his records. He had joined the Corps right out of high school (in fact, several months before; his high school diploma had come to him while he was at Parris Island and was entered into his record then), had served for three months with the Fleet Marine Force at San Diego, and then been shipped to the 4th Marines in Shanghai, where they'd made him an assistant gunner on a water-cooled .30-caliber Browning machine gun.

He had by and large kept out of trouble since arriving in China. And he got along all right with his corporal and his sergeant, who both described him as "a good man."

But there were several things out of the ordinary: He didn't have a Chinese girl, for one thing. But he had had a Chinese girl, so there didn't seem to be reason to suspect he was queer. He didn't have a buddy, either, which was unusual.

But some men were by nature loners, himself included, and this McCoy seemed to be another of them. There was nothing wrong with that, it was just a little unusual.

What was most unusual, though, was his skill as a typist and his language ability. Banning was a little chagrined to discover that Dog Company had a natural linguist who could type seventy-five words a minute assigned to a machine gun. If he had known that, PFC McCoy would have found himself assigned to headquarters company. Skilled typists were in short supply, but not nearly as short supply as people who could read and write French and Italian and Chinese.

Banning decided that McCoy, more than likely with the connivance of his first and gunnery sergeants, had wanted these skills kept a secret. Gunnery sergeants were concerned with having good men on the machine guns and cared very little for the personnel problems of the chairwarmers at regimental headquarters. And McCoy himself was probably one of those kids who did not want to be a clerk.

When he was convinced he had learned all he could about PFC Kenneth J. McCoy from his service records and those around him, Captain Banning went to the infirmary to see the accused face-to-face.

McCoy's medical records showed that he had been admitted to the dispensary at 2310 hours 2 January 1941 suffering cuts and abrasions and a penetrating wound of the upper right thigh possibly caused by a small-caliber bullet. A surgical procedure at 0930 hours 3 January 1941 had removed a lead-and-brass object, tentatively identified as a .25-caliber bullet, from the thigh. The prognosis was complete recovery, with return to full duty status in ten to fifteen days.

Captain Banning found PFC McCoy in a two-bed infirmary room. He was sitting in a chair by the window, using the windowsill as a desk while he worked the crossword puzzle in the *Shanghai Post*. An issue cane was hanging from the windowsill.

"As you were!" Banning barked, when McCoy saw him and started to rise. "Keep your seat!"

Banning could not remember ever having seen McCoy before, which was not that unusual. There were a number of young privates and PFCs in the 4th Marines who looked very much like PFC McCoy.

Captain Banning introduced himself and told McCoy he had been appointed his defense counsel. Then he made sure that McCoy understood his predicament. He told it as he saw it, that he didn't think there was any chance that McCoy would be found guilty of first-degree murder, which required serious elements such as previous intent, but that it was very likely that he would be found guilty of what was known as a "lesser included offense."

There was no question that there were two dead Italian marines or that McCoy had killed them. Neither was there any question that they had been killed with his knife. Banning then explained that while authority might—and did—look away at the illegal carrying of a concealed deadly weapon so long as nothing happened, when something did happen, the offense could no longer be ignored.

There were two lesser included offenses, Banning continued: "Manslaughter," which was the illegal taking of human life, and "Negligent Homicide," which meant killing somebody by carelessness.

"I haven't discussed this with Major DeLaney, who will serve as prosecutor, McCoy," Captain Banning said. "Because I wanted to talk to you first. But this possibility exists: When you come to trial, you have the option of pleading guilty to a lesser included offense. I feel reasonably sure that Major DeLaney would have no objection if you pleaded guilty to manslaughter, and perhaps I could persuade him to accept a plea of guilty to involuntary manslaughter."

PFC McCoy did not respond.

"If you did plead guilty to either of the lesser included offenses," Banning said, "the court-martial board would then decide on the punishment. No matter what they decided, the sentence would be reviewed both by the colonel and by General Butler, both of whom have the authority to reduce it."

"Sir, it was self-defense," McCoy said.

"Let me try to explain this to you," Banning said. "You would be better off if you had knifed two American Marines. But you killed two Italian marines, and they have to do something about it. The Italian Consul General and the Italian marine colonel are going to be at your court-martial. They want to be able to report that the U.S. Marine who killed two of their marines was found guilty and will be punished. Am I getting through to you?"

"Sir, it was self-defense," McCoy repeated doggedly.

"You don't have any witnesses," Banning said.

"There was the rickshaw boy and twenty, thirty Chinese that saw it."

"How do you plan to find them?" Banning asked.

McCoy shrugged his shoulders. "Ask around, I suppose."

There was no sense arguing with him, Banning decided. He just didn't understand the situation.

"Let me tell you what I think is going to happen," he said. "I think I can get Major DeLaney to accept a plea of guilty to a charge of manslaughter. You will be sentenced, and you might as well understand this, the sentence will be stiff. Maybe twenty years to life."

"Jesus Christ!" McCoy said.

"That will satisfy the Italians," Banning said. "You understand that's necessary?"

McCoy gave him a cold look but said nothing.

"The sentence is then subject to review by the colonel," Banning said. "He will take his time reviewing it, I think, to let things cool off a little. Then, he will decide that you're not really guilty of manslaughter, but of the lesser included offense of involuntary manslaughter, and he will reduce the punishment accordingly."

"To what?"

" 'To what, *sir*,' " Banning corrected him.

"To what, sir?" McCoy repeated, dutifully.

"The maximum punishment for involuntary manslaughter is five years."

"I've heard about Mare Island and Portsmouth," McCoy said, grim faced.

He had not appended "sir" as military courtesy required, but Banning did not correct him. It was Banning's personal opinion that the Naval Prisons at Mare Island, California, and Portsmouth, New Hampshire, where the brutality under Marine guards was legendary, were a disgrace to the Marine Corps.

"The next step in the process," Banning went on, "is the review of the sentence by General Butler. I think it's very possible that General Butler would reduce the sentence even further, say to one year's confinement. And then, by the time you got to the states, the Navy Department would review the sentence still again, and I'm sure that they would pay attention both to your previous service and to the letters recommending clemency that your company and battalion commanders tell me they will write in your behalf. Your sentence could then be reduced again to time already served.''

"In other words, sir," McCoy said, with a "sir" that bordered on silent insubordination, "I could count on being a busted Marine looking for a new home?"

"For Christ's sake, McCoy, you killed two people! You can't expect to get off scot-free!"

"Sir," PFC McCoy said, "no disrespect intended, but they gave me the court-martial manual to read, and in there it says I can have the defense counsel of my choice."

Banning felt his temper rise. The sonofabitch was a guardhouse lawyer on top of everything else.

"That is your right," he said, stiffly. "Who would you like to have defend you?"

"My company commander, sir."

"You can't have him, because he is your company commander. Neither can you have your platoon leader."

"Then Lieutenant Kaye, sir, the assistant supply officer."

With a massive effort, Captain Banning kept his temper under control.

"McCoy," he said. "I'm going to give you twenty-four hours to think this over. I want you to carefully consider your position."

"Yes, sir," PFC McCoy said.

(Three)

On the way to his office from the infirmary, Captain Banning's anger rose. Among other things, he was going to look like a goddamned fool in front of the colonel when he had to go to him and tell him this knife-wielding PFC had refused his services as defense counsel. It was of course the kid's right, but Banning could not remember ever hearing of anything like this happening.

And PFC McCoy was not doing himself any good. If he went to trial and pleaded not guilty, he was digging his own grave. He was not being tried for stabbing the two Italians, but to make the point to the other Marines that they couldn't go around killing people.

If he went along with that, in three months he would be a free man at San Diego or Quantico, with only the loss of a stripe to show for having killed two men.

If he annoyed the court-martial board, they would very likely conclude that he was somebody who needed to be taught a lesson and sock him with a heavy sentence. If the colonel was annoyed, he would find nothing wrong with the sentence when it was reviewed. And if General Butler smelled that McCoy was a troublemaker, he wouldn't find anything wrong with the sentence, either.

PFC McCoy stood a very good chance of finding himself locked up in the Portsmouth Naval Prison for thirty years to life.

Captain Banning's rage lasted through lunch. And then he considered the situation from McCoy's point of view. The kid actually believed—since it was the truth—that he had acted in self-defense. It was therefore his own duty, Banning decided, to at least pursue that as far as it would go.

To prove self-defense he would need witnesses. The only witnesses right now were two Italian marines. *They* were prepared to testify that they were minding their own business when McCoy drew a knife on them, whereupon one of their number drew a pistol in self-defense.

When he went back to his office after lunch, Banning told his clerk to see if he could get a car from the motor pool. He had to go into town.

Banning hoped to find Bruce Fairbairn at the headquarters of the Shanghai Municipal Police. He knew him, and could explain the problem to him. But when he got to police headquarters, Fairbairn was not available, and neither was Chief Inspector Thwaite, who was the only other Shanghai Police officer he knew well enough to speak to with complete frankness.

He wound up talking to a Detective Sergeant Chatworth.

Chatworth sat at an old wooden desk covered with papers. As Banning approached, he shuffled angrily through them, searching for something he had apparently mislaid.

Banning introduced himself and told him what he had come for.

"Right," Chatworth said, looking at Banning with a screwed-up face. He seemed surprised to hear Banning's story. "You Yanks always seem to have to wear white," he said after a moment while searching through his pocket for a near-empty package of vile Chinese cigarettes. "Fag?" he offered, holding one out.

"Thanks, no," Banning said.

"I mean, Christ," he went on, lighting up. "Don't you have any loyalty towards your own? For the sake of Italians? Really!" He inhaled deep, savoring it. Then blew out. "And besides, I know the boy. McCoy is a good one. Protect him. You don't find his class all that often."

"That may be." Banning shrugged, stiffening. He did not like Chatworth very much. "But Italian pride has been badly hurt. They've gone to the foreign service boys at the consulate. One thing has led to the other. And the consequence is that there is nothing we can do but court-martial PFC McCoy.

"And then on top of that," Banning continued, "McCoy is being difficult. He thinks he did it all in self-defense; and he simply refuses to understand that without witnesses, he can't possibly get away with that plea."

"So?" Chatworth said, beginning to understand.

"And so, Sergeant, I'm desperate. Could you people possibly help us and see if you can find some Chinese who (a) saw the fight and (b) would be willing to testify in McCoy's behalf at his court-martial?"

Rather abruptly, Detective Sergeant Chatworth turned his attention back to his papers.

"I'll look into the matter," he said, dropping the now-dead cigarette on the floor and snuffing it out with his heel. "And I'll be in touch with you in due course."

Banning saw that Chatworth did not like him any more than he liked Chatworth. And Banning also realized that Chatworth knew even better than he did that there was virtually no chance of finding a Chinese who would be willing to testify that he had seen the fight between the Big Noses. And it would matter to the Chinese not at all that the U.S. Marine Big Nose had clearly been the aggrieved party. Detective Sergeant Chatworth had abruptly dismissed him because he was wasting Detective Sergeant Chatworth's valuable time.

Banning did not go back to the office. He went to the

apartment. Milla was there, giving a Chinese woman hell because she had not ironed several of Banning's shirts to what Milla thought were Marine sartorial standards. She was acting wifely, and that upset him, too, and he got drunk.

And he told Milla about McCoy.

She was sympathetic. To *him*. She felt sorry for him that he had a problem with McCoy.

Later she consoled him in bed, which was usually enough to make him happy as hell. But not this time.

As he watched her get dressed to go to work, he tormented himself with fantasies of other men watching her naked, as she was now. And touching her naked flesh, as he had just done . . . which was sure as hell going to happen if he didn't marry her and get himself booted out of the Corps.

After she left, he hit the whiskey again, and ended up with some drunken ideas. He could go to trial and try to play on the sympathy of the court-martial board, paint PFC McCoy as a saint in uniform who was the innocent party in this whole mess. He could try to convince the court-martial that the reason PFC McCoy went around with a Fairbairn dagger in his sleeve was that he collected butterflies. He'd throw the fucking knife at them and pin their wings. The poor fucking Wops had fallen onto the blade of the knife when they slipped on a banana peel.

(Four)

At eight-fifteen the next morning, as Captain Banning drank his third Coca-Cola of the day in a vain attempt to extinguish the fire in his stomach, his clerk came into his office with the first batch of the day's official correspondence from the message center.

Among the items which required his initials was a communication from Headquarters, United States Marine Corps: A promotion board having been convened to consider candidates for promotion to the grade of corporal had reached the end of its deliberations. There were thirty names on the list and there were twelve vacancies within the Marine Corps for corporals. Therefore, commanding officers of the first twelve names on the list were herewith directed to issue promotion orders for the individuals concerned. As additional vacancies occurred, authority would be granted to promote individuals on the list numbers 13 through 30.

The second name on the list was PFC Kenneth J. McCoy, Company "D," 4th Marines.

The Navy, and thus the Marine Corps, was governed by common law of the United States, and a pillar of that code of justice was that an accused was presumed innocent until proven guilty.

The colonel had just been directed by Hq, USMC, to promote PFC McCoy to Corporal McCoy, an action that would be very difficult to explain to the colonel commanding the Italian marines and to the Consul General of the King of Italy at Shanghai. It would look as if the punishment for stabbing to death two Italians was promotion to corporal.

Captain Banning wondered whether it was his duty to bring the problem to the colonel's attention himself, or whether the S-1 would consider it part of his duty as personnel officer. Most likely, the problem would skip the G-1's attention, Banning decided. The Colonel was going to be furious when he found out about this, and the S-1 knew it, too.

He was still considering the problem, and half expecting his telephone to ring with a call from either the S-1 or the colonel's sergeant-major, when his clerk knocked at the door, put his head in, and announced that Detective Sergeant Chatworth and two Chinese were in the outer office.

As incredible as it sounded, had Chatworth turned up two witnesses? In so short a time?

"Ask him to come in, please." Banning said.

Chatworth came in with two coolies. Banning's heart sank again. The court-martial would not take the word of two coolies over that of two Italian marines.

"Good morning, Captain," Detective Sergeant Chatworth said. "May I present Constable Hang Chee and Senior Patrolman Kin Tong?"

The two coolies bowed their heads.

"Constable Hang and Patrolman Kin were fortunately in a position to see the McCoy incident from start to finish. Tell the captain what you saw, Hang."

Constable Hang spoke English very softly, but well. He reported that PFC McCoy had just stepped out of his rickshaw near the compound gate when he was beset by the five Italians and had no choice but to defend himself.

"He was three blocks from the compound," Banning said, "when four Italian marines overturned the rickshaw."

"Now that you mention it," Constable Hang said, "that's right. There were four Italian marines and the assault took place several blocks from the compound entrance."

It was clear to Banning that they had no more seen the fight than he had.

"What's going on, Sergeant Chatworth?" Banning asked.

"You wanted witnesses, I found them," Chatworth said. "Will a sworn statement suffice, do you think, or will these officers have to testify in court?"

I don't want McCoy to go to Portsmouth, either. But I am a Marine officer, and I can't close my eyes and pretend I believe Chatworth's Chinese.

"I could not put these men on the stand," Banning said, disliking Chatworth more than ever. "I think you misunderstood the purpose of my visit yesterday."

"You're a bloody fool, then, Banning," Chatworth said, coldly.

"Good day, Sergeant Chatworth," Banning said.

"I'll send the report of these officers concerning the incident they witnessed to you via the British Consulate," Chatworth said. "It'll take two, three days to get here, I'd suppose."

"I told you: as much as I might personally like to, I can't put these men on the stand."

"Why not?" Chatworth asked.

"Being very blunt, I'm not sure I believe your men. Goddamn it, I know I don't believe them."

"That's not really for you to decide, is it?" Chatworth said. "And, if you don't let these men testify, wouldn't that be 'suppression of evidence'?"

"Why the hell are you doing this?" Banning asked.

"We're just doing our duty as we see it," Chatworth said, sarcastically. "I can only hope that you're not one of those bloody fools who doesn't know he's in Shanghai and thinks he can go by the bloody book."

"How dare you talk to me that way?" Banning flared.

"What are you going to do about it?" Chatworth asked calmly.

"I tell you now, Sergeant Chatworth, that I intend to discuss this with Captain Fairbairn."

"Odd that you should mention his name," Chatworth said. "Constable Wang and Patrolman Kin are members of Captain Fairbairn's Flying Squad."

Banning's temper flared. He reached for the telephone, actually intending to call Fairbairn. But reason prevailed. He instead had the operator connect him with the colonel.

"Sir," he said. "There has been a rather startling development. When PFC McCoy was attacked by the Italian Marines, the whole incident was witnessed by two Chinese police officers of Captain Fairbairn's Flying Squad. They are prepared to testify that it was clearly a case of self-defense."

"That's bloody well more like it," Detective Sergeant Chatworth said.

II

(One)
4th Marine Infirmary
Shanghai, China
6 January 1941

PFC Kenneth J. McCoy, wearing issue pajamas and a bathrobe, was stretched out on his bed working at a crossword puzzle in the *Shanghai Post* when Captain Banning walked into his room. Banning saw that they had brought him his breakfast on a tray, and that he had eaten little of it.

"As you were," Banning said, as McCoy started to swing his legs out of the bed.

McCoy looked at him warily.

"I want a straight answer to this question, McCoy," Banning began. "How well do you know a Sergeant Chatworth of the Shanghai Municipal Police?"

McCoy, Banning noticed with annoyance, debated answering the question before replying, "I know him, sir."

"Good friend of yours, is he?" Banning pursued.

"I wouldn't say that, sir," McCoy said. "I know him."

"Sergeant Chatworth has come up with two witnesses to support your allegation of self-defense," Banning said. "They saw the six Italians attack you when you got out of the rickshaw at the compound gate."

McCoy's eyebrows went up, but he said nothing.

This is a very bright young man, Banning thought. Bright and tough, who knows when to keep his mouth shut.

"The two witnesses were Chinese police officers of Captain Fairbairn's Flying Squad," Banning went on. "They have appeared before the adjutant and made sworn statements. The statements bring the number of Italian marines

28

down to four, and say that your rickshaw was turned over where you said it was.''

McCoy looked at Captain Banning without expression.

"The statements are so much bullshit, of course," Banning said, "and you know it."

"Sir, so were the statements of the Italians."

"The first thing I thought, McCoy, was that you and Chatworth were involved in something dishonest, and it was a case of one crook helping another. But I just came from seeing Captain Fairbairn, and he tells me that Chatworth is a good man. Off the record, he told me that if Chatworth was getting you out of the mess you're in, that speaks highly for you, because he doesn't normally do things like that.''

"I don't know, sir, what you expect me to say," McCoy said.

"You think I'm a sonofabitch, don't you?''

McCoy, his face expressionless, met Banning's eyes, but he said nothing.

"If I were in your shoes, and the officer appointed to defend me against a charge I was innocent of tried to talk me into pleading guilty, I'd think he was a sonofabitch," Banning said.

"You're an officer, sir," McCoy said.

The implication of that, Banning thought, is that all officers are sonsofbitches. Do all the enlisted men think that way, or only the ones smart enough, like this one, to know when somebody's been trying to fuck them?

"And in this case, I was a sonofabitch," Banning said. "I'm going to give you that, McCoy. It's the truth. I am not exactly proud of the way I handled this. It's pretty goddamned shaming, to put a point on it, for me to admit that it took an English policeman to remind me that a Marine officer's first duty is to his men. I'd like to apologize.''

"Yes, sir," McCoy said.

"Does that mean you accept my apology? Or that you're just saying 'Yes, sir'?" Banning asked. "It's important that I know. I would like a straight answer. Man to man.''

"I didn't expect anything else," McCoy said. "And I've never had an officer apologize to me before.''

"I guess what I'm really asking," Banning said, "is whether

you do accept my apology, or whether you're just going to bide your time waiting for an opportunity to stick it in me.''

''Am I carrying a grudge, you mean? No, sir.''

''I really hope you mean that, McCoy, because you are going to be in a position to stick it in me,'' Banning said.

''Sir?''

''When your friend Chatworth came up with witnesses to your innocence, the colonel decided that there was no reason to go ahead with your court-martial. It would have been a waste of time and money. In light of the new evidence, all charges against you have been dropped. As soon as the surgeon clears you, you'll go back to duty.''

''Aye, aye, sir,'' McCoy said. ''Thank you, sir.''

''But not to Dog Company,'' Banning said. ''The colonel has given you to me. You're being transferred to Headquarters Company.''

''I don't understand,'' McCoy said.

''The colonel said that a man with your many talents, McCoy,'' Banning said, dryly, ''the typing and the languages—not to mention your ability to make friends in the international community—was wasting his time, and the Corps' time and money, on a machine gun. A man like you, McCoy, the colonel said, should work somewhere where his talents could be better utilized. Like S-2.''

''I don't want to be a clerk,'' McCoy said.

''What you want, McCoy, is not up for debate,'' Captain Banning said. ''But for your general information, I don't have any more choice in the matter than you do. What went unsaid, I think, was that the colonel wants me to make sure you don't stick that knife of yours in anyone else.''

''Aye, aye, sir.''

''There's more. As soon as you feel up to making the trip, you're going to Peking for a while. A month, six weeks.''

''Get me out of Shanghai?'' McCoy asked, but it was more thinking out loud than a question.

Banning nodded.

''You're a problem, McCoy,'' Banning said. ''The Italians want you punished. Now that we can't do that, we want to get you out of sight for a while.''

''Captain,'' McCoy said, ''the surgeon told me that if there was going to be infection, I would have it by now. There's no reason for me to be in here."

"Do you feel up to going that far in a truck?" Banning asked.

"I thought we moved people by water between here and Tientsin," McCoy said.

"From time to time, we send a truck convoy up there," Banning said. "One is leaving on Thursday. Didn't you hear that?"

"The word is," McCoy said, "that what the convoys really do is spy on the Japs."

"And that would bother you?"

"No, Sir," McCoy said. "That sounds interesting. I asked my Gunny[1] how I could get to go, and he told me to mind my own business."

"Military intelligence isn't what you might think it is from watching Errol Flynn or Robert Taylor in the movies," Banning said.

"I didn't think it was," McCoy said, evenly.

"Are you familiar with the term 'Order of Battle'?" Banning asked.

"No, sir."

"It is the composition of forces," Banning said. "What units are where and in what condition. By that I mean how they are armed, equipped, fed, whether or not they're up to strength, whether or not there are any signs of an impending move. You understand?"

"Yes, sir."

"One of my responsibilities is to keep up to date on the Japanese Order of Battle," Banning said. "One of the ways I do that is give the officer in charge of the Tientsin-Peking convoys a list of things to look for. That does not mean, I should add, breaking into a Japanese headquarters in the middle of the night to steal secret plans, the way Errol Flynn operates in the movies. My instructions to the officer are that his first duty is to not get caught being nosey."

"I guess the Japanese watch him pretty closely?"

"Of course they do," Banning said.

"They'd be less likely to pay attention to a PFC," McCoy

---

[1]Gunnery Sergeant. A senior noncommissioned officer.

said. "They judge our PFCs by the way they treat their own. And their PFCs can't spit without orders."

"The low regard the Japanese have for their own enlisted men works both ways," Banning said. "They would shoot one of our PFCs they caught snooping around, and then be genuinely surprised that we would be upset about it."

"Then the thing for our PFCs to do is not get caught," McCoy said.

"Didn't you ever hear that the smart thing to do is never volunteer for anything?" Banning asked.

"There's always an exception to that," McCoy said. "Like when you think it might do you some good to volunteer."

"Go on," Banning said.

"I think I'm going to be on the corporals' promotion list," McCoy said. "I also think what I did is liable to fuck me up with getting promoted. Maybe I could get off the shit-list by doing something like snooping around the Japs."

"You're on the corporals' list," Banning said. "The promotion orders will be cut today. A separate order, by the way, hoping the Italians won't find out about it and think that we're promoting you for cutting up their marines. You will be a very young corporal, McCoy."

"Then maybe, if I volunteer for this and do it right," McCoy said, "I can get to be a very young sergeant."

"And maybe you'd fuck up and embarrass the colonel and give him an excuse to bust you," Banning said. "I don't think busting you would make him unhappy."

"And maybe I wouldn't," McCoy said. "I'll take that chance."

"Right now, McCoy, and understand me good, all you are to do when you go on the convoy is sit beside the driver. I don't want you snooping around the Japanese unless and until I tell you what to look for. Do you understand that?"

"Aye, aye, sir," McCoy said. "I'm not going to charge around like a headless chicken and get you in trouble, Captain."

"As long as we both understand that," Banning said.

"Yes, sir," McCoy said.

"Unless you have any questions, then, that seems to be about it. I want you to stay in here until Wednesday, when you can go to your billet and pack your gear for the trip. You are not to leave the compound. And I think it would be a good idea if you didn't sew on your corporal's chevrons until you are out of Shanghai.''

"Aye, aye, sir," McCoy said.

"Any questions?"

"Do I get my knife back?"

"So you can slice somebody else up?" Banning flared.

"I wasn't looking for trouble with the Italians," McCoy said. "But when it found me, it was a damned good thing I had that knife."

"Tell me something, McCoy," Banning said. "Does it bother you at all to have killed those two men?"

"Straight answer?"

Banning nodded.

"I've been wondering if something's wrong with me," McCoy said. "I'm sorry I had to kill them. But you're supposed to be all upset when you kill somebody, and I just don't feel that way. I mean, I'm not having nightmares about it, or anything like that, the way I hear other people do."

"It says in the Bible, 'Thou shalt not kill,' " Banning said.

"And it also says, 'An eye for an eye and a tooth for a tooth,' " McCoy said. "And that 'he who lives by the sword shall die by the sword.' "

Banning looked at him for a long moment before he spoke.

"I'm not absolutely sure about this," he said finally. "Your knife was evidence in a court-martial. But now that there's not going to be a court-martial, maybe I can get it back for you."

"Thank you," McCoy said. "I'd hate to have to buy another one."

(Two)

On the way back to his office, Captain Banning wondered why in their meeting PFC/Corporal McCoy had not said "Yes, sir" as often as he was expected to—using the phrase as sort of military verbal punctuation.

And he wondered why he himself, except that once, hadn't called him on it. The fact, he concluded after a while, was that McCoy was neither intentionally discourteous nor insolent; and that the discussion had been between them as men, not officer and PFC. In other words, the kid had understood—

either from instinct or from smarts—what was the correct tone to take with him.

The more he saw of McCoy, the more he learned about him, the more impressed he became both with his intelligence (his score on the written promotion examination should have prepared him for that, but it hadn't) and with his toughness. He was a very tough young man. But not entirely. Within, there was a soft center of young boy, who wished to sneak off and be a spy—for the pure glamour of it, and the romance.

He could not, of course, permit him to snoop around the Japanese, both because he would get caught doing it (always an embarrassment with the Japanese) and because it was very likely that the Japanese would in fact "accidentally" kill him . . . or, if they wanted to send a message to the Americans, behead him with a sword, and then arrange for his head to be delivered in a box.

Before the convoy left for Tientsin and Peking, Banning took McCoy aside and made it as clear as he could that he was to leave what espionage there was to Lieutenant John Macklin, who was the officer charged with conducting it. He was to go nowhere and do nothing that the other enlisted men on the convoy did not do.

McCoy said, "Aye, aye, sir."

Banning felt a little sorry for him when he saw him climb into the cab of a Studebaker truck. While it was true that the danger of infection of the small caliber wound was over, it was also true that the little slug had caused some muscle damage, and the operation to remove the slug much more. What muscle fibers weren't torn were severely bruised. It was going to be a very painful trip over a long and bumpy road.

Almost a month to the day later, the convoy returned.

Two days later Lieutenant Macklin furnished Banning with a neatly typed-up report—a report that exceedingly dissatisfied him. Because he had acted with much too much caution, Macklin had not found out what Banning had told him to find out. And he had, for all his caution, been caught snooping by the Japanese.

They hadn't actually caught Macklin in a situation where they could credibly claim espionage, they just found him somewhere that the officer in charge of a supply convoy should not have been.

There were a number of legalities and unwritten laws involving the relationship between the Japanese Imperial Army in China and the military forces of the French, the Italians, the English, and the Americans. Captain Banning had come to China briefed on many of them. And his years in China had taught him much more. He had a pretty good sense by now of the rules of the game.

What the Japanese had done when they caught Macklin was what they had done before.

They had, as brother officers, courteously invited him to visit their headquarters. They then took him on an exhausting inspection of the area, with particular emphasis on the garbage dumps, rifle ranges, and other fascinating aspects of their operation. Then they brought him to the mess, where several profusely apologetic Japanese officers spilled their drinks on him while they got him drunk. At dinner they managed to spill in his lap a large vessel of something greasy, sticky, and absolutely impervious to cleaning.

The idea was to make him lose face. As usual, they succeeded.

Corporal Kenneth J. McCoy came to the S-2 office just after noon the day Banning received Macklin's report. He apologized for taking so long. But he explained that his gunnery sergeant had run him over to S-1 to take care of the paperwork that went with his promotion to corporal. This had not been taken care of when he had been shipped off to Peking.

"How's your leg?" Banning asked. "Bother you on the trip?" He didn't seem bothered by McCoy's delay in reporting to him—or else he didn't believe the kid would have anything worth reporting.

"It was rough on the way up, sir," McCoy said.

"All right now, though?"

"Yes, sir," McCoy said.

"Well, whether or not you like it, McCoy," Banning said, "I'm going to have to use you as a clerk."

"I thought that was probably going to happen," McCoy said.

"I'm sorry you're not pleased," Banning said. "But that's the way it's going to have to be."

"Captain, I've got something to say, and I don't know how to go about saying it."

"Spit it out," Banning said.

"The 111th and 113th Regiments of the 22nd Infantry Division are going to be moved from Süchow to Nantung, where they are going to be mobilized."

"Mobilized?" Banning asked, confused.

"I mean they're going to get trucks to replace their horses."

"You mean motorized," Banning corrected, chuckling.

"Yeah, motorized," McCoy said. "Sorry, sir. And then," he went on, "the 119th Regiment is going to stay at Süchow, reinforced by a regiment, I don't know which one, of 41st Division. Then, when the 111th and 113th come back, the 119th'll go to Nantung and get their trucks, and the other regiment will go back where it came from. When the whole division has trucks, they're going to move to Tsinan."

"You're sure of this?" Banning said, sarcastically.

"A couple of whores told me," McCoy said. "And I checked it out."

"Now, Corporal McCoy, why do you suppose Lieutenant Macklin's report doesn't mention this?"

As he spoke, Banning almost kicked himself for coming to Macklin's defense. And yet he knew he couldn't really help himself: Macklin was an officer, and officers do not admit to enlisted men that any other officer is less than an officer should be. But more important, there was bad chemistry between himself and Macklin. And Banning felt guilty about it, guilty enough to protect the lieutenant when he really shouldn't be protected.

Banning just did not like Macklin. He was a tall, dark-haired, fine-featured man, who fairly could be called handsome, and whose face seemed as bright and intelligent as it was handsome. The problem was that he was not nearly as bright as he looked—much less than he thought he was. The first time Banning had laid eye~ on him, he had pegged him as the sort of man who substituted charm for substance, someone who spoke very carefully, never causing offense, never in a position he couldn't escape from by claiming misunderstanding.

"Well, I told you I didn't know how to say it," McCoy said. "I told him what I heard, and he laughed at me. But he's wrong. Whores know."

The truth was, Banning knew, that whores did indeed know.

"You said you 'checked it out,' " Banning said.

"Yes, sir."

"How?"

"I checked it out, sir," McCoy replied.

"You said that, and I asked you how."

"Sir, you told me not to go snooping around the Japs, and I'm afraid you're going to think I did anyhow."

"Why would I think that?" Banning asked.

"Well," McCoy said uneasily, "I got pretty close to them." He paused and then blurted, "I went to Nantung, Captain."

"You're telling me you went to Nantung? Without orders?"

"There was a Texaco truck going in," McCoy said. "With a load of kerosene. I gave the driver fifty yuan to take me with him. And then bring me back."

"And what did you do, Corporal McCoy, when you were in Nantung?" Banning asked.

The question seemed to surprise McCoy.

"I told you," he said. "I went to a whorehouse. One that the Jap officers go to."

"And there were Japanese officers in this brothel?"

"Yes, sir."

"And what did the Japanese officers think when they found a Marine Corps corporal in their whorehouse?" Banning asked. But before McCoy could reply, he went on: "They obviously did not see you, or you wouldn't be here. Did it occur to you, McCoy, that if they did see you, and they didn't slice your head off at the Adam's apple, I would have your ass if and when you came back?"

"They saw me," McCoy said, "They thought I was an Italian that works for Texaco. One of them had been in Rome and thought he talked Italian."

"Goddamn you, McCoy," Banning said. "You were ordered to leave the snooping to Lieutenant Macklin."

"You said not to go near them," McCoy said. "I thought you meant I wasn't to get near the compound. I didn't. I went to a whorehouse. And you made it sound like finding out about the trucks was important."

"And you're sure they didn't suspect you were a Marine?" Banning asked.

Dumb fucking question, Banning. If they suspected he was a Marine, he wouldn't be here.

"They thought I was Angelo Salini, from *Napoli*," McCoy said, both matter-of-factly and a little smugly. "I went to high school with a guy with that name."

"And they told you about the trucks?" Banning asked.

"No, sir," McCoy said. "We just had a couple of drinks and messed around with the whores. The *whores* told me about the trucks."

Do I bring him up on charges for disobeying what was a direct order? Or do I commend him for his initiative?

"And did the ladies tell you what kind of trucks?" Banning said. "Or how many?"

"Just 'army trucks,' " McCoy said. "And since I couldn't go near the compound, I couldn't find out," McCoy said.

"Why should I believe this whorehouse scuttlebutt?" Banning asked.

"I don't know if you should or not, Captain," McCoy said. "But that's what I found out, and since Lieutenant Macklin wasn't going to report it, I figured I should."

Which means, of course, that he first told this to Macklin. Which means that Macklin knew McCoy had done something he wasn't supposed to do, and which Macklin should have reported to me. But if Macklin did report him, his own failure would be even more conspicuous. Sonofabitch!

"And did your lady friends tell you when all this is going to happen?"

McCoy nodded.

"By the time the next convoy goes through Süchow, one or the other of the regiments will probably be gone," McCoy said. "Maybe on the way back, one of them will already be back, and you could count the trucks."

"If you were on the next convoy, do you suppose you could count the trucks?" Banning asked.

"Yes, sir."

"I'm going to rephrase the question," Banning said. "Being fully aware of the risks involved—which means that if the

Japanese catch you, they will more than likely break every bone in your body with clubs, and then behead you—would you be willing to try to get some photographs of the trucks, of their motorpool, photographs close enough up so that the bumper markings could be read?''

''I don't have a camera, Captain.''

''I'll get you a camera, McCoy,'' Banning said.

''Then, yes, sir,'' McCoy said.

The cold-blooded decision, Banning realized, was whether or not it was worth it to determine if the Japanese were motorizing one of their divisions. It would be more than embarrassing if the Japanese caught this corporal. What he'd told McCoy would happen to him if he were caught was not hyperbole.

''Take the rest of the day off, McCoy,'' Banning said. ''I want to have another talk with Lieutenant Macklin, and I want to think about this.''

''He's liable to be pissed I went over his head,'' McCoy said.

''Don't worry about that,'' Banning said. ''You're assigned to S-2. You work for me.''

''Thank you, sir,'' McCoy said.

The moment McCoy walked out of his office, Banning had further thoughts about what he had just said. There was no question in his mind that the Japanese knew his name, as well as the names of everybody who worked closely with S-2. If it came to their attention that a corporal of his was making another trip on the Tientsin-Peking run, they were liable to drag him out of a truck on general principles.

But, he realized, they'd believe they had an officer in a corporal's uniform. Japanese corporals were not dispatched on missions of espionage, and therefore they could not imagine that Americans would do it either.

He realized he had already decided to send McCoy back to Peking on the next convoy.

Very early the next morning, Banning was summoned to the colonel's office. The colonel was in a near-rage.

''Are you aware, Banning, that there was a 'Welcome Home, Killer McCoy' party at the club last night? Complete with a banner saying exactly that?''

The club was called the ''Million-Dollar Club,'' because it

had allegedly cost that much to build fourteen years earlier, before the 4th Marines had come to China. It was on Bubbling Well Road, on the way to Shanghai's elegant race track.

"No, sir," Banning said. "I was not."

"What it looks like to the Italians is that we promoted him for stabbing those people," the colonel said. "If they haven't heard about it yet, the Italians soon will. We're going to have to get that kid out of Shanghai again, and quickly."

"I'd planned to send him back to Peking with the next convoy, sir," Banning said.

"When does it go?"

"On Thursday, sir."

"Is there any way it can leave sooner, say tomorrow?"

"I'll have to check with the S-4, sir, to be absolutely sure, but offhand I can't think of any reason it can't."

"Check with him. If there's any problem, let me know."

"Aye, aye, sir."

"What about the last trip?" the colonel asked. "Anything interesting?"

"I have some fairly reliable information, sir, say seven on a scale of one to ten, that the 22nd Infantry at Süchow is being motorized."

"That is interesting," the colonel said. "Wonder what the hell that's all about? Do they have that many trucks?"

"I'll be able to make a better guess when I have more information, sir. I'm going to try to get some photographs."

"Make sure whoever you send is a good man," the colonel said.

"Aye, aye, sir," Banning said. "I think he is."

"And get that damned Killer McCoy out of here as soon as possible. I don't want him waved like a red flag in front of the Italians."

"Aye, aye, sir."

(Three)
Headquarters, 4th Regiment, USMC
Shanghai, China
11 May 1941
When his sergeant opened the office door to tell him that Lieutenant Sessions had arrived, Captain Edward J. Banning, USMC, was looking out the window of his office at the trees

just coming into bloom. He had been thinking about Milla. If it wasn't for this character Sessions he was waiting for, he could be with her in the apartment. He had forced the image of Milla in her underwear out of his mind by reminding himself that the price they were going to have to pay for the beauty of spring would be the smell that would shortly come from Shanghai's infamous sewers.

"Ask him to come in, please, Sergeant," Banning said.

He turned and hoisted himself onto the window ledge. He was high enough off the floor for his feet to dangle.

Lieutenant Edward Sessions, USMC, marched into the office. He was wearing civilian clothing, a seersucker suit and a straw hat with a stiff brim. He looked, Banning decided, like another Macklin, another handsome sonofabitch with a full head of hair and nice white teeth.

And Lieutenant Sessions was clearly a little surprised to find, on this momentous occasion, the Intelligence Staff Officer of the 4th Marines sitting with his feet dangling like a small boy rather than solemnly behind a desk.

Sessions was not only fresh off the boat from the States, but he was fresh from Headquarters, USMC, and he was on a secret mission. All of these, Banning decided, had perhaps naturally made him just a little bit impressed with his own role in the scheme of things.

Fuck him!

Captain Banning was not awed by Lieutenant Sessions (whom he now remembered having once met years ago at Quantico), nor by the fact that he was fresh from Hq, USMC, nor by his secret mission. And he believed, in fact, that the secret mission itself was a little insulting to him, personally. Not only had he been in China four years and earned, he thought, a reputation for doing his duty the way it should be done, but his own man had been the reason why this whole secret-mission business had started.

Killer McCoy not only returned undetected from his second trip by motor convoy to Peking, but he came back with six rolls of 35-mm film. The Japanese 22nd Division had then been in the process of exchanging its horse-drawn transport for three kinds of trucks—a small truck, smaller even than an American pickup truck; a Japanese copy of a Ford ton-and-a-half stake-body truck; and a larger Mitsubishi two-ton, which was capable of towing both field pieces and ammunition trailers.

Banning had had the film processed, and then sent the negatives and a set of prints by the fastest means available (via the *President Wilson* of U.S. Lines to Manila, where it had been loaded aboard one of Pan American Airways' Sikorsky seaplanes bound for Hawaii and San Francisco) to Headquarters, USMC.

The first response to that had been a cryptic radio message:

HQ USMC WASHINGTON DC VIA MACKAY RADIO FOR COMMANDING OFFICER 4TH MARINES SHANGHAI FOR BANNING REFERENCE PHOTOS WELL DONE STOP THE MORE THE MERRIER STOP MORE FOLLOWS COURIER STOP FORREST BRIG GEN USMC

Brigadier General Horace W. T. Forrest, Assistant Chief of Staff, Intelligence, Headquarters, USMC, was not only so pleased with Killer McCoy's photographs that he wanted more, but he was sending additional information (which he was reluctant to send via Mackay Radio) by courier.

That communication had taken nine days to arrive:

There are several possible ramifications to the Japanese motorization of divisional-strength units which should be self-evident to you. Among these is the possibility that, considering the road network of China, it is the intention of the Japanese to employ these units elsewhere. It is therefore considered of the greatest importance that you continue to furnish this headquarters with the latest information available concerning actual, or projected, motorization of Japanese formations.

Additionally, intelligence gathered in this area will serve to reflect the Japanese industrial capability.

It has been learned from other sources that Germany will furnish to the Japanese an unknown quantity of so far unidentified field artillery. It is considered of the highest importance that information regarding the specific type of such German field artillery, the quantity of such artillery and ammunition stocks, and the identity of troop units to which such German artillery has been assigned be developed as soon as possible.

Lieutenant Edward Sessions has been detached from Hq, USMC to assist in the gathering of this intelligence. He will

*be traveling to, and within, China, bearing a passport identi-
fying him as a missionary of the Christian & Missionary
Alliance. He will bring with him an encryption code, which,
after the intelligence he develops concerning German artillery
in Japanese hands is compiled with information you will have
generated concerning Japanese motorization of tactical and
logistical units, you will use to transmit refined intelligence
data to this headquarters. This encryption code will be used
for no other purpose, and you will continue to transmit data
you generate as in the past.*

*You will furnish to Lieutenant Sessions such support as is
within your capability. Disbursal of confidential funds in this
connection is authorized. Although Lieutenant Sessions will
be functioning as a staff officer of this headquarters, he will
be under your orders while in China.*

Why it was considered necessary for them to send an
officer to China to see if any German artillery pieces were in
Japanese hands was interesting. Finding out what equipment
the Japanese had was something that Banning had been doing
all along. So Sessions's arrival meant one of two things:
Either they didn't like the way he was handling things, or
Lieutenant Sessions had friends in high places, and a secret
mission to China would look good on his record when the
next promotion board sat.

When Lieutenant Sessions walked into the office, Captain
Banning was not surprised to see on his finger the ring
signifying graduation from the United States Naval Academy
at Annapolis. The conclusion to be drawn was that Sessions
indeed was well connected politically.

"Lieutenant Sessions, sir," Sessions said, standing to
attention.

Banning pushed himself off the windowsill and offered his
hand.

"We met, I think, at Quantico in 'thirty-five," he said.
"Nice to see you again, Sessions. Nice voyage?"

"Yes, sir," Sessions said, "I remember meeting the captain. And the trip was first class, long, but with first-class
food and service to make it bearable."

"I came out here on the *Shaumont*," Banning said. "And I
have good reason to believe that she'll be back here just in
time to take me home."

Sessions was sure there was more to that statement than was on the surface. It was a dig at him for being ordered to China on a passenger ship rather than on the *Shaumont,* one of the two Navy Transports (the other was the *Henderson*) that cruised around the world, stopping at every Naval base or port with a sizable Navy or Marine detachment from Portsmouth, New Hampshire, to Shanghai.

If I were in his shoes, Sessions thought, *I would be more than a little pissed-off myself. If I were the S-2, and they sent a major to "help" do what I am supposed to, it would be insulting. And I'm a lieutenant.*

"The *President Madison* was part of the plan, sir," Sessions said, "so that no questions would be raised if I suddenly joined the Christian & Missionary Alliance people here."

"I thought it might be something like that," Banning said dryly.

"There are seven Christian & Missionary Alliance missions in China," Sessions explained. "Six of them are located between here and Peking. They are regularly resupplied twice a year with both stores and personnel. That will be the cover for this operation. We will visit each of the six missions on the route. We'll drop off supplies and replacement personnel and pick up some missionaries who are due for a vacation in the United States. It is believed that I can simply blend in with the other missionaries and not attract Japanese attention."

"Well, you could pass for a missionary, I'll say that," Banning said.

"Sir, do I detect some sarcasm?"

The people in Washington who dreamed up this operation, Banning thought, *have apparently spent a lot of time watching Humphrey Bogart and Robert Taylor spy movies.*

"The people who dreamed up this idea, Sessions," Banning said, "left one important factor out of the equation."

"Sir?"

"With your passport and in civilian clothing, I have no doubt that the Japanese will indeed believe you are an American missionary," Banning said. "The trouble with that is that so far as the Japanese are concerned, all Americans, including missionaries, are spies."

"I don't know what to say, sir," Sessions said.

"In my judgment, Lieutenant Sessions," Banning went on,

"this brilliant Washington scheme is tantamount to hanging a sign from both sides of the missionaries' trucks, 'CAUTION!! SPIES AT WORK!' "

He gave Sessions a moment to let that sink in, and then went on.

"But you and I are Marine officers, Lieutenant," he said. "And when we are given an order, we carry it out."

"Aye, aye, sir," Sessions said, uncomfortably.

"There is one small loophole in the Japanese perception of Americans," Banning said, "that I have had some success in exploiting. The Japanese believe—and I'm not sure if this is their code of Bushido or whether they picked it up from the British—that enlisted men come from the peasant class, and therefore can be presumed to be too stupid to have anything to do with intelligence."

"I'm not sure I follow you, sir," Sessions said.

"Bear with me," Banning replied. "What I'm going to do is inform Major Akkaido, who is the Japanese liaison officer, that I have been directed by higher authority to provide an escort for the Christian & Missionary Alliance vehicles. I am going to try very hard to convince Major Akkaido, as one soldier to another, that I am annoyed by this, and that, whether or not it is convenient for the missionaries, I am going to send the missionaries along with one of our regular Peking truck convoys."

"I think I'm beginning to see," Sessions said.

"The regular supply convoy consists of four Studebaker trucks and a GMC pickup that we've rigged up as sort of a half-assed wrecker. It can drag a broken-down truck, presuming it hasn't lost a wheel or broken an axle. If the motor officer can spare another Studebaker, we'll send that too, empty, to take the load if one of the other trucks breaks down."

"Presumably, there will be mechanics along?" Sessions asked.

"Each truck carries two people," Banning said, "one of whom is allegedly a mechanic. They give the trucks a pretty good going-over before they leave. But most of the difficulty we experience is with tires. There's nothing that can be done about them until they go flat or blow out. We carry spare tires and wheels, as well as an air pump, on the pickup and hope they will cover whatever trouble we have on the road.''

"You're thinking the Japanese will pay less attention to the missionary vehicles and me, if we are part of a regular convoy?" Sessions asked.

"The picture I hope to paint for the Japanese," Banning said, "one I devoutly hope they buy, is that the regular, routine, no-longer-very-auspicious supply convoy is carrying with it this time a handful of missionaries and their supplies."

"I think that's a good idea," Sessions said.

"The convoy is under the command of an officer. These we rotate, both to give them a chance to see the landscape between here and Peking and to keep the Japanese from becoming suspicious of any particular man."

"I understand," Sessions said. "And whoever this officer is, you intend to make him aware of the mission?"

"No, I don't think that will be necessary," Banning said. "But I will tell him what I'm now going to tell you. There will be a Corporal McCoy along on the convoy. They call him 'Killer.' And Killer McCoy works for me. And when Killer McCoy makes a suggestion about what route the convoy is to take or not to take, or what the personnel on the convoy are or are not to do, that suggestion is to be interpreted as being an order from me."

" 'Killer' McCoy? Why do they call him 'Killer'?"

"They call him 'Killer,' " Banning said, matter-of-factly, "because four Italian marines attacked him. He killed two of them with a Baby Fairbairn."

"Excuse me? With a what?"

"There's a rather interesting Englishman, Captain Bruce Fairbairn, on the Shanghai Municipal Police," Banning explained. "He knows more about hand-to-hand combat, jujitsu, and the other martial disciplines than anybody else. He invented a knife, a long, narrow, sharp-as-a-razor dagger—which incidentally General Butler tried to get the Corps to buy and issue. Anyway, there is a smaller, more concealable version. The big knife is called the 'Fairbairn,' and the smaller one the 'Baby Fairbairn.' "

"And your noncom killed two people with it?"

"Two Italian marines," Banning said.

"And there was no court-martial?" Sessions asked. Banning shook his head no. "He knifed two people to death, and that's it?"

"It was self-defense," Banning said. "There were witnesses, two plainclothes Chinese policemen. That was the end of it. The Italians are still—this happened right after the New Year—pretty upset about it. And McCoy is something of a celebrity among the troops. Including the Japanese, who admire that sort of thing. The Japanese don't know that he works for me, of course. Only a few people do. On paper, he's assigned to the motor pool."

"I can hardly wait to meet this man," Sessions said.

"I think, Lieutenant Sessions, that you will find Corporal McCoy very interesting, and perhaps even educational," Banning said. "He speaks Chinese and Japanese, and even reads a little bit of it. And he's been making this run twice a month for six months. He's a good man. He uncovered the whole motorization business; and he took the photographs I presume you've seen."

"I've seen the photographs," Sessions said.

"I'm a little worried about the reaction of the missionaries to Corporal McCoy," Banning said.

"Why do you say that?"

"As a general rule of thumb, Lieutenant Sessions," Banning said, "I have found that most missionaries consider the Marines the tools of Satan. Our enlisted men fornicate with Chinese women, and our officers support the sinful repression of the natives. Now the Japanese enlisted men rape the Chinese women, and Japanese officers order the heads sliced from Chinese they judge unenthusiastic about the Greater Japanese Co-Prosperity Sphere. But that doesn't bother the missionaries, for the Japanese are heathens, and that sort of thing is to be expected of them."

"The Reverend Feller does not quite fit that picture, Captain," Lieutenant Sessions said. "He really hates the Japanese."

"Oh?"

"During his previous service here, he saw enough of the Japanese to see them for what they are. He was present at the rape of Nanking, for example, and believes that the promise of China can only be realized after the Japanese are expelled. He recognizes that can only happen with our assistance."

"I presume he knows that we're neutral in this war?" Banning asked, dryly.

"Apparently, he believes we're going to get in it sooner or later," Sessions said. "And in the meantime is anxious to help, even when that means a personal sacrifice."

"What does that mean?"

"It would have been far more convenient for him to remain in the United States and simply send for Mrs. Feller."

"I have no idea what you're talking about," Banning said.

"The Reverend Feller was summoned home for conferences with his superiors. While he was there, his church decided that he would not be returning to China."

"You mean he got fired?"

"No. He was given a bigger job. His wife remained in China when he went to the United States. She could have returned to the United States by herself, which would have been far more convenient for all concerned. But he elected instead to make the voyage over here 'to settle his replacement in his job,' to help me in my mission, and to take Mrs. Feller back with him. This was all really unnecessary, but he did it anyway."

"A real self-sacrificing patriot, huh?" Banning said, wondering what the Reverend's real purpose was. There were stories of missionaries accumulating chests of valuable Chinese antiques, so many stories that all of them could not be discounted. And what better way to carry valuable antiques out of China than under protection of the U.S. Marine Corps?

"I don't think that's quite fair, sir," Sessions said.

Banning didn't want to get into a discussion of missionary antiques, and changed the subject.

"Christ, I hope both the Reverend and you are wrong about us getting into a war with the Japs," he said.

Sessions looked at him in surprise. It was not the sort of remark he expected from a Marine officer.

"Lieutenant," Banning said, patiently, "certainly you can understand what a logistic horror it would be to attempt to field one division over here. This isn't Nicaragua. China could swallow the entire World War I American Expeditionary Force without a burp."

"I've thought about that, sir," Sessions said.

Banning looked at Sessions with annoyance. *Another Always-*

Agree-with-the-Superior-Officer ass-kisser like Macklin. Then he changed his mind. Sessions was just saying what he was really thinking.

"Have you?" Banning asked.

"Eventually, we may have to face that logistic horror," Sessions said. "I really thought we were going to take action when the Japanese sank the *Panay*[2]."

"Tell me more about the Reverend Feller," Banning said. There was no point in discussing whether a force large enough to do any good could be deployed in China with an officer who had just gotten off the boat.

"He is willing to help us in any way he can," Sessions said, "consistent, of course, with his religious principles."

Banning thought, but did not say, that there was very little then that the good Reverend would be able to do. The principles of religion seemed to disagree almost entirely with the principles and practice of gathering intelligence. The more he thought about it, the more he thought it was likely that the Reverend Feller's motive in returning to China had less to do with patriotism than it did with transporting a case, or cases, of Chinese antiques back to the States.

"As a practical matter, Lieutenant," Banning said, "I am more concerned with the Reverend Feller's reaction to Corporal McCoy."

"I don't think I follow you."

"For one thing, on the way back and forth to Peking, McCoy spends a lot of time drunk, usually in brothels. I don't want the Reverend, or anyone else, interfering with that. Or anything else that McCoy might do."

"I understand, sir," Sessions said immediately.

Banning looked at him and was somewhat surprised to see that he did, in fact, understand why McCoy spent a lot of time in brothels.

"Did the missionaries weather the trip well?" Banning asked. "How soon can they be ready to start?"

"They're in the Hotel Metropole," Sessions said. "They can leave just as soon as their vehicles have been serviced."

[2]The U.S.S. *Panay*, a gunboat of the Yangtze River Patrol, was attacked and sunk, with many Americans killed and wounded, by Japanese aircraft in 1937.

"I'll send McCoy over to the hotel in the morning,"
Banning said. "The Japanese will hear of it immediately, of
course. But they won't think anything about it after I tell
them that he will be taking your missionaries with him to
Peking. What he'll do at the hotel is what he would be
expected to do."

"Which is?"

"Get the missionary vehicles in condition to roll. Tell the
Reverend Feller that it will be his responsibility to bring his
vehicles here to be examined and to provide two extra wheels
and four extra tires and tubes for each of them. That sort of
thing."

"Where is Feller going to get wheels and tires?"

"You can buy anything you want in Shanghai," Banning
said.

"Wouldn't it make more sense to have Corporal McCoy
get the wheels and tires for him? I have some funds . . ."

"The only reason a corporal of Marines would go shopping
for a missionary," Banning said, "would be if he were
ordered to. And the Japanese would then wonder why the
Marines were going out of their way to be nice to a couple of
missionaries—why these missionaries were different from any
of the others."

Sessions winced, and exhaled audibly.

"I've got a lot to learn, don't I?"

"I'm sure that Corporal McCoy will be happy to point out
the more significant rocks and shoals to you," Banning said.

"The most dangerous shoal would be getting caught in a
compromising position," Sessions said. "What would happen if the Japanese detain or arrest me and charge me with
espionage?"

"The thing to do, of course, is not get yourself arrested.
And the way to do that is to listen to Killer McCoy. If he says
don't go somewhere, don't go somewhere."

III

(One)
The Metropole Hotel
Shanghai, China
12 May 1941

None of his peers was surprised when Corporal Kenneth J. "Killer" McCoy, USMC, took an off-the-compound apartment immediately after his return from the first "Get Him out Of Sight" trip to Peking.

He was now a corporal, and most of the noncommissioned officers of the 4th Regiment of Marines in Shanghai had both a billet and a place where they actually lived. McCoy's billet, appropriate to a corporal, was half of a small room (not unlike a cell) in one of the two-story brick buildings that served the Headquarters Company, First Battalion, as barracks. It was furnished with a steel cot (on which rested a mattress, two blankets, two sheets, a pillow and a pillow case), a wall locker and a footlocker filled with the uniforms and accoutrements prescribed for a corporal of Marines.

With the exception of an issue mirror mounted to the door, that was all. There was not even a folding chair.

McCoy shared his billet with a staff sergeant assigned to the office of the battalion S-4 officer[1]. The two of them split the cost of a Chinese room boy (actually a thirty-five-year-old man) who daily visited the room, polished the floor, washed the windows, tightened the blankets on the bunks, touched up the gloss of the boots and shoes, polished the brass, saw that the uniforms and accoutrements were shipshape, and in every way kept things shipshape.

[1]Supply.

Before inspections that Corporal McCoy and Staff Sergeant Patrick O'Dell were obliged to attend (and there was at least one such scheduled inspection every month, on payday) Chong Lee, the room boy, would remove from the wall locker and the footlocker those items of uniform and accoutrements that were required by Marine regulation and lay them out on the bunks precisely in the prescribed manner.

To prepare for the monthly inspection of personnel in billets, it was only necessary for Staff Sergeant O'Dell and Corporal McCoy to go to the arms room and draw their Springfield Model 1903 rifles and the bayonets for them, ensure they were clean, and proceed to their billet.

The gunnery sergeant of Headquarters Company, First Battalion, 4th Marines, was a salty old sonofabitch who drew the line at some fucking Chink having access to the weapons. His men would fucking well clean their own pieces.

The assignment of Staff Sergeant O'Dell and Corporal McCoy to the same room was a matter of convenience. They did not like each other. And sometimes the only time they spoke was when they met, once a month for the scheduled inspection. The only thing they had in common was that neither of them had responsibility for the company supervision of subordinates. The six other enlisted men assigned to battalion S-4 were supervised outside the office by the assistant S-4 corporal, Corporal Williamson.

After his promotion and return from the first "Get Him out of Sight" trip to Peking, Corporal McCoy had been officially transferred from Dog Company to Headquarters Company and assigned to the motor pool.

Whether—as some reasoned—it had been decided to continue to keep him out of sight of the Italians, or whether—as others reasoned—that to get right down to it McCoy didn't know his ass from left field about being a motor pool corporal, he had been given the more or less permanent assignment of riding the supply convoys to Peking.

That kept him out of town more than he was in Shanghai. The result was that since he didn't have a shack job and since he was gone so often, the first sergeant and the gunny had decided there was no sense in putting him on duty rosters if more often than not he wouldn't be around when the duty came up.

And then after sometimes three or four weeks spent bouncing his ass around in the cab of a Studebaker truck, it seemed only fair to give him liberty when he was in Shanghai.

For all practical purposes, then, he didn't have any company duties when he wasn't off with one of the supply convoys. And it was understandable that he didn't want to hang around the billet waiting for some odd job to come up. When he was in Shanghai he stood the reveille formation. After that nobody saw him until reveille the next morning. He *needed* an apartment. You couldn't spend all day in bars and whorehouses.

Most of his peers found nothing wrong with the way McCoy was playing the game. Most of them had themselves made one or more trips away from Shanghai in truck convoys. For the first couple of hours, maybe even the first couple of days, it was okay. But then it became nothing but a bumpy road going on for fucking ever, broken only by meals and piss calls. And the meals were either cold canned rations or something Chink, like fried chunks of fucking dog meat.

But there were a few—generally lower-ranking noncommissioned officers with eight or more years of service—who held contrary opinions: The Goddamned Corps was obviously going to hell in a handbasket if a candy-ass sonofabitch with Parris Island sand still in his boots gets to be a corporal just starting his second fucking hitch, for Christ's sake, instead of having his ass shipped in irons to Portsmouth for cutting up them Italian marines.

What his peers did not know—and what McCoy was under orders not to tell them—was that not only did he have an apartment with a telephone but that the Corps was paying for it. The less the other enlisted men knew about the real nature of McCoy's S-2 duty, the better. Getting him out of the billets would help. And there was another secret from the troops, shared only by the colonel (who had to sign the authorizations), Captain Banning, and the finance sergeant: McCoy had been given a one-time cash grant of $125 for "the purchase of suitable civilian clothing necessary in the performance of his military duty" and was drawing "rations and quarters allowance."

Corporal Kenneth J. McCoy's apartment was on the top floor of a three-story building in P'u-tung. It was not at all elaborate. And it was small, one large room with a bed in a curtained alcove, and a tiny bathroom (shower, no tub) in another. There was no kitchen, but he had installed an electric hot plate so that he could make coffee. And he had an icebox to cool his beer.

But there was a tiny balcony, shielded from view, large enough for just one chair, on which he could sit when he had the time and watch the boat traffic on Soochow Creek.

There was a restaurant in the adjacent building. If he wanted something to eat, all he had to do was put his head out the window and yell at the cook, and food would be delivered to him. He often got breakfast like that, yelling down for a couple of three-minute eggs and a pot of tea. And sometimes late at night, when he was hungry, he'd call down for some kind of Chinese version of a Western omelet, eggs scrambled with onions, bits of ham, and sweet pepper.

He rarely ate in the NCO mess of the 4th Marines, although the chow there was good. It was just that there were so many places in Shanghai to eat well, and so cheaply, that unless he just happened to be near the mess at chow time, it didn't seem worth the effort to take a meal there.

The building on the other side was a brothel, the "Golden Dragon Club," where he had run an account for nearly as long as he'd been stationed in Shanghai. It was through his friend Piotr Petrovich Muller he had found the apartment. Piotr had known the proprietor of the Golden Dragon in the good old days, back in Holy Mother Russia.

The man had an unpronounceable name, but that didn't matter, because he liked to be called "General." He claimed (McCoy was sure he was lying) that he had been a General in the Army of the Czar.

When he had first moved into the apartment, McCoy had played "Vingt-et-Un" with the General long enough for the both of them to recognize the other was not a pigeon to be plucked. They had become more or less friends afterwards, despite the differences in their age and "rank."

Most of the items on the monthly bill the General rendered were for services not connected with the twenty-odd girls in the General's employ. The General's people cleaned McCoy's apartment and did his laundry. And then there were bar charges and food charges. The girls themselves were more than okay. Mostly they were Chinese, who ranged from very pretty to very elegant (no peasant wenches in the General's establishment), but there were a few Indochinese and two White Russians as well.

McCoy actually believed that the General, who exhibited a certain officer-type arrogance, had most probably been an officer, if not officially a general, in the Czarist Army. Something like captain or maybe major was what he probably had been when, like so many other White Russian "generals," he had come penniless and stateless to Shanghai twenty years before. McCoy didn't like to think how the General had survived at first—probably as a pimp, possibly by strong-arm robbery—but he was now inarguably a success.

He had an elegant apartment in one of the newer buildings, to which he sometimes invited McCoy for a Russian dinner. He drove a new American Buick, and he had a number of successful business interests now (some of them perfectly legal) in addition to the Golden Dragon.

There were eight sets of khakis hanging in the wardrobe when McCoy, naked, and still dripping from his shower, walked across the room and opened it. They were not issue. His issue khakis hung in his wall locker at the barracks. These uniforms were tailor-made. The shirts had cost him sixty cents, American, and the trousers ninety. The field scarves[2] had been a nickel, and the belt (stitched layers of khaki) a dime. The belt was not regulation. Regulation was web. But McCoy knew that the only time anything would ever be said about it was at a formal inspection, and he hardly ever stood one of those anymore.

Neither were his chevrons regulation. Regulation chevrons were embroidered onto a piece of khaki and then sewn onto the shirt. McCoy's chevrons (and those of the gunnery sergeant) had been embroidered directly onto their shirts. If it was good enough for the gunny, McCoy had reasoned, it was good enough for him. And now that he had made corporal, he

---

[2]Neckties.

knew that the shirts would be worn out long before he would make sergeant.

The shirt and trousers were stiffly starched. They would not stay that way long. It was already getting humid. Shanghai was as far south as New Orleans, and every bit as muggy. Before long the starch would wilt, and it was more than likely that he would have to change uniforms when he went to the compound, which is where he had to go after he introduced himself to the Reverend Feller, who was staying at the Hotel Metropole. He did not wish to give the assholes in Motor Transport any opportunity to spread it around that Killer McCoy had shown up in a sweaty uniform looking like a fucking Chinaman.

When he was dressed, with his field scarf held in place with the prescribed USMC tie clasp, there was no longer any question that he would need another uniform before the day was over. He decided that it made more sense to take one with him than to use one of the issue uniforms in his billet. He could change in the motor pool head and avoid going to the barracks at all.

Carrying an extra uniform on a hanger, he left the apartment and trotted down the stairs. He did not lock the apartment. The way that worked was that there were some Westerners whose apartments were robbable, and some whose apartments were not. It had nothing to do with locks on doors and bars over windows. The trick was to get yourself on the list of those whose apartments were safe. One way to do this was to have it known that you were friendly with a Shanghai policeman, and the other was to be friendly with the chief of the tong whom the association had granted burglary privileges in your area.

McCoy's apartment was twice safe. When he was in town, he continued to gamble regularly with both Detective Sergeant Lester Chatworth of the Shanghai Police, and (not at the same time, of course, but when the local celebrity honored the Golden Dragon with his presence) with Lon Ci'iang, head of the Po'Ti Tong.

On the crowded street, he stopped first to buy a rice cake, and then flagged down a rickshaw.

He told the boy, a wiry, leather-skinned man of maybe twenty-five, to please take him to the Hotel Metropole, and the boy swung around to look at him in unabashed curiosity. It always shocked the Chinese to encounter a white face who spoke their language.

When the rickshaw delivered him in front of the Hotel Metropole, there were several Europeans (in Shanghai, that included Americans), among them a quartet of British officers, standing on the sidewalk there. The civilians looked at him with distaste, the officers with curiosity. When McCoy saluted crisply, one of the officers, as he returned the salute with a casual wave of his swagger stick, gave him a faint smile.

He is giving me the benefit of the doubt, McCoy thought, *deciding that I wouldn't be coming here unless I were on duty. The civilians just don't like a place like this under any circumstances fouled by the presence of a Marine enlisted man.*

He went to the desk and asked for the room number of the Reverend Mr. Feller. Captain Banning had been specific on the telephone about that. The missionary named Sessions was really a Marine lieutenant, but McCoy was to deal with a Reverend Feller and not the lieutenant.

As he crossed the lobby to the elevators, one of the bellboys offered to relieve him of the spare uniform, but McCoy waved him away.

The elevators were contained within an ornate metal framework, and the cage itself was glassed in. As it rose, it gave McCoy a view of the entire lobby: the potted palms, the leather couches and chairs, the hotel guests, the men already in linen and seersucker suits, and the women in their summer dresses. He could see the outlines of underwear beneath some of the dresses; and in the right light, some of the women—the younger ones mostly—showed ghostly, lovely legs.

McCoy saw few European women. He hadn't, he thought, spoken to a European woman in over six months, the only exceptions being the General's two Russian whores, and they didn't really count.

He walked down the wide, carpeted corridor to 514, and knocked at the door.

"Who is it?" an American female voice called after a moment.

"Corporal McCoy, ma'am," he called out. "Of the Fourth Marines. I'm here to see Reverend Feller."

"Oh, my!" she said. He heard in the tone of her voice either displeasure or fright that he was here. He wondered what the hell that was all about.

The door opened.

"I'm Mrs. Moore," she said. "Please come in. I'll have to fetch the Reverend. He's with Mr. Sessions."

She was a large woman, big boned, just on the wrong side of fat. She was, McCoy judged, maybe forty. With the well-scrubbed, makeup-free face of a woman who took religion seriously. She had light brown hair, braided and pinned to the side of her head. And she wore a cotton dress, with long sleeves and buttons fastened up to the throat. Hanging from her neck was a four-inch Christian cross, made of wood.

"Thank you," McCoy said.

"Are you the man who was originally supposed to come?" she asked.

"I don't think I understand you," McCoy said.

"It doesn't matter," she said. "I'll go fetch the Reverend Feller," she added, smiling uneasily at him. She slid past him to the door, as if she were afraid he would pick her up, carry her into the adjacent bedroom, throw her on the bed, and work his sinful ways on her. The thought amused him, and he smiled, which discomfited her further.

He decided he'd have a word with the people in the convoy to watch what they said and did with her around. If somebody said "fuck," she would faint. Then her husband would bitch to the lieutenant in civilian clothes, and he would make trouble.

A minute later, the Reverend Glen T. Feller entered the room. He wore a broad, toothy smile, and his hand was extended farther than McCoy believed was anatomically possible.

He was of average height, slim, with dark hair plastered carefully to his skull, and a pencil-line mustache. He was immaculately shaven, and McCoy could smell his after-shave cologne.

"I'm the Reverend Feller," he said. "I'm happy to meet you, Corporal, and I'm sorry I wasn't here when you came."

"No problem, sir," McCoy said. The Reverend Feller's

hand was soft, clammy, and limp. McCoy was a little repelled, but not surprised. It was the sort of hand he expected to find on a missionary.

Mrs. Moore moved around them, so as to stand behind the Reverend and put him between herself and McCoy.

There was a rap at the door, and then "Mr." Sessions entered the room.

Even in the civilian clothes, McCoy decided, *this guy looks like he's an officer. But like a regular platoon leader, not a hotshot intelligence officer from Headquarters, USMC, in Washington.*

"You're Corporal McCoy?" Sessions asked, surprised. "The one they call 'Killer'?"

"Some people have called me that," McCoy said, uncomfortably.

"You're not quite what I expected, Corporal, from the way Captain Banning spoke of you," Sessions said.

Well, shit, Lieutenant, neither are you.

"Well, I'm McCoy," he said.

He was aware that Mrs. Moore was looking at him very strangely; he decided she had heard all about the Italian marines.

"How long have you been in the Corps, Corporal?" Lieutenant Sessions asked.

"About four years," McCoy said.

"There aren't very many men who make corporal in four years," Sessions said. "Or as young as you are."

McCoy looked at him, but said nothing.

"How old are you, Corporal?"

"Twenty-one, sir," Corporal Killer McCoy said.

"Presuming Captain Banning was not pulling your leg, Ed," the Reverend Feller said, laughing, "we must presume the Killer's bite is considerably worse than his bark."

I don't like this sonofabitch, McCoy thought.

"Killer," the Reverend Feller said, "we place ourselves in your capable hands."

"I said some people call me that, Reverend," McCoy said. "I didn't mean you could."

"Well, I'm very sorry, Corporal," the Reverend Feller said. He looked at Sessions, as if waiting for him to remind Corporal McCoy that he was speaking to a high-ranking missionary. When Sessions was silent, Feller said, "I don't want us to get off on the wrong foot. No hard feelings?"

"No," McCoy said.

(Two)
Motor Pool, First Bn, 4th Marines
Shanghai, China
14 May 1941

The Christian & Missionary Alliance vehicles had been taken from the docks to the motor pool of the First Battalion, 4th Marines, where they were carefully examined by Sergeant Ernst Zimmerman, who was the assistant motor transport supervisor and would be the NCOIC[3] of the Peking convoy.

The vehicles were greased and their oil was changed. And just to be on the safe side, Ernie Zimmerman changed the points and condensors and cleaned and gapped the spark plugs. Zimmerman, at twenty-six, was already on his third hitch, and had been in China since 1935.

He was a phlegmatic man, stocky, tightly muscled, with short, stubby fingers on hands that were surprisingly immaculate considering that he spent most of his duty time bent over the fender of one vehicle or another doing himself what he did not trust the private and PFC mechanics to do.

He lived with a slight Chinese woman who had born him three children. She and the children had learned to speak German. Though he understood much more Chinese than he let on, Zimmerman spoke little more than he had the day he'd carried his sea bag down the gangway of the Naval Transport U.S.S. *Henderson* more than six years before.

At 0700 hours, two hours before the convoy was to get underway, a meeting was held in the motor pool office, a small wooden building at the entrance to the motor pool. The motor pool itself was a barbed-wire-fenced enclosure within the First Battalion compound.

Present were Lieutenant John Macklin, who would again be the officer in charge of the convoy; Sergeant Zimmerman; Corporal McCoy; and the eight other enlisted men of the convoy detail. They had just spread maps out on the dispatcher's table when they were joined by Captain Edward Banning.

[3]Noncommissioned Officer In Charge.

The usual route the convoy traveled could not be followed on this trip, because of the necessity to stop at the six Christian & Missionary Alliance missions. The first deviation would be to Nanking. Normally they turned off the Shanghai-Nanking highway onto a dirt road just past Wuhsi. Fifty miles down that road was the ferry across the Yangtze River between Chiangyin and Chen-chiang.

It would now be necessary to enter Nanking, drop off supplies for the Christian & Missionary Alliance there, and pick up the Reverend Feller's wife, her luggage, and their household goods. It was a hundred miles from where they normally turned off, a two-hundred-mile round trip, because it still made good sense to cross the Yangtze between Chiangyin and Chen-chiang.

"It has been suggested, sir," Lieutenant Macklin said to Captain Banning, "that at the turnoff point for Chiangyin we detach from the convoy one of the Studebaker automobiles, the wrecker, and the missionary truck with the Nanking supplies. The rest of the convoy would go onto Chiangyin and wait for the others to return from Nanking there. That would mean spending the night in Nanking."

There was no question in Sergeant Ernst Zimmerman's mind who had made the suggestion, and he was not at all surprised when Captain Banning said, "That seems to make more sense than having the whole convoy make the round trip." Banning continued, "Why don't you have McCoy drive the civilian car? That would make sort of a Marine detachment, with the wrecker, to accompany the missionary vehicles."

"Aye, aye, sir," Lieutenant Macklin said.

There was therefore, Sergeant Ernie Zimmerman concluded, some reason for McCoy to go to Nanking, as there was obviously some reason why McCoy had been given the convoy as kind of a primary duty. He had not been told what that reason was, and he had no intention of asking. If they wanted him to know, they would have told him. He believed the key to a successful career in the Corps was to do what you were told to do as well as you could and ask no questions. And to keep your eyes open so that you noticed strange little things, like the fact the regimental S-2 paid a lot of attention to a truck convoy that was really none of an intelligence officer's business, and that the real man in charge of the convoys was not whichever officer happened to be sent along, but Corporal "Killer" McCoy.

It took about an hour to decide—and mark on the three maps they would take with them—where the convoy would leave their normal route to visit the other five missions where they would be stopping.

Then Lieutenant Macklin sent the enlisted men to the arms room to draw their weapons. Each Marine drew a Colt Model 1911A1 .45 ACP pistol with three charged magazines. Two PFCs drew Browning Automatic Rifles, caliber .30-06, together with five charged twenty-round magazines. Sergeant Zimmerman and Corporal McCoy drew Thompson submachine guns, caliber .45 ACP with two fifty-round drum magazines. Everybody else took their assigned Springfield Model 1903 rifles from the arms room. There was also a prepacked ammo load, sealed cases of ammunition for all the weapons, plus a sealed case of fragmentation grenades.

There never had been any trouble on the Peking convoys. Sergeant Zimmerman, unaware that he was in complete agreement with the colonel, believed this was because the convoy detail was heavily armed.

There were nine vehicles in the convoy when it rolled out of the First Battalion compound: four Marine Corps Studebaker ton-and-a-half trucks, with canvas roofs suspended over the beds on wooden bows; two Christian & Missionary Alliance trucks, also Studebakers, differing from the Marine trucks only in that they did not have a steel protective grill mounted to the frame; two gray Studebaker "Captain" sedans, with the Christian & Missionary Alliance insignia (a burning cross) and a legend in Chinese ideograms painted on their doors; and bringing up the rear was the homemade pickup/wrecker, stacked high with spare tires and wheels.

Sergeant Zimmerman drove the wrecker. He usually rode in it as a passenger, but its normal driver was at the wheel of one of the missionary trucks. The second missionary truck was driven by a Marine who ordinarily would have been assistant driver on one of the trucks. Lieutenant Macklin drove one of the missionary Studebakers, and Corporal McCoy the other.

As the trucks made their way through heavy traffic toward

the Nanking Highway, the passenger cars left the convoy and went to the Hotel Metropole to pick up the missionaries. Zimmerman was not surprised when they had to wait by the side of the Nanking Highway for more than an hour for the missionaries. Missionaries were fucking civilians, and fucking civilians were always late.

The first hundred miles went quickly. The Japanese Army kept the Nanking Highway and the rail line that ran parallel to it in good shape. Every twenty miles or so, near intersections, there were Japanese checkpoints, two or three soldiers under a corporal. But they just waved the convoy through. Long lines of Chinese, however, were backed up at every checkpoint.

It was less a search for contraband, McCoy thought, than a reminder of Japanese authority.

Just past Wuhsi, two and a half hours into the journey, the convoy rolled through another Japanese checkpoint, then turned off the highway onto a gravel road which led, fifty miles away, to the ferry between Chiangyin and Chen-chiang.

Once they had reached the ferry, the Reverend Feller, Mr. Sessions, and Mrs. Moore got in the back seat of the Studebaker McCoy was driving, and (trailed by one of the missionary trucks) headed down the highway for Nanking.

The rest of the convoy, led by Lieutenant Macklin in the other missionary Studebaker, started off toward Chiangyin. It was the rainy season, and, predictably, it began to rain buckets. The road turned slick and treacherous, and it took them nearly as long to make that fifty miles as it had to come from Shanghai to Wuhsi.

(Three)
Christian & Missionary Alliance Mission
Nanking, China
1630 Hours 14 May 1941

Nanking was a curious mixture of East and West, ancient and modern. The tallest building in the city, for instance, was not a modern skyscraper but the Porcelain Tower, an octagon of white glazed bricks 260 feet tall, built five hundred years before by the Emperor Yung Lo to memorialize the virtues of his mother.

Recently, from 1928 until 1937, Nanking had been the capital of the Republic of China. But in 1937 the Japanese had captured it in a vicious battle followed by bloody carnage. Their victory was soon known as "The Rape of Nanking."

There had nevertheless still been time for Chiang Kaishek's Kuomintang government to make their modern mark on it. Outside of town was the Sun Yat-sen mausoleum, honoring the founder of the Chinese Republic. And within the city half a dozen large, Western-style office buildings were built on wide avenues to house governmental ministries. There was also a modern railroad station and a large airport.

After "The Rape of Nanking," in the correct belief that representatives of the foreign press (whom they could not bar from China) would all immediately head for Nanking, the Japanese had made a point of keeping Nanking peaceful. Only a handful of military units were stationed there, and they were on their good behavior. When, in the interests of furthering the Greater Japanese Asian Co-Prosperity Sphere it became necessary to slice off some heads, the persons designated were first removed from Nanking.

The Christian & Missionary Alliance mission was in an ancient part of town, close to the Yangtze and within sight of the cranes on the docks. The mission covered a little more than two acres, which were enclosed by walls. Directly across from the gate a four-hundred-year-old granite-block building had been converted to a chapel. A wooden, gold-painted cross sat atop it.

There were two large wooden crates in the courtyard of the mission, obviously the household goods of the Fellers. Captain Banning had told McCoy of his suspicions about their contents, and now he wondered idly if the captain was right. Then, more practically, he wondered how they were going to load the crates onto the trucks. The damn things probably weighed a ton.

A woman who was almost certainly Mrs. Feller appeared in the courtyard as the truck and car drove through the gate. She was more or less what McCoy expected, a somewhat thinner, somewhat younger copy of Mrs. Moore—a wellscrubbed, makeup-free do-gooder. She even wore her hair the same way, braided and then pinned to the sides of her head. But unlike Mrs. Moore, McCoy noticed, she had good-looking legs, trim hips, and an interesting set of knockers.

She kissed her husband like a nun kisses a relative. On the cheek, as if a little uncomfortable with that little bit of passion.

When the Reverend Feller marched her over to the car and introduced her, McCoy was surprised that her hand was warm. He had expected it to be sort of clammy, like her husband's.

She had a boy show McCoy and PFC Everly (the tall, gangly hillbilly driving the missionary truck) where they were to sleep. Except for a Bible on a bedside table and a brightly colored framed lithograph of Jesus Christ gathering children around his knee, it was very much like McCoy's billet in the First Battalion compound in Shanghai. A steel cot, bed-clothes, a chair, and nothing else.

Sessions came to the room shortly after the mission boy left them there.

"Could I have a word with you, Corporal McCoy?" he asked.

"Take a walk, why don't you, Everly?" McCoy ordered.

"Where am I supposed to go?"

"See if you can scout up a decent-looking place for us to eat. Come back in fifteen minutes."

When he was gone, Sessions said, "Mrs. Feller has asked you to supper, McCoy."

"Everly and I will get something," McCoy said.

"She meant the both of you, of course," Sessions said. "You're welcome, you understand? She's really a very nice person."

"Lieutenant, I didn't come here to eat supper with missionaries," McCoy said. "I'm going out on the town."

"In the line of duty, of course," Sessions said, sarcastically.

"The Corps's paying for it," McCoy said. "Why not?"

"Yes, of course," Sessions said. "Is there anything of interest here that I could credibly have a look at?"

"There's Kempei-Tai[4] watching this place. They're not going to think much if two Marines leave here to get their ashes hauled. They might get very curious if a newly arrived missionary did the same thing."

"I wasn't thinking of going to a brothel," Sessions replied,

[4]The Japanese Security Police.

chuckling. "I was suggesting that it would be credible if the Fellers, while I was here, showed me the sights. And that while so doing, I might come across something of interest."

"If the Japs have German artillery, it's not going to be here in Nanking," McCoy said flatly. "And I think the less attention you call to yourself, the better it would be."

"McCoy, I am simply trying to do my job," Sessions said, annoyed at what he considered McCoy's condescension. He wondered what Captain Banning had told McCoy about him.

"That's all I'm trying to do, Lieutenant," McCoy said. "Captain Banning said I was to do what I could for you, and that's what I'm trying to do."

As the whores later confirmed, nothing was happening in Nanking. So at half past ten, McCoy decided that there wasn't anything more to be gained from spending the night in the whorehouse. He put on his clothes, paid off his girl, and went to the room Everly had taken.

"I'm heading back in," he told Everly, who was standing there in the doorway a little dazzled by the interruption. He had wrapped a towel around his middle. It threatened to fall.

"Do I have to?" he said.

"Just be at the mission at five o'clock," McCoy said, after a moment. Everly was a fucker, not a fighter; and he didn't drink dangerously. There was little chance that he would get in trouble. On the other hand, if he spent the night in the whorehouse, it would give the Kempei-Tai agents who had trailed them something to do. And the report they would write would state that a Marine had hired a whore for the night and stayed with her.

He returned to the mission and searched in vain through the small mission library for something that had nothing to do with Christianity. Then, disappointed, he retreated to his room, undressed to his skivvies, and took from his musette bag one of the copies of the *Shanghai Post* that had accumulated during his last trip to Shanghai. After he'd read it, he started in on the crossword puzzle.

Someone knocked at the door. Certain that it was the boy, he called permission to enter in Chinese.

It was Mrs. Feller, a very different Mrs. Feller from the tight-assed lady he had met that afternoon. She was wearing a cotton bathrobe over a silk gown; and her hair was free now, hanging halfway down her back. It was glossy and soft, as though she had just brushed it. Then he noticed—more than noticed—the unrestrained breasts under her thin night clothes. . . . The Reverend was about to get a little, after what presumably was a long dry spell.

"Do you speak Chinese?" she asked, in Chinese.

"Some," McCoy said, in English.

"I just wanted to see if you or the other gentleman needed anything," she said.

"No, ma'am," McCoy said, chuckling. "We're fine, thank you."

"Why are you chuckling?" she asked, smiling.

"Hearing you call Everly 'the other gentleman,' " McCoy said.

"Where is he?" she asked.

When McCoy didn't reply, her face flushed.

"Mrs. Moore told me an incredible story about you," she said. "I can't believe it's true."

"What did she tell you?"

"Now I'm sorry I brought this up," she said. "I shouldn't have."

He nodded his acceptance of that.

"But do they call you 'Killer'? Or were they just teasing my husband and Mr. Sessions?"

"Some people call me that," McCoy said. "I don't like it much."

"But you're just a boy," she said, after deciding that the rest of the story was also probably—if incredibly—true.

"I don't like to be called a boy, either," McCoy said. "I'm a corporal in the Marine Corps."

"I'm really sorry I brought the whole thing up," she said. McCoy nodded.

"Breakfast will be at six-thirty," she said. "My husband wants to get on the way early. Is that all right with you?"

"Yes, ma'am," he said. "We'll be there. Thank you."

"Then I'll say good night," she said.

He thought that he would really have liked to get a look at her teats. Chinese women, by and large, didn't have very big teats, and it had been a long time since he had seen an American woman's teats.

Come to think of it, he had seen very few American women's teats. Before he had come to China it had been a really big deal to get a look at a set of teats—not to mention actually getting laid. But getting laid in China was about as out-of-the-ordinary as blowing your nose. And in fact he had come to see there was no big difference between Chinese women and American (the story that their pussies ran sideward had turned out to be so much bullshit); but it would still be kind of nice to make it with a real American.

He would, come to think of it, really like to jump Mrs. Feller, though he immediately recognized that dream as the same kind of fantasy as wishing he would make sergeant next week . . . out of the goddamned question for two hundred different reasons.

He turned his attention back to the crossword puzzle.

(Four)
The Christian & Missionary Alliance Mission
Nanking, China
0830 Hours 15 May 1941

The Christians of the mission put on a little farewell ceremony for Mrs. Feller. After maybe fifty Chinese had manhandled the wooden crates onto the bed of the Studebaker, they went to one side of the courtyard and stood in some kind of a formation. McCoy settled into the front seat of the car, and watched.

Next came maybe fifty little Chinese kids dressed in middie-blouse uniforms (which reminded McCoy of the uniform of the Italian marines). They lined up in four ranks. Finally, the missionary equivalent of the officers appeared—all the white Christians and half a dozen suit-wearing Chinese Christians. They sat down on a row of chairs set up on a sort of platform against a wall. One of them rose and said a prayer. Then the Chinese kids sang a hymn in Chinese. McCoy recognized the melody but could not recall the words.

One of the Chinese Christians gave Mrs. Feller a present. She thanked him, and they sang another hymn, this time in English. The Reverend Feller then gave what was either a sermon or a very long prayer. Then came another hymn.

All this time, McCoy was looking up Mrs. Feller's dress. He hadn't started out to do that. But the way she was sitting up on the platform, and the way he was looking out the Studebaker window, that's where his eyes naturally fell. And then it got worse. He was originally looking at a lot of white thigh. But then she had uncrossed her knees, and put her feet flat on the little platform just far enough apart to show all the way up. And she wasn't wearing any pants.

He didn't believe what he saw at first. Ladies didn't go around without their underpants, and she was not only a lady, she was a lady missionary. But there was no question about it. She was sitting there with everything showing.

And then Lieutenant Sessions came over and sat beside McCoy. The minute he did, Mrs. Feller crossed her legs.

Did she suddenly remember how she was sitting? Or didn't it matter, since only an enlisted man was getting an eyeful? Or was she playing the cockteaser with me, and stopped only because Sessions showed up?

When the ceremony was finally over, and the officer-type Christians walked with Mrs. Feller to the Studebaker, McCoy did not get out from behind the wheel to open the door. He had a hard-on.

Mister/Lieutenant Sessions, obviously anxious to get the show on the road again, opened the door and motioned for Mrs. Feller to get in.

"If you don't mind, Mr. Sessions," Mrs. Feller said. "I'll sit with Corporal McCoy. I get woozy if I ride in backseats."

She got in beside McCoy and smiled at him.

"I'm sorry you had to wait," she said.

"No sweat," McCoy said, devoting all of his attention to starting the engine.

"I always wondered how you did that," she said.

"Did what?" he asked. In spite of his misgivings, curiosity forced him to look at her.

She was holding up his hat press[5]. He had put his campaign hat in it when he'd got in the car. It was the rainy season, and humidity was hell on fur felt hats.

"Oh," McCoy said. "That."

She put the hat press back where it had been.

"Very clever," she said.

"Okay to go?" McCoy asked.

---

[5] A device that keeps the brim of the felt campaign hat from curling.

"Get the show on the road, McCoy," Sessions said.

Mrs. Feller waved to the Christians, and blew several of them a kiss.

For somebody who got screwed as much as she probably got screwed last night, having been away from the Reverend all that time, McCoy thought, *she don't look all that worn out.*

Then he realized he was wrong about that. The reason she was going around without any underpants was that she and the Reverend had screwed it sore.

She half turned on the seat, pulling her dress above her knees in the process, and started talking to Sessions. "Where are you from?" And "Where is your wife from?" And "How much do you like the Marine Corps?" That sort of thing.

McCoy kept his eyes off her knees as much as he could.

He had it made now, he told himself. It would be real dumb fucking that up by doing something dumb with this missionary woman. He had probably the best duty of any corporal in the Corps. For all practical purposes, he didn't have anybody telling him what to do. And the Corps was paying all his expenses, even what he spent getting laid. And it was even better than that:

When he filled out the "report of expenses" Captain Banning made him do about once a month, he put down on it usually twice (sometimes three times) what it really cost him. He wasn't greedy, and Captain Banning probably thought he was getting a bargain. But the prices McCoy listed on the report were what Marines would be expected to pay for a room, a meal, a whore, or whatever. Marines who spoke Chinese didn't pay half what Marines who didn't speak Chinese did. Not a month had passed since he'd gone to work for Banning that he hadn't been able to add a hundred dollars to his retirement-fund account at Barclays Bank. And that didn't include his gambling money.

They always spent two days in the Marine Compound at Tientsin on the way to Peking, then two days in Peking, and then another day at Tientsin on the way back to Shanghai. As regular as clockwork, he'd been taking ten, fifteen dollars a night from the Tientsin and Peking Marines. He hadn't been greedy, which wasn't easy, because there were Tientsin and

Peking Marines who played poker so bad it was sometimes hard not to clean them out.

It was hard to believe how much money he had in Barclays Bank.

And he could fuck the whole thing up by doing something stupid with this missionary who went around without her underpants.

When they were out of Nanking, the humidity started to close in so bad that the outside of the windshield kept clouding over and he had to run the wipers every once in a while. It would be better whenever it started to rain. He wished it would start soon.

Mrs. Feller glanced at McCoy to make sure he had his eyes on the road. Then she took a little bottle of perfume or cologne from her purse and shook a tiny dab of it on a handkerchief. She touched her temples with it, and her ears, and her forehead, and then quickly opened a couple of buttons on her dress and rubbed a little in the crack between her breasts.

McCoy's erection was painful.

He was sure, to make it worse, that she had seen him looking.

Goddamn these missionaries anyway! If the Corps had wanted to find out if the 11th Jap Division had German artillery pieces, I could have found out, without dragging a bunch of fucking missionaries around with me.

It finally started to rain, a steady, soft rain that meant it would probably go on forever.

And now the inside of the windshield started to steam up. Mrs. Feller, trying to be helpful, kept wiping it with a handkerchief. Sometimes when she leaned over to wipe his window, her hand rested on his knee. And every time he could see her boobs straining against her brassiere and the thin cotton of her dress.

It was still raining when they reached the Yangtze ferry at Chiangyin. McCoy was not pleased with what he found. Not only was one of the two ferries that normally worked the crossing tied up at a wharf and out of service, but none of the other vehicles in the convoy had crossed over.

Several hundred Chinese were milling around. A few drove trucks, and half a dozen had oxcarts. But mostly there were hand-pulled carts, and people carrying huge bundles on their backs. That meant that they would have to post a guard on every truck. Otherwise, if they blinked, they would have an empty truck.

Zimmerman told McCoy that when he tried to load the vehicles the night before, Lieutenant Macklin wouldn't let him. Macklin thought it would be better to wait on this side of the Yangtze for the car and truck from Nanking.

Officer-type thinking, McCoy decided. *You had to keep your eyes on the bastards all the time, or they would think of something smart like this.*

The remaining ferry was going to require three trips to transport all of the vehicles, so it was going to be at least an hour, probably closer to an hour and a half, before they were all across the river, which was at least four miles across at that point.

McCoy went to Lieutenant Macklin and told him he thought it would probably be a good idea if he took one of the cars, two Marine trucks, and one missionary truck on the first trip. Two of the three remaining trucks could cross on the second trip. And the remaining truck, the pickup/wrecker, and the other car could cross on the third . . . if that was all right with Lieutenant Macklin.

There was a nice little restaurant in Chen-chiang on the far shore, and McCoy could see no reason to remain on the near shore hungry, while there was a commissioned officer and gentleman (two, if you counted Sessions) available to supervise the loading of the rear echelon.

And if he was just a little lucky, he'd be able to overhear a conversation (or perhaps even join in one) in the restaurant that might tell him something about Japanese activity farther up the road.

Lieutenant Macklin thought that was as good a way to do it as any.

"Sergeant Zimmerman can handle it by himself, sir," McCoy said, "if you'd rather cross with the first load."

"I'll bring up the rear, McCoy," Lieutenant Macklin said, as McCoy had been eighty percent sure he would. "You and Sergeant Zimmerman go over and see what you can do to get the men something to eat."

"Aye, aye, sir."

Might as well let Zimmerman feed his face first, too. McCoy liked Zimmerman. He was a placid, quiet German who had found a home in the Corps, started a family with a Chinese girl, and did not resent McCoy's unofficial—if unmistakable—authority on the convoys the way some other senior noncoms did.

Ernie had some kind of rice bowl going on the Peking trips, McCoy was sure, but whatever it was, he did it quietly. And he didn't get fall-down drunk in a whorehouse as soon as there was the chance. Ernie understood Chinese, too, although for some strange reason, he pretended he didn't.

He was also faster on the pickup than you'd expect. For instance, he caught on right away to what McCoy wanted when McCoy suggested that he eat at a different restaurant from the big one McCoy was going to. Ernie would pick up whatever he could learn about any Japanese activity farther up the road while he sipped slowly on a beer. Too bad Lieutenant Macklin wasn't as sharp, McCoy thought.

The other two drivers McCoy took on the first ferry were PFCs, and they were on their best behavior because making the trips got them out from under the harassment of the motor pool. McCoy gave them his ritual "one beer, no more, or I'll have your ass" speech, confident that he'd be obeyed.

When Ernie came into the big restaurant (six tables, plus a low counter), McCoy was gnawing on a nearly crystallized piece of duck skin. Ernie took off his wide-brimmed campaign hat, gave it several violent shakes to knock the water loose from the rain cover, and then looked for and found McCoy.

Ernie was a man of few words: "The other Studebaker car's on the ferry."

McCoy nodded, and Ernie left. McCoy shoved the rest of the crisp duck skin in his mouth, daintily dipped his fingers into a bowl of warm water, dried them, and reached for his hat. He put it on at the prescribed angle, twisted his head around to seat the leather strap against the back of his head, and started out of the restaurant.

Then he changed his mind.

Fuck him. So Macklin and/or Sessions sees me eating and having a beer, so what?

He gave the proprietor a large bill and told him he would be back for his change after he'd returned the empty beer bottle and the napkin he was taking with him.

Then he walked quickly to the ferry, keeping himself (more importantly, the campaign hat) out of the rain as much as possible.

He didn't know why Lieutenant Macklin had decided to come in the second car rather than the third ferry trip, but it didn't matter: It was a to-be-expected thing for an officer—any officer—to do. No matter what an enlisted man decided, it could be improved upon by any officer. That's why they were officers.

McCoy paid little attention to the Studebaker until it was off the ferry and, with its wheels slipping and skidding, had made it up the road from the ferry slip. Then he stepped out from beneath the overhang of a building where he had been sheltered from the rain, went into the middle of the road, and made more or the less official Corps hand signals to tell Lieutenant Macklin where the car should be parked.

But Macklin wasn't driving the Studebaker. The lady missionary, Ol' No Underpants, Perfume on the Teats herself, was at the wheel. And she was alone.

What the hell's going on?

McCoy reclaimed the beer bottle he had been prepared to discard for either of the officers and walked nimbly—avoiding puddles where possible—to where Ol' No Underpants had parked.

She saw him coming and opened the door for him as he approached. The way she leaned over the seat to reach the door, he could see down her dress, down where she'd wiped perfume between her teats.

"I hope I'm not interfering with anything, Corporal McCoy," she said. "Lieutenant Macklin said it would be all right if I came now."

"Yes, ma'am," McCoy said.

"I also thought," she said, "that since there was no restaurant on that side, maybe there would be one on this one. I'm hungry."

"Yes, ma'am," McCoy said. "There's a restaurant here."

"Could you take me there?"

"Yes, ma'am."

"I've got an umbrella," she said, and reached into the backseat for it. He noticed that her breasts got in the way.

When she had it, she handed it to him.

"No, ma'am," McCoy said. "Thank you just the same."

"You mean you'd get wet?"

"I mean that Marines don't use umbrellas," McCoy said.

"It's against the rules, you mean?"

"Yes, ma'am."

"Don't you ever break the rules, Corporal?" she asked.

"Sometimes," he said.

"Everybody breaks them sometime," she said. "And this seems to be a good time for you to break this one."

He thought that sounded a little strange coming from a missionary, but decided to share the umbrella with her. There was no one here to see him who counted, and it was raining steadily.

Accepting the umbrella from her, McCoy got out of the car, opened the umbrella, and walked around to the driver's side. She slid out of the Studebaker, stepped under the umbrella, closed the door, and then took his arm. Her arm pressed against his, and he could feel the heaviness of her breast.

He marched with her back to the restaurant, shifting course to avoid the larger puddles.

The eyes of the proprietor widened without embarrassment when he saw the woman. Blond hair simply fascinated Orientals.

He came to the table for their order.

"What do you recommend?" she asked.

"I had the duck," McCoy said, almost blurted, "the way they fix it in Peking. I don't like the duck much, but the skin's first rate."

"Then I'll have that," she said. "Are you going to have anything?"

"I've had mine, thank you," McCoy said.

"Not even another beer?"

"I told the men they could have one beer," McCoy said. "It wouldn't be right if I had two."

"I'm sorry to hear that," she said.

"Why?" he asked, surprised.

"Because I would like a beer," she said. "But I can't have one. My husband doesn't like me to drink."

"What you mean is, you could have had a sip of mine?"

She nodded her head conspiratorially.

There was something perversely pleasant in frustrating the morality of a missionary, McCoy thought. He told the proprietor to put a bottle of beer in a tea pot and to bring the lady a cup to go with it.

When it was delivered she said, "I thought that you were telling him something like this."

"You did?" he asked.

"Your eyes lit up like a naughty boy's," she said.

He didn't know what to make of this missionary lady. She was being much too friendly. And he was well aware of the kind of relationship possible between American women and Marines in China: none. American women, probably because there were so few of them, were on a sort of pedestal. They were presumed to be ladies. They wore gloves and hats and did no work. And they did not speak to enlisted Marines, who were at the opposite end of the American social structure— only a half step above the Chinese. Most American women in China pretended that Marines were invisible. They did not walk arm in arm with them under umbrellas, or sit at tables with them in restaurants, or look directly—almost provocatively—into their eyes.

He could only come up with two explanations for Mrs. Reverend Feller's behavior. She could simply be acting according to her private idea of what it meant to be Christian; in other words, treating him as a social equal out of some strange notion that everybody was really equal in the sight of God. Or else maybe she was in fact flirting with him, or at least pretending to.

There were a couple of reasons that she might be doing just that. One was that she had caught him looking at her when she was putting perfume on her teats and thought it was funny. If that was the way it was, then she knew she could tease him and have her fun in perfect safety, because she knew that only a goddamned fool of a Marine would make a pass at an American lady missionary. And might even be hoping that he would say or do something out of line, so that she could run and tell the Reverend about it.

He'd heard about that happening. Not with a missionary lady, but with the wives of American businessmen. They'd catch their husband with a Chinese girl and decide to make it look like they were paying him back by getting some Marine to start hanging around and panting with his tongue hanging out. They had no intention of giving the poor fucker any; they just wanted to let their old man know there was a Marine with the hots for them. And then if the old man went to the colonel and the Marine wound up on the shit list, that was his problem.

Whatever Mrs. Reverend Feller was up to—even if she was just being Christian—it made him uncomfortable, and he wanted nothing to do with it. He changed the subject.

"There's one good thing about the bad road," McCoy said. "We can stay at Chiehshom tonight. It's going to be too dark to go any farther today."

"What's at Chiehshom?" she asked, looking at him over the edge of her teacup of beer.

"A nice hotel," he said, "built by a German. The plumbing works, in other words, and the kitchen's clean. It's on a hill over the lake."

"You always stay there?" she asked.

"Normally we get a lot farther than this," he said.

"When you don't have to carry missionaries with you, you mean?"

"I didn't say that," McCoy said.

"No, but that's what you meant," she said.

McCoy stood up and put his campaign hat on. "I'll go down to the ferry and see what's up," he said. "You can stay here. You'll be all right."

IV

While the Reverend Feller, Lieutenant Macklin, and "Mr." Sessions ate in the "big" restaurant, and the Marine drivers at one of the tiny stalls, Ernie Zimmerman took the opportunity once again to carefully check the vehicles, paying particular attention to the tires. Changing a tire on a muddy road was bad enough, but changing one in the rain, at night, was a royal fucking pain in the ass.

Zimmerman found a couple of tires that looked as if they might blow, one on a truck, the other on one of the Studebaker sedans, and ordered them changed. McCoy and Zimmerman were watching a PFC remove the wheel of the car when Lieutenant Macklin and Sessions walked up to them.

"We about ready to roll, Sergeant?" Lieutenant Macklin asked.

"Aye, aye, sir," Zimmerman said.

"Well, get everyone loaded up, please," Macklin said. "We'd like a word with Corporal McCoy."

"Aye, aye, sir," Zimmerman said, and walked off toward the food stalls where the drivers were eating. Macklin and Sessions walked out of earshot of the driver changing the tire, and McCoy followed them.

"Under the circumstances, McCoy," Sessions said, "I decided that it was necessary to make Lieutenant Macklin aware of my real purpose in being here."

"Yes, sir," McCoy said.

He was not annoyed, but neither was he surprised. Sessions was more than a little pissed about their conversation in

Nanking; and it was clear that Sessions was about to put him in his place. As missionaries have no authority to order Marine corporals around, it was necessary to let Macklin know who he actually was. He had thus told Macklin that he was an officer on a secret mission, and now they were both thrilled about their importance in the scheme of things—and prepared to deal with a lowly corporal who was standing in the way of their doing their duty. Captain Banning had warned him this was likely to happen.

"And we've been looking at the map," Sessions said. "Lieutenant Macklin thinks we can make it to Chiehshom before it gets dark. Do you agree with that?"

"Yes, sir," McCoy said. "It's a good place to spend the night. There's a good hotel there."

"So Lieutenant Macklin tells me," Sessions said. "More importantly, McCoy, it's not too far from Yenchi'eng, is it?"

McCoy's eyebrows went up as he looked at him. The Japanese 11th Infantry Division was at Yenchi'eng.

"No, sir," he said, "it's not."

"Have you ever been to Yenchi'eng, McCoy?" Sessions asked.

"Yes, sir," McCoy said.

"Do you know how the divisional artillery of the 11th Japanese Infantry is equipped?"

"Yes, sir," McCoy said. "They've got four batteries, they call it a regiment, of Model 94s. That's a 37-mm antitank cannon, but the Japs use it as regular artillery because they can throw so much fire. And the Chinese have damned little to use for counterfire."

"I want to check that out, McCoy," Lieutenant Sessions said.

"Sir?"

"I want to find out if the 11th Division has been equipped with German PAK38[1] cannon."

"They haven't," McCoy said. "What they've got, Lieutenant, is maybe thirty-five Model 94s. Eight to a battery, plus spares."

"You seem very sure of that, McCoy," Lieutenant Macklin said.

---

[1]PAK38: *Panzerabwehrkanone*, caliber 5cm, Model 1938.

"Yes, sir, I am."

"You know the difference between the two cannon?" Macklin pursued, more than a little sarcastic.

"The PAK38 is bigger, with a larger shield and larger wheels than the Model 94," McCoy said, on the edge of insolence, Lieutenant Macklin thought. "And it has a muzzle brake. They're not hard to tell apart."

"And you're absolutely sure the 11th Division doesn't have any of those cannon?" Sessions asked.

"I took some pictures of their artillery park a couple of weeks ago," McCoy said. "That's what they've got, Lieutenant. Thirty, maybe thirty-five 94s. Captain Banning sent the pictures to Washington."

"But we have no way of knowing, do we, Corporal McCoy, whether or not the Japanese have received German cannon since your last visit? Without having another look?" Macklin asked sarcastically.

"We have people watching the docks, and the railroad, and the roads. If the 11th Division had gotten any new artillery, we'd have heard about it."

" 'We'?" Macklin asked sarcastically.

"Captain Banning," McCoy said, accepting the rebuke, "has people watching the docks and the railroads and the roads."

"Under the circumstances—and after all, we are so close—I'm afraid I can't just accept that," Lieutenant Sessions said. "How long would you say it is by car from Chiehshom to Yenchi'eng?"

"If you drive down there, Lieutenant," McCoy said, "they're going to catch you, and you'll find yourself being entertained by the Japs for a couple of days."

"What do you mean by 'entertained'?"

"They'll take you on maneuvers," McCoy said. "Walk you around in the swamps all night, feed you raw fish, that sort of thing." He stopped, and then his mouth ran away with him: "Some of them have got a pretty good sense of humor. They had Lieutenant Macklin three days one time."

"That's quite enough, McCoy!" Macklin flared.

"Well then, we'll just have to make sure they don't catch us, won't we?" Lieutenant Sessions said.

"Lieutenant, I'm not going to Yenchi'eng with you," McCoy said. "I'm sorry."

"How long did you say it will take us to drive from Chiehshom to Yenchi'eng, Corporal?" Sessions asked.

"It's about a two-hour drive, maybe two and a half, with the roads like this."

"And you presumably can manage the road at night?"

"Sir, I'm sorry, but I'm not going to Yenchi'eng with you," McCoy said.

"I didn't ask you if you had volunteered, Corporal," Lieutenant Sessions said reasonably. "The decision to go has been made by Lieutenant Macklin and myself. Your presence will lend your knowledge of the terrain to our enterprise. I don't have to remind you, do I, that despite your special relationship with Captain Banning, you still remain subject to the orders of your superiors?"

"Lieutenant," McCoy said, "you're putting me on a spot."

"The only spot you'll be on," Macklin flared, "is if you persist in your defiance."

McCoy looked at him, shrugged, and took an envelope from his hip pocket. He extended it toward Sessions.

"I think you better take a look at this, Lieutenant," he said.

"What is that?" Sessions asked.

"My orders, sir, in writing," McCoy said. "Captain Banning said I wasn't to give them to you unless I had to. I think I have to."

Sessions took the envelope, tore it open, and unfolded the sheet of paper inside. He glanced at the sheet and then shook his head.

"What is it?" Lieutenant Macklin asked.

"It's a set of letter orders," Sessions said, and then read it aloud: 'Headquarters, 4th Marines, Shanghai, 13 May 1941. Subject, Letter Orders. To Corporal Kenneth J. McCoy, Headquarters Company, First Battalion, 4th Marines. Your confidential orders concerning the period 14 May 1941 to 14 June 1941 have been issued to you verbally by Captain Edward Banning, USMC. You are reminded herewith that no officer or noncommissioned officer assigned or attached to the 4th Regiment, USMC, is authorized to amend or countermand your orders in any way.' " Sessions looked at Macklin. "Corporal McCoy's letter orders are signed by the colonel."

"Well, I'll be damned," Macklin said. "I never heard of such a thing."

"Lieutenant," McCoy said to Macklin. "I wish you'd read those orders."

"Just what the hell do you mean by that?" Macklin snapped.

"With respect, sir," McCoy said. "I'd like to burn them."

"Go ahead and burn them," Macklin said coldly.

Sessions handed the orders back to McCoy, who ripped the single sheet of paper into long strips, which he then carefully burned, one at a time, letting the wind blow the ashes and unburned stub from his fingers.

"I presume your 'confidential verbal orders' forbid you to go to Yenchi'eng?" Macklin asked, when he had finished.

"No, sir, except that Captain Banning said I was to use my own judgment if you wanted me to do something like that."

"Then you have not been forbidden to go to Yenchi'eng? You've taken that decision yourself?" Sessions asked.

"That's about the size of it, sir," McCoy said.

A very self-confident young man, Sessions thought. *Highly intelligent. He almost certainly believes in what he's doing. So where does that leave us?*

"I presume you have considered, Corporal," Macklin said, icily, "that Lieutenant Sessions's interest in the cannon of the 11th Division is not idle curiosity? That he has been sent here by Headquarters, USMC?"

"Yes, sir," McCoy said. "Captain Banning told me all about that."

"And you are apparently unimpressed by my decision that knowing that for sure is worth whatever risk is entailed in going to Yenchi'eng?" Macklin asked, coldly furious.

"I'm convinced there's no way you could go there without getting caught," McCoy said. "You have to go by road. The first checkpoint you pass, they'll phone ahead to the Kempei-Tai, and that will be it."

"There are ways of getting around checkposts and the Kempei-Tai," Macklin said. "You have done so."

"That was different," McCoy said.

"That was different, *sir*," Macklin corrected him.

"That was different, sir," McCoy parroted.

"Well, then, perhaps you'd be good enough to tell Mr. Sessions and myself how you would go to Yenchi'eng."

"If I told you that, it would look like I thought you could get away with it, Lieutenant," McCoy said.

"So you refuse even to help us?" Macklin said, incredulously.

McCoy pretended he hadn't heard the question.

"And I don't see any point in taking the risk of going myself," he said. "If they had any German cannon, I'd know about it."

"Corporal," Lieutenant Macklin said, icily sarcastic, "I stand in awe of your self-confidence."

"Yes, sir," McCoy said.

"You will, I hope, tell us what you can about the location of the artillery park?" Lieutenant Sessions asked conversationally. "How we can find it?"

"Aye, aye, sir," McCoy said. "I hope you'll make it clear to Captain Banning, sir, that I told you you're going to get caught?"

"Oh, yes, Corporal McCoy," Lieutenant Macklin said. "You can count on our relating this incident to Captain Banning in detail."

(Two)
Chiehshom, Shantung Province, China
15 May 1941

The three classes of accommodation at the Hotel am See at Chiehshom had (in descending order) been originally intended for Europeans, European servants, and Chinese servants. On McCoy's first couple of trips to and from Peking, all the enlisted Marines had been put up in the rooms set aside for European servants. But on the last couple of trips, like this one, the management had made quite a show of giving the noncoms "European" rooms—small ones, to be sure—in the main wing of the hotel.

McCoy realized that the proprietor had figured out that the sergeant, rather than the officer-in-charge, was the man who really decided (by speeding up or slowing down) where the convoy and its ten-man detail would stop for the night. That meant the sale of ten beds and twenty meals, plus whatever they all had to drink. There wasn't all that much business anyway.

McCoy really liked to stay at the Hotel am See. The food was good and the place was spotless. And even the small rooms they gave the noncoms had enormous bathtubs with apparently limitless clean hot water. He would take a bath at night, a long soak, and then a shower in the morning. It was the only shower he'd had in China that made his skin sting with the pressure. All the others were like being rained on.

After settling into his room, McCoy had hoped to have dinner with Ernie Zimmerman and be gone from the dining room before the officers and the Fellers came down for dinner. That would give him a chance both to avoid Lieutenants Macklin and Sessions and to steel himself for another meeting with them that was scheduled for after dinner. They wanted him to go over their route to and from Yenchi'eng. As pissed as the both of them were with him, that was going to be bad enough without having dinner in the same room (where they didn't think enlisted Marines had any right to be anyway) with them.

But Ernie Zimmerman got hung up somehow getting the other Marines bedded down and was ten minutes late. Zimmerman and McCoy had no sooner sat down in the dining room when the officers and the Fellers showed up. Mrs. Feller said something to the Reverend, and he came over and insisted that they all have dinner together.

McCoy thought the officers would be pissed. Eating in the same room with enlisted Marines was bad enough, but not as bad as having to share a table with them. But they weren't. They were playing spy again, McCoy saw, and the dinner table gave them a stage for the playacting they thought was necessary.

"Mr." Sessions announced that he had asked Lieutenant Macklin if it would be all right if they spent two nights in Chiehshom, instead of the one originally planned. The Christian & Missionary Alliance was considering opening another mission in Yenchi'eng, and they wanted to take advantage of being close to it to have a good look at it.

He's a goddamned fool, McCoy thought. *They're all goddamned fools. They think they will look more innocent brazening it out, two missionaries and a Marine officer in full uniform simply out for a ride looking for a new place to save souls. It will take the Japs about ten minutes to learn they've left here, and there will be a greeting party waiting for them long before they get anywhere near Yenchi'eng.*

The only thing more dangerous than an officer convinced he's doing what duty requires is two officers doing the same thing. Two officers and a missionary.

They would be back in Chiehshom by nightfall, Sessions said, and spending the extra day would give Sergeant Zimmerman and his men the chance to go over the vehicles and make sure everything was shipshape.

"You're not going with them, Corporal McCoy," Mrs. Feller asked, "to drive the car?"

"No, ma'am," McCoy said. "I'm not going along."

Ernie Zimmerman, uncomfortable in the presence of the officers, and fully aware there was some friction between them and McCoy, bolted down his food and pushed himself wordlessly away from the table.

McCoy went after him.

"Ernie, jack up one of the trucks and drop the drive shaft," McCoy said.

"What the hell for?" Zimmerman demanded.

"Just do it, Ernie, please," McCoy said.

"What are they up to?" Zimmerman asked.

"You heard it," McCoy said.

"What was that bullshit anyway?"

"Just get somebody to drop a drive shaft, Ernie. And make sure one of the cars is gassed and ready to go," McCoy said. Then he went to his room to mark the route the damned fools should take to Yenchi'eng.

When McCoy met with the three of them in Sessions's room, they made no further attempt to get him to take them to Yenchi'eng. This surprised him until he realized they'd concluded that their brilliant inspiration of brazening it out was going to work, and they didn't need him.

After they came back from successfully spying on the Japs, they'd be in a position to rack his ass with Banning for refusing to go with them. They would have been right all along, and he would have been nothing but an insolent enlisted man with the gall to challenge the wise judgment of his betters.

There was nothing he could do to stop them, of course, and (except for having one of the missionary trucks jacked up and the drive shaft dropped so that it might fool the Kempei-Tai watching the hotel) there was nothing he could do to help them either.

But he set his portable alarm clock for half-past four and went down to the courtyard to see them off. Mrs. Feller was there too, the nipples of her teats sticking up under her bathrobe and her blond hair, now unbraided, hanging down her back.

Jesus Christ, without her hair glued to her head, she's a hell of a good-looking woman. I would give my left nut to get in the sack with her.

The officers and the missionary were a little carried away with the situation. They saw themselves, McCoy thought contemptuously, as patriots about to embark on a great espionage mission. McCoy had to temper his scorn, however, when Sessions took him aside and told him, dead serious, that no matter what happened today he wanted him to understand that he understood his position.

"This is one of those situations, Corporal, where we both must do what we believe is right. And I want you to know that I believe you thought long and hard about your obligations before you decided you couldn't go with me."

He's not so much of a prick as a virgin.

"Good luck, Lieutenant," McCoy said, and offered his hand.

What the hell, it didn't cost anything to say that. And if Sessions means what he said, then on the off chance they don't get bagged and Macklin tries to get me in trouble, maybe it'll help.

As they walked back to the hotel, Mrs. Feller's leg kept coming out of the flap of her bathrobe, and she kept trying to hold the robe closed. He remembered that all through dinner she had kept bumping her knee "accidentally" against his.

McCoy was now convinced she was just fucking around with him, getting some kind of sick kick out of trying to make him uncomfortable, the way some people get a sick kick out of teasing a dog. He intended to stay as far away from her as he could.

"Is there any interesting way you can think of to kill the

time until they get back?'' she asked, when they were inside the hotel.

She goddamned well knows there are two or three meanings I could put on that.

"Until it starts to rain, which should be about noon, you could fish, I suppose," McCoy said. "They've got tackle. I've got to work on the trucks."

"That doesn't sound very exciting," she said.

"I guess not," he said, turning and walking away from her down the corridor to his room.

He didn't see her at breakfast, and he ate with the Marines at lunch. They asked him where the officers and the Christer had gone, and how long that would keep them all in Chiehshom. Zimmerman had already told them he didn't know, they said, or else he wouldn't tell them. McCoy told them he didn't know, either.

At half-past three, a boy came to his room and told him that Sergeant Zimmerman wanted to see him in the lobby. When McCoy went down, there were two Japanese soldiers with Zimmerman, a sergeant and a corporal. They were both large for Japanese, and they were wearing leather jackets and puttees. Goggles hung loosely from leather helmets. Motorcycle messengers.

They bowed to McCoy and then saluted, and he bowed back and returned the salute. Then Zimmerman gave him two envelopes, one addressed to him and the other to Mrs. Feller.

"This is addressed to you," McCoy said.

"I can read," Zimmerman said. "And they want me to sign for it. I thought I better ask you."

One of the Japanese soldiers then handed McCoy some kind of a form to sign. He saw that it was just a message receipt form.

"Sign it," he said to Zimmerman.

"What is it?"

"A confession that you eat babies for breakfast," McCoy said.

Zimmerman, with obvious reluctance, carefully wrote his name on the form. He gave it to the Japanese sergeant, who bowed and saluted again, then marched out of the lobby with the other Japanese hopping along after him.

As he tore open the envelope and took out the message, McCoy heard their motorcycle engines start.

From what his note said, Lieutenant Macklin had obviously decided that the Japanese were going to read it before they delivered it:

Yenchi'eng
Sergeant Zimmerman:
The Reverend Mr. Feller, Mr. Sessions and I have accepted the kind invitation of the commanding general of the 11th Division of the Imperial Japanese Army to inspect the division.
I will send further orders as necessary.
R.B. Macklin 1/Lt. USMC

McCoy realized there was absolutely no "I Told You So" pleasure in his reaction. He felt sorry for them, and he felt a little sorry for himself. Sooner (if he could get through on the telephone now) or later, Captain Banning was going to eat his ass out for letting them get their asses in a crack.

"Well, what the hell does it say?" Zimmerman asked.

McCoy handed him the note.

"I figured it was something like that," Zimmerman said. "How come you didn't go? You knew they was going to get caught?"

McCoy shrugged.

"You figure the Japs'll find out Sessions is an officer?"

"What makes you think he's an officer?"

"Come on, McCoy," Zimmerman said.

"Christ, for his sake, I hope not."

"What do we do now?"

"We wait twenty-four, maybe forty-eight hours to see what the Japs do."

"Then what?"

"Then I don't know," McCoy said. "There's reason the guys have to hang around here, but I don't want them getting shitfaced in case we need them."

"Okay," Zimmerman said. He walked out of the hotel lobby, and McCoy went up the wide stairs to the second floor and knocked on Mrs. Feller's door.

When she opened it, her hair was up in braids again, and

she was wearing a pale yellow dress just about covered with tiny little holes.

He handed her the letter addressed to her. She raised her eyebrows questioningly and then tore open the envelope.

Even with her hair up again, she still looks pretty good. And Christ, what teats!

When she had read the letter, she raised her eyes and looked at him, obviously expecting some comment from him.

"Nothing to be worried about," he said. "They'll show them marching troops and barracks, and feed them food they know they won't like; and tonight they'll probably try hard to get them drunk. But there's no danger or anything like that. If there was, they wouldn't have let them send the letters."

"My husband doesn't drink," she said.

"He probably will tonight," McCoy said.

She seemed to find that amusing, he saw.

"His letter says that you will look after me," she said. "Are you going to look after me?"

"Yes, ma'am," he said.

"Starting at dinner? I missed you at lunch."

"I had something to do over lunch," he said. "And I'm afraid I'll be busy for dinner, too. If you'd like, I can ask Sergeant Zimmerman to have dinner with you."

"That won't be necessary," she said coldly.

Fuck you, too, lady!

"Are you going to do anything about this?" she asked. "Notify someone what's happened?"

"If I can get through on the phone," McCoy said.

It turned out he couldn't get through to Captain Banning in Shanghai, which didn't surprise him—and was actually a relief. Getting your ass chewed out was one of those things the longer you put off, the better.

And then he realized there was a way he could avoid it entirely. He thought it over a minute and went looking for Ernie Zimmerman.

(Three)
The Hotel am See
Chiehshom, Shantung Province
0815 Hours 17 May 1941

McCoy had just finished a hard day and night in the country

and was now lowering himself all the way into a full tub hot clean water when there was a knock at his door.

"Come back later," he yelled in Chinese.

"It's Ellen Feller," she said.

"I'm in the bathtub."

Her response to this was a heavy, angry-sounding pounding on the door.

"Wait a minute, wait a minute," he called. "I'm coming."

McCoy hoisted himself out of the tub, wrapped a towel around his waist, and walked dripping to the door.

The moment it was opened a crack, she pushed past him into the room. She was wearing her robe, and her hair was again unbraided and hanging nearly to her waist. When he came back she must have seen him from her window talking to Ernie Zimmerman in the courtyard, he decided.

She walked to his small window, turned, and glared at him.

"Close the door, or someone will see us in here," she ordered.

In his junior year in St. Rose of Lima High, there had been a course in Musical Appreciation. They had studied *Die Walküre* then. That was what Mrs. Ellen Feller looked like now, McCoy thought, smiling. Obviously pissed off, she stood stiff and strident-looking, with her long hair flowing, her cheeks red, and her teats awesome even under her bathrobe—a goddamned Valkyrie.

"What are you smiling about?" she demanded furiously. Then, without waiting, demanded even more angrily, "And where have you been?"

"I don't think that's any of your business," McCoy said.

"You've been laying up with some almond-eyed whore in the village," she accused furiously. "You've been gone all night!"

"Don't hand me any of your missionary crap," McCoy said angrily. "Where I have been all night is none of your goddamned business. What did you do, come looking for me?"

He could tell from the look in her eyes that she had, indeed, come to his room looking for him.

"Why?" he asked. "What's happened?"

She shook her head. "Nothing," she said. "I just wondered where you were," she added awkwardly.

McCoy was still angry. "So you could start playing games
with me again?" he asked.

"I don't know what you're talking about," she said
automatically.

"You know goddamned well what I'm talking about," he
said.

"So that's what you thought," she said, after a moment.

"Go find some clown in the mission," he said, warming to
his subject, "if you get your kicks that way. Just leave people
like me out of it."

"How can you be so sure it was a game?" she asked.

"Huh!" McCoy snorted righteously.

"Maybe you should have considered the possibility that it
wasn't a game and that you didn't have to go buy a woman,"
she said. "Maybe what you need, Corporal Killer McCoy, is
a little more self-confidence."

"Jesus Christ!" he said.

"What's your given name?" she asked.

"Ken, Kenneth," he said without thinking. Then, "Why?"

"Because if I'm going to get in that bathtub with you and
scrub the smell of your whore off you, I thought it would be
nice to know your name."

"There was no whore," he said.

She looked intently at him and almost visibly decided he
was telling the truth. She nodded her head.

"Then the bath can wait till later," she said. "Lock the
door."

(Four)
Room 23
The Hotel Am See
Chiehshom, Shantung Province
1015 Hours 18 May 1941

"This is very nice," Ellen Feller said, picking the camera up
from the chest of drawers and turning to look at him. She was
naked. "Very expensive." That was a question.

"It's a Leica," he said. "It belongs to the Corps."

She held it up and pretended to aim it.

"Pity we can't use it," she said. "I would like to have a memento of this. Of us."

"For your husband to find," he said.

She laughed and put the camera down. It had been practically nonstop screwing (with breaks only for meals and trips to make sure none of the Marines had gone off on a drunk someplace); but this was the first time either of them had mentioned her husband.

"It's possible he could walk in any minute," McCoy said. "And catch us like this."

"You don't have to worry about him," she said. "But I wouldn't want to get you in trouble with your officers. Are they really likely to come back soon?"

"Can't tell. Why wouldn't I have to worry about him?"

"You mean you couldn't tell? Not even from the way he looked at you?"

"What are you saying, that he's a fairy?"

She shrugged.

"Then why do you stay married to him?" he asked. "Why did you marry him in the first place?"

"That's none of your business," she said. She leaned against the chest of drawers and arched her back.

She inhaled and ran her fingers across the flat of her belly. And then she told him.

"When I was fourteen, my father had a religious experience," she said. "Do you know what that means?"

"No," he admitted.

"He accepted the Lord Jesus Christ as his personal saviour," Ellen Feller said, evenly. "And brought his family, my mother and me, into the fold with him. She didn't mind, I don't suppose, although I suspect she's a little uncomfortable with some of the brothers and sisters of the Christian & Missionary Alliance. And I just went along. Girls at that age are a little frightened of life anyway; and when the hellfire of eternity is presented as a reality, it's not hard to accept the notion of being washed in the blood of the lamb."

"Jesus Christ," McCoy said.

"Yes," Ellen said wryly. "Jesus Christ."

She pushed herself off the chest of drawers and walked to the bed. Then she leaned over him and ran the balls of her fingers over his chest.

"So I passed through my high school years convinced that when I had nice thoughts about boys, it was Satan at work trying to get my soul."

"I was a Catholic," McCoy said. "They tried to tell us the same thing."

"Did you believe it?" she asked.

"I wasn't sure," he said.

"I was," she said. "And I went through college that way. It wasn't hard. I was surrounded with them. Whenever anyone confessed any doubts, the others closed ranks around her. Or him. We prayed a lot, and avoided temptation. No drinking, no dancing, no smoking. No touching."

She moved her hand to his groin and repeated, "No touching."

"So how come you married him? Where did you meet him?"

"I was a senior in college," she said. "The Christian & Missionary Alliance is, as you can imagine, big on missionaries; and he came looking for missionary recruits. Came from here, I mean. With slides of China and all the souls the Alliance was saving for Jesus. He told us all about the heathens and how they hungered for the Lord. Very impressive stuff.

"And then that summer, right after I graduated, he came to our church in Baltimore . . . I'm from Baltimore . . . to give his report to our church. My father is a pillar of our church, and he was important to my husband, because my father is pretty well off. He stayed with us while he was in Baltimore."

"And made a play for you," McCoy said. "Jesus, that feels good!"

She chuckled deep in her throat and bent over him and nipped his nipple with her teeth. He put his hand on her breast and dragged her down on top of him.

"Do you want to hear this, or not?" she asked.

"Yeah," he said.

"It's all right with me if you don't," she said.

"Finish it," he said.

"What I thought I was getting was a life toiling in the Lord's Vineyard," Ellen went on. "With a man of God. Saving the heathen Chinese from eternal damnation. What he knew he was getting was a wife, and a wife who would not only put to rest unpleasant suspicions that had begun to crop up, but a wife whose father would more than likely be very generous to his mission . . . he had the mission in Wang-Tua, then . . . but probably to him personally."

"When did you find out he was a faggot?" McCoy asked.

"We were married at nine o'clock in the morning," she said. "At noon, we took the train to New York. And then from New York, we took the train to San Francisco. I decided that it was wrong of me to think that anything would happen on a railroad train. And we boarded the *President Jefferson* for Tientsin the same day we arrived in San Francisco."

"And nothing happened on the ship?"

"*Something* happened on the ship," Ellen said. "I was not surprised that I didn't like it very much, and that it didn't happen very often."

"Then he can get it up?" McCoy asked.

"Not like this," she said, squeezing him so hard that he yelped. "But he can, yes. I suspect he closes his eyes and pretends I'm a boy."

"So why the hell did you stay married to him?"

"You just don't understand. I just didn't know. I was innocent. Ignorant."

He snorted.

"Meaning I'm not innocent now?" she asked.

"No complaints," McCoy said.

"There was somebody else, obviously."

"Who?"

"None of your business," she said, but then she told him: A newly ordained bachelor missionary with whom she'd been left alone a good deal when the Reverend Feller had been promoted to Assistant District Superintendent. They had been caught together. They had begged forgiveness. After prayerful consideration, the Reverend Feller had decided the way to handle the situation was to send the young missionary home, as "unsuited for missionary service," which happened often. A church would be found for him at home. As a guarantee of impeccable Christian behavior in the future, there was a written confession of his sinful misbehavior left behind in the Reverend Feller's safe.

McCoy was sure there'd been more than one "somebody else." She had done things to him he hadn't thought American women even knew about. Things that one missionary minister wouldn't have taught her. But he could hardly expect her to provide him with a list of the guys she had screwed. She wasn't like that. He was somewhat surprised to realize that he had come to like Ellen Feller.

"After that," Ellen went on, "he never came near me. I thought he was either disgusted with me or was punishing me."

"You still didn't know he was queer?"

"I didn't find out about that, believe it or not, until just before the Alliance called him home for consultation. That was the reason I didn't go home with him."

"How'd you find out?"

"I walked in on him," she said, matter-of-factly.

He was aware that she'd stopped manipulating him and he had gone down. She still had her hand on him, though, possessively, and he liked that.

"What did he say?" McCoy asked.

"Nothing," she said. "He didn't even stop. So I just closed the door and left. Very civilized."

"Why didn't you leave him?" McCoy asked.

"It's not that simple, my darling," Ellen said.

McCoy liked when she called him "my darling," even though it embarrassed him a little. He couldn't remember anyone ever saying that to him before. It was a lot different from a whore calling him "honey" or "sweetheart" or "big boy."

"Why not?" he asked.

"Well, there's Jerry's detailed, written confession, for one thing," she said, as if explaining something that should have been self-evident.

"So what?"

"He would show it to my father."

"So what? Tell your father he's queer."

"I wouldn't be believed," she said. "He's a man of God. My father is very impressed with him. He would think I made the accusation in desperation, to excuse my own behavior."

"Then fuck your father," McCoy said.

Her eyebrows went up. "I know how you meant that," she said.

"Jesus!" he said.

"I'm thirty years old," she said. "I have no money. I can play every hymn in the hymnal from memory on the piano. I speak Chinese. Unless I could find a job as a Chinese-speaking piano player, I don't know how I could support myself."

Thirty years old? At first I thought she was older than that. Then I thought she was younger. Thirty is too old for me. What the hell am I thinking about? In a week, she'll get on a ship, and that will be the last I'll ever see her.

"Can you type?" McCoy asked. She nodded. "Then get a job as a typist, for Christ's sake."

"For my own sake, you mean," she said. Then she added, mysteriously, "I have something else that might turn out. I won't know until I get to the States."

"Like a couple of thousand-year-old vases, for example?" McCoy asked. "Or some jade?"

Her face clouded, and she took her hand from his crotch and covered her mouth with it. "What did you do, look in the crates?"

"No. A stab in the dark," McCoy said.

"My God, does anybody else know?"

"My officer thinks that's the real reason your husband came back to China," McCoy said. "He doesn't believe the selfless patriot business."

"I have three Ming dynasty vases and some jade my husband doesn't know about," Ellen said. "I thought I could sell them and use the money to get a start."

"You probably can, if you can get them through customs," McCoy said.

"Your . . . officer . . . isn't going to say anything?"

"It's none of his business," he said.

"And the other officers? Do they know?"

"You've just seen how smart they are," McCoy said.

"It left us alone, my darling," she said.

"I like it when you say that," McCoy said. She looked into his eyes and it made him uncomfortable. "And I like it when you put your hand on my balls."

She stiffened. She didn't like him to talk that way, he thought. But she shifted on the bed and cupped her hand on him again.

"I would like it, too, if you said that to me," she whispered.

"Said what?"

"My darling."

"My darling," McCoy said, and flushed. It made him uncomfortable. "And I like to suck your teats," he added almost defiantly.

She stiffened again, and he wondered why he said that, knowing it would piss her off.

"I like the thought but not the vocabulary," she sighed. "Cows have teats, ladies have breasts."

"Pardon me," McCoy said.

"You're forgiven," she said.

"Move closer, so I can play with them," McCoy said.

"Why, you wicked little boy, you," she said, but she pushed herself closer to him, so that his hands and his mouth could reach her breast.

The "my darling" business was over, McCoy realized. First with relief, then with sadness.

She took her nipple from his mouth a moment later and kissed him lasciviously, then moved her head down his body. She was just straddling him when there was a knock at the door.

"Come back later," McCoy called in Chinese.

"It's Lieutenant Sessions, McCoy, open the door!"

Breathing heavily, Ellen reluctantly hauled herself off him and scurried around the room, picking up her clothing. McCoy watched her moves—lovely and graceful. She was the best-looking piece of ass he'd ever had, he had realized sometime during the last twenty-four hours. And the best.

He wondered how she was going to handle Sessions. She was not going to be able to holler rape, which was what usually happened when an American woman got caught fucking a Marine. Not only wouldn't she be able to get away with it (how could she explain being in his room?); but she had called him 'my darling' and he knew somehow that she meant it. He meant more to her than a stiff prick. She was not going to cause him any trouble, and he knew he didn't want to cause her any.

"Come on, Corporal, I have business with you!" Sessions called.

McCoy waited until she'd gone into the bathroom, then

pushed himself out of the bed and went to the door, pulling on his shorts en route.

Lieutenant Sessions wore two days' growth of beard, and his seersucker suit was badly soiled. The Japanese knew that it embarrassed Americans not to be clean-shaven, so razors were not made available. And there was evidence of an "accident" at a meal. McCoy was amused at the Japanese skill in embarrassing their unwanted guests (and so was Captain Banning), but it was apparent that Lieutenant Sessions was not.

"Sergeant Zimmerman said he had no idea where you were," Sessions accused as he pushed past McCoy into the room.

McCoy didn't reply.

"I presume that you have reported our detention by the Japanese to Shanghai?" Sessions asked.

"No, sir," McCoy said.

"Why not, Corporal?" Sessions asked angrily.

"I thought I'd wait to see what the Japs decided to do," McCoy said.

"You 'thought you'd wait'?" Sessions quoted incredulously. "Good God! And it's pretty clear, isn't it, how you passed your time while you were waiting? What the hell have you been doing in here, McCoy? Conducting an orgy?"

McCoy didn't reply.

"A round-the-clock orgy," Sessions went on, looking at the debris, food trays, bottles of beer, and towels on the floor. He sniffed the air. "It smells like a whorehouse in here. Is she still here, for Christ's sake?"

McCoy nodded.

"Goddamn it, Corporal, in my absence you were supposed to take charge, not conduct yourself like a PFC on payday. You are prepared to offer no excuse at all for not getting in touch with Shanghai and reporting what had happened to us?"

"I was trying not to make waves," McCoy said.

"And what the hell is that supposed to mean?"

The bathroom door opened and Ellen Feller came into the room. She was in her bathrobe, and her hair fanned down her shoulders.

She looked directly at Lieutenant Sessions as she walked through the room and out the door.

"Well, that really does it," Sessions said coldly, almost calmly, when she had gone. "Instead of doing your duty . . . Jesus Christ! I'm going to have your stripes for this, McCoy. I'd like to have you court-martialed!"

McCoy walked across the room to the chest of drawers and picked up the Leica camera.

"Goddamnit, Corporal, don't you turn your back on me when I'm talking to you!" Sessions said furiously.

McCoy rewound the film, opened the camera, and slipped the film out. He held the small can of film between his thumb and index finger and turned to face Lieutenant Sessions.

"I hope you didn't lose your temper like that in Yenchi'eng," McCoy said. "So far as the Japs are concerned, you lose a lot of face when you lose your temper."

"How dare you talk to me that way?" Sessions barked, both incredulous and furious.

"Lieutenant, as I see it, you have two choices," McCoy said. "You can make a by-the-book report of what happened: That against my advice, you went to Yenchi'eng and got yourself caught, and that when you came back here, you found out that I hadn't even reported that the Japs had you . . ."

" 'Had completely abandoned your obvious obligations' would be a better way to put it," Sessions interrupted.

"And had 'completely abandoned my obvious obligations' " McCoy parroted.

"That's Silent Insolence[2] on top of everything else!" Sessions snapped.

"And that you found Mrs. Feller in my room," McCoy said.

"What the hell were you thinking about in that connection?" Sessions fumed. "Good God, man, her husband is a missionary!"

"Who will say that his wife was in here reading the Bible to me," McCoy said calmly. "He's a faggot."

Surprise flashed over Sessions's face.

"She is a married woman, and you damned well knew she

---

[2]Prior to 1948 the Universal Code of Military Justice included the offense "Silent Insolence." Among the offenses therein embraced was a "mocking attitude" to military superiors.

was," Sessions said, somewhat lamely. This confrontation was not going at all the way he had expected it would.

"The other choice you and Lieutenant Macklin have," McCoy said, "is to report that you have proof the Japs don't have any German PAK38 50-mm cannons, at least not in the 11th Division."

That caught Sessions by surprise.

"What are you talking about?" he asked. "What proof?"

"If they had German cannon, they would have turned in their Model 94s," McCoy said. "They didn't." He held up the can of film. "I took these at first light yesterday morning," he said. "I was lucky: The Japs were up before daylight lining them up and taking the covers off. Probably weekly maintenance, something like that."

It took Sessions a moment to frame his thoughts.

"So you went yourself. And of course didn't get caught. That was very resourceful of you, McCoy," he said.

McCoy shrugged.

"How the hell did you do it?" Sessions asked.

"The German's got a truck," he said.

"German? Oh, you mean the man who owns the hotel?"

McCoy nodded.

"You just borrowed his truck and drove into Yenchi'eng, that's it?"

"Not exactly," McCoy said. "I went into Yenchi'eng last night. On a bicycle. I told the boy who drives the German's truck there was a hundred yuan in it for him if he picked me up at a certain place on the road at half-past six yesterday morning."

"And then he just brought you back?"

"No, we had to go into town first. He picks up stuff—vegetables mostly, sometimes a pig and chickens. I had to go in with him."

"How did you keep from being seen?"

"I didn't," McCoy said. "When I'm around the Japs, I play like I'm an Italian."

"How do you do that? Do you speak Italian?"

McCoy nodded.

"Christ, you're amazing, McCoy!" Sessions said.

"It was stupid, me going in there like that," McCoy said. "I should have known better."

"Why did you go?" Sessions asked.

"You acted like it was important," McCoy said. "Anyway, it's done. And if you were to tell Captain Banning that you and Macklin and the Reverend were making a diversion, that you knew I was going to Yenchi'eng, I wouldn't say anything," McCoy said.

"You're not, I hope, suggesting, McCoy, that I submit a patently dishonest report," Sessions said.

"Rule one, doing what we're doing," McCoy said, "is don't make waves. Either with the Corps or with the people you're watching. You tell them what really happened, you're going to look like a . . ."

The next word in that sentence was clearly going be "horse's ass," Sessions thought. He stopped himself just in time from saying, "How dare you talk to me that way?"

A small voice in the back of his skull told him quietly but surely that he had indeed made a horse's ass of himself already—in China ten days and already grabbed by the Japanese doing something he had been told not to do, and digging himself in still deeper every time he opened his mouth.

He had been a Marine eleven years. Never before had an enlisted man—not even a Master Gunnery Sergeant when he had been a wet-behind-the-ears shavetail—talked to him the way this twenty-one-year-old corporal was talking to him now.

And the small voice in the back of his skull told him McCoy was *not* insolent. Inferiors are insolent to superiors. McCoy was tolerantly contemptuous, as superiors are to inferiors. And the painful truth seemed to be that he had given him every right to do so.

He had been informed—and had pretended to understand—that he would have to learn to expect the unexpected. And he hadn't. Because he was a thirty-two-year-old officer, he had presumed that he knew more than a twenty-one-year-old enlisted man.

If he followed the book—the code of conduct expected of an officer and a gentleman, especially one who wore an Annapolis ring—he would immediately grab a telephone and formally report to Captain Banning that—against McCoy's advice—he had taken the Reverend Feller and Lieutenant

Macklin to Yenchi'eng, been detained by the Japanese, had a pot of some greasy rice substance dumped in his lap, and then had returned to find that not only was Corporal McCoy fornicating with the missionary's wife (conduct prejudicial to good military order and discipline) but was silently insolent to boot. And that he just incidentally happened to have a roll of 35-mm film of the 11th Japanese Division's artillery park.

"I need a bath, a shave, and a clean uniform, Corporal," Lieutenant Sessions said. "We'll settle this later."

"Aye, aye, sir."

"I'd like to get started again first thing in the morning," Sessions went on. "Will there be any problems about that?"

"No, sir," McCoy said. "Now that you're back, we can move anytime you want to."

Sessions realized he was still making an ass of himself and that he had to do something about it.

"What I intend to do when we get somewhere with secure communications, Corporal McCoy," he said, "is advise Captain Banning that I went to Yenchi'eng against your advice and was detained by the Japanese. I will tell him of your commendable initiative in getting the film of the Japanese artillery park. I can see no point in discussing your personal life. I would be grateful, when you make your own report, if you would go easy on how I stormed in here and showed my ass."

"I hadn't planned to say anything about that, sir," McCoy said.

"And I'm sure," Sessions said, searching for some clever way to phrase it, "that . . . you will not permit your romantic affairs to in any way cast a shadow on the Corps' well-known reputation for chastity outside marriage."

"No, sir," McCoy said, chuckling. "I'll be very careful about that, sir." And then he added: "I'd be grateful if you didn't tell Lieutenant Macklin about Mrs. Feller."

Sessions nodded. "Thank you, McCoy," he said, then turned and walked out of the room.

V

(One)
The Hotel am See
Chiehshom, China
2215 Hours 18 May 1941

McCoy could not sleep. The smell of Ellen was inescapably on the sheets. And her image was no less indelibly printed on his mind.

Earlier, he found himself next to her at dinner. The moment he sat down, her knee moved against his.

There wasn't anything particularly sexy about her touch, and she didn't try to feel him up under the table—or he her—or anything like that. She just wanted to touch him. She didn't say two words to him either, except "please pass the salt." But she didn't take her knee away once.

All too soon, the Reverend Feller announced, "Well, we have a long day ahead of us." Ellen rose after him and followed him out . . . leaving McCoy with a terrible feeling of loss.

Later, McCoy and Zimmerman went to the European servants' quarters to make sure none of the drivers had shacked up in town. Afterward, Zimmerman asked matter-of-factly, "Sessions find out you're fucking the missionary lady?"

He had *not* been "fucking the missionary lady." It had started out that way, but it wasn't that way now. McCoy couldn't bring himself to admit he was in love, but it was more than an unexpected piece of ass, more than "fucking the missionary lady." And she had called him "my darling," and had meant it. And he had meant it, too, when she made him say it back.

"Yeah," McCoy said.

"And?"

"And what?"

"What's he going to do about it?"

"He's not going to do anything about it," McCoy said. "He's all right."

"You're lucky," Zimmerman said. "If that bastard Macklin finds out, McCoy, you're going to find yourself up on charges."

"One good way for him to find out, Ernie, is for you to keep talking about it."

"You better watch your ass, McCoy," Zimmerman said.

"Yeah," McCoy said. "I will."

Jesus Christ, what a fucking mess!

He turned the light back on and reached for the crossword puzzles from the *Shanghai Post.* He did three of them before he fell asleep sitting up. Then, carefully, so as not to rouse himself fully, he turned the light off, slipped under the sheet, and felt himself drifting off again.

When he felt her mouth on him, he thought he was having a wet dream—and that surprised him, considering all the fucking they had done. And then he realized that he wasn't dreaming.

"I thought that might wake you up, my darling," Ellen Feller said softly.

"What about your husband?"

"What about him? As you so obscenely put it," she said, "fuck him."

"You mean he knows?"

"I mean he sleeps in a separate bed, and when I left him, he was asleep."

"I had a hard time getting to sleep," McCoy said, "thinking about you."

"I'm glad," she said. She moved up next to him and put her face in his neck. "I would have come sooner," she said, "but he insisted on talking."

"About what?"

"That his being detained by the Japanese was a good thing, that it will probably make it easier to get the crates on the ship. Without having them inspected, I mean."

The thought saddened him. In nine days she would leave, and that would be the last he would ever see of her.

"You'd better set your alarm clock," she said practically. "I don't want to fall asleep in here."

He set the alarm clock, but it was unnecessary. They were wide awake at half-past four. Neither of them had slept for more than twenty minutes all through the night.

(Two)
Huimin, Shantung Province
27 May 1941

It took them another nine days to reach Huimin, nine days without an opportunity for McCoy and Ellen to be together.

The days on the way to Huimin were pretty much alike. They would start out early and drive slowly and steadily until they found a place where they could buy lunch. Failing that they stopped by the side of the road and picnicked on rice balls, egg rolls, and fried chicken from the hoods and running boards of the trucks and cars.

The road meandered around endless rice paddies. The inclines and declines were shallow, but the curves were often sharp, thus making more than twenty miles an hour impossible. Sometimes there was nothing at all on the road to the horizon, and sometimes the road was packed with Chinese, walking alone or with their families or behind ox-drawn carts.

The Chinese were usually deaf to the sound of a horn. So when the road was narrow, as it most often was, it was necessary to crawl along in low gear until the road widened enough to let them pass the oxcarts. But sometimes at the blast of the horn, the slowly plodding pedestrians would jump to the side of the road and glower as the convoy passed.

When they had to picnic by the side of the road, McCoy tried to stop when there was no one else on the road. But most of the time, in spite of McCoy's intentions, they were surrounded by hordes of Chinese within five minutes. Some stared in frank curiosity, and others begged for the scraps.

Or for rides. And that was impossible, of course. If they allowed Chinese in the backs of the trucks, the beds would be stripped bare within a mile.

At Ssuyango, T'anch'eng, and Weifang, McCoy spent the hours of darkness trying to find out whether various Japanese units had indeed received German field artillery pieces. And at T'anch'eng, he somewhat reluctantly took Lieutenant Sessions with him.

Sessions skillfully sandbagged him into that. He came to McCoy's room after supper, while McCoy was dressing: black cotton peasant shirt, trousers, and rubber shoes, and a black handkerchief over his head. It was less a disguise than a solution to the problem of crawling through feces-fertilized rice paddies. A complete suit cost less than a dollar. He wore one and carried two more tightly rolled and tied with string that he looped and fastened around his neck.

When he came out of a rice paddy smelling like the bottom of a latrine pit, he would strip and put on a fresh costume. It didn't help much, but it was better than running around soaked in shit.

During the stopover at Ssuyango, McCoy made a deal with a merchant: five gallons of gasoline for eight sets of cotton jackets and trousers. When Sessions came to his room at T'anch'eng, he still had three left, not counting the one he was wearing.

Sessions was politely curious about exactly what McCoy intended to do, and McCoy told him. It wasn't that much of a big deal. All he was going to do was make his way down the dikes between the rice paddies until he was close to the Japanese compound. Then he would slip into the water and make his way close enough to the compound to photograph the artillery park and motor pool. Then he would make his way out of the rice paddie, change clothes, and come back.

"How do you keep the camera dry?" Sessions asked.

"Wrap it in a couple of rubbers," McCoy said.

Sessions laughed appreciatively.

"Do you go armed?"

"I have a knife I take with me," McCoy told him. "But the worst thing I could do is kill a Jap."

Sessions nodded his understanding. Then he said, "Tell me the truth, McCoy. There's no reason I couldn't go, is there? If you were willing to take me, I mean."

"Christ, Lieutenant, you don't want to go."

"Yes, I do, McCoy," Sessions had said. "If you'll take me, I'll go."

Then he walked to the bed and picked up the peasant suit.

"I'd like to have a picture of me in one of these," he said. "It would impress the hell out of my wife."

He looked at McCoy and smiled.

"I really would like to go with you, McCoy," he said. It was still a request.

"Officers are supposed to be in charge," McCoy said. "That wouldn't work."

"You don't have to worry about that," Sessions said. "You're the expert, and I know it. It's your show. I'd just like to tag along."

"Once you get your shoes in a rice paddy, they'll be ruined," McCoy said. It was his last argument.

"Okay," Sessions said. "So I wear old shoes."

So he took Sessions with him. It went as he thought it would, and the only trouble they had was close to the Jap compound. Sessions panicked a little when he hadn't heard McCoy for a couple of minutes and came looking for him, calling his name in a stage whisper.

They didn't find any German PAK38s, but neither did they get caught. And McCoy was by then convinced that the PAK38s existed only in the imagination of chairwarming sonsofbitches in Washington, bastards who didn't have to crawl around through rice paddies or fields fertilized with human shit.

Sessions was so excited by his adventure that when they got back to the Christian & Missionary Alliance Mission, he insisted on talking about it until it was way too late to even think of getting together with Ellen for a quickie before breakfast.

After it was light, they killed the roll of film in the camera by taking pictures of each other dressed up like Chinamen.

McCoy hoped that the pictures of Sessions dressed up that way might get the guy off the hook in Washington. They might decide to forget that the Japs had caught him if they saw that he had at least tried to do what they'd sent him to do.

The next night, however, McCoy refused to take Sessions with him when he went to see what he could find near the mission at Weifang. It was a different setup there, the Japs ran perimeter patrols, and he didn't want to run the risk of the both of them getting caught. Sessions didn't argue. Which made McCoy feel a little guilty, because the real reason he didn't want to take Sessions along was that he slowed McCoy down. If Sessions wasn't along, maybe he could get back to the mission in time for Ellen to come to his room.

That hadn't done any good. When he got back, Sessions was waiting for him. Sessions kept him talking (even though there hadn't been any German cannon at Weifang, either) until it was too late to do anything with Ellen. It was really a royal pain in the ass doing nothing with her during the day but hold hands on the front seat for a moment, or touch legs under a table, or something like that. Or he would catch her looking at him.

He decided to take Sessions with him to look at a motorized infantry regiment, the 403rd, near Huimin, because it was the last chance they would have on this trip. If there were some of these German cannons at Huimin, Sessions might as well be able to say he found them. Otherwise—having gotten himself caught by the Japanese—he was going to come off this big-time secret mission looking like an asshole. The pictures of him dressed up like a Chinaman weren't going to impress the big shots as much as his report that he had been caught.

McCoy was beginning to see that Sessions wasn't that much of your typical Headquarters, USMC, sonofabitch. What was really wrong with him was that he didn't know what he was doing. And he could hardly be blamed for that. They didn't teach "How to Spy on the Japs" at the Officer School in Quantico. It was a really dumb fucking thing for the Corps to do, sending him over here the way they had; but to be fair, that was the Corps' fault, not his.

And at Huimin, they found PAK38s. The 403rd Motorized Infantry Regiment (Separate) of His Imperial Majesty's Imperial Fucking Army had eight of them. And the eight had the wrong canvas covers. So they'd taken covers from the Model 94s and put them over the PAK38s.

They didn't fit. The muzzle of the PAK38s, with its distinctive and unmistakable muzzle brake, stuck three feet outside the two small canvas covers. And with the Model 94s parked right beside them—looking very small compared to the PAK38s—there was absolutely no question about what they were.

McCoy shot two thirty-six-exposure rolls of 35-mm black and white film in the Leica, and then a twenty-exposure roll of Kodacolor, although he suspected that one wouldn't turn out. Kodacolor had a tendency to fuck up when you used it at first light—McCoy had no idea why.

Sessions was naturally all excited, and had a hard time keeping himself under control. But he didn't order McCoy, he asked him whether it would be a good idea to send somebody—maybe him, maybe Zimmerman—right off to Tientsin with the film. Or to take the whole convoy to Tientsin instead of making the other stops.

And Sessions just accepted it when McCoy told him that if he or Zimmerman took off alone with the film, the Kempei-Tai, who had been following them around since they crossed the Yangtze River, would figure there was something special up, and that would be the last time he or Zimmerman would ever be seen.

"Chinese bandits, Lieutenant," McCoy said. "Since there really aren't any, the Japs have organized their own."

"And similarly, taking the whole convoy to Tientsin right away would make them think something was out of the ordinary?"

"Yes, it would," McCoy said. "They probably would leave the whole thing alone, but you couldn't be sure. If we do what we told them we're going to do . . ."

"That would be best, obviously," Sessions concluded the sentence for him.

"Aye, aye, sir."

And it will give us another night on the road, maybe more if I get lucky and one of the trucks breaks down. And maybe that will mean maybe more than one other night with Ellen. Christ knows, I've done all the crawling through rice paddies I'm going to do on this trip.

He had no such luck. They spent the next night in a Christian & Missionary Alliance mission, where he was given a small room to share with Sergeant Zimmerman. Since he was in a different building from the officers and missionaries, there was just nothing he could do about getting together with Ellen.

He wondered if he might get lucky in Tientsin. He hoped

so. It would probably be the last time in his life he would
ever have a woman like that.

It was about two hundred miles from Huimin to Tientsin.
About halfway there, there was another ferry. This one crossed
a branch of the Yun Ho River. It wasn't much of a river,
maybe two hundred yards across, and the ferry was built to
fit. He thought for a minute that he and Ellen were going to
get to cross first, which meant they would be alone for a little
while. There probably was no place where they could screw—
except maybe the backseat of the Studebaker. But he would
have willingly settled for that.

At the last minute, though, Sessions decided to go too, and
climbed in the backseat. And then, as McCoy was about to
drive down the bank onto the ferry, Sessions had another
officer inspiration.

"Sergeant Zimmerman!" he called. "Would you come
with us, please?"

A moment later, he leaned forward.

"I don't think it's a good idea for us to be all alone over
there," he said, significantly. "Do you?"

"No, sir," McCoy said. "I guess not."

*What does he think is going to happen over there? I
shouldn't have told him about the Chinese/Japanese bandits.
If I hadn't, he would have stayed behind, and I could have
had fifteen, twenty minutes alone with Ellen.*

When Ellen turned to smile at Ernie Zimmerman as he
moved into the back beside Sessions, she caught McCoy's
hand in both of hers, and held it for a moment in her lap. He
could feel the heat of her belly.

On the other side of the river, he drove the Studebaker far
enough up the road to make room for the convoy to reform
behind it as they came off the ferry.

And then Lieutenant Sessions did something very nice.

"McCoy, you stay here in the car with Mrs. Feller. Sergeant Zimmerman and I will walk back to the river to wait for
the others."

"Aye, aye, sir," McCoy said.

He took Ellen's hand as soon as they were out of the car.
She held it in both of hers and drew it against her breast.

McCoy watched the rearview mirror very carefully until

Sessions and Zimmerman had disappeared around a bend. Then he turned to her and put his arms around her.

"What are we going to do?" Ellen asked against his ear.

"I don't know," he said. "At least I got to put my arms around you."

She kissed him, first tenderly, then lasciviously, and then she put her mouth to his ear as she applied her fingers to the buttons of his fly.

"I know what to do," she said. "Just make sure they don't suddenly come walking back."

After a moment, she sat up to let him reach down and open her dress. Then he slipped his hand behind her, unclasped her brassiere, and freed her breasts.

And then, all of a sudden, the hair on the back of his neck began to curl, and he felt a really weird sensation—of chill and excitement at once.

He was being a goddamned fool, he told himself. He was just scared that the two of them would be caught together doing what they were doing.

And with a strange certainty, he knew that wasn't it at all.

He lifted himself high enough on the seat to look in the backseat. Zimmerman's Thompson was on the floorboard. That left Zimmerman and Sessions with nothing but Zimmerman's pistol.

"What are you doing?" Ellen asked, taking her mouth off him.

"There's a Thompson in the backseat," McCoy said. "You grab it and run after me."

He pushed his thing back in his pants and took his Thompson from the floorboard.

"What's the matter?" Ellen asked.

"Goddamnit, just do what I tell you!" he snapped, and sprang out of the car. As he trotted down the road, he chambered a cartridge in the Thompson.

I'm going to race the hell down there and find the two of them sitting on a bench waiting for the ferry. And they are both going to think I've lost my fucking mind.

But they weren't sitting on a bench when he trotted around the bend.

They were up against a steep bank, and there were twenty, twenty-five Chinese, dressed as coolies, crowding them.

The convoy would be broken in pieces in only one place between Huimin and Tientsin. The only place, therefore, where it could credibly be reported that Chinese bandits had attacked it. And the Japanese had damned well figured that out.

And they had handed the Japs the opportunity on a silver platter. Sessions and Zimmerman were isolated and practically unarmed. After the 'bandits' finished with them, they would have come to the car.

Zimmerman had the flap on his .45 holster open, but hadn't drawn it.

"Take the fucking thing out, for Christ's sake," McCoy called out.

The Chinese looked over their shoulders at him. Several of them took several steps in his direction. Several others moved toward Zimmerman and Sessions.

McCoy was holding the Thompson by the pistol grip, the butt resting against the pit of his elbow, the muzzle elevated. He realized that he was reluctant to aim it at the mob.

Goddamnit, I'm scared! If I aim it at them, the shit will hit the fan!

He pulled the trigger. The submachine gun slammed against his arm, three, four, five times, as if somebody was punching him. He could smell the burned powder, and he saw the flashes coming from the slits in the Cutts Compensator on the muzzle.

Everybody froze for a moment, and then the Chinese who had been advancing on Zimmerman and Sessions started to run toward them. After that the shit did hit the fan. Pistols were drawn from wherever they had been concealed. McCoy saw that at least two of the pistols were Broomhandled Model 98 Mausers, which fire 9-mm cartridges full automatic.

McCoy put the Thompson to his shoulder, aimed very carefully, and tapped the trigger. The Thompson fired three times, and one of the Chinese with a Broomhandle Mauser went down with a look of surprise on his face. McCoy found another Chinese with a Broomhandle and touched the trigger again. This time the Thompson barked only twice, a dull blam-blam, and the second Chinese dropped like someone who'd been slugged in the stomach with a baseball bat.

As he methodically took two more Chinese down with two- and three-round bursts from the Thompson, he saw Zimmerman finally get around to drawing his pistol and working the action.

A movement beside him startled him, frightened him. He twisted and saw that Ellen was standing a foot behind him. Everything seemed to be in slow motion. He had time to notice that she had her breasts back inside her brassiere, but that there was something wrong with her dress. Then he figured out that she hadn't gotten the right button in the right hole.

She had Zimmerman's Thompson in her hands, holding it as if she was afraid of it. And around her shoulder was Zimmerman's musette bag. The bulges told him there were two spare drum magazines in it. Her eyes were wide with horror.

He returned his attention to the mob, and fired again.

"Shoot, for Christ's sake!" McCoy shouted. Zimmerman looked baffled.

Sessions finally did something. He snatched the Colt from Zimmerman's hand. Holding it with both hands he aimed at the ground in front of the Chinese. He fired, and then fired again. McCoy heard a slug richochet over his head.

That dumb sonofabitch is actually trying to wound them in the legs!

He put the Thompson back to his shoulder and emptied the magazine in four- and five-shot bursts into the mob of Chinese. There was no longer time to aim. He sprayed the mob, aware that most of his shots were going wild. And then when he tugged at the trigger, nothing was happening. The fifty-round drum was empty.

Conditioned by Parris Island Drill Instructors to treat any weapon with something approaching reverence—abuse was *the* unpardonable sin—he very carefully laid the empty Thompson on the ground and only then took Zimmerman's Thompson from Ellen.

When he had raised it to his shoulder, he saw that the mob had broken and was running toward the ferry slip. For some reason that produced rage, not relief. Telling himself to take it easy, to get a decent sight picture before pulling the trigger, he fired at individual members of the now-fleeing mob. He was too excited to properly control the sensitive trigger, and the Thompson fired in four-, five-, and six-shot bursts until the magazine was empty. By then there were five more Chinese down, some of them sprawled flat on their faces, one of them on his knees, and another crawling for safety like a worm, his hands on the gaping wound in his leg.

McCoy ejected the magazine and went for the spares in the musette bag around Ellen's shoulders. He snared one on the first grab, but as he did so he dislodged the top cartridge from its proper position in the magazine. He put the magazine to his mouth and yanked the cartridge out with his teeth. Then he jammed the magazine into the Thompson and put it back in his shoulder. Two Chinese were rushing toward him, one with a knife, the other with what looked like a boat pole. He took both of them down with two bursts. One of the 230-grain .45 slugs caught the second one in the face and blew blood and brains all over the road.

And then it was all over. No Chinese were on their feet; and when he trained the Thompson on the ground, the ones down there seemed to be dead. Except one, who was doggedly trying to unjam his Broomhandle Mauser. McCoy took a good sight on him and put two rounds in his head.

There were more than a dozen dead and wounded Chinese on the ground. Some were screaming in agony.

Lieutenant Sessions ran over to McCoy, looking as if he was trying to find something to say. But nothing came out of his mouth for several moments.

"My God," he whispered finally.

McCoy felt faint and nauseous. But forced it down. Then Ellen slumped to her knees and threw up. That made McCoy do the same thing.

"What the hell was that all about?" Sessions finally asked.

"Shit!" McCoy said.

Ellen looked at him, white-faced, and he thought he saw disgust in her eyes.

"I guess the Japs decided you're not really a Christer, Lieutenant," McCoy said.

"Jesus Christ, the film!" Sessions said. "Where is it?"

"Goddamn it," McCoy said, and started to run back to the car.

He was halfway to the car when he heard shots and then a scream. He spun around. Zimmerman had finally got his shit together. He had put a fresh magazine in McCoy's Thompson and was walking among the downed Chinese, methodically firing a couple of rounds into each of them to make sure they were dead.

Ellen was doing the screaming, while Lieutenant Sessions held her, staring horrified at what Zimmerman was doing.

And McCoy saw the cavalry finally galloping to the rescue.

The ferry was in midstream. Lieutenant Macklin, who had found his steel helmet somewhere, stood at the bow with his pistol in his hand and a whistle in his mouth. Behind him were the two BAR men, and behind them the rest of the drivers, armed with Springfields. McCoy did not see the Reverend Mr. Feller.

He ran the rest of the way to the car. The film was where he had left it, in the crown of his campaign hat, concealed there by a skivvy shirt.

He got behind the wheel and backed up to where Ellen stood with Lieutenant Sessions. Sessions opened the back door, and she got in and slumped against the seat, white-faced and white-eyed.

The ferry finally touched the near shore, and Lieutenant Macklin, furiously blowing his whistle, led the cavalry up the road to them.

(Three)

Lieutenant Sessions learned quick, McCoy decided. You had to give him that. He took charge, the way an officer was expected to. Lieutenant Macklin was running around like a fucking chicken with his head cut off. The first thing he was worried about was that the Chinese would "counterattack." They were a bunch of fucking bandits, more than half of them were dead. Military units counterattacked. What was left of the Chinese were still running.

The second thing that worried Macklin was what the colonel would think. His orders were to avoid a "confrontation" at all costs. There had obviously been a "confrontation."

"There's sure to be an official inquiry," Macklin said. "We're going to have to explain all these bodies. God, there must be a dozen of them! How are we going to explain all these dead Chinese?"

"There's eighteen," McCoy said helpfully. "I counted them. I guess we're just going to have to say we shot them."

Both Sessions and Macklin gave him dirty looks. Sessions still didn't like it that McCoy was contemptuous of Macklin, who was after all an officer. And Macklin thought that Killer McCoy was not only an insolent enlisted man, but was more than likely responsible for what had happened.

What bothered Macklin, McCoy understood, was not that they had almost gotten themselves killed, but that he himself was somehow going to be embarrassed before the colonel. He was, when it came down to it, the officer in command.

"Corporal," Macklin snapped. "I don't expect you to understand this, but what we have here is an International Incident."

"You weren't even involved, Lieutenant," McCoy said. "You were on the other side of the river. By the time you got here, it was all over."

"That's enough, McCoy!" Sessions snapped.

"I'm the officer in charge," Macklin flared. "Of course, I'm involved!"

"Aye, aye, sir," McCoy said.

Macklin sucked in his breath, in preparation, McCoy sensed, to really putting him in his place.

Sessions stopped him by speaking first.

"The important thing, Macklin," he said, while Lieutenant Macklin paused to draw in a breath, "is to place the rolls of film McCoy took into the proper hands at Tientsin. That's the primary objective of this whole operation."

"Yes, of course," Macklin said impatiently, itching to launch into McCoy. "But—"

Sessions cut him off again.

"Next in importance is the physical safety of the Reverend and Mrs. Feller."

"Yes, of course," Macklin repeated.

"And as you point out, there is the problem of the bodies," Sessions said.

"Obviously," Macklin said. "McCoy's latest contribution to the death rate in China."

Sessions smiled at that.

"We can't just drive off and leave eighteen bodies in the road," Sessions said. "And I think McCoy and I should separate, in case something should happen to one or the other of us—"

Now Macklin interrupted him: "You do think there's a chance of a counterattack, then?"

"I think it's very unlikely," Sessions said, "but not impossible."

He's humoring the sonofabitch, McCoy thought.

"As I was saying," Sessions went on, "I think we should do whatever we have to, to make sure that either McCoy or I make it to Tientsin, to be a witness to the fact that there are German PAK38s in Japanese hands."

"I take your point," Macklin said solemnly. "What do you propose?"

Just as solemnly, Sessions proposed that McCoy, two Marine trucks, and all the extra drivers be left behind in a detachment commanded by Lieutenant Macklin, while he and Sergeant Zimmerman and everybody and everything else immediately left for Tientsin.

"I think that's the thing to do," Macklin solemnly judged.

McCoy was almost positive the Japanese would not try anything else. They would think the Americans had something else in mind—like an ambush—when they stayed behind with the bodies. The Japanese would have left the bodies where they fell, he knew, unless they felt ambitious enough to throw them into the river.

But just to be sure, he set up as good a perimeter guard as he could with the few men he had. Meanwhile Lieutenant Macklin relieved him of the Thompson submachine gun. He kept it with him where he spent the night in the cab of one of the trucks.

Early the next morning a mixed detachment of French Foreign Legionnaires, Italian marines, and Tientsin Marines showed up.

McCoy was a little uncomfortable when he saw the Italians, but if they knew who he was, there was no sign. Somewhat reluctantly, they set about loading the bodies on the trucks they had brought with them.

It was dark before they got to the International Settlement in Tientsin, and there was no way McCoy could get away to try to go see Ellen Feller in the Christian & Missionary Alliance mission. The Tientsin officers kept him up all night writing down what had happened at the ferry.

Some of their questions made him more than uncomfortable.

First, they went out of their way to persuade him to admit that he had been more than a little excited. If he hadn't been a little excited (We're not suggesting you were afraid, McCoy. Nobody's saying that. But weren't you *really* nervous?) the "confrontation" could have been avoided.

"Sir, there was no way what happened could have been avoided. I was scared and excited, but that had nothing to do with what happened."

When they realized they weren't going to get him to acknowledge—even obliquely—that the incident was his fault, they dropped another, more uncomfortable accusation on him:

"Mrs. Feller tells us that you and Sergeant Zimmerman went around shooting the wounded, McCoy," one of them asked. "Was that necessary?"

McCoy had been around officers long enough to know when they were up to something. They were trying to stick it in Zimmerman. Zimmerman had a Chinese wife and kids. He couldn't afford to be busted.

"Nobody shot any wounded, Captain. Not the way you make it sound."

"Then why do you suppose both Mrs. Feller and Lieutenant Macklin both say that's what happened?"

"I don't know," McCoy said. "Lieutenant Macklin didn't even show up there until it was all over. So far as I know, Sergeant Zimmerman didn't fire his weapon. Lieutenant Sessions and I had to shoot a couple of them after they were down."

"Why did you feel you had to do that?"

"Because there was three of us and fifty of them, and the rest of the convoy was still across the river. Those guys that were down were still trying to fire their weapons."

"You don't say 'sir' very often, do you, Corporal?"

"Sir, no disrespect intended, sir," McCoy said.

"You say both you and Lieutenant Sessions found it necessary to shoot wounded men again?"

"Yes, sir."

"Mrs. Feller obviously confused you with Sergeant Zimmerman," the officer said, and McCoy knew that was the last anybody was going to hear about making sure the Chinese were really dead.

The next morning, a runner came after him while he was having breakfast in the mess. Lieutenant Sessions was waiting for him in the orderly room.

Sessions told him there that since the Japanese would by now suspect he was not a missionary, he had decided there was no point to his staying in China for the several months he had originally planned. So he was now going to take the *President Wilson* home with the Fellers.

"I'd like to say good-bye to her, Lieutenant," McCoy said.

"I'm not sure that's wise," Sessions said then. But in the end Sessions changed his mind and decided to be a good guy and told the Tientsin officers he wanted to speak to McCoy aboard the ship before he left.

On the way, he handed McCoy a thick envelope.

"This is for Captain Banning," he said. "I want you to deliver it personally."

"Aye, aye, sir," McCoy said, wondering why he hadn't given whatever it was to Macklin to deliver—until he realized that whatever it was, Sessions didn't want Macklin to see it.

"It's a report of everything that happened on the trip, McCoy," Sessions said. When he saw McCoy's eyebrows go up, he chuckled and added: "Everything of a duty, as opposed to social, nature, that is."

"Thank you, sir," McCoy said.

"I was up all night writing it," Sessions said. "There just wasn't time for the other letter I want to write. But that's probably just as well. I'll have time to write it on the ship, and it would probably be better coming from someone more important than me."

"I don't know what you're talking about, Lieutenant," McCoy said.

"You're going to get an official Letter of Commendation, McCoy," Sessions said. "For your record jacket. I'm going to write it, and I'm going to try to get someone senior to sign it. If I can't, I'll sign it myself."

"Thank you," McCoy said.

"No thanks are necessary," Sessions said. "You performed superbly under stress, and that should be recorded in your official records."

What Sessions meant, McCoy knew, was that without the

sixth sense—or whatever the hell it was—that something was wrong, he wouldn't have shown up when he had, and Sessions would probably be going back to the States in a coffin in the reefer compartment of the *President Wilson*.

Sessions meant well, McCoy decided, but he doubted if there would be a Letter of Commendation. Even if Sessions really remembered to write one, he doubted if Headquarters, USMC, would let him make it official. From the way the officers here were acting (and the higher-ranking the officer, the worse it was), what had happened at the ferry was his fault. In their view he had "overreacted to a situation" which a more senior and experienced noncom would have handled without loss of life.

The letter report he was carrying to Captain Banning was nevertheless important. He trusted Sessions now: The report would tell it like it happened, and Banning would understand why he had done what he had.

At the gangplank of the *President Wilson,* Sessions got him a Visitor's Boarding Pass, and then asked the steward at the gangplank for the number of the Fellers' cabin.

When they reached the corridor leading to the Fellers' cabin, Sessions offered his hand.

"I'll say good-bye here, McCoy," he said. "I want to thank you, for everything, and to say I think you're one hell of a Marine."

"Thank you, Lieutenant," McCoy said. He was more than a little embarrassed.

"We'll run into each other again, I'm sure," Sessions said. "Sooner or later. Good luck, McCoy."

"Good luck to you, too, sir," McCoy said.

As he looked for the Feller cabin, he felt pretty good. He was beginning to believe now that there might be a Letter of Commendation. It would be nice to have something like that in the official records when his name came up before the sergeant's promotion board.

The good feeling vanished the moment Ellen answered his knock at her cabin door. The look on her face instantly showed she'd hoped she'd seen the last of him. Being the fucking fool he was, though, he didn't want to believe what he saw on her face and in her eyes. He told himself that what it was was surprise.

He started out by asking her if maybe she would write him. "Maybe, you never can tell, we'll be able to see each other again sometime." He ended up telling her he loved her. "I think it's still possible for me to buy my way out of the Corps," he went on. "I'll look into it, I have the money. And I do really love you."

She got stiff when he started talking, the way she did when he talked crude to her; and by the time he was telling her he loved her, her face was rigid and her eyes cold.

"How dare you talk to me like that?" she said when he had finished, with a voice like a dagger.

So what she wanted after all was nothing but the stiff prick her fairy husband couldn't give her. The funny thing about it was that he wasn't mad. He was damned close to crying.

He turned and walked out of her cabin, vowing that he would never make a fucking mistake like that again. He'd never mistake some old bitch with hot pants for the real thing. He didn't give a shit if she fucked Lieutenant Sessions eight time a day all the way across the Pacific. If she couldn't get Sessions, she'd grab some other dumb fucker. And failing that, she'd get herself a broomhandle.

(Four)
Headquarters, 4th Marines
Shanghai, China
11 June 1941

Once given permission to enter the office of Captain Edward Banning, Lieutenant John Macklin marched in erectly, came to attention before Banning's desk, and said, "Reporting as directed, sir."

The formalities over, he stepped to the chair in front of Banning's desk, sat down in it, and crossed his legs.

"Getting hot already, isn't it?" he asked.

"I don't recall giving you permission to sit down, Lieutenant," Captain Banning said, almost conversationally, but with a touch of anger in his voice.

Macklin, surprised, took a quick look at Banning's face and then scrambled to his feet. When he was again at the position of attention, he said: "I beg your pardon, Captain."

"Lieutenant," Banning said, "I have carefully read your report of the Tientsin-Peking trip, paying particular attention to those parts dealing with your detention at Yenchi'eng and the incident at the ferry.''

"Yes, sir?"

"I have read with equal care the report Lieutenant Sessions wrote on the same subjects,'' Banning said.

"Sir?" Macklin asked.

"There was a caveat in Lieutenant Sessions's report," Banning said. "He wrote that he was writing in the small hours of the morning because he hoped to finish it before he went home. Thus he was afraid there would be some small errors in it because of his haste.''

"I wasn't aware that Lieutenant Sessions had made a report, sir,'' Lieutenant Macklin said. "May I suggest that it might be a good idea if I had a look at it, with a view to perhaps revising my own report?''

Banning's temper flared again when he recalled Macklin's report. It boggled his mind to think that the man blamed the detention at Yenchi'eng on McCoy's "cowardly refusal to do what duty clearly required"; and that the "tragic events" at the river crossing could have been avoided if only Lieutenant Sessions had heeded his warning that "Corporal McCoy clearly manifested paranoid tendencies of a homicidal nature and had to be carefully watched.''

And then, in the presumption that Sessions was on the high seas and safely removed from rebuttal, he'd even gone after him:

"The possibility cannot be dismissed that Lieutenant Sessions acquiesced, if he did not actually participate, in the brutal slaughter of the wounded Chinese civilians."

Banning waited a moment for his temper to subside.

"You are a slimy creature, aren't you, Macklin?" Banning asked calmly. "How the hell have you managed to stay in the Corps this long?"

"I don't know what you mean, sir," Macklin said.

"You know what a slimy creature is, Macklin. In the Marine Corps, a slimy creature is an officer who tries to pass the blame for his own failures onto the shoulders of a brother officer. I don't know of a phrase obscene enough to describe an officer who tries to cover his own ass by trying to blame his failures on an enlisted man. And you probably would have gotten away with it, you slimy sonofabitch, if Sessions hadn't spotted you for what you are and sent his report back with McCoy.''

"There may be, Captain, some minor differences of judgment between the two reports, but nothing of magnitude that would justify these insulting accusations—''

"Shut your face, Lieutenant!" Banning shouted. It was the first time he had raised his voice, and his loss of temper embarrassed him. Glaring contemptuously at Macklin, he took time to regain control before he went on.

"If I had my druthers, Lieutenant," Banning said, "I'd bring charges against you for conduct unbecoming an officer. Or for knowingly uttering a false official statement. But I can't. If I brought you before a court-martial, we would have to get into security matters. And we can't do that. What I can do, what I will do, is see that your next efficiency report contains a number of phrases which will suggest to the captain's promotion board that you should not be entrusted with a machine-gun crew, much less with command of a company. It will be a very long time before you are promoted, Lieutenant. You're a smart fellow. Perhaps you will conclude that it would be best if you resigned from the Marine Corps.''

"Captain Banning," Macklin said after a moment. "There is obviously a misunderstanding between us.''

"There's no misunderstanding, Macklin," Banning said, almost sadly. "What's happened here is that you have proved you're unfit to be a Marine officer. It's as simple as that. The one thing a Marine officer has to have going for him is integrity. And you just don't have any.''

"I'm sure I'll be able to explain this misunderstanding to the colonel," Macklin said. "And that is my intention, sir.''

Banning looked at him for a moment and then picked up his telephone and dialed a number.

"Captain Banning, sir," he said. "I have Macklin in here. I have just informed him of the contempt in which I hold him. He tells me that he believes he can explain the misunderstanding to you.''

There was a hesitation before the colonel replied.

"I suppose he is entitled to hear it from me," the colonel said. "Send him over.''

"Aye, aye, sir," Banning said, and replaced the telephone in its cradle.

"You're dismissed, Macklin," Banning said. "The colonel will see you, if you wish."

Macklin did an about-face and marched out of his office.

Banning knew what sort of a reception Macklin was going to get from the colonel. He had had to argue at length with him to talk him out of a court-martial. It was only Banning's invocation of the Good of the Corps that finally persuaded the colonel to reluctantly agree that the only way to deal with the problem was to immediately relieve Macklin of duty until such time as he could be sent home.

(Five)
Headquarters, First Battalion, 4th Marines
Shanghai, China
12 June 1941

The first sergeant sent a runner into town to McCoy's apartment by rickshaw. Liberty or no liberty, the first sergeant wanted to see him right away.

McCoy shaved and put on a fresh uniform and went to the compound.

"I hope you're packed, McCoy," the first sergeant said when he walked into the company office. Then he handed him maybe twenty copies of a special order, held together with a paper clip.

HEADQUARTERS
4th Regiment, USMC, Shanghai, China

10 June 1941
Subject: Letter Orders
To: Cpl Kenneth J. MCCOY 32875 USMC
Hq Co, 1st Bn, 4th Marines

1. Reference is made to cable message, Hq, USMC, Washington, D.C., subject, "McCoy, Kenneth J., Transfer Of", dated 4 June 1941.

2. You are detached effective this date from Hq Co 1st Bn, 4th Marines, and transferred in grade to 47th Motor Transport Platoon, USMC, U.S. Navy Yard, Philadelphia, Penna.

3. You will depart Shanghai aboard the first available vessel in the Naval service sailing for a port in the United

States. On arrival in the United States you will report to nearest USMC or U.S. Navy base or facility, who will furnish you with the necessary transportation vouchers to your final destination.

4. You are authorized the shipment of 300 pounds of personal belongings. You are NOT authorized the shipment of household goods. You are NOT authorized delay en route leave. You will carry with you your service records, which will be sealed. Breaking the seal is forbidden.

5. You will present these orders to the officer commanding each USMC or USN station or vessel en route. Such officers are directed to transmit by the most expeditious means to Hq, USMC, Washington, D.C., ATTN Q3-03A, the date of your arrival, the date and means of your transportation on your departure, and your estimated date of arrival at your next destination.

BY DIRECTION:

> J. James Gerber
> Major, USMC
> Adjutant

"What the hell is all this?"

"I guess the Corps wants to get you out of China, Killer, before they run out of people for you to cut up or shoot," the first sergeant said.

"Jesus Christ," McCoy said.

" 'The first available vessel in the service of the U.S.'," the first sergeant quoted, "is the *Whaley*[1]. She sails Friday morning. You will be aboard. You know the *Whaley,* McCoy?"

"I know the *Whaley*," McCoy said. "Fucking grease bucket."

"It's going to Pearl Harbor, not the States," the first sergeant said. "They'll put you aboard something else at Pearl. With a little bit of luck, you could spend two, three weeks in Pearl," the first sergeant said.

---

[1] The U.S.S. *Charles E. Whaley* was a fleet oiler that regularly called at Shanghai to replenish the fuel supplies of the vessels of the Yangtze River Patrol and the half dozen small pigboats of SUBFORCHINA (U.S. Navy Submarine Force, China).

"Top, I don't want to go home," McCoy said.

The first sergeant's reaction to that was predictable: "You don't want to go home?"

"You know what I mean, Top," McCoy said. "I just shipped over to stay in China."

"McCoy, I don't know how you got to be a corporal without figuring this out for yourself . . . I don't know, come to think of it, how you got be a corporal, period . . . but this is the Marine Corps. In the Marine Corps the way it works is the Marine Corps tells you where you go, and when."

There really wasn't any point in arguing with the first sergeant, and McCoy knew it, but he did so anyway, thinking that maybe he could get an extra few days, an extra two weeks.

If he had that much time, maybe he could think of something.

"For Christ's sake, Top, I got stuff to sell. I'll have to give it away if I have to get rid of everything by Friday. How about letting me miss the *Whaley* and catch whatever is next?"

"Like what, for instance, do you have to get rid of cheap? I'm always on the lookout for a bargain."

"Come on, Top, you could fix it if you wanted to."

"Fuck you, McCoy," the first sergeant said. "A little time on a tanker'll be good for you."

"Can I tell Captain Banning about this?" McCoy asked.

"You go tell him, if you think it'll do you any good," the first sergeant said. "And then get your ass back here and start packing. When the Gunny tells me your gear is shipshape, then maybe I'll think about letting you go into town and see about selling your stuff."

Captain Banning waved him into his inner office as soon as he saw him coming through the door.

"I guess you've just got the word from your first sergeant?" he asked.

"Yes, sir."

"Before you start wasting your breath, McCoy, let me tell you that not only is the colonel overjoyed at your departure, but he has told me to make sure, personally, that you get on the *Whaley*."

"I'm on his shit list, am I?"

"Let us say that you have been the subject of considerable cable traffic between here and Headquarters, Marine Corps, following the shootout at the O.K. Corral. If you plan to make a career of the Marine Corps, Killer, you're going to have to restrain your urge to cut people up and shoot them.''

"That's unfair, Captain," McCoy said.

"Yeah," Captain Banning said. "I know it is, McCoy. You didn't start that fight, and according to Sessions, you handled yourself damned well once it started. For what it's worth, I argued with the colonel until he told me to shut my face. But he's still getting crap from the Italians, and the Consul General's been all over his ass about you. I was there when he asked whether you were just a homicidal maniac, or whether you were trying to start World War II all by yourself.''

"So for doing what I was told to do, keep Sessions and Macklin alive, I get my ass shipped home in disgrace.''

"That's about the sum of it," Banning said. "But you don't have everything straight. First of all, the colonel's not shipping you home in disgrace or otherwise. I think underneath, he sort of admires you. You were ordered home by the Corps. I suspect that the Consul General had something to do with it—raised hell about you through the State Department, or something like that—but the colonel didn't do it. And you're not going home in disgrace. Not only do you get to keep your stripes, but your company commander is going to give you an efficiency report that makes you sound like Lou Diamond, Jr.[2] I know, because I wrote it.''

McCoy was obviously puzzled by that, and it showed on his face.

"It doesn't say anything about your working for me, McCoy," Banning said. "You understand that you can't talk to anybody, in or out of the Corps, about that?''

"Aye, aye, sir.''

"But it should impress the hell out of your new commanding officer," Banning said.

"I'm going to a truck company," McCoy said. "A goddamned truck company. I'm a machine-gunner.''

"I'm going home in a couple of months myself," Banning said. "You keep your nose clean in the truck company, and when I get settled, I'll see what I can do for you. Either

[2]Master Gunnery Sergeant Diamond was a Corps-wide Marine legend, the perfect Marine.

working for me, or doing something else interesting. Or, if you really want to, getting you back in a heavy-weapons company.''

"Thank you," McCoy said.

"What are you going to do about the stuff in the apartment?"

"As soon as my Gunny decides my gear is shipshape, the first sergeant said I could go into town."

"I'll call your first sergeant and tell him I'm sending you into town," Banning said. "Take whatever time you need to do what you have to do. And then go back to your company. I want to put you aboard the *Whaley* first thing Friday morning. If you're not on her, McCoy, the colonel will have my ass."

"I'll be aboard her, sir," McCoy said.

VI

(One)
U.S. Marine Corps Base
San Diego, California
9 July 1941

The U.S.S. *Charles E. Whaley* was as miserable a pile of
rust and rivets as McCoy expected it would be. Since she was
not a man-of-war, there was no Marine detachment aboard,
which translated to mean that he had hardly anybody to talk
to. Sailors don't like Marines anyway, and there were six
pigboat swab jockeys from SUBFORCHINA being shipped to
Pearl Harbor, and they really hated China Marines. The only
swabbie who gave him the time of day was a bald, hairy
machinist's mate second class who quickly let him know that
he didn't mind spending a lot of time at sea far from women.

Reeking of diesel fuel, riding light in the water, the *Whaley*
took seventeen days to make Pearl Harbor—swaying and
pitching even in calm seas.

There was plenty of time to think things over and conclude
that he'd been handed the shitty end of the stick. Again. Like
always.

Starting with Ellen Goddamn-the-Bitch Feller.

And getting sent home from China was also getting the
shitty end of the stick, too. Christ, he'd practically given
away the furniture in the apartment. And despite the efficiency report that was supposed to make him sound like Lou
Diamond, even a bunch of dumb fuckers in a fucking truck
company would smell a rat about somebody who was sent
home from China just after he shipped over for the 4th
Marines and got promoted.

And the new assignment stank, too. A goddamned truck

company at the Navy yard in Philly. Philly was the last fucking place he wanted to go. It was too close to Norristown, and he never wanted to go there again, period. And there was no question in his mind that he was going to walk into this fucking truck company in Philly and immediately be on everybody's shit list. There weren't that many corporal's billets in a Motor Transport platoon, and sure as Christ made little apples, the people in Philly had planned to give this billet to some deserving asshole of a PFC with hash marks[1] halfway to his elbow.

McCoy had been in the Corps long enough to know that Stateside Marines didn't like China Marines[2] and here would be a China Marine, a corporal three months into his second hitch, showing up to fuck good ol' PFC Whatsisname out of his promotion.

When the U.S.S. *Charles E. Whaley* finally tied up at Pearl Harbor, there was a Master at Arms and two Shore Patrol guys waiting for him at the foot of the gangplank. He wasn't under arrest or anything, the Master at Arms told him (although he really should write him up for his illegal, embroidered to the sleeves chevrons). It was just that The U.S.S. *Fenton* was about to sail for Diego, and they didn't want him to miss it.

The U.S.S. *Fenton* turned out to be an old four-stacker destroyer that was tied up the other side of Pearl. Ten minutes after he was shown his bunk in the fo'c'sle, a loudspeaker six inches from where he was supposed to sleep came to life:

"Now Hear This, Now Hear This, Off-Duty Watch Stand to in Undress Whites to Man The Rail."

That fucking loudspeaker went off on the average of once every ten minutes all the way across the Pacific to Diego.

The only kind thing McCoy could think of to say about the U.S.S. *Fenton*, DD133, was that it made San Diego six days out of Pearl. She was carrying a rear admiral who didn't like to fly and knew that with his flag aboard nobody was going to

---

[1]Oblong bars, one for each four years of satisfactory service, worn on the lower sleeve of outer garments.

[2]The tales—amplified in the retelling—of houseboys to clean billets, of custom made uniforms, of exotic women available for the price of a beer, of extra retirement credit, et cetera, tended to cause some resentment toward China Marines among their Stateside peers.

ask questions about fuel consumed making twenty-two knots. It must have been great on the bridge, turning the tin can into a speedboat. But where he was, McCoy thought, he had trouble staying in his bunk. And his body was bruised black in half a dozen places from bumping into bulkheads and ladder rails when he misjudged where the tin can was going to bounce.

But Diego was next, and he would soon be on land again, and there was no reason he couldn't get a nice berth on the train from San Diego to Philly. The Corps probably wouldn't pay for it, but he could do that himself. In his money belt he had a little over three hundred dollars in cash: the hundred he'd started with, plus the hundred ninety he'd won—ten and twenty dollars at a time—from the pigboat sailors on the *Charles E. Whaley* and the ten he'd won in the only game there had been on the tin can.

Plus an ornately engraved "Officer's Guaranteed Checque" on Barclays Bank, Ltd., Shanghai, for $5,102.40. That came from the last crazy thing that had happened in Shanghai. When he'd gone to the apartment to sell his stuff, the "General" said he'd make it easy for him. He'd take everything off his hands for five hundred dollars American. McCoy had jumped at that. Then the General pushed a deck of cards at him and demanded, "Double or nothing."

McCoy cut the deck for the jack of clubs to the General's eight of hearts.

"Once more," the General demanded.

"Just so long as it's *once* more," McCoy said. "I'm not going to keep cutting the deck until you win and quit."

He got a dirty look for that.

"Once more," the General said. "That's it."

McCoy cut the five of clubs. The General smiled, showing his gold teeth . . . until he cut the three of hearts.

But he paid up, even though he had to go to the bank to get that kind of cash.

McCoy added the General's two thousand American to the money already in Barclays Bank and then asked for a cashier's check for the whole thing. After a moment they understood that what he wanted was what they called an "officer's checque."

He made them make it payable in dollars. The Limeys

were in a war, and he didn't want to take the chance that they'd tell him to wait for his money until the war was over when he went to cash it.

He could goddamned well afford a Pullman berth from California to Philly, even if they would't give him credit for the government rail voucher and he had to pay for the whole damned thing himself.

McCoy had taken boot camp at Parris Island, and he'd shipped to China out of Mare Island, in San Francisco. So this was his first time in Diego. His initial impression of the place—or anyway of the part that he saw, which was the Marine Corps Recruit Depot—was that it was a hell of a lot nicer-looking, at least, than Parris Island, although he supposed that that didn't make a hell of lot of difference to boots. They probably had the same kind of semiliterate, sadistic assholes for DIs here that they did at Parris Island.

There was a bullshit legend in the Corps that after you finished boot camp, you would understand why the DIs treated you like they did, how it had been necessary to make a Marine out of you, and how you'd now respect them for it. As he watched a Diego DI jab his elbow in the gut of some kid who wasn't standing tall enough, or who had dared to look directly at the DI, or some other chickenshit offense, McCoy remembered his own Parris Island DI.

If I ever see Corporal Ellwood Doudt, that vicious shit-kicking hillbilly again, he thought, *I'll make him eat his teeth, even if I have to go after him with a two-by-four.*

McCoy found the Post Transportation Office without trouble in a Spanish-looking building with a tile roof. He set his seabags down and presented his orders to a sergeant behind a metal-grilled window, like a teller's station in a bank.

"You need a partial pay, Corporal?" the sergeant asked.

"Let it ride on the books," McCoy said. "I was a little lucky on the ship."

"Your luck just ran out," the sergeant said. "I hate to do this to you, Corporal, but you report to the brig sergeant."

"What?"

"They'll explain it over there," the sergeant said. "I just do what I'm told."

"All I want from you is a rail voucher to Philadelphia," McCoy said.

"You would have been smarter to pay your own way and put in for it when you got there. But you didn't. You came here, and my orders are to send the next three corporals who come in here over to the brig. There's a shipment of prisoners headed for Portsmouth. The guard detail needs a sergeant and three corporals. Now that you're here, they can go."

"Give me a break. Forget I came in."

"I can't," the sergeant said. "I got to send a TWX to Washington saying you're in the States. You read the orders."

The brig sergeant was a forty-year-old gunnery sergeant, a wiry, tight-lipped man with five hash marks and a face so badly scarred that McCoy wondered how the hell he managed to shave.

"What did you do, Corporal, fuck up in China?" he said, when McCoy gave him his orders.

"Not as far as I know, Gunny," McCoy said. "I'm being transferred in grade."

"Well, we got sixteen sailors headed for Portsmouth," he said. "Mostly repeat ship-jumpers, one deserter, one assault upon a commissioned officer, one thief, and three fags. You, plus a second lieutenant, a staff sergeant, and two other corporals are going to take them there. And all the time you thought the Corps didn't love you, right?"

"There's no way I can get out of this?"

"You're fucked, Corporal," the Gunny said. "You just lucked out."

In addition to the other corporals, the sergeant, and the lieutenant, the guard detail consisted of seven privates and PFCs. The other corporals and the sergeant were at least ten years older than McCoy. The lieutenant was McCoy's age, a muscular, crew-cut, tanned man who—to prove his own importance, McCoy thought—went right after McCoy.

"You're a little young to be a corporal, aren't you? Have you had any experience with a detail like this?"

"No, sir."

"You've qualified with the shotgun?"

"No, sir."

"Why not?"

"I don't know, sir."

"What's your skill?"

"Motor transport, sir."

"They must be pretty generous with motor transport promotions in China," the lieutenant said.

"I guess so, sir."

"Frankly, I'd hoped to have a more experienced noncom," the lieutenant said. "One at least who has qualified with the shotgun."

"I'm an Expert with the Springfield and the .45, sir. I think I can handle a shotgun."

"You can't handle a shotgun, Corporal, until you're qualified with the shotgun," the lieutenant said, as if explaining something to a backward and unpleasant child. "I'll have the gunnery sergeant arrange for you to be qualified."

"Aye, aye, sir."

A corporal drove McCoy to the range in a pickup truck. The same corporal watched him fire ten brass-cased rounds of 00-buckshot from a Winchester Model 1897 12-gauge trench gun at a silhouette target at fifteen yards. He then drove him back to the brig and told McCoy it was SOP to clean a riot gun whenever it had been fired. That meant it had to be detail stripped . . . McCoy couldn't just run a brass brush and then a couple of patches though the bore.

As careful as McCoy was, he managed to spot his shirt, tie, and trousers with bore cleaner, which meant that he might as well use them for rags or throw them away, because no matter how many times you washed them, you couldn't get bore cleaner out of khakis.

When he reported back to the lieutenant, the lieutenant told him that he had a soiled uniform.

"Aye, aye, sir, I'll change it."

"When you do change it, Corporal, make sure you have a shirt with regulation chevrons."

"Sir?"

"Get rid of those Tijuana stripes, Corporal."

McCoy decided to take a chance; he had nothing to lose anyway.

"Sir, embroidered-to-the-garment chevrons are regulation in China."

"You're no longer in China, Corporal," the lieutenant said. "And I don't want to debate this with you. I expect to see you here at 0730 tomorrow in the correct uniform."

"Aye, aye, sir."

"And, Corporal, I've inquired; and regulations state that at my discretion the noncoms may be armed with the pistol. Since you say you are an Expert with the pistol, I think you had better draw one rather than arm yourself with a trench gun."

"Aye, aye, sir," McCoy said.

The 47th Motor Transport Company at Philadelphia, McCoy thought, had to be an improvement over what he was doing now. Otherwise he was going to belt some chickenshit sonofabitch like this before his discharge came and get dragged to Portsmouth with a trench gun pointed at his back.

He went to the clothing store and bought three shirts and had regulation chevrons sewn to their sleeves. And then he fought down the temptation to get a hotel room in Diego. The way his luck was running lately, he'd get in a fight or something and get his ass in a crack.

The duty NCO at the brig found a cot for him, and he slept there.

In the morning, the lieutenant gave everybody detailed instructions and a little pep talk, then they went to the brig gate to take over the prisoners. The prisoners were in blue denim, with a foot-high "P" stenciled on the knee of the trousers and on the back of the jacket. They each carried a small cotton bag, which contained a change of underwear and socks, another set of "P"-marked denims, a toilet kit, less razor (since attempted suicide was a possibility, especially among the 'deviates,' they would shave themselves under the supervision of their guards), and their choice of either New Testament or Roman Catholic missal.

They were handcuffed: the right wrist of one man to the left wrist of the man beside him. And their ankles were chained, which made them walk in a shuffle.

On the brig bus, the lieutenant informed the guard detail that if a prisoner escaped, Marine Corps regulations stated that the guard responsible for that prisoner would be confined in his place.

McCoy knew that was bullshit. But he wondered if the lieutenant really believed it or whether it was just one more instance of an officer believing the troops in line were so stupid he could tell them anything he wanted.

The brig bus delivered them to the San Diego railroad station.

A U.S. Army Troop Car had been made available to the Marine Corps for the trip. It was attached to the train immediately behind the locomotive.

McCoy marched his guard detail—their riot guns at port arms—and the fourteen handcuffed and shackled prisoners through the crowded concourse and down the platform to the Army Troop Car.

He tried to tell himself that all he was doing was his duty, that these guys had fucked themselves up, that they had no one to blame but themselves for the mess they were in. But it didn't work. None of the fourteen prisoners was old enough to vote. Most of them looked not only frightened and humiliated but insignificant—like little boys. And so did most of their guards.

He was going to have to have a quiet word with the guards on his shift to make sure that one of the little boys didn't without goddamned good reason turn his shotgun on another of the little boys.

McCoy was relieved when they were all inside the Army car. He could not ever remember being so uncomfortable—so ashamed of himself was more like it—than when he had marched this pathetic little band through the station.

The sergeant showed up just before the train pulled out to show McCoy and the other corporals where he and the lieutenant would be sleeping and to explain the arrangements the lieutenant had come to with the conductor regarding chow. The dining car would make available "sandwich meals" for the prisoners, which would have to be picked up by the guard detail.

"When things settle down, maybe you corporals can get a meal in the dining car, but for now the lieutenant says he doesn't want you to leave the car."

The lieutenant made four ritual appearances every day, at 0600, 1200, 1800, and 2400 hours. He stayed about ten minutes, making sure that every prisoner had eaten, washed, and shaved, and had washed his previous day's uniform and underclothing.

McCoy managed to eat in the dining car only once. The waiters made it perfectly clear by lousy service and exaggerated courtesy what kind of shit they considered the guards to be. He didn't need any more reminding.

He took every other meal in the U.S. Army Troop Car, which meant that he ate nothing but sandwiches and coffee all the way across the North American continent.

It wasn't what he had dreamed about on the Pacific: a plush seat in a Pullman car and meals and drinks in the club car, as America the Beautiful rolls past the windows.

But that, of course, was fantasy. This was reality. This was the fucking United States Marine Corps.

(Two)
Boston, Massachusetts
1630 Hours 16 July 1941

McCoy had to change trains at Boston for the Philadelphia train. He had plenty of time. The Boston & Maine from Portsmouth had put him into Boston at five minutes to three. By quarter after three, he had a reserved seat on the club car. They'd given him a train voucher to Philly and two meal tickets at the Portsmouth Naval Prison, but he'd torn them into tiny pieces and thrown the pieces into a trash bucket.

He didn't want a fucking thing to do with anything concerning the Portsmouth Naval Prison. Or, more importantly, with the Fucking United States Marine Corps. He had made that decision somewhere between Diego and Chicago and still wondered why he hadn't thought of it before. For his *own* sake. Not in connection with any dumb fucking ideas he had about doing something with Ellen Goddamn-the-Bitch Feller. He had five thousand fucking dollars. There was absolutely no reason he had to stay in the Marine Corps and put up with all the shit.

He could buy his way out of the Corps and get a job. Things were better now, and he had a high school diploma. Maybe even go back to Shanghai and see if he couldn't work something out with Piotr Petrovich Muller, or the "General."

Five thousand simoleons plus was a lot of money. Even if he spent whatever it cost for passage back to Shanghai, he would have enough left over not to have to worry about getting a job right that minute. He could look around, see what looked good, and move into that.

So it was really a good thing in the end that the fucking

Corps had sent him home as a fuck-up for doing what he was supposed to do, and even a better thing that he had gotten involved in the prisoner-escort detail. It had convinced him to get the hell out of the fucking Corps. Otherwise, he would have stayed in China sticking his neck out, and sooner or later the Japs would have done to him what they tried to do to Sessions.

The prisoner-escort detail had gotten worse toward the end after they'd changed trains in Boston for New Hampshire, and really rough when they actually got to Portsmouth.

There had been another bus with bars over the windows waiting for them along with three Marines carrying pistols in white web gear and three-foot-long billy clubs they kept slapping in the palms of their hands.

All the prisoners were scared shitless, and two of them—one of the fairies and the great big guy who was going to do ten years before he was dishonorably discharged for slugging an officer—had actually cried.

There was a little ceremony when the prison signed for the prisoners. Then one of them tried to ask a question and got the end of a billy club in his gut for it. Hard enough to knock the wind out of him and knock him down.

And that fucking lieutenant just stood there and made believe nothing had happened. He knew goddamned well it was a violation of Rocks and Shoals[3] to hit somebody with a billy club like that, but the chickenshit sonofabitch didn't do a thing about it.

He was more concerned with important things like taking McCoy aside and telling him he was willing to admit a mistake about him and that he had probably been put off by McCoy's Tijuana chevrons. Anyhow, the lieutenant went on, he wanted to tell McCoy his deportment during the trip was all and more that could be expected of a good Marine noncom and that when he got back to San Diego he was going to write his commanding officer a letter of commendation.

What that was going to mean after he got to this fucking truck company in Philly (and McCoy believed the chickenshit sonofabitch was serious about writing the letter) was that whenever some poor sonofabitch had to be transported to

[3]The Disciplinary Code for the Governance of the Naval Service.

Portsmouth, that shitty detail would go to Corporal McCoy since he was so good at it. But fuck that. The first thing he was going to do when he got to the 47th Motor Transport Platoon was ask the first sergeant for the forms to buy himself out of the Corps.

There was a bar in the station in Boston, and McCoy walked by it half a dozen times waiting for the Philly train without going in. He wanted a drink. He wanted lots of drinks, but he was going to wait until he was safe on the train—had left Portsmouth Naval Prison behind him for good—before he took one.

The first time he noticed the guy looking at him was on the platform. He was a regular candy-ass, about his age, wearing a regular candy-ass seersucker suit; and McCoy thought he was probably a kid going home from college, except that it was now the middle of July, and colleges were closed for the summer.

The candy-ass wasn't just looking at him, he was sort of smiling at him, as if goosing up his courage to talk to him. Christ, there were fairies all over. Goddamn-the-Bitch Ellen Feller's husband wasn't the only one. And he never would have guessed that hairy machinist's mate second on the *Whaley* was a cocksucker. And now here was this kid making eyes at him who looked like an Arrow Shirt Company advertisement for a choirboy Boy Scout.

On the train the club car steward put McCoy in a velvet plush chair by a little table and handed him a menu. Fifty cents (not counting tip) was a hell of a lot of money for one lousy drink of Scotch whiskey; but he didn't give a fuck what it cost, he was entitled. He'd been thinking about this drink practically from the moment he went aboard that fucking fleet oiler in Shanghai. Just as the waiter was about to take his order, the guy who had been making eyes at him on the platform walked up.

"This free?" he asked, putting his hand on the back of the velvet plush armchair on the other side of the table.

"Help yourself," McCoy said.

How am I going to get rid of this pansy without belting him?

"Scotch," McCoy said to the waiter. "Johnnie Walker. Soda on the side."

"Same for me, please," the pansy said.

McCoy gave him a dirty look.

"I'm about to be a Marine myself," the pansy said.

"You're what?" McCoy asked, incredulously.

"I'm about to join the Marine Corps," the pansy repeated.

"I'm about to get out of the Marine Corps," McCoy said.

"You are?" the pansy-who-said-he-was-about-to-enlist asked, surprised. "I thought all discharges were frozen."

"I'm getting out," McCoy said firmly. He remembered hearing rumors of a freeze, or a year's extension, or something like that, but he hadn't paid a hell of a lot of attention.

Jesus Christ! What if this candy-ass is right? Then what?

"You sound as if you're not happy in the Marine Corps," the young pansy said.

He doesn't talk like a pansy, and wave his hands like a woman, but then, neither did the machinist's mate second.

"Do I?" McCoy replied, unpleasantly.

"Then you're just the guy I want to talk to," the young man said. "The way the recruiters talk, it's paradise on earth. All the food you can eat, all the liquor you can drink, and all the prettiest girls throwing themselves at you."

"You're really going in the Corps?" McCoy asked, his curiosity aroused—and his suspicions diminished just a little by the pretty girls.

"I'm really going in the Corps," the young man said. He put out his hand. "Malcolm Pickering," he said.

McCoy took it.

"Ken McCoy," he said. Pickering's grip was firm, not like a pansy's.

The steward set their drinks on the table.

"Put that on my tab," Pickering said.

"I can buy my own drink," McCoy said.

"Put the next round on your tab," Pickering said reasonably.

McCoy nodded. He twisted the cap off the miniature bottle and wondered idly if putting it in its own little bottle was how they got away charging half a buck for one lousy drink. He picked it up and read the lable. It held 1.6 ounces. That brought it down to 37.5 cents an ounce, which was still a hell of a lot more than he was used to paying for liquor.

"Can I ask you a question, Corporal McCoy?" Malcolm Pickering asked.

McCoy looked at him and nodded.

"I saw you in Chicago on the track with some strange-looking guys," Pickering said. "What was that all about?"

Chicago? What the hell does he mean by that?

And then he understood. There had been an hour's wait while the railroad switched locomotives. The lieutenant had the bright idea that the prisoners should exercise. Since they couldn't do calisthenics or close-order drill handcuffed and with their feet shackled, what the lieutenant had done was send them shuffling up and back down the track for half a mile or so. This Pickering guy had obviously seen that.

"We were exercising the prisoners," he said. "That what you mean?"

"What did they do?" Pickering asked.

"Three of them were fags," McCoy said. "One of them slugged an officer. The rest of them found out the hard way that once you enlist, you're in until they let you out."

"They were Marines?"

"Sailors," McCoy said. "The Marine Corps does the Navy's dirty work, like guarding and transporting prisoners."

"What happened to them?"

"We took them to the Naval Prison at Portsmouth, New Hampshire, to serve their sentences," McCoy said.

"Is that what you do in the Marine Corps?" Pickering asked.

"No," McCoy said. "I just got to San Diego when they needed a couple of corporals for the guard detail."

"What do you do?" Pickering asked.

"I'm a motor transport corporal," McCoy said. Though he didn't like the sound of it, that's what he was on paper. "I work in the motor pool."

"You like it?"

"No. I told you, I'm just waiting to get out of the Marine Corps."

"Then what will you do?"

McCoy didn't want to tell this nosy guy that he was going back to China. That would trigger a whole new line of questions. And aside from going back to China, he couldn't think of a thing he was likely to do. He had been in the

Marine Corps since he was seventeen. It was the only thing he had ever done.

"What made you join the Corps?" McCoy asked.

"My father was a Marine," Pickering said. "In the World War."

"And he didn't warn you off?" McCoy said.

"He was a corporal," Pickering said. "What he warned me to do was get a commission."

Then he realized what he had said.

"I didn't mean to offend . . ." he began.

"Your father was right," McCoy said.

"So, with war coming, I figured I had better get one," Pickering said. "A commission, I mean."

"You seem sure that we're going to get into this war," McCoy said.

"You don't?"

"Christ, I hope not," McCoy said.

"We're probably going to have to do something about the Japanese," Pickering argued.

"The Japs are probably thinking the same thing about us," McCoy said. "And you wouldn't believe how many of the bastards there are."

"But they're not like Americans, are they?" Pickering asked.

"The ones I've seen are first-class soldiers," McCoy said. He saw the surprise on Pickering's face.

"The ones you've seen?" Pickering asked.

"I just came from China," McCoy said. "I was with the Fourth Marines in Shanghai."

Now why the fuck did I start in on that?

"I'd like to hear about that," Pickering said.

"I'd rather talk about something else," McCoy said.

"Like what?" Pickering said, agreeably.

"I'm going to be stationed in Philly," McCoy said. "For a while, I mean, say a month or six weeks, until I can get my discharge. If you know anything about it, why don't we talk about the best way to get laid in Philadelphia?"

"The best way, I've found," Pickering said, "is to use a bed. But there is a school of thought that says that turning them upside down in a shower is the way to go."

McCoy looked at him for a moment and then laughed out loud.

"You tell me about the Marines in China, McCoy," Pickering said. "And then I will tell you about getting laid in Philadelphia. Maybe with a little luck, when we get there—that's where I'm going, too, to the Navy Yard, to give them my college records—we could conduct what they call a 'practical experiment.'"

If I keep drinking with this guy and then start chasing whores with him, I am probably going to get my ass in deep trouble, But right now, I don't give a fuck.

He raised his hand above his head, snapped his fingers at the steward for another drink, and turned to Malcolm Pickering.

"You can buy a fourteen-year-old virgin in Shanghai for three dollars," he said. "What's the going rate these days in Philly?"

"There are no fourteen-year-old virgins in Philadelphia," Malcolm Pickering said solemnly.

I'll be goddamned if I don't really like this candy-ass civilian.

(Three)
The Bellevue Stratford Hotel
Philadelphia, Pennsylvania
0905 Hours 17 July 1941

The first thing McCoy remembered when he woke up was that there had been a woman in bed with him, which meant he was likely to find his money and his watch gone.

The second thought was more frightening: The "Guaranteed Officer's Checque" from Barclays Bank, Ltd., Shanghai, had been in his money belt with the three hundred bucks. The whore probably wouldn't be able to cash it; but sure as Christ, she would have taken it, and it was going to be a real pain in the ass to get it replaced.

When he sat up, his head hurt like a toothache, as if his brain had shrunk and was banging around loose inside his skull. His lips were dry and cracked and the tip of his tongue felt like the sole of a boot.

How the hell am I going to get from wherever the hell I am to the Navy Yard without any fucking money? Or for that matter, out of the hotel? Jesus Christ, I hope at least they made me pay in advance!

He looked around the room, and that made it worse. This was no dollar-a-night hot-sheet joint. This was not only a real hotel, but a fancy-hotel hotel. Great big fucking room, drapes over the windows, a couch and a couple of armchairs, and Christ only knows what he had paid for the bottles sitting on a chest of drawers across the room. Before the whore got his money, he thought, at least he'd spent a hell of a lot of it.

And then he saw the money belt. It was on the little shelf over the wash basin in the bathroom. That figured. Just before she left, the whore had taken the money belt into the bathroom, just in case he should wake up and see her going through it. Once she'd emptied it, she hadn't given a damn where she left it.

He needed a glass of water, and desperately. Maybe, if he hadn't been rolled, too, he could borrow say, ten bucks, from Pickering. It wasn't the end of the fucking world. He had his pay record with him, and he had at least two months' back pay on the books. All he had to do was come up with enough money to get from here to the Philadelphia Navy Yard, and he could draw enough money to keep him going.

And he would go to some bank and ask them what you were supposed to do when you lost a 'Guaranteed Officer's Checque.' He would say he lost it. And since he hadn't signed it, they would have to sooner or later make it good.

He staggered across the room to the bathroom and saw that it was really a high-class place. There was a little button marked ICE WATER that operated a tiny little chrome water pipe. And when you pushed the button, it really produced ice water.

He drank one glass of ice water so quickly it made his teeth ache. He drank a second glass more slowly, from time to time looking at his reflection in the mirror over the sink. His eyes were bloodshot, and—he had to check twice to make sure what it was—his ears were red with lipstick.

He looked down at other parts of his body.

Well, I apparently had a very good time, even if I can't remember the details.

There was something under the empty money belt, making

a bulge. Idly curious, he pushed the money belt off it. It was his watch.

"I'll be goddamned," McCoy said, then told himself that just because the whore hadn't stolen the watch, it didn't mean she hadn't helped herself to the cash and the "checque." It wasn't that good a watch, he knew. He had bought it primarily because it had a lot of radium paint on the hands, so that he could see them at night. He picked up the money belt and worked the zipper. There was money in it, $250, and the "checque."

"I'll be goddamned," he said again.

Now he had a cramp in his bladder, so he went to the toilet and relieved himself. He saw that the bathroom had two doors: one led in from his fancy bedroom, and one went out into some other room. When he was finished taking a leak (an incredibly long leak), he tried the knob. It was unlocked, and he pushed it open.

Malcolm Pickering (McCoy remembered at that moment that sometime during last night, Pickering had told him to call him " 'Pick'") was on his back on a double bed, stark naked. His arms and legs were spread. And he was awake.

"Please piss a little more quietly," Pick Pickering said. "I woke up thinking our ship was going down."

"Shit." McCoy laughed.

"I have come to the conclusion, Corporal McCoy," Pick Pickering said, "that you are an evil character who rides on railroads leading innocent youth such as myself into sin."

"It looks like we had a good time," McCoy said.

"Yeah, doesn't it?" Pickering said. "What time is it?"

"A little after nine," McCoy said.

"I treat my hangovers with large breakfasts and a beer," Pickering said. "That sound all right to you?"

"I don't want to report smelling of beer," McCoy said.

"They have Sen-Sen," Pickering said, and suddenly sat up. "Jesus!" he said, and then he swung his feet to the floor and reached for the telephone. "Room service," he ordered, and then: "This is Malcolm Pickering, in 907. Large orange juice, breakfast steak, medium, corned-beef hash, eggs up, toast, two pots of coffee, and two bottles of Feigenspann ale. Do that twice, please, and the sooner the better."

Very classy, McCoy thought. *That'll probably cost three, four, maybe five dollars. But what the hell, I've still got most of my money.*

"What's this place costing us?" McCoy asked.

"I probably shouldn't tell you this, Killer," Pickering said. "It is only because I am an upstanding Christian that I do. We flipped for it last night, and you won. It's not costing you a dime, and I don't want to think about what it's costing me."

McCoy was surprised that Pickering called him "Killer." The only way he could have known that was if he had told him. And the only way he would have told him, as if he needed another proof, was that he was pretty drunk.

"I want to pay my share," McCoy said.

"Don't be a damned fool. If that quarter had landed on the other side, you would have paid," Pickering said. He got to his feet and walked across the room. "But since I am paying, I get first shot at the shower."

If anything, McCoy decided, Pickering's room was larger than his. And then he noticed that a door and not just the bathroom connected both rooms. He went back to his own room, found his seabags in a closet, and took out a clean uniform. It was clean but mussed. He hated to report in a mussed uniform, even if the first thing he was going to do when he reported in was ask for the buy-out papers.

"What the hell," he said aloud and picked up the telephone. He didn't give a damn what it cost, he was going to have it pressed. So far, he hadn't spent much money at all.

A waiter and a bellboy delivered the breakfast on a rolling table. By the time he'd eaten everything and put down both bottles of ale, he felt almost human again.

When he was dressed, Pick Pickering lifted up the telephone and told them to send up a boy for the luggage and to have a cab waiting.

The MP at the gate to the Navy Yard took one look at McCoy's campaign hat and went back in the guard shack for his pad of violation reports.

"Got to write you up, Corporal, sorry," the MP said. "Maybe they'll let it ride because you just got back."

The Officer Procurement Board was in a three-story red-brick building near the gate, and McCoy said good-bye to Pickering there.

"Well, maybe we'll bump into each other again," Pickering said.

"I hope by then I'm a civilian. Otherwise, I'll be standing at attention and calling you 'sir,'" McCoy said.

"So what?" Pickering said.

"It doesn't work that way, Pick," McCoy said, giving him his hand. "As you are about to find out, this is the U. Fucking S. Fucking Marine Corps. But it was fun, and I'm glad the quarter landed the way it did."

"Good luck," Pickering said, and squeezed McCoy's hand a little harder, then got out of the cab and walked up the sidewalk to the big red-brick building.

The 47th Motor Transport Platoon was in a red-brick barracks building not far from the river. Two Marines were very slowly raking the small patch of carefully tended lawn between the sidewalk and the building.

McCoy paid the cab driver and then stood by the open truck.

"You guys want to give me a hand with my gear?" he called to the guys with the rakes.

He was still a corporal, a noncommissioned officer. Noncommissioned officers don't carry things if there are privates around to carry things. They looked at him curiously, not missing the out-of-uniform campaign hat and the illegal chevrons. Then they stepped over the chain guarding the lawn and shouldered his seabags and followed him into the barracks building.

The linoleum deck inside glistened, and the brass doorknobs and push plates were highly polished. This was the States, McCoy thought, where American Marines—not Chinese boys—waxed the decks and polished the brass. And Marine corporals watched them to make sure they did it right.

There was a sign on the orderly room door. KNOCK, REMOVE HEADGEAR, AND WAIT FOR PERMISSION TO ENTER.

McCoy checked his uniform to make sure it was shipshape, removed his campaign hat, knocked, and waited for permission to enter.

"Come!" a voice called, and he pushed the door open and walked in.

There was a company clerk, a PFC, behind his desk, and a first sergeant, a squeaky-clean guy of about thirty-five behind his. Behind the first sergeant was a door marked LT A.J. FOGARTY, USMC, COMMANDING.

"You must be McCoy," the first sergeant said. "You was due in day before yesterday."

"At Portsmouth they told me I had forty-eight hours to get here," McCoy said. "I'm not due in until noon tomorrow."

"What were you doing at Portsmouth?" the first sergeant said.

"I was in a squad of prisoner-chasers from Diego," McCoy said.

"Shit!" the first sergeant said. "Nobody told us anything about you going to Portsmouth. You went on the Morning Report as AWOL this morning. Now we'll have to do the whole fucking thing over."

Well, I'm stepping right off on the wrong foot. Not only did I have to take those poor bastards to Portsmouth, but it put me right on the first sergeant's shit list.

"We can submit an amended report," the company clerk said.

"When I want your advice, I'll ask for it," the first sergeant said. He looked at McCoy. "Sit," he said. "You know that campaign hat's nonregulation?"

"No, I didn't," McCoy said.

"Well, it is," the first sergeant said. "And so are them chevrons."

"I just got a violation written by the MP at the Main Gate," McCoy said. "For the hat. He didn't say anything about the stripes."

"It'll take a week, ten days, to come down through channels," the first sergeant said. "I don't know nothing about violations until the message center delivers them. And sometimes they get lost. You want a cup of coffee?"

I'll be a sonofabitch, he's not entirely a prick.

"Yes, please, thank you."

The first sergeant picked up the telephone on his desk and dialed a number.

Then, while it was ringing, he covered the mouthpiece with his hand and spoke to the PFC: "You heard the corporal," he said. "Get him a cup of coffee and if they got any, a doughnut."

The PFC scurried from the orderly room.

"Sergeant-Major, this is Quinn," the first sergeant said to the telephone. "Corporal McCoy wasn't AWOL. They stuck him with a prisoner-chaser detail to Portsmouth. He just reported in a day early. I got him on the Morning Report as AWOL. How do you want me to handle it?"

Whatever the sergeant-major replied it didn't take long, for the first sergeant broke the connection with his finger and dialed another number.

"First Sergeant Quinn," he announced. "Is Lieutenant Fogarty there?"

A moment later, Lieutenant Fogarty apparently came on the line, for Quinn delivered the report that McCoy had arrived, that he wasn't AWOL, and that he'd caught the Morning Report before it left for Washington and was going to make out a new one.

"The Old Man says wait," First Sergeant Quinn said when he hung up. "You want to read the newspaper?"

He pushed a neatly folded *Philadelphia Bulletin* across his desk toward McCoy.

"Top," McCoy said, "what I'd really like is to get buy-out papers filled out."

"What?"

"No offense, but I've have enough of the Corps."

The first sergeant laughed, not unpleasantly.

"All discharges have been frozen," he said. "Nobody's getting out of the Corps except on a medical discharge. Didn't they know that in China?"

"Shit," McCoy said.

"There's some people thinks there's going to be war," the first sergeant said.

"I didn't know discharges had been frozen," McCoy said lamely.

Half an hour later, a young PFC came into the orderly room (without knocking, McCoy noticed).

"If you're Corporal McCoy," he said, "the Old Man's outside in the staff car."

McCoy looked at the first sergeant, who jerked his thumb in a signal for him to go with the driver.

The Old Man was about twenty-four, McCoy judged, a well-set-up, ex-football player–type. He returned McCoy's salute, motioned him into the backseat of the staff car, and then, as it moved off, turned to face McCoy.

"I'm glad it turned out you weren't AWOL, Corporal McCoy," he said. "That really would have disappointed a lot of people."

"Sir, I didn't volunteer to go to Portsmouth," McCoy said.

"I didn't think you did." Lieutenant Fogarty laughed.

They went back to the building where Pick Pickering had gone to deliver his college records to the Officer Procurement Board. That seemed a lot longer ago than an hour before, McCoy thought.

He followed Fogarty into the building and up two flights of stairs to the third floor. Fogarty pushed open a door and went into an office, holding the door open for McCoy. Then he spoke to a staff sergeant behind a desk.

"The not-really-AWOL Corporal McCoy," he said.

"You go right in and report to the captain, Corporal," the staff sergeant said. "He's been waiting for you."

Since I'm not going to be able to get out of the Corps, I'd better do what Captain Banning told me to do: Keep my nose clean in this truck platoon and hope that when he comes home from Shanghai, he'll remember his promise to see about getting me out of it.

That meant reporting according to the book. McCoy went to the closed door, knocked, was told to enter, and marched erectly in. Carefully staring six inches above the back of the chair that was facing him, so that whenever the captain spun around in it, he would be looking, as custom required, six inches over the captain's head. He came to attention and barked: "Corporal McCoy reporting to the captain as directed, sir!"

The chair slowly spun around until the captain was facing him.

"With that China Marine hat, Killer," Captain Edward Sessions, USMC, said, "I'm surprised they didn't keep you in Portsmouth. Aside from that, how was the trip?"

McCoy was literally struck dumb.

"You seem just a little surprised, McCoy," Sessions said,

chuckling. "Can I interpret that to mean Captain Banning didn't guess what we had in mind for you?"

"What's going on here?" McCoy said.

"For public consumption, we're part of the administrative staff of the Marine Detachment, Philadelphia Navy Yard. And you were assigned to the 47th Motor Transport Platoon because that was a good way to get you to Philadelphia without a lot of questions being asked. What this really is—not for public consumption—is the Philadelphia Detachment of the Office of the Assistant Chief of Staff, Intelligence, of the Marine Corps."

"I don't understand," McCoy said.

"I'm disappointed," Sessions said. "Two things, McCoy. The first is that my boss believes you know a lot about the Japanese in China that no one else knows, including Captain Banning; and we want to squeeze that information out of you. Secondly, he thought the Japanese would probably decide to do to you what you kept them from doing to me. Either reason would have been enough to order you home."

"So what happens to me here?"

"I hope you have a clear head," Sessions said. "Because there are two officers here who are about to pump it dry."

"And then what?"

"Then, there are several interesting possibilities," Sessions said. "We'll get into that later."

"When did you make Captain?" McCoy asked, and belatedly added, "Sir?"

"I was a captain all the time," Sessions said. "The orders were cut two days after I sailed for Shanghai." He leaned across his desk and offered McCoy his hand. "Welcome home, McCoy. Welcome aboard."

VII

(One)
Golden's Pre-Owned Motor Cars
North Broad Street
Philadelphia, Pennsylvania
1 August 1941

There was no doubt in Dickie Golden's mind that despite the seersucker suit, the kid looking at the 1939 LaSalle convertible coupe on the platform was a serviceman. For one thing, he had a crew cut. For another, he was deeply tanned. For another, he didn't look quite right in his clothing. He was wearing a seersucker suit, but he was obviously no college kid.

He was probably a Marine from the Navy Yard, Dickie Golden decided. They looked somehow different from sailors. He was too young to be more than a PFC; but maybe, just maybe, he was a lance corporal; and the finance company would sometimes write up a lance corporal if he could come up with the one-third down payment. There was of course no way this kid could come up with one-third down on the LaSalle convertible, even though it was really one hell of a bargain at $695.

Cadillac had stopped making LaSalles as of 1940, which really cut into their resale value. And the last couple of years Cadillac made them, they had practically given them away. But that hadn't worked, and LaSalles were orphans now. A 1939 Cadillac convertible like this one, with the same engine . . . about the only real difference between a little Cadillac and a LaSalle was the grill and the chrome . . . would sell for twelve, thirteen hundred.

The down payment on this would have to be at least $250,

and the odds were the kid looking at it didn't have that kind of money. Dickie Golden did the rough figures in his head. Say he had the $250, that would leave $500 over two years plus a hundred a year for insurance. A $700 note over two years at 6% was right at $29 a month. They paid Marine privates $21 a month. He didn't know what they paid lance corporals, but it wasn't much more.

But, Dickie Golden decided, what the hell; it was an up. It was possible the kid had just come off a ship or something, with money burning a hole in his pocket from a crap game. He just might have $300 for a down payment. More likely, he could switch the kid over to something he could afford. If he wanted an open car, there was a '37 Pontiac convertible at $495 and a '33 Ford—a little rough, needed a new top—for $229.

He walked over to the kid.

"Good-looking car, isn't it?" Dickie Golden said. "I've been thinking of buying it myself for the little woman."

McCoy didn't reply to that.

"You got the keys?" he asked.

McCoy had just about decided to buy the LaSalle. Everything else was crazy, why not buy a crazy car?

McCoy had just come from dinner with an officer and his wife. That was why he was wearing a suit. Maybe an apartment in a tall building at 2601 Parkway wasn't like officer's quarters on a base, and maybe there was some difference between a regular officer and an intelligence officer, but he was a corporal, USMC, and Sessions was a captain, USMC; it was the first time he had ever heard of a captain's wife "insisting" that a corporal come to dinner.

More than that. Grabbing him by the arms, and hugging and kissing him on the cheeks . . . with her husband watching.

She was a good-looking woman. *Decent* looking. Wholesome. She looked a lot like Mickey Rooney's girl friend in the Andy Hardy movies.

"Ed told me what you did at the ferry, Ken," Mrs. Sessions said. "I can call you 'Ken,' can't I?"

"Yes, ma'am," he said.

"Well, you can't call me 'ma'am,' " she said. "I won't have that. You'll call me Jean."

He hadn't replied. On the wall was an eight-by-ten enlargement of the picture he'd taken of Sessions in the black cotton peasant clothes.

"I want to thank you for my husband's life," Mrs. Sessions said when she noticed him looking at it, and then when she saw how uncomfortable she had made him, she added: "I know he's not much, but he's the only one I have."

Then Captain Sessions put a drink in his hand, and soon afterward they fed him, first-class chow that McCoy had never had before: one great big steak for all of them served in slices. Mrs. Sessions (he was unable to bring himself to call a captain's wife by her first name) told him they called it a "London broil."

Since they were both being so nice to him, he had been very careful not to say or do anything out of line. He watched his table manners and went easy on the booze (there was wine with the London broil and cognac afterward). And as soon as he thought he could politely get out of there, he left.

Which had put him all dressed-up on North Broad Street at eight o'clock at night with no place to go but a bar; and he didn't want to go to a bar. Drinking at a bar and trying to pick up some dame and get his ashes hauled did not seem like the right thing to do after a respectable dinner with a Marine Corps officer and his lady in their home.

So he had figured he would walk up North Broad Street and maybe see if he could find a car in one of the used-car lots—at least get an idea of what they were asking for iron these days. And then he'd seen the LaSalle and decided, what the hell, why not see what he could do?

"The down payment on a car like this would be $300, maybe a little more," Dickie Golden said, not wanting to let the kid take the car for a ride if there was no way he could handle it, "and the payments, including insurance, about thirty bucks a month over two years. Could you handle that much?"

"Yeah," McCoy said. "I could handle that much."

"You're a Marine, aren't you?" Dickie Golden said. One more fact out of him, and he would go get the keys.

"Yeah," McCoy said.

"The finance company don't like to make loans on a car like this to anybody's not at least a lance corporal."

"I'm a corporal," McCoy said. "And I can make the down payment, okay? You want to let me hear the engine, take it for a ride?"

Dickie Golden put out his hand. "I'm Dickie Golden, Corporal . . . I didn't catch the name?"

"McCoy," McCoy said.

"Well, I'm pleased to meet you, Corporal McCoy," he said. "You really know how to spot a bargain, I'll tell you that."

You bet your candy-ass I do, you sonofabitch. I grew up on a goddamned used-car lot. You're about to be had, buster, presuming the engine isn't shot in this thing.

"Seven hundred dollars seems like a lot of money for an orphan like this," McCoy said.

"Well, maybe we can shave that a little, if you don't have a trade," Dickie Golden said.

The battery was almost dead, and went dead before the engine would crank. A colored man with a battery on a little wheeled truck was called. Dickie Golden said he would replace the battery.

"Maybe all it needs is a charge," McCoy offered helpfully.

You dumb sonofabitch, if you knew what you were doing, you'd not only make sure there was a hot battery in here, but you'd start it up every couple of days. These flat-head 322-cubic-inch V-8s are always hard to start.

"No," Dickie Golden said, grandly, "I want this car to be right." He told the colored man to replace the battery. And then "while they were waiting" he suggested they take the information for the finance company down on paper.

He was obviously pleased with the facts McCoy gave him: That he was a corporal, unmarried, and had no other "installment loans" outstanding. McCoy decided he was going to come down $100 from the $695 and make it back by slipping the paper to some finance company who would give him half of the fifty back and make it up by charging eight percent, maybe ten. That would make the car $595. Then he would sell him insurance through some shyster outfit that would charge twice what it was worth—making it part of the easy payments—and slip Dickie Golden another twenty-five bucks back under the table. Then there would be a credit-check charge, and Christ only knew what else.

After McCoy's first look at the LaSalle, he went to another used-car lot and gave the wash boy there a dollar to go in the office and borrow the Blue Book for him. The Blue Book told him the LaSalle was worth $475 wholesale, the average retail was $650, and the average loan value was $400. McCoy decided he would pay $525 for the car.

Dickie Golden wanted to ride along with him, of course, when he took the test drive. McCoy handled that by passing the salesman three hundred in cash—enough for the down payment—"to hold." And when Dickie Golden said he still thought he'd better go along, McCoy turned indignant and asked if Dickie Golden didn't think he could drive; and Dickie Golden backed down.

McCoy drove up Broad Street until the engine was warm and then pulled in a gas station on a side street and gave the guy running it a buck to let him put it up on the grease rack and lend him some tools.

He could find nothing wrong with the car and would have been surprised if he had. It needed points and a condenser, and an oil change, and the wheels aligned, but there was nothing seriously wrong with it. The heads had never been off, and the engine was just as dirty as it ought to be. If it had required work it would have showed.

He drove back to Golden's Pre-Owned Motor Cars.

Dickie Golden told him he had been getting worried.

McCoy told him he thought the clutch was going.

Dickie Golden said he didn't think so, but that it was not much to worry about anyway, since they had a thirty-day fifty-fifty fix-anything policy. That meant they would pay half of the cost of anything that needed fixing or replacing in the next thirty days. And besides he was going to knock $100 off the price because Corporal McCoy didn't have a trade-in.

He showed McCoy the papers, already made out. With everything included, after a $300 down payment, the payments would come out to $27.80 over thirty months."

"I talked them into going thirty months," Dickie Golden said, "to keep your payments down."

You just hung yourself, Buster. You must really get kick-backs from every sonofabitch and his brother. So much that you won't mind going down another $70 on the basic price.

"I'll give you $500 for it," McCoy said.

"You got to be kidding," Dickie Golden said.

"That's all I can afford," McCoy said.

"Then I guess we don't have a deal," Dickie Golden said.

"I guess not," McCoy said. "You want to give me my $300 back?"

"I guess I could ask my partner," Dickie Golden said. "I don't think he'll go along with this, but I'd like to see you in the LaSalle, and I could ask him. If I can catch him at home . . ."

If you've got a partner, at home or anywhere else, I'll kiss your ass at high noon at Broad and Market.

"Why don't you ask him?" McCoy said.

Dickie Golden was gone twenty minutes. When he came back, he had a whole new set of papers all made out.

"My partner says $525 is as low as we can go," Dickie Golden said. "That's less than wholesale."

McCoy read the finance agreement with interest. Then he handed Dickie Golden $225.

"Deal," he said.

"What's this?" Golden said, looking at the money but not picking it up.

"I already gave you $300," McCoy said. "That's the other $225."

"No, this deal was to finance the car and for you to buy your insurance through us."

"What do you want me to do, call a cop? It's against the law in Pennsylvania to take kickbacks from finance companies and insurance companies."

"What are you, some kind of wise guy?"

"You just write on there, paid in full in cash," McCoy said. "Or we call the cops."

"Give me those papers back and get your ass off my lot!"

"I'll walk just as far as the pay-phone booth down the block," McCoy said. "With the papers."

"I ought to kick your ass!" Dickie Golden said, but when McCoy handed him the papers, he wrote "paid in full" on the Conditions of Sale.

McCoy was pleased with himself when he drove the LaSalle off the lot and onto North Broad Street. Not only was the LaSalle a nice car, but he had just screwed a used-car dealer. McCoy hated used-car dealers: Patrick J. McCoy of Norristown, Pennsylvania, Past Grand Exalted Commander of the

Knights of Columbus, Good ol' Pat, everybody's pal at the bar of the 12th Street Bar & Grill, Corporal Kenneth J. "Killer" McCoy's father, was a used-car dealer.

(Two)

The next morning was a Saturday, but there was no reveille bugle, at least not one the enlisted members of the Philadelphia Detachment of the Office of the Assistant Chief of Staff for Intelligence had to pay any attention to. Reveille sounded and ten minutes later first call; and the truck drivers and mechanics of the 47th Motor Transport Platoon went down and out on the street and lined up for roll call.

But the seven enlisted men in the three rooms on the attic floor set aside for the "Special Detachment" didn't even get out of bed until the bugler sounded mess call. In addition to McCoy, there were two gunnery sergeants, a staff sergeant, and three PFCs. The PFCs were clerks. The staff sergeant worked for Captain Sessions. McCoy didn't know where the gunnery sergeants worked. The only time one of the gunnery sergeants spoke to him since he reported in was when one of them told him he didn't have to stand any formations, but that he had to be in the red-brick office building every morning at oh-eight-hundred.

What happened there was that from the very first day they sat him down in an upholstered chair he suspected had been stolen from a Day Room and talked to him about what he knew about the Imperial Japanese Army in China.

There were usually three of them: Captain Sessions, another captain, and two lieutenants. The other captain was pretty old—and an old Marine—because the first thing he asked McCoy was whether he had known Major Lewis B. "Chesty" Puller in Shanghai.

"He commanded the Second Battalion, sir," McCoy said. "I knew who he was."

Puller was a real hard ass. Fair, but a hard-ass. He acted as if he thought the Second Battalion was going to war the next day and trained them that way.

"He's pretty good with a Thompson himself," the old captain said. "I thought maybe you two had got together and compared techniques."

Aside from recognizing it as a reference to the incident at the ferry, McCoy didn't know what the old captain was driving at.

"No, sir," he said.

Sometimes it was all the officers at once, sometimes it was a couple of them, and sometimes it was just one of the young lieutenants by himself. Always there was one of the PFCs to take care of changing the tubular records on a Dictaphone.

However many of them there were, the interrogation went generally the same every day.

They came with folders, notebooks, and pencils. And they had thumbtacked maps of Kiangsu, Shantung, Honan, and Hopeh provinces to a cork board. The locations of Japanese units were marked on each map. The wall beside the cork board was painted white, and they used that as a screen for a slide projector. Sometimes there were photographs, including some he took himself. Some of these were blowups, and some had been converted to slides.

And they asked question after question about the Japanese forces. McCoy was surprised at how wrong their information was about the Jap order of battle. And he could tell they didn't like some of his answers about the Japanese. It was as if they hoped he was going to tell them the Japs were nothing but a bunch of fuck-ups who had done so well against the Chinese because the Chinese were fucked up even worse.

But he told them what he knew and what he thought: The Chinese were *not* lousy soldiers, but they just didn't give a damn because they knew they were getting screwed by their officers, who would sell the day's ration if they could find a buyer. The Jap officers, on the other hand, were generally honest. Mean as hell, they thought nothing of belting the enlisted men—sergeants, too—in the mouth. But they didn't sell the troops' rations, and the rest of the Jap system seemed to work well. If a Jap soldier was told to do something, he did it, period.

One of the young lieutenants had studied Japanese in college. When he was alone with McCoy, he spoke a few words of Japanese to him. He didn't speak it all that well, but he spoke better Japanese than the old captain (who had done eight years, 1927–1935, with the 4th Marines in Shanghai) spoke Chinese.

McCoy learned (they didn't tell him, but he learned) that none of the young lieutenants was a regular. They had all come into the Corps right after college. McCoy wondered what the hell they were doing sitting around asking an enlisted man questions. As young lieutenants without any experience, they should instead have been out with troops in the field.

Once, a couple of civilians, an old one and a young one, dropped in while he was standing in a skivvy shirt by a map of Honan Province (the room was right under the roof and was hot as hell). When they entered the room, McCoy stopped talking, not knowing who they were.

"Don't let me interrupt," the older civilian said.

"Carry on, McCoy," the old captain ordered. So he carried on.

That was the day he was straightening them out about how good the Japanese soldiers were, and he went on with that. From time to time the old civilian would snort, as if he didn't think McCoy knew what the hell he was talking about, but McCoy decided to let the old guy fuck himself. The civilians stuck around until he was finished. When they were gone, McCoy asked who they were. For some reason, the officers thought that was funny. They laughed at him, and he never got an answer.

McCoy had no idea how long the "interviews" were going to go on. At first, he'd hoped they would go on forever. But by the end of the second week, he knew he was just about talked-out. If there was something he knew about China they hadn't gotten out of him, he couldn't think of what it was.

When first call blew that Saturday morning, he got out of bed and took a shower. Standing under the shower, shaving, reminded him of China and made him a little homesick for it. The only time in China he'd had to shave himself was when he was on a convoy. The rest of the time there'd been Chinese boys to do it for him.

After he was dressed, he went down to the mess for breakfast, and then he walked to the gate. When he had tried to bring the LaSalle onto the Yard the night before, the guard at the gate wouldn't let him, because he didn't have either a Yard sticker, license plates, or proof of insurance. But the guard had let him park the LaSalle inside the gate and had explained to McCoy that he could get a sticker on Saturday morning from the provost marshal if he got there before noon with proof of insurance and license plates.

McCoy started the LaSalle and drove to an office of the Pennsylvania Motor Vehicle Bureau, where he registered the car and got a cardboard temporary license plate until they mailed him a real one from Harrisburg. Then he went to an insurance agency and bought insurance. It was still early, and he didn't like the way the wear on the tires looked, so he found a Cadillac dealer. While they were aligning the front end, he went to the parts department and bought a set of points and condensers and a set of spark plugs and a carburetor rebuild kit.

Finally, on the way back to the Navy Yard, he saw a Sears, Roebuck where he bought a small set of tools on sale. Later he got a sticker from the provost marshal and drove to the barracks.

He would spend the weekend rebuilding the carburetor and changing the points and the plugs, and maybe giving it a good shine with Simoniz. Dickie Golden for sure had used some quickie polish, which made it look good but wouldn't last more than a week.

What he was doing, he knew, was not what he should really be doing. Working on the car was a dodge, an escape: He should *really* be going back to Norristown, even if he had to ride there on the Interurban Rapid Transit.

But he didn't want to go home now or next week or maybe ever. So maybe he would get lucky between now and next weekend. Maybe something would happen that would keep him from going home then. Like a transfer to the West Coast. Or maybe getting run over by a truck.

(Three)
United States Navy Yard
Philadelphia, Pennsylvania
0830 Hours 4 August 1941

"Close the door, Ken," Captain Sessions said, "and then help yourself to coffee if you'd like. I want to talk to you."

McCoy expected that Sessions was going to talk to him about the LaSalle. He knew there was scuttlebutt around about it: Where the hell did a corporal come up with enough money to buy a car like that? Scuttlebutt had a way of getting around—and that meant to the officers. So he thought it had finally become official.

He poured black coffee in a china cup. When he turned around, Sessions waved him into a chair.

"Have you given any thought, Ken, about what you'd like to do next?"

That meant that the "interviews," as McCoy suspected, were now over.

"Yes, sir," McCoy said.

Sessions made a "come on" gesture with his hand.

"Captain Banning said that when he gets home, he would try to find a home for me," McCoy said. "He said I should keep my nose clean, and he would either get me to work for him again or send me back to heavy weapons."

"Have you ever considered becoming an officer?" Sessions asked.

McCoy thought that over a moment before answering.

There were a number of officers around the Corps who had been enlisted men. And a number of noncoms had at one time or another been officers. An even larger number of old noncoms had been officers in the Haitian Constabulary, where the troops they'd commanded had been Haitians. McCoy had sometimes imagined that there would probably be a chance somewhere down the road after he had more time in, for him to get to be a warrant officer, and maybe even a commissioned officer. But he sensed that Sessions wasn't talking about some time in the future.

"You're talking about now, sir?" McCoy asked.

Sessions nodded.

"The Corps is about to really expand, McCoy. Even if we don't get in the war, the Corps is going to be five times as big as it is now. We're going to need large numbers of officers. And many of them are going to come from the noncommissioned officer corps. People like yourself, in other words. Are you interested?"

"I don't know," McCoy said, more thinking aloud than a direct reply.

"There are a number of people, myself included, Ken, who believe that you have what it takes."

"I hadn't even thought about now," McCoy said. "Maybe later."

"The process is simple," Sessions said. "You apply. Sergeant Davis has your application all typed up. All you have to do is sign it. Then you appear before a board of officers. The purpose of that is to give them a chance to see how well you can think under pressure. The board then votes on you; and if they approve, you'll be ordered to Marine Corps Schools in Quantico and run through the final phase of the Platoon Leader's Course. If you get through that, you'd be commissioned a second lieutenant."

"I never heard of the Platoon Leader's Course," McCoy said.

"The primary source of officers will be young men who have spent their college summer vacations going through officer training courses. The first summer they go through what amounts to boot camp. And the rest of the time we give them everything from customs of the service to the platoon in the assault. If you went to Quantico, you would be sent through the final phase with a group of them."

"College boys?" McCoy said, thinking of Pick Pickering. That's how Pickering was going to become an officer.

"Going through college is not a disease, McCoy," Sessions said. "You'd be surprised how many people have gone to college. Nice people. Jean went to college. I met her there."

McCoy smiled at him.

"I meant, I'm not sure I could hack it in that kind of company," McCoy said. "All I've got is a high school diploma."

"And four years in the Corps," Sessions said. "Which I think would give you a hell of an advantage at Quantico."

"You think I could make it through?" McCoy asked.

"I do," Sessions said. "But the only way to find out for sure is for you to apply, pass the board, and go."

"It's worth a shot, I guess," McCoy said, thinking aloud. "What have I got to lose?"

"Sergeant Davis has your application all typed up," Sessions repeated. "I'll approve it, of course."

"Thank you," McCoy said, simply.

(Four)

After he signed his name to the applications Staff Sergeant Davis had typed up for him, he put the whole business from his mind, convinced that like all other paperwork he'd seen in the Corps, it would take forever and a day to work its way through the system. He had more important things on his mind than the possibility that the application might, some months down the pike, be favorably acted upon . . . or that some further months down the pike he would be facing a board of officers—which probably wouldn't approve him anyway. After a while, in fact, he'd come to the conclusion that the incident at the ferry had a lot more to do with the whole business than Sessions's brilliant insight that he would make an officer. Sessions was being nice to him. The officers he would face on the board, when and if he got to face it, wouldn't think they owed him a thing.

And besides, he had three much more immediate problems to face, all of them connected. The first was what was going to happen to him now that the "interviews" were over. He didn't want to go to the Motor Transport Platoon, but on the other hand that would be a good place to keep his nose clean until Captain Banning came home from Shanghai. And he didn't really want to go to a heavy weapons platoon as a machine-gunner either. Since he'd be transferring in grade, they would try to bust him on general principles; and that would fuck up going back to work for Captain Banning.

He could also ask Captain Sessions to keep him around the detachment. Sessions would probably do it—as a favor. But that would mean he'd have to work as a clerk and push a typewriter and he was still not anxious to do that. And more important, if he stayed in Philadelphia, he'd have to deal with his two other problems: He had made up his mind to go home and face that and get it the hell over with once and for all. But going home once was not the same thing as having home so close to where he was stationed . . . Christ, Norristown was only an hour away in the LaSalle.

These were the thoughts that were occupying his mind, not the remote, way-down-the-pike possibility of being called before a board of officers who would make up their minds whether or not he stood a chance of keeping up with a bunch of college boys at Quantico.

On Monday morning, he signed the application papers. On Wednesday morning, Staff Sergeant Davis came to the barracks and told him to put on his best uniform and report to the board at 1330.

"Sit down, Corporal," a major, who was the president of the board, said. The five officers of the board were sitting behind two issue tables pushed together. One was a second lieutenant who was functioning as secretary. Two of them were first lieutenants (Lieutenant Fogarty, the 47th Motor Transport Platoon commander was one of them). Captain Sessions was the fourth. And the last was the major McCoy was seeing for the first time.

McCoy sat down at attention in a straight-backed wooden chair facing the tables.

"We have before us what is apparently a well-turned-out corporal of the regular Marine Corps," the president of the board said, "who, with his shady reputation, his illegal chevrons, and his equally illegal campaign hat, is just about what we expected of a China Marine so highly recommended by Captain Sessions. And others."

"Come on, Major." Captain Sessions chuckled. "The lieutenant's going to write that all down."

"Strike everything after—what did I say?—'well-turned-out corporal of the regular Marine Corps,' Lieutenant," the president ordered.

"Aye, aye, sir," the lieutenant said, and smiled at McCoy.

"Who comes to us not only recommended by Captain Sessions but by another member of this board, Lieutenant Fogarty, whose recommendation is based on his long-time evaluation—it must be three weeks now—as the corporal's platoon leader. The corporal's qualifications having, after due evaluation, been judged to be more than adequate, we now turn to the real question. In your own words, Corporal, would you tell this board why you feel yourself qualified, after proper training, to serve your country and the Marine Corps as a commissioned officer?"

"I'm not sure I do, sir," McCoy said.

"That's the wrong answer, Corporal," the president of the board said. "You want to try again?"

"Tell us why not, McCoy," Captain Sessions said.

This whole fucking thing is unreal. How am I supposed to answer that?

He paraphrased what was in his mind: "I'm not sure I know how to answer that question, sir," he said.

"You've known second lieutenants, McCoy," Sessions said. "Pick out any one of them except this one, and tell us why you doubt your ability to do anything he can do."

"Sir, all I've got is a high school education," McCoy said.

"You speak Chinese, I have been told?" the president asked. "And Japanese? And several European languages?"

"I don't speak Japanese as well as Chinese, sir. And I can hardly read it at all."

"Well, here's a given for you, Corporal. So far as the Marine Corps is concerned, fluency in almost any foreign language is worth more than a bachelor's degree. Anything else?"

"I wouldn't know how to behave as an officer, sir."

"They'll teach you that at Quantico," the president said. "Anything else?"

"Sir, Captain Sessions just sprung this whole idea on me."

"Answer this question. Think it over first—yes or no. No qualifications. Do you want to be an officer or don't you?"

McCoy thought it over. For what seemed to him like a very long time. The president of the board began to tap his fingertips impatiently on the table. Captain Sessions's left eyebrow was arched, a sign of impatience, often followed by an angry outburst.

"Yes, sir," McCoy said.

"You are temporarily dismissed, Corporal," the president said, "while this board discusses your application. There may be other questions for you. Please wait in the corridor."

"Aye, aye, sir," McCoy said. He stood up, did an about-face, and marched out of the room. He had just managed to close the door when he broke wind. It smelled like something had died.

"The board will offer comments in inverse order of rank," the president said. "Lieutenant?"

"Sir, I'm a little concerned about his attitude," the second lieutenant said. "He certainly took his time thinking it over when you asked him straight out if he wanted to become an officer.''

"It has been my experience, Lieutenant," the major said, "that what's wrong with most junior officers is that they leap into action without thinking things over carefully.''

"Yes, sir," the lieutenant said.

"Lieutenant Bruce?"

"So far as I'm concerned," Lieutenant Bruce said, "he's what we're supposed to be looking for. A noncom of proven ability who can handle a wartime commission.''

"Lieutenant Fogarty?"

"I'm impressed with him," Fogarty said simply. "He's a little rough around the edges, maybe, but they can clean up his language and teach him which fork to use at Quantico.''

"Ed?" the president asked, turning to Captain Sessions.

"I admit of course to a certain personal bias. He saved my life. One finds all sorts of previously unsuspected virtues in people who do that.''

There was laughter along the table.

"But even if he hadn't saved my skin, and even if a certain unnamed very senior officer had not made his desires known, I would enthusiastically recommend McCoy for a commission," Sessions added.

"Does he know about the general?"

"I'm sure he doesn't. The general and his aide were in civilian clothing, and they weren't introduced," Sessions said. "Being as objective as I can, I believe the Corps needs officers like McCoy.''

"Because he's a linguist, you mean?" the President asked.

"He'd be a linguist anyway," Sessions said. "But that would be a waste of his talents, even though people who speak Chinese and Japanese are damned hard to come by.''

"We will now vote in the same order," the president said. "Unless someone wants to call him back and ask him something else?"

He looked up and down the table.

"Lieutenant?" he asked, when he saw that no one had any additional questions.

"I vote yes, sir," the lieutenant said.

One by one, the others said exactly the same thing.

"This board, whose president is not about to put his judgment in conflict with that of the Assistant Chief of Staff for Intelligence, USMC . . . ,'' the president said, and waited for the expected chuckles.

After they came, he went on: "Especially after he said— slowly, carefully, and with great emphasis—'I think we ought to put bars on that boy's shoulders, if for no other reason than he seems to be the only one in the Marine Corps besides me and Chesty Puller who doesn't think the Japs can be whipped with one hand tied behind us.' ''

He waited again for the chuckles, then concluded: "This board has in secret session just unanimously approved the application of Corporal McCoy to attend the Platoon Leader's Course at Quantico. Lieutenant, you are directed to make the decision known to the appointing authority."

"Aye, aye, sir," the lieutenant said.

"Call him back in here, will you?" the president said.

The lieutenant went to the door, opened it, and motioned McCoy back into the room. McCoy marched in and stood to attention beside the straight-backed wooden chair.

"Corporal," the president said, "this board has considered your application carefully, and after review by the appointing authority, that decision will be made known to you through channels. In the meantime, you will continue to perform your regular duties. Do you have any questions?"

"No, sir."

The president rapped his knuckles on the table. "This board stands adjourned until recalled by me."

McCoy, thinking he had been dismissed again, started to do another about-face.

"Hold it, Corporal," the president said. "Sit down a minute."

McCoy sat down, more or less at attention.

"Corporal, unofficially, what that Platoon Leader's Course actually is is Parris Island for officers. What it's really all about is to make Marines—Marine *officers*—out of civilians. To do that, they're going to lean hard on the trainees. That might be harder for a Marine corporal to take than it would for some kid straight from college. It would be a shame if some Marine corporal who a lot of people think would make a good officer were to say, 'I'm a corporal; I don't have to put up with this crap. They can stick their commission.' Do I make my point?''

"Yes, sir.''

"Now, while I cannot tell you how this board has acted on your application, or whether or not the appointing authority will concur with its recommendation, I can mention in passing that the next Platoon Leader's Course begins at Quantico One September, and if I were you I wouldn't make any plans for the period following One September. Perhaps between now and One September, your platoon commander could see his way clear to putting you on leave.''

"Yes, sir,'' Lieutenant Fogarty said. "No problem there, sir.''

"Well, that's it then,'' the president said. "Unless anyone else has something?''

"I want to see the corporal a minute when this is over,'' Captain Sessions said. "Stick around, please, Killer.''

"'Killer?''' the president asked, wryly. "Is that what you call him? My curiosity is aroused.''

"With respect, sir, that is a little private joke between the corporal and myself,'' Captain Sessions said.

(Five)
Norristown, Pennsylvania
10 August 1941

Norristown was dingier, dirtier, grayer, and greasier than McCoy remembered; and he had a terrible temptation just to say fuck it and turn the LaSalle around and go back to Philly.

In China, McCoy had told himself more than once that he would never go back home, because as far as he was concerned there was nothing left for him there. That had been all right in Shanghai, but it hadn't been all right once the Corps had sent him to Philly. He knew he was at least going to have to make an effort to go see his sister Anne-Marie, who was probably a regular nun by now, and his brother Tommy, who was now eighteen and probably almost a man, and maybe even the old man.

McCoy told himself that at least he was not going back to Norristown the way he left . . . on the Interurban Rapid Transit car to Philly with nothing in his pocket but the trolley transfer the Marine recruiter had given him to get from the Twelfth Street Station in Philly to the Navy Yard.

He was coming home in a LaSalle convertible automobile; he was wearing a candy-ass college boy seersucker suit like Pick Pickering wore; and he had a couple of hundred bucks in his pockets and a hell of a lot more than that in the Philadelphia Savings Fund Society bank.

At the convent, a pale-faced nun behind a grille told him that she was sorry she couldn't help him but she had never heard of anyone named Anne-Marie McCoy. A moment later, the door over the grill was once more shut and locked. After that he went to the rectory at Saint Rose of Lima's.

A young priest opened the door. He was a dark-eyed, dark-haired guy, who looked like he could be either some kind of a Mexican or maybe a Hungarian. He was only wearing a T-shirt; but the black slacks and shoes gave him away. Besides, McCoy could have told you this one was a priest even if he was naked in a steambath. He had *that* look. Still, McCoy was a little let down that the guy wasn't wearing a white collar and a black front.

''Can I help you?'' the young priest asked.

''Is Father Zoghby in?'' McCoy asked.

Standing in exactly this spot, he recalled, he had asked that same question at least a couple of hundred times before: When he was an altar boy. Later when he was in some kind of trouble in school and the sisters or the brothers sent him to see ''the Father.'' And later still on the night when the old man went apeshit and came after him with crazy eyes, swinging the bottom of the lamp. McCoy came here that night because he hadn't known where else to go or what else to do.

''I'm sorry,'' the young priest said. ''Father Zoghby's no longer at Saint Rose's.''

''Where is he?'' McCoy asked.

''He's in Saint Francis's, I'm sorry to say,'' the young priest said, and repeated, ''Can I help you?''

Saint Francis's was a hospital near Philadelphia. It was where they sent you if you were going to die, or if you went crazy.

''I'm looking for Anne-Marie McCoy,'' he said. ''She used to be in this parish, and then I heard she was at the

Sisters of the Holy Ghost as a novice. But when I asked at the convent, they told me she wasn't there. And they wouldn't tell me where she went."

"What's your interest in her?"

"She's my sister," McCoy said. "I've been away."

"I see," the priest said.

There was recognition now in his eyes. McCoy thought the young priest had probably heard all about the grief and pain the incorrigible son had inflicted on good ol' Pat McCoy before they ran the incorrigible off to the Marines. Nobody but his family would believe it, but when good ol' Pat wasn't glad-handing people at the used-car lot or the KC or the 12th Street Bar & Grill, good ol' Pat McCoy was pouring John Jamieson's into his brain. Only his wife and kids knew it, but good ol' glad-hand Pat was a mean, vicious drunk who got his kicks slapping his wife and his kids around. Sometimes he beat them because there was some kind of reason like not showing the proper respect, or for bad grades or a note from one of the Sisters or the Brothers, or for leaving polish showing when you'd waxed one of the cars on the lot. More often he beat them for no reason at all.

Kenneth J. McCoy would never forget the time when good ol' Pat had dragged him in front of the judge: "God knows, Your Honor," Pat McCoy told the judge, the Honorable Francis Mulvaney, a fellow knight at the KC, "I have tried to do my best for my family. God knows that. I sent them to parochial school when it was a genuine sacrifice to come up with the tuition. I made them take Mass regular. I tried to set an example."

He paused then to blow his nose and wipe his eyes.

"And now this," his father went on. "Maybe God is punishing me for something I done in my youth. I don't know, Your Honor."

"I'll hear your side of this," His Honor said to the incorrigible.

Who replied that good ol' Pat had slapped his eldest—just turned seventeen—son one time too many. And his eldest son (otherwise known to this court as the accused, Kenneth J. McCoy) had seen red and given him a shove back. And good ol' Pat, the loving father who had sent the accused to parochial school even when that had been a genuine financial sacrifice, had been so drunk that he fell down and tore his cheek when he knocked over the coffee table.

And that had made ol' loving Father so pissed that he came after the accused with the base of the table lamp. After he'd demonstrated his willingness to use it by smashing the Philco radio and the glass in the bookcases and the plaster statue of the Sacred Heart of Jesus, the accused had fled the premises and sought refuge in the rectory of Saint Rose of Lima Roman Catholic Church. There he had remained until, accompanied by the good Father Zoghby, he surrendered himself to the Norristown Police to face charges. Good ol' loving Father Pat McCoy had accused his eldest son of assault with intent to do bodily harm as well as general all-around incorrigibility and heathenism and ungrateful sonism.

"I'm sorry he cut his face," the accused mumbled to the judge.

"That's all?"

"Yes, sir."

It had already been arranged, Father Zoghby had told him when he'd come to the jail. He'd had a word with the judge. To spare his family any further shame and humiliation, the judge would drop all charges on condition that the accused join the U.S. Marine Corps for four years.

Later he'd tried to send his civvies home in the box they gave you at Parris Island, but it had come back marked REFUSED. So had the letters he'd written at first to his mother and Anne-Marie and Tommy. Then there had been a letter from Father Zoghby: His father could not find it in his heart to forgive him, and had started telling people he had no son named Kenneth. It would be better, Father Zoghby continued, if Kenneth stopped writing until things had a time to settle. He would pray that his father would in time forgive him, and he would keep him posted if anything happened he should know.

While McCoy was still running the water-cooled .30-caliber Browning in Dog Company, First Battalion, 4th Marines, Father Zoghby had written him one more letter: His mother was dead; Anne-Marie had a vocation and was a novice at the Convent of the Sisters of the Holy Ghost; Tommy had gone to

Bethlehem, where the steel mills had reopened and there was work; and his father had remarried.

"Anne-Marie left the convent at least two years ago, I'm sorry to say," the young priest said. "I'm sure your father would know where she is."

"I can't ask him," McCoy said.

The priest looked at him for a moment, and McCoy sensed that he was making up his mind. Then the priest stepped outside and closed the rectory door after him.

"Maybe I can help you," he said.

He led him past the church building, then down the cracked concrete walkway to the school buildings—the grammar school to the left and the larger, newer Saint Rose of Lima High School building to the right—and finally to the nun's residence.

He spoke first to Sister Gregory, who recognized McCoy as she looked down at him from the steps of the residence, but acted as if she had never seen him before in her life. She went back inside, and a minute later Sister Paul appeared at the door and walked down the steps to where McCoy and the young priest stood.

"How are you, Kenneth?" Sister Paul said.

"I'm all right, Sister," McCoy said. "How are you?"

"Have you made things right between you and God, Kenneth?"

"I don't know, Sister," McCoy said.

"You're not going to make trouble are you, Kenneth?" she asked.

"I just came home from China," McCoy said. "I want to see Anne-Marie."

"You were in China, were you?"

"Yes, Sister."

"Anne-Marie left the Sisters of the Holy Ghost," Sister Paul said, "and I'm sorry to tell you, she has also abandoned the Church."

"Do you know where she is?"

"Here in Norristown," Sister Paul said. "She's taken up with a Protestant."

"Excuse me?"

"She chose to marry a young man outside the Church. He's a Protestant whose name is Schulter. He has the Amoco station at Ninth and Walnut. They have two babies, a little girl and a little boy.''

"Thank you, Sister Paul," McCoy said.

"I don't want you to do anything, Kenneth, that will cause your father more pain," she said. "I hope you've had time to grow up, to think things through."

VIII

(One)

The man who walked out to the pump island when McCoy drove in wore an Amoco uniform: a striped shirt and trousers with a matching billed cap. There was an Amoco insignia on the brow of the cap and a nameplate, "Dutch," was sewn to the shirt breast. The man was about thirty, McCoy judged, and already wearing a spare tire.

"Fill it with high-test, sir?" he asked.

McCoy nodded. After Dutch had opened the hood, McCoy got out of the car.

"You must have just had the oil changed," Dutch said, showing McCoy the dipstick. "Clean as a whistle and right to the top."

"Your name Schulter?" McCoy asked.

"That's right," Dutch said, warily curious.

"I'm Anne-Marie's brother," McCoy said.

Dutch hesitated a moment and then put out his hand. "Dutch Schulter," he said. "I heard—she told me—you was in the Marines."

"I am," McCoy said.

"You must be doing all right in the Marines," Dutch Schulter said, making a vague gesture first at the LaSalle, and then at McCoy himself.

"I do all right," McCoy said.

The gas pump made a chugging noise when the automatic filler nozzle was triggered. Dutch Schulter moved to the rear of the car, topped off the tank, then hung the hose up. McCoy looked at the pump. Eleven point seven gallons at 23.9 cents a gallon: $2.79. He took a wad of bills from his pocket and peeled off a ten-dollar bill.

Dutch Schulter handed the change to him, together with a Coca-Cola glass.

"They're free with a fill-up," he said.

"How do I get to see my sister?" McCoy said.

Schulter looked at him for a moment as if making up his mind, and then raised his voice: "Mickey!"

A kid in an Amoco uniform appeared at the door of the grease-rack bay.

"Hold the fort, Mickey," Dutch called. "I got to go home for a minute."

Home was a row house on North Elm, a little wooden porch in front of a fieldstone house that smelled of baby shit, sour milk, and cabbage.

Anne-Marie looked older than he expected. She was already getting fat and lumpy, and she had lost a couple of teeth. She cried when she saw him, and hugged him, and told him he had really growed up.

Dutch touched his shoulder, and when McCoy turned to look at him, handed him a bottle of beer.

"You're an uncle, Kenny," Anne-Marie said. "We got a boy and a girl, but I just got them to sleep, and you'll have to wait to see them. You can stay for supper?"

"I thought I'd take you and Dutch out for supper," McCoy said.

"You don't want to do that," she protested. "You won't believe what restaurants ask for food these days."

"Yeah, I do," McCoy said.

"What I should have done," Dutch said, "is had him follow me in the truck. You want to run me back by the station? Could you find your way back here again?"

"Why don't you take my car?" McCoy said. "I've got no place else to go."

"You got a car, Kenny?" Anne-Marie asked, surprised.

"He's got a goddamned LaSalle convertible, is what he's got," Dutch said.

She looked at him in surprise.

"You been doing all right for yourself, I guess," she said.

"I've been doing all right," McCoy said.

"I'll put it up on the rack, and grease it," Dutch said. "And then have the kid works for me, you saw him, Mickey, wash it."

"Thank you," McCoy said, and tossed him the keys.

Dutch Schulter returned a few minutes after six, as soon as the night man came on at the station. McCoy was glad to see him. Anne-Marie was getting on his nerves. She was a god-damned slob. He had to tell her to change the diaper on the older kid; he had shit running down his leg from under his diaper.

The sink was full of unwashed dishes. McCoy remembered that, come to think of it, his mother had been sort of a slob herself. Many of the times the old man had slapped her around, it had started with him bitching about something being dirty.

She told him she would really rather make his supper herself. When Dutch returned with his car, she said, he could take her down to the Acme and she would get steaks or something; but she didn't mean it, and McCoy didn't want to eat in her dirty kitchen, off her dirty plates.

She asked him if he had been to see "Daddy," and he told her no. And she told him she hadn't seen him either. He had been mad at her since she left the convent (and boy, could she tell him stories about what went on in that place!); and after she had married Dutch, outside the church and all, it had gotten worse.

Dutch was a good man, she said. She had met him when she was working in the Highway Diner on the Bethlehem Pike after she left the convent. He had been nice to her, and one thing had led to another, and they'd started going out. Then they got married and started their family.

McCoy did the arithmetic in his head, and decided she had the sequence wrong: She and Dutch started their family, and then got married. The old man could count, too, which might be one of the reasons he was pissed-off at her.

How dare she embarrass Past Grand Exalted Commander Pat McCoy of the KC? She not only leaves (or gets kicked out of?) the convent, but she gets herself knocked up by some Dutchy she meets slinging hash at the Highway Diner.

Dutch came home with the LaSalle all greased and pol-ished, then took a bath and got dressed-up in a two-tone sports coat and slacks. Anne-Marie had on a too-tight spotted dress with a flowery print. They loaded the kids in the car and went looking for someplace to eat.

Anne-Marie said the food in the 12th Street Bar & Grill was always good, and they didn't ask an arm and a leg for it. McCoy knew she was less concerned with good food and saving his money than she was in going where the old man would be hanging out so he'd see them together all dressed-up, and him driving a LaSalle.

"I saw a place on the way into town, Norristown Tavern . . . Inn . . . that looked nice," McCoy said.

"They charge an arm and a leg in there," Anne-Marie said.

"Yeah, they do, Kenny," Dutch agreed. He did care, McCoy decided, what it was going to cost.

"What the hell, I don't get to come all that often," McCoy said.

When they were in the Norristown Inn, in a booth against the wall, Anne-Marie looked up from trying to force a spoonful of potatoes into the boy and whispered, "There's Daddy."

Good ol' Pat McCoy was at the bar, with a sharp-faced female, her hair piled high on top of her head, her lipstick a red gash across her pale face . . . obviously the second Mrs. Patrick J. McCoy.

McCoy thought it over, and when they were on their strawberry shortcake, he got up from the table without saying anything and walked to the bar.

"Hello," he said to his father.

His father nodded at him. The second Mrs. McCoy looked at him curiously.

He's not surprised to see me, which means that he saw me at the table with Anne-Marie and Dutch. And didn't come over.

"You're home, I see," McCoy's father said.

"About ten days ago."

McCoy's father moved his glass in little circles on the bar.

"Learn anything in the Marine Corps?" McCoy's father asked.

That told his new wife who I am. Now she doesn't like me either.

"I learned a little," McCoy said.

"So what are you doing now, looking for a job?"

"Not yet."

"Maybe the Dutchman'll give you one pumping gas," his

father said. He laughed at his own wit and turned to his wife for an audience. She dutifully tittered.

"Maybe he will," McCoy said, and walked back to the table.

"What did he say?" Anne-Marie asked.

"Not much," McCoy said.

He told himself he was being a prick when the bill came and he got mad that Anne-Marie had ordered one of everything on the menu. He'd offered to take them to dinner; he shouldn't bitch about what it cost.

He told Anne-Marie and Dutch that he had to go back to Philadelphia, so he couldn't stay over on the foldaway bed. But he promised to write. Then he dropped them at their row house. Before he left, he asked for Tommy's address.

They were obviously pressed for dough, and he considered slipping Anne-Marie fifty bucks "to buy something for the kids," but decided against it. She'd already started moaning abut how hard it was to make it with two kids on what Dutch brought home from the Amoco station. If he gave her money, she would be back for more.

He didn't return to Philly. He never intended to. Though he wasn't on leave, he didn't have to go back or make the reveille formation or anything. Lieutenant Fogarty had pointedly told him that no one was going to be looking for him around the platoon, and that if he didn't want to use up his leave time, he could sack out in the barracks whenever and check in with the first sergeant every couple of days.

He just wanted to get away from the row house and the stink of baby shit and cabbage.

He stopped outside of town, put the roof up, then drove to Bethlehem and checked into the Hotel Bethlehem. It wasn't the Bellevue Stratford, but it was nice, and when he went down to the dining room in the morning, they had breakfast steaks and corned beef hash on the menu. He ordered it up, fuck what it cost.

Tommy lived in a rooming house, a great big old rambling building built on the side of a hill. He wasn't there, of course; but the landlady, a big pink-cheeked Polack woman told him he could probably catch him at the walk bridge over the railroad tracks when his shift was over, and that if he missed him there, he could find him at the Lithuanian Social Club.

He drove around town. He saw Lehigh University and, just for the hell of it, drove inside. There really wasn't much to see. He was disappointed, and wondered why. What had he expected?

He went back to the Hotel Bethlehem, and checked out. When the eight-to-four shift let out, he was standing at the end of the bridge over the railroad tracks hoping he would be able to spot Tommy.

Tommy spotted him first. Tommy had changed so much he had let him walk right by him. But Tommy saw him out of the corner of his eye, and came back—even though the last fucking person in the fucking world he expected to see was his fucking brother on the fucking bridge wearing a fucking suit.

They went to the Lithuanian Club, and drank a lot of beer. Once Tommy told the guys his fucking big brother was a fucking corporal in the fucking Marines, it was all right with them despite the fucking suit that made him look like a fucking fairy.

The Lithuanian Club reminded McCoy of the Million Dollar Club in Shanghai. Not in looks. The Lithuanian Club was a dump. It smelled of beer and piss. But the Million Dollar Club was the place where Marines went because they had nowhere else to go and nothing else to do but get drunk when the duty day was over. And that's all the Lithuanian Club was, too, a place where the enlisted men from the steel mill went because there was no place else to go when they came away from the open hearths, and nothing to do but get drunk.

Tommy reminded McCoy of a lot of Marines he knew, particularly in the line companies.

They wound up in a whorehouse by the railroad station. McCoy paid for the all-night services of a peroxide blonde not because he was really all that interested in screwing her, but because the alternative was worse: He was too shit-faced to get in his car and drive back to Tommy's rooming house or the Hotel Bethlehem.

The Corps was hell on drunk driving and/or speeding. He still hadn't accepted the possibility that he could become an officer. Which was the main reason why he hadn't said anything about Quantico to either Anne-Marie or Tommy. Besides, they probably wouldn't believe it. Which was easy to understand; he didn't quite believe it himself. But getting arrested for drunk driving or speeding would be the end of it. He wanted to give it a shot, anyway.

Tommy pulled him out of the whore's bed at half-past six in the morning and said he had to go to fucking work and needed a fucking ride and some fucking breakfast: He couldn't work eight fucking hours on the fucking open hearth with nothing in his fucking stomach.

They went to a greasy spoon and had eggs and home fries and coffee. He dropped Tommy off at the walk bridge over the railroad tracks and drove back to the Navy Yard.

(Two)
The San Mateo Club
San Mateo, California
27 August 1941

The building that housed the San Mateo Club had been built, in 1895, as the country residence of Andrew Foster, Sr. It so remained until 1939, when Andrew Foster, Jr., seventy, on the death of his wife, moved into the penthouse atop the Andrew Foster Hotel in San Francisco and put the estate on the market.

It had been quickly snapped up by the board of directors of the San Mateo club. Not only was the price right and the house large enough for the membership then rather crowded into the "old clubhouse," but the money was there. A very nice price had been offered for the "old club" by developers who wanted to turn its greens and fairways into a housing development.

The Foster Estate ("the new club") contained land enough to lay out twenty-seven holes (as opposed to eighteen at the old club), as well as gently rolling pastures right beside the polo field that could accommodate far more ponies than the old club could handle. And old Mr. Foster, Jr. had thrown in all of the furnishings, except for those in his private apartment, which had moved to the hotel penthouse with him.

The woman was lanky and fair-haired. She wore a wide-brimmed straw hat, a pale blue dress, and white gloves. From where she was standing, by the foot of the wide staircase leading to the second floor of the clubhouse, she could see the reserve supply of champagne. It was practically, if somewhat inelegantly, stored by the door to the passageway to the kitchen in ice-filled, galvanized-iron watering troughs for horses.

She took a delicate bite of her hors d'oeuvre, a very nice pâté on a crisp cracker, sipped at her champagne, and seriously considered just picking up one of the bottles and carrying it upstairs. He would probably find that amusing.

But it would be difficult to explain if she met someone coming down the stairs. Without the champagne, it would be presumed that she was going up to use the john. There were inadequate rest room facilities for ladies on the main floor of the San Mateo Club. The men had no similar problem. What had been a private study off the library had been equipped with the proper plumbing and that was it.

Which meant that when nature called, the men could conveniently take a leak not fifty feet from the bar. But the women, when faced with a similar requirement, more often than not would find their small downstairs facilities occupied and would have to seek release in an upstairs john. The silver lining in that cloud was that no one looked curiously at a woman making her way up the wide, curving staircase.

She put her empty champagne glass on the tray of a passing waiter, smilingly shook her head when he offered her a fresh glass, and started up the stairs.

No one was in the upstairs corridors, which she thought was fortuitous. But she hurried nevertheless, and quickly entered, without knocking, a door halfway down the right corridor. There was a brass number on the door, 14. The numbered rooms were an innovation of the House Committee; before they had been put up, people spending the night or the weekend in the "new clubhouse" had been unable to find their own rooms.

She closed the door and fastened the lock. She could hear the sound of the shower and of his voice, an entirely satisfactory tenor. She smiled at that, then walked to the bed, saw that he had tossed his clothing on it, sniffed, and wrinkled her nose. She delicately picked up the sweat-soaked blue polo shirt (a cloth letter "2" still safety-pinned to it) and an equally sweat-soaked pair of Jockey shorts and dropped them onto the floor beside a very dirty pair of breeches, a scarred and battered pair of riding boots, and a pair of heavy woolen socks.

Then she pulled the cover off the bed and turned it down. She looked toward the bathroom, wondering how long he had been in there, how soon he could come out to find her.

Surprise! Surprise!

Then she had an even better idea. She walked to a credenza and pulled her hat and gloves off and dropped them there. Then she took off her wedding and engagement rings. And, very quickly, the rest of her clothing. It would be amusing only if she was finished undressing.

But when she had finished that, he still hadn't come out. The last time she'd seen him, she remembered, he had really needed a bath. He had been reeking with sweat; and perspiration was literally dripping off his chin. But enough was enough.

She examined herself in a mirror and smiled wickedly at herself, walked to the bathroom door, opened it, and went inside. There was no shower stall. One corner had been tiled. The tiled area was so large that water from three shower heads aimed at the corner did not splash beyond it.

His head and face were covered with lather. Still singing cheerfully, he was rubbing the tips of his fingers vigorously on his scalp. She saw a shower cap on a hook and quickly stuffed her hair under it. Then she stepped into the tiled area, hunching her shoulders involuntarily as the water, colder than she expected, struck her. Then she dropped to her knees, reached out, and put it in her mouth.

"Jesus Christ!" Pick Pickering said, "Are you crazy?" And then he yelped. "Christ, I got soap in my eyes!"

He stepped away from her abruptly to turn his face to a shower stream. Slipping and almost falling, the woman rose to her feet. She went to him, pressed her body against him, and nipped his nipple.

"Where the hell is your husband?" Pick Pickering asked.

"In the bar, I suppose," the woman said. "I got bored."

She put her hand on it and pumped it just a few times until it filled her hand.

"You want to try doing it standing up?" she asked. "It would be sort of like doing it in the rain."

"Dorothy!" Pick said.

She tried to arrange herself so he could penetrate her, and failed.

"I don't think that's going to work," she said, matter-of-factly.

Pick Pickering picked her up and carried her to the bed. Penetration there proved simple.

Three minutes later, he jumped out of bed.

"Wham, bam, thank you, ma'am?" she said. "That's not very nice."

"You're out of your mind, Dorothy, do you know that?"

"Where are you going?"

"I am due in town right now," he said.

"Who is she? Anyone I know?"

He didn't reply.

"No goddamned underwear!" He cried as he pawed through a canvas overnight bag. "I didn't bring any underwear!"

"How sexy!" Dorothy said.

"What the hell am I going to do?"

"Do without," she said. "I do that all the time."

He looked at her and smiled.

"You would crack wise at the moment your husband shot us both with a shotgun," he said.

"That presumes his being sober enough to hold a shotgun," Dorothy said. "You really do have to go, don't you?"

"The only reason I played at all today is because Tommy Whitlock canceled at the last minute."

He pulled a fresh polo shirt over his head, and then started to pull on a pair of cotton trousers.

"How lucky for the both of us," she said.

He looked at her and smiled again.

"Be careful with the zipper," she said. "I wouldn't want anything to get damaged."

"Neither would I," he said.

"I'm not going to see you again, am I?" she asked.

"I don't see how," Pick said.

"I'll miss you, baby."

"I'll miss you too, Dorothy," he said. He found his wrist-watch on the bedside table and strapped it on. "Christ, I am late!" he said.

He looked down at her, and she pushed herself onto her elbows. He leaned over and kissed her.

"I really am going to miss you," she said.

"Me, too," he said.

"Be careful, baby," she said.

He jumped up and, hopping, pushed his bare feet into a pair of loafers.

Then he left, without looking back at her.

Thirty minutes later he was in San Francisco by the entrance to the parking garage of the Andrew Foster Hotel. A sign had been placed on the sidewalk there: SORRY, BUT JUST NOW, WE NEED ALL OUR SPACE FOR OUR REGISTERED GUESTS!"

Like everything else connected with the Andrew Foster Hotel, it was not an ordinary sign. It was contained within a polished brass frame and lettered in gold. And the frame was mounted in an ornate cast-iron mounting. The Andrew Foster was one of the world's great hotels (the most prestigious as well as the most expensive hotel in San Francisco), the flagship of the forty-two-hotel Foster Hotel chain. Certain standards would have been expected of it even if Andrew Foster were not resident in the penthouse.

Andrew Foster was fond of quoting the "One Great Rule of Keeping a Decent Inn." It was not the sort of rule that could be written down, for it changed sometimes half a dozen times a day. It could be summarized (and was, behind his back) as immediately correcting whatever offended his eye at the moment.

What offended Andrew Foster could range from a smudge on a bellman's shoes ("The One Great Rule of Keeping a Decent Inn is that the staff must be impeccably turned out. If you do that, everything else will fall into place."); to an overdone medium-rare steak ("The One Great Rule of Keeping a Decent Inn is to give people at table what they ask for. If you do that, everything else will fall into place."); to fresh flowers starting to wilt ("The One Great Rule of Keeping a Decent Inn is to keep the place from looking like a rundown funeral home! If you can do that, everything else will fall into place!").

The gilt-lettered sign appeared on the sidewalk shortly after Mr. Andrew Foster spotted a simple GARAGE FULL sign. Everything else would fall in place if people were told (by means of a sign that didn't look as if it came off the midway of a second-rate carnival) why they couldn't do something they wanted to and were offered the inn's apologies for the inconvenience.

Ignoring the sign, Pick Pickering drove his car, a black Cadillac convertible, roof down, a brand new one, into the parking garage. He quickly saw that the garage was indeed full; there was not sufficient room for the rear of the car to clear the sidewalk.

One of the neatly uniformed (after the fashion of the French Foreign Legion) parking attendants rushed to the car.

"May I park your car for you, sir?" the attendant asked, very politely.

Pick Pickering looked at him and grinned.

"Would you please, Tony?" he asked. "I'm really late."

"No!" the attendant said, in elaborate mock surprise. "Is that why everybody but the Coast Guard's looking for you?"

"Oh, Christ," Pickering said.

" 'The One Great Rule of Keeping a Decent Inn,' " Tony quoted.

" 'Is That People Are Where They Are Supposed to Be, When They Are Supposed to Be There,' " Pickering finished for him.

"You've heard that, Pick, have you?" Tony asked. "You want me to let him know you're here?"

"Please, Tony," Pickering said and walked quickly, almost ran, between the tightly packed cars to a door marked STAFF ONLY.

Behind it was a locker room. Pickering started pulling the polo shirt off his head as he pushed the door open. He had his pants off before he stopped before one of the battered lockers.

Two dinner jackets were hanging in the locker, and three dress shirts in cellophane bags fresh from the hotel laundry, but there was no underwear where there was supposed to be underwear. And not even any goddamned socks!

Moving with a speed that could come only of long practice, he put suspenders on the trousers, studs and cufflinks in the shirt; and as he hooked the cummerbund around his waist, slipped his bare feet into patent leather shoes.

Ninety seconds after he opened the locker door, Pick Pickering tied the knot in the bow tie as he waited impatiently for an elevator.

The elevator door opened. The operator, a middle-aged black woman, stared at him and said, ''You've got lipstick on your ear, Pick, and the tie's crooked.''

''Would you believe this?'' he said, showing her his bare ankles as he stepped into the elevator and reached for a handkerchief to deal with the lipstick.

''Going to be dull around here without you,'' she said, laughing.

''I understand he's in a rage,'' Pickering said. ''Is there any special reason, or is he just staying in practice?''

''You know why he's mad,'' she chided. ''Where were you, anyway?''

''San Mateo,'' he said. ''I was delayed.''

''I could tell,'' she said, then added, ''You may wish you called him and told him.''

Most of the ''passenger waiting'' lights on the call board were lit up, but the elevator operator ignored them as she took him all the way up without stopping. Pick watched annoyed and angry faces as the car rose past people waiting.

''Your ears are clean, but don't give him a chance to look at your feet,'' the operator said, as she opened the door.

Pickering was surprised to see that the foyer outside the elevator was full of people. Normally the only thing to be found in it were room service or housekeeping carts. He should have known the old man had more in mind than a lamb chop when he said he wanted Pick to have supper with him before he went.

Someone recognized him and giggled, and then applauded. That seemed like a good idea to the others, and the applause caught on like a brushfire. Pick clasped his hands over his head like a victorious prize fighter. That caused more laughter.

''I believe the Marine Corps has landed,'' Andrew Foster's voice boomed. ''An hour late, and more than likely a dollar short.''

''I'm sorry, Grandfather,'' Pick Pickering said.

''I assume that she was worth it,'' the old man said. ''I can't believe you'd keep your mother and your father, not to mention your guests and me, waiting solely because you were riding around on a horse.''

(Three)
Bethlehem, Pennsylvania
21 August 1941

Two cops came to the cell.

"Okay, Joe Louis, on your feet!" one of them said, as the other signaled for the remotely operated door to be opened.

One of the cops came in the cell and stood over Tommy McCoy as he put his feet in his work shoes. When Tommy finally stood up, the cop took handcuffs from a holder on his belt.

"Put your hands behind you," he said.

"Hey, I'm all right now," Tommy said.

"Put your hands behind you," the cop repeated.

As he felt the manacles snap in place around his wrist, Tommy asked, "What happens now?"

The cop ignored him. He took his arm and sort of shoved him out of the cell, then out of the cellblock. They stopped at the property room and picked up their revolvers, then ripped open a brown manila envelope. They tucked his wallet, handkerchief, cigarettes, matches and change in his pockets, and led him out of the building to a parking lot in the rear.

"When do I get something to eat?" Tommy asked.

The cops ignored that question too.

He wasn't so much hungry as thirsty, Tommy thought. He'd really put away the boilermakers the night before, and the only water in the cell had been warm, and brown, and smelled like horse-piss.

What he really needed was a couple of beers, maybe a couple of boilermakers, to straighten himself out.

They took him to the mill to the small brick building just inside the gate. It looked like a regular house but was the place where the mill security police had their office. In there was also a dispensary where they took people until the ambulance arrived.

They led him into the office of the chief of plant security. He wasn't surprised to see him, but he was surprised to see Denny Walkowicz, Assistant Business Manager of Local 3341, United Steel Workers of America, a big, shiny-faced Polack.

No one said hello to Tommy, or offered him a chair.

"What's all this?" Tommy asked.

"You broke his nose, you might like to know," the chief

of plant security said. "He said you hit him with a beer bottle."

"Bullshit," Tommy said.

"What do they call that?" the plant security chief said.

"We got him charged with 'assault with a dangerous object,' " one of the cops said.

"That's all?"

"Public drunkenness, resisting arrest," the cop said. "There's more."

"Nobody's asked for his side of it," Denny Walkowicz said.

"His side don't mean a shit, Denny. Let's not start that bullshit all over again."

Another man came into the room. One of the fucking white-collar workers from Personnel. Little shit in a shiny blue suit.

He had an envelope in his hand, which he laid on the table.

"Denny Walkowicz stood up for you, McCoy, Christ only knows why," the plant security chief said. "Here's what we worked out. There's two weeks' severance pay, plus what you earned through last Friday. You take that."

"Or what?"

"Or they take you back to jail."

"You're facing ninety days in the can, kid," Denny Walkowicz said. "At least, maybe a lot more. And it ain't only the time, it's a criminal record."

"For getting in a fight?"

"You don't listen, do you, McCoy?" the plant security chief said. "You hit a guy with a beer bottle, it's not like punching him."

"I told you, I didn't use no bottle."

"Yeah, you said that, but other people say different."

"Well, fuck you!"

"I'm glad you were here and the cops are to hear that, Denny," the chief of plant security said. " 'Using profane or obscene language to a supervisor or member of management shall be grounds for dismissal for cause,' " he quoted.

"He's got you, McCoy," Denny Walkowicz said. "You gotta learn to watch your mouth."

"Take him back to jail," the chief of plant security said, and then picked up the brown envelope and handed it back to the white-collar guy from administration. "Do what you have to," he said. "No severance pay."

"Now wait a minute," Denny Walkowicz said. "We had a deal, we worked this out."

"Nobody tells me, 'fuck you,' " the plant security chief said.

Denny Walkowicz took the envelope back from the white-collar guy.

"You," he said to Tommy McCoy, "keep your fucking mouth shut!"

Then he led him out of the room, with the cops following.

The cops took the handcuffs off him.

"If it was up to me," the larger one said, "you'd do time."

"Yeah, well it ain't up to you, is it?" Denny Walkowicz said.

"If you're smart, McCoy, you won't hang around Bethlehem," the cop said. "You know what I mean?"

As Denny Walkowicz drove Tommy to the boardinghouse in his blue Buick Roadmaster, he said: "You better pay attention to what the cop said. They're after your ass. It took three of them to hold you down, and you kicked one of them in the balls. They're not going to take that."

"That was all the union could do for me?"

"You ungrateful sonofabitch!" Denny Walkowicz exploded. "We kept you from going to jail!"

Tommy went to bed the minute he got to his room. He slept the rest of the day, and except for going out for two beers and some spaghetti about ten that night, slept right around the clock.

At ten-thirty the next morning, he went down to the post office and talked to the recruiter. The guy was especially nice to him after he told him his brother was a Marine, too. He told Tommy that if he enlisted for the duration of the present emergency plus six months, he could fix it for him to be assigned to the same unit as his brother. And when Tommy said that he had always wanted to be a pilot, the recruiter said he could arrange for that, too.

Thomas Michael McCoy was sworn into the United States Marine Corps at 1645 hours that same afternoon. He was transported by bus to the U.S. Navy Yard, Philadelphia,

Pennsylvania, the next morning. At Philadelphia, he learned that the recruiter had been something less than honest with him. He wasn't going to be trained as a pilot, but as an infantryman. And the corporal in Philadelphia told him he stood as much chance of being assigned with his brother as he did of being elected pope.

But the corporal felt that professional courtesy to a fellow corporal required that he inform Corporal McCoy that his little brother was on the base awaiting transport to Parris Island. He called Post Locator, and they told him that Corporal McCoy had been the day before transferred to Marine Corps Schools, Quantico, Virginia.

Then the corporal made the connection. This dumb Mick's brother was the China Marine in the campaign hat driving the LaSalle convertible, the one they were sending to officers' school. They sure as Christ made little apples were not two peas from the same pod, he thought.

(Four)
Office of the Deputy Chief of Staff for Personnel
Headquarters, United States Marine Corps
Washington, D.C.
29 August 1941

The wooden frame building—designed for no more than five years' usage—had been built during the Great War (1917–18). The Chief of Company-Grade Officer Assignments stood waiting in one of the doorways to catch the eye of the Deputy Chief, Assignments Branch. The doorway sagged.

The Chief of Company-Grade Officer Assignments, a balding, stocky man, had taken off the jacket of his cord suit and rolled up the sleeves of his sweat-soaked white shirt. Standing there with his suspenders exposed, he didn't look much like the captain of Marines he was. He held two documents at his side. One was that week's listing of actual and projected billet vacancies. The other was the service record of MACKLIN, John D., 1st Lt.

The Deputy Chief, Assignments Branch, had been reading with great interest an interoffice memorandum which compared projected Company-Grade Officer Requirements for Fiscal Year 1942 against projected officer recruitment for

Fiscal Year 1942 and was wondering where the hell they were going to dig up the 2,195 bodies that represented the difference between what they needed and what they were likely to get. Finally he noticed the Chief of Company-Grade Officer Assignments standing in his door and motioned him inside with a wave of his hand.

The Deputy Chief, Assignments Branch, who had also removed his jacket, was a major—although he looked, and sometimes felt, more like a bureaucrat than a Marine officer.

"How would you like me to handle this, sir?" the Chief of Company-Grade officer assignments asked. He handed the major the documents in his hand.

The major opened the service-record jacket of MACKLIN, John D., 1st Lt.

There was a file of orders concerning the officer in question bound to the record jacket with a metal expanding clip. The order on top, which made it the most recent one, had been issued by the 4th Marines. Lieutenant Macklin, having been decreed excess to the needs of the command, was relieved of duty and would proceed to the United States of America aboard the U.S.S. *Shaumont,* reporting on arrival to Headquarters, USMC, Washington, D.C., for further assignment. A thirty day delay en route leave was authorized.

Macklin was not really expected to physically report in Washington. His orders and his records would be sent to Washington. When Washington decided what to do with him, either a telegram or a registered letter would be sent to his leave address telling him where to go and when to be there.

In a manila folder were copies of Lieutenant Macklin's efficiency reports, mounted in the same manner as his orders.

"I wonder what he did?" the major asked, without expecting an answer, as he turned his attention to Lieutenant Macklin's most recent efficiency report. Officers were rarely decreed excess to the needs of a command. Commands, as a rule of thumb, generally sent a steady stream of justifications for the assignment of additional officer personnel to carry out their assigned missions.

A civilian, reading the efficiency report, would probably have concluded that it was a frank, confidential appraisal of the strengths and weaknesses of what a civilian would probably think was a typical Marine officer.

He was described as a "tall, lean, and fit" officer of "erect bearing" with "no disfiguring marks or scars." It said that Lieutenant Macklin was "slightly below" the average of his peers in professional knowledge; that he had "adequately discharged the duties assigned to him"; that there was "no indication of abuse of alcoholic beverages or other stimulants"; and that Lieutenant Macklin had "a tendency not to accept blame for his failures, but instead to attempt to shift the blame to subordinates." In this connection, it said that Lieutenant Macklin was prone to submit official reports that both omitted facts that might tend to make him look bad, and "to present other facts in such a manner as to magnify his own contribution to the accomplishment of the assigned mission." It said finally that Lieutenant Macklin "could not be honestly recommended for the command of a company or larger tactical unit at this time."

A civilian would doubtless think that here was a nice-looking erect young man, who was mostly competent, did what he was told to do, and had no problem with the bottle. If there was anything wrong with him at all, it was a perfectly understandable inclination to present only his best side to his superiors. If he could not be recommended to be a company commander at this time, well, he was young, and there would be a chance for that later. In the meantime, there were certainly other places where his "slightly below average professional knowledge" could be put to good use.

In the Corps, Macklin's efficiency report was lethal.

"Jesus, I wonder what the hell he did?" the major repeated.

"The endorsing officer is Chesty Puller," the captain said. "Puller's a hardnose, but he's fair. And you saw how he endorsed it."

" 'The undersigned concurs in this evaluation of this officer,' " the major quoted.

"So what do we do with him?" the captain asked.

"Maybe he got too friendly with some wife?" the major asked.

"I think he got caught writing a false report," the captain said.

"In which he tried to shaft somebody . . ."

"Somebody who worked with him, you saw that remark about 'shifting blame to subordinates?' "

"And got caught," the major agreed. "That would tee Chesty Puller off."

"So what do we do with him?"

"Six months ago, I would ask when he planned to resign," the major said. "But that's no longer an option, is it?"

"No, sir."

"What's open?" the major asked.

"I gave you the list, sir."

The major consulted the week's listing of actual and projected billet vacancies for company-grade officers.

"It says here there's a vacancy for a mess officer at the School Battalion at Quantico. I thought we sent that kid from the hotel school at Cornell down there? Ye Olde Round Peg in Ye Olde Round Hole?"

"He developed a hernia," the captain said. "They sent him to the Navy hospital at Norfolk. It'll be more than ninety days before he's fit for full duty, so they transferred him to the Detachment of Patients."

"I would hate to see someone who has graduated from the Cornell Hotel School assigned anywhere but a kitchen," the major said.

The captain chuckled.

"I've sort of penciled in when he's available for assignment, assigning him to the Marine Barracks here. He'd make a fine assistant officers' club officer."

"Don't let him get away," the major said. "And in the meantime, I think we should send Lieutenant Macklin to Quantico, at least for the time being. All a mess officer does anyway—Cornell Hotel School graduates excepted—is make sure nobody's selling the rations."

"Aye, aye, sir," the chief of company-grade officer assignments said. And then he thought of something else: "We've got another one, sir."

"Somebody else with an efficiency report like that?" the major asked, incredulously.

"No, sir. Another hotelier. Is that right?"

The major nodded.

"One of the kids starting the Platoon Leader's course listed his current occupation as resident manager of the Andrew Foster Hotel in San Francisco. That sounded a little odd for a twenty-one-year-old, so I checked on it."

"And he really was?"

"He really was. And not only because he's Andrew Foster's grandson."

"Our cup runneth over," the major said. "Don't let that one get away, either. Maybe something can be done about the quality of the chow after all."

"Aye, aye, sir," the captain repeated with a smile.

IX

The man at the wheel of the spotless Chevrolet pickup truck was Master Gunnery Sergeant Jack (NMI)[1] Stecker, USMC. Stecker was a tall, muscular, tanned, erect man of forty-one who looked the way a master gunnery sergeant, USMC, with twenty-five years in the Corps, was supposed to look.

He was in stiffly starched, impeccably pressed khakis. A vertical crease ran precisely through the buttons of the shirt pockets to the shoulder seam on the front of the shirt. There were four creases on the rear: One ran horizontally across the back of his shoulders. The other three ran down the back, one on each side, and one down the middle. There were a total of six pockets on his khaki shirt and trousers. Two were in use. Stecker's left hip pocket held his wallet; and his right shirt pocket held a small, thin notebook and a silver-plated Parker pen-and-pencil set. The other pockets were sealed shut with starch, and would remain sealed shut.

The keys to his office, to his quarters, and to his personal automobile, a 1939 Packard Phaeton, as well as a Saint Christopher medal, were on a second dogtag cord worn around his neck.

Stecker did not think it fitting that the uniform of a master gunnery sergeant, USMC, should bulge in any way. There was a handkerchief in his left sock. Sometimes, not often,

---

[1] No Middle Initial.

when he knew he would be away from another source of smoking material for a considerable period of time, he carried a package of Lucky Strike cigarettes and a book of matches in his right sock. Mostly, he kept his smoking material in various convenient places—the glove compartment of the pickup, his desk drawer, and sometimes (if he knew he was not going to have to remove his campaign hat) in the crown of the hat.

Master Gunnery Sergeant Jack Stecker, USMC, turned off the macadam Range Road and slowed the Chevrolet pickup as he approached the barrier, a weighted pole, barring access to the ranges.

As it often is in Virginia in late August, it was hot and muggy, and Jack Stecker had rolled the driver's-side window down. But as he approached the Known Distance Rifle Range close enough to hear the firing, he rolled the window up. The crack of .30-caliber rifle fire does more than make your ears ring; it permanently damages your hearing if you get enough of it.

A large red flag hung limply from a twenty-five-foot pole, signaling that the range was in use. A young Marine had been assigned to bar access to the range by unauthorized personnel, and to raise the barrier to pass authorized personnel. He was about twenty-one, his nose was sunburned, and he wore utilities, a World War I-style helmet, a web cartridge belt (from which hung a canteen and a first-aid packet), and had a U.S. Rifle, Caliber .30, Model 1903A3, slung over his shoulder by its leather sling.

When Master Gunnery Sergeant Jack Stecker first saw him, the young man with the sunburned nose was standing five feet from the flagpole. And Jack Stecker had no doubt that the young man (who looked like a boot about to graduate from the Recruit Depot at Parris Island, but who was in fact an officer candidate about to graduate from the Platoon Leader's Course and become a commissioned officer, second lieutenant, in the Marines) had probably been leaning on the pole. He had also probably propped the Springfield against the flagpole.

Stecker was not offended. What was important was that he had not caught him failing in his duties as a guard. He would have burned him a new asshole if he had caught him doing what he damned well knew he had been doing, but he had not.

When the trainee, recognizing Master Gunnery Sergeant Stecker's Chevrolet pickup, had quickly raised the weighted pole barrier, he was rewarded for his efforts by a slight but unmistakable nod of Stecker's head. The trainee nodded back, and smiled shyly—and with some relief. He had been forced to make a decision, and it had turned out to be the right one.

When he first recognized the pickup as Master Gunnery Sergeant Stecker's, he hadn't been sure whether Stecker expected him to raise the barrier immediately, or to bar Stecker's path until he had satisfied himself that Master Gunnery Sergeant Stecker indeed had official business on the range.

He had decided in the end that the safest course was to presume that whatever Master Gunnery Sergeant Stecker wanted to do on the Quantico reservation was official business and that it was not his role to question him about it.

It had not been difficult to differentiate Master Gunnery Sergeant Stecker's pickup from the perhaps fifty identical 1940 Chevrolet pickups on the Quantico reservation. Stecker's personal pickup was very likely the cleanest, most highly polished pickup in the Marine Corps, perhaps in the world.

When Master Gunnery Sergeant Stecker telephoned the motor sergeant to announce that he was through for the day with his transport, a motor pool corporal went to Base Headquarters to fetch it. He then drove it to the motor pool, where he examined the odometer to see how many miles Stecker had driven that day. He then filled out the trip ticket with probable, if wholly imaginary, destinations to correspond with the miles driven. It was universally recognized that Master Gunnery Sergeant Stecker had more important things to do with his time than fill out forms like a fucking clerk.

With that done, the vehicle went through prescribed daily maintenance. The fuel tank was filled; the tire pressure checked; and the oil level and radiator water replenished. The vehicle was then turned over to whatever enlisted men had run afoul of Rocks and Shoals; had gone to Office Hours; and were now performing punitive extra duty in the motor pool.

They washed the vehicle with soap and water, every inch of it, inside and out—except for the glove compartment, which was off limits. When the vehicle was washed and dried, it was swept out with whisk brooms, making sure there was no dust or sand in the cracks of the rubber covering of the running board or between the wooden planks of the bed. The vehicle was then inspected by the motor transport corporal. If the wax polish seemed to need touching up, the pickup was waxed. When it was finally judged likely to meet Master Gunnery Sergeant Stecker's standards, it was parked overnight inside, in the hoist section of the garage.

In the morning, a motor transport corporal drove the pickup to Base Headquarters, where he parked it in a space marked FOR OFFICIAL VISITORS ONLY, so that it would be available should Master Gunnery Sergeant Stecker need transport.

When the first Trucks, one-quarter ton, four-by-four, General Purpose (called "Jeeps") had been issued to Quantico, it had been proposed to Master Gunnery Sergeant Stecker that one be assigned to him, with a driver, for his use. Stecker had somewhat icily informed the motor transport sergeant that even though he could doubtless spare someone to spend most of his duty day sitting around with his thumb up his ass waiting to drive somebody someplace, he certainly could find real work for him to do that would be of value to the Corps.

Master Gunnery Sergeant Stecker had other reasons to refuse the assignment of a jeep and driver. One of them was that a driver would come to know where he went, and why, and talk about it at night in the barracks. The less the men knew where he went and what he did, the better. Neither could Master Gunnery Sergeant Stecker see any reason why he should exchange a perfectly satisfactory vehicle, which came with nicely upholstered seats and roll-up windows, for a small open truck with thin canvas-covered pads to cushion his bottom.

There was absolutely nothing that Stecker could find wrong, which is to say unmilitary, in finding comfort wherever it might be found. In his twenty-five years of service, he had been acutely uncomfortable on more occasions than he liked to remember. And there was no question whatever in his mind that he would be made acutely uncomfortable again—possibly, the Corps being what it was, as soon as tomorrow.

It was not necessary to train to be uncomfortable. That came naturally, like taking a leak.

When Master Gunnery Sergeant Stecker reached the Known Distance rifle range itself, he put wax plugs in his ears to protect them from the damaging crack of riflefire, and then got out of his pickup and approached the Range Tower. Pretending not to see the range officer, a young lieutenant who was in the tower itself, he examined the firing records, checked over two weapons that had failed to function, and the general police of the area; then discreetly inquired of the range sergeant how the new range officer was working out.

"He's all right, Gunny," the range sergeant said. "Better than most second lieutenants, to tell you the truth."

Stecker nodded. Then, with hands folded against the small of his back and the range sergeant trailing him, he marched to one end of the firing line, pausing now and again when the targets were marked or to stand behind one prone rifleman and his coach. Then he reversed course and marched to the other end. He found nothing that required correction. He really hadn't expected to. Except for the general truth that the way to keep things running smoothly was to keep your eye on them, there had really been no reason for him to "have a look" at the range.

Then he returned to the pickup and drove back to his office.

There was a glistening LaSalle convertible in one of the "Official Visitor" parking spaces. Stecker had almost bought a LaSalle convertible. Although he considered his Packard Phaeton to be a fine piece of machinery, sometimes he wished he had gone to the LaSalle. It wouldn't have cost nearly so much money, and it was, under the skin, a Cadillac. And there would not have been so many eyebrows raised at a Master Gunnery Sergeant driving a LaSalle.

The question was how could an enlisted man, even one in the highest enlisted grade, afford the monthly payments on a Packard Phaeton? The answer was that there were no monthly payments. He had paid cash on the barrel head for it. And the reason cash was available to pay for it was that shortly after he had married, when he was a twenty-one-year-old sergeant, he had gone out on payday and got tanked and blown most of his pay in a poker game.

Elly gave him what he later came to call "her look." Then she put it to him simply: Not only was he a damned fool, but she was in the family way, and if the marriage wasn't going to work, it would be better if they faced it and called it off. Either she would handle the money from now on, or she was going home to Tatamy the next day.

She then put him on an allowance, like a little boy, and kept him on it even later, when he'd gotten more stripes. When the kids were big enough, she'd gotten her teacher's certificate and gone to work. And it wasn't just her making the buffalo on the nickels squeal before she parted with one; Elly put the money to work.

Right from the first, she had started buying and selling things. She would read the "Unofficial" section of the Daily Bulletin looking for bargains for sale. She didn't only buy things to use (like kid's clothes and from time to time a nice piece of furniture), she bought things to resell. And she was good at buying things and selling them. She told him once that she had a twenty-five percent rule: She wouldn't buy anything unless she could buy it for twenty-five percent less than what somebody was asking for it, and she wouldn't sell it for less than twenty-five percent more than she had paid for it.

So the boy's college fund kept growing. Elly was determined from the beginning that the boys would go to college. And then, as the fund grew, her determination changed to "the boys would go to a *good* college."

In '34, when the Depression was really bad (Jack Stecker was a staff sergeant then), the bank had foreclosed on her brother Fritz's house in Tatamy. Elly took a chance and put in a bid at the sheriff's auction. Most everybody else in Tatamy had been laid off from Bethlehem Steel, too, and not many people wanted an old three-family row house anyway. So she got it at a steal and without the down payment really making a big dent in the boys' college fund.

Fritz went on living in what had been his apartment, and his oldest son and his family in another—neither of them paying rent, because they were out of work—but the third was rented out for nearly enough money to make the mortgage payment.

Jack Stecker hadn't said anything to her, because he always considered the boys' college money to really be Elly's money, and if she wanted to help her family out when they were in a bind, he understood that, too.

He came later to understand that what Elly had really done was put the money to work, and that if it also made things a little easier for her brother and nephew, fine, but that wasn't the reason she had bought the house.

Neither Fritz nor his kid paid any rent until they got called back by Bethlehem Steel, Fritz in '37, his kid not until '39. When Fritz complained that paying back rent was a hell of a thing for a sister to ask of her own brother, Elly told him that she was charging him two percent less than the bank would have charged him, that he knew damned well that the bank would not have loaned a laid-off steel worker a dime, and that he and his family would have been put out on the street.

Then she offered to sell him the house back at what an appraiser called the "fair market value." And she would carry the mortgage herself. So they had the house appraised and added what Fritz and his son owed for back rent to that, and Fritz was paying it off by the month at six percent interest. Not to Elly anymore. Elly had sold the mortgage to the Easton Bank & Trust Company. And that money had gone into the boys' college fund.

And then, as it turned out, they didn't need the boys' college fund at all. He'd gone home one afternoon and saw her with "her look." But Elly waited until he had changed out of his uniform, taken his beer from the icebox, and listened to the "Burns & Allen" program on the radio. Then she made room for herself on the footstool and handed him a paperbound book.

"You ever see this?" she asked.

Sure, he'd seen it. It was the catalog of the United States Naval Academy.

"You ever read it?" she asked.

"I glanced through it," he said, somewhat defensively. It was difficult for a master gunnery sergeant, USMC, to admit to anyone, including his wife, that there was any aspect of the Naval Service of the United States with which he was not intimately familiar.

"God, Jack," Elly said, disgusted. "You sometimes are a really thick-headed Dutchman!"

She handed him the catalog, open, with a passage marked in red ink.

"Additionally, an unlimited number of appointments are available noncompetitively to sons of winners of the Medal of Honor."

Jack Stecker never wore the Medal, but it was in the strongbox, together with a copy of the citation, and a non-yellowing photograph of General "Black Jack" Pershing hanging it around his neck.

> In the name of the American people, the Congress of the United States awards the Medal of Honor to Sergeant Jack NMI Stecker, USMC, for valor in action above and beyond the call of duty in the vicinity of Belleau Wood, near Château-Thierry, France, during the period June 6 to June 9, 1918. CITATION: Sergeant (then Corporal) Stecker, in command of a squad of United States Marines participating in an assault upon German positions on June 6, was grievously wounded in the leg. When it became necessary for American forces to temporarily break off the attack and reform prior to a second attack, Sergeant Stecker refused evacuation and, despite his wounds, established himself in a position from which he could bring rifle fire to bear upon the enemy.
>
> During the nights of June 6 through June 8, without regard to either his wound or the great risk to his life posed by incessant small arms and artillery fire, Sergeant Stecker searched the area between the lines of the opposing forces (commonly referred to as "no-man's land") for other U.S. Marines who had also been unable or unwilling to withdraw to safe positions.
>
> Not only did Sergeant Stecker save the lives of many of these wounded men by administering first aid to them, but, inspiring them by his personal example of valor in the face of overwhelming odds, formed them into a 24-man-strong fighting force and established a rifle and machine-gun position from which, when the second, successful assault

was launched on June 9, he laid a withering fire on German positions which otherwise would have been able to bring fire to bear on attacking American Forces with a resultant great loss of life.

During the fighting involved during the second assault, Sergeant Stecker was wounded twice more, and suffered great loss of blood and excruciating pain. Despite his wounds and pain, Sergeant Stecker remained in command, inspiring his subordinates with his courage and coolness under fire until he lost consciousness.

Sergeant Stecker's valor and dedication to duty are in keeping with the highest traditions of the United States Marine Corps and the Naval Service.

Entered the Naval Service from Pennsylvania.

So the boys had gone to service academies, Jack Jr. to Annapolis, and Richard to West Point. Jack was an ensign on the Battleship *Arizona* in the Pacific Fleet in Pearl Harbor, and Richard would graduate next June and take a commission as a second lieutenant of Marines.

Elly had waited until she was sure the boys were set, then she had used some—not much—of what was now "the retirement fund" to buy him the Packard Phaeton. He was entitled, she said, and you only live once.

Three people were waiting outside Master Gunnery Sergeant Jack Stecker's office when he reached it: a staff sergeant, a PFC, and a corporal. He nodded at them, said, "Be with you in a minute," and went inside. When his clerk delivered his coffee, he would tell Stecker what they wanted.

He knew the staff sergeant; he was from Post housing, and that was personal, so it could wait. And he supposed the PFC was carrying some kind of message, and that could wait too. But the corporal was completely unfamiliar to Stecker, and he was a little curious about him.

The coffee (black, brewed no more than thirty minutes before; Stecker could not stand stale coffee) was delivered in a white china mess-hall mug within sixty seconds of his sitting down behind his desk.

"Sergeant Quinn's here about your quarters," Stecker's

clerk, a corporal, said. "The PFC was sent by the first sergeant of 'B' Company. Your wife called and said if you could come home early that would be nice. And the colonel says he'd like to see you when you have time, nothing important."

"And the China Marine?" Stecker asked.

"You mean the corporal?" the clerk asked. Stecker nodded, barely perceptibly. "How do you know he's a China Marine?"

"What does he want?" Stecker asked, deciding that he would not mention the young corporal's embroidered-to-his-shirt chevrons, one of the marks of a China Marine.

"Wouldn't say," the clerk said. "Wants to see you. I seen him drive up. You see that LaSalle convertible when you come in?"

"Send the corporal in," Stecker said.

(Two)

Corporal Kenneth J. "Killer" McCoy walked into the room, looked at Stecker, and said, "Thank you, Gunny."

Stecker liked that. The kid hadn't tried to kiss his ass with "Good afternoon, Sergeant, I'm sorry to bother you" or some candy-ass remark like that. But he was polite, and recognized that Master Gunnery Sergeants were busy men, and that he appreciated this one giving him a little bit of his time.

Stecker liked what else he saw. Aside from the embroidered-to-the-garment chevrons and the khaki fore-and-aft cap this young corporal looked the way Stecker liked his young corporals to look. Neat, trim, and military. And as far as the China stripes were concerned, if he had his way everybody would wear them.

"When did you ship home from China?" Stecker asked.

"It shows, does it?" McCoy said, smiling.

"Yeah," Stecker said. "Could you use some coffee?"

"Sure could," McCoy said.

"Doan!" Stecker raised his voice. "One java!"

"Reporting in, are you?" Stecker guessed, and then guessed again: "With a problem?"

"I've got until midnight tomorrow," McCoy said.

"Between now and midnight tomorrow," Stecker said, "get yourself a campaign hat."

McCoy chuckled.

"That's funny?"

"I just came from the Navy Yard in Philly," McCoy said. "The first thing the first sergeant said to me there was 'get rid of the campaign hat.'"

"That was there, this is here," Stecker said. "What were you doing in Philly? You ship home the long way around?"

"I shipped home to Diego on a tincan," McCoy said. "Diego shipped me to Philly via Portsmouth."

"Prisoner-chasing?" Stecker asked, and when McCoy nodded, went on: "Then you must just have bought the LaSalle."

He enjoyed the look of surprise on the kid's face, but left him wondering until after Doan delivered the coffee and left. "My clerk doesn't miss much," he said.

"Just bought it," McCoy said.

"Like it?"

"Except that it drinks gas, I like it fine," McCoy said.

"What kind of a rice bowl did you have going for you in China?" Stecker asked, and again enjoyed the look of surprise on the kid's face. "To bring home enough money to buy a car like that?"

"I spent a lot of time on back roads, drawing ration money," McCoy said.

"Motor transport?"

"Sort of," McCoy said.

"What do you mean, 'sort of'?"

"That's my skill," McCoy said.

"And you made corporal on one hitch, driving a truck?"

"Yeah," McCoy said.

"Why don't I believe that?" Stecker asked.

"I don't know," McCoy said. "It's the truth."

"You must have got along pretty good with the motor officer," Stecker said. The translation of that was, "You must have had your nose pretty far up his ass."

"Most of the time, I worked for an officer at regiment," McCoy said.

"I did a hitch, '35–'37, with the Fourth Marines," Stecker said. "I guess I still know some of the officers. Who did you work for?"

"Captain Banning," McCoy said.

Stecker was very pleased to hear that. It reconfirmed his

first judgment of the young corporal. (His second, more negative judgment sprang from questions about his making corporal in one hitch in motor transport.) Ed Banning was the China Marines' S-2. If this kid had been made a corporal by Banning, that was a whole hell of a lot different from making it as an ass-licker.

"Ed Banning and I were in Nicaragua together in '29," Stecker said. "He was a lieutenant then. He was a good officer."

"He is a good officer," McCoy agreed.

"Well, what can I do for you, Corporal?" Stecker asked.

"Got a problem, Gunny," McCoy said, and added wryly: "And when I was a young Marine, at Parris Island, they told me whenever I had a problem I couldn't deal with myself, I should take it to the gunny."

Stecker smiled at him. The kid had a sense of humor.

"Just think of me as your father, son, and tell Daddy all," Stecker said.

"I need to get that LaSalle registered on the post," McCoy said.

"What's the problem? Unsafe? Or inadequate insurance?"

"No, I'm sure it'll pass the safety inspection, and I'm insured up to my ass."

Those were two of the three problems with a corporal getting a POV (Privately Owned Vehicle) registered on the post. Stecker now asked about the third:

"You lost your driver's license. Speeding or drunk driving?"

"I'm in the Platoon Leader's Course," McCoy said. "And a fat-bellied PFC over in Vehicle Registration got his rocks off telling me that means I can't have a car on the post."

Now Stecker was surprised. The Platoon Leader's Course was designed to turn college kids, not China Marine corporals, into second lieutenants. But now that he thought about it, he'd heard that starting with this class, they were going to slip some young Marines in with college kids. It was sort of an experiment, to see if they could hack it. The Marines in the course would be like this one, on their first hitch, or maybe starting their second, kids without enough experience to get a direct commission, but who had been judged to be above average.

"He's right," Stecker said. "You can't. No cars, civilian clothes, personal weapons, or dirty books or pictures."

"What am I supposed to do with it?"

"You should have read the instructions, Corporal," Stecker said, "the part where it said, 'don't take no POV's, civvies, weapons or dirty pictures.' "

"I don't have any instructions," McCoy said. "I don't even have any orders. I'm traveling VOCO (Verbal Order Commanding Officer)."

"He must have been pretty sure you were selected," Stecker said.

"He was on the board," McCoy said. "And as fast as this has gone, I've been wondering if the Corps didn't ship me home from China for this officer shit."

"Officer shit?" Stecker parroted. "You don't want to be an officer?"

"I didn't mean that the way it sounded, Gunny," McCoy said. "But I walked over and had a look at the school before I came over here. It reminded me that I'm a China Marine, not a college boy."

"You better not tell anybody that when you start the course," Stecker said. "One of the things they expect is enthusiasm. You better act as if your one great desire in the whole world is to pin a gold bar on your shoulder, or you'll get shipped out so quick it'll take your asshole six weeks to catch up with you."

McCoy chuckled. "That's what I mean about being a Marine, and not a college boy. I *know* about second lieutenants. Would you want to be second lieutenant, Gunny?" McCoy challenged.

Stecker thought, *No, I wouldn't want to be a second lieutenant. I really don't want to be an officer, period.*

"Then you shouldn't have applied," Stecker said.

"The ways were greased," McCoy said.

"What do you mean by that?"

"I mean that an officer I knew in China asked me at nine o'clock one morning if I had ever heard of the Platoon Leader Program. I was through with the selection board before lunch three days later," McCoy said.

"But if you don't want to be an officer, then I guess

you've wasted his effort, and the Corps' money and time coming here at all," Stecker said.

"Don't get me wrong, Gunny," McCoy said. "I'm going to go through that course. The minute I report in, I'm going to be the eagerest sonofabitch to get a commission they ever saw."

"Why?"

"Well, I thought that over, driving down here," McCoy said. "Asked myself what the fuck I was doing, why I hadn't told them what they could do with a gold bar in Philly. The answer is, why not? I'm a good Marine. I'll probably make as good a temporary officer as most of the college kids, and probably better than some of them. And since they greased the ways like they have—at least a couple of officers think I would make a good second lieutenant—who the hell am I to argue with them?"

"You seem pretty sure you won't bilge out of the course," Stecker said.

"Gunny, I'm a good Marine. I'll get through that course. My problem is what do I do with my car when I'm over there being eager as hell?"

"Where you from?"

"Pennsylvania, Norristown."

"If you left now, you could drive there, leave the car, catch a train, and be back here by midnight tomorrow. If you were a little late, so long as it was before reveille on the second, I could take care of that."

"I got no place to leave it."

"I thought you said your home was in Norristown."

"I said 'I'm from Norristown,' " McCoy said. "My home is the Corps."

"Then I guess you'll have to park it outside the gate," Stecker said.

"Yeah, and have it either stolen or fucked up, the roof cut."

"Hey, you're a Marine corporal, wants to be a Marine officer, you don't know a regulation's a regulation?"

McCoy looked at him, and Stecker saw anger, regret, and resignation in his eyes. But he didn't say anything, and he didn't beg.

"Thanks for the coffee, Gunny," McCoy said. "And your time."

He got up and walked toward the door.

"McCoy," Stecker called, and McCoy stopped and turned around.

"Forget what I said about getting a campaign hat. That was before I knew you were going to be a student. Students wear cunt caps like that [a soft cap, sometimes called an "overseas" cap]. Makes them easy to tell from Marines."

"Thanks," McCoy said.

"Doan!" Stecker called, raising his voice. "Send in the sergeant from Post Housing."

The sergeant came into the office with all the paperwork involved in turning in one set of government quarters and their furnishings so as to draw another set of quarters and furnishings. Stecker was moving—moving up. Though he thought about *that* pretty much the way McCoy did. Stecker took his Parker pen from his shirt pocket and began to write his signature, in a neat; round hand, where the forms were marked with small penciled *x*s.

Then he suddenly sat up straight in his chair and spun it around so that he could look out the window. He saw Corporal McCoy unlocking the door of the pretty LaSalle convertible that sure as Christ made little apples was going to get all fucked up if he had to leave it parked outside the gate.

Master Gunnery Sergeant Stecker leaned out the window.

"Corporal McCoy!" he bellowed.

McCoy looked around for him.

"Hold it right there, Corporal McCoy!"

He sat down again and, as quickly as he could, signed the rest of the forms. Then he stood up and went in the outer office.

"I'm going," he said.

"You going to see the colonel first?" Doan asked.

"I have an appointment with the colonel at oh-eight-thirty the day after tomorrow. Whatever's on his mind will have to wait until then."

"You coming back?" Doan asked.

"No. Have the motor pool fetch the truck," Stecker ordered.

"Is there anything else I can do for you?" Doan asked.

"Not a goddamned thing, Corporal Doan," Stecker snapped. "Not a goddamned thing."

He glowered at him a moment, and then added: "But I'll tell you this, Doan. I told the colonel that it was possible that under all your baby fat, there just might be a Marine, and that he could probably do worse than making you a sergeant. You're on orders as of 1 September. Try, at least, to act like a sergeant, Doan."

Now why the hell did I tell him? It was supposed to be a surprise.

"What do I tell anybody who calls?" Doan asked.

The fat little fucker is so surprised at the promotion that he looks like he might bawl. Hell of a thing for a Marine sergeant to be doing.

"Tell them to take a flying fuck at a rolling doughnut," Stecker said and, pleased with himself, marched out of the office."

He walked up to Corporal McCoy, where he was waiting by his LaSalle.

"I have a black Packard Phaeton machine, Corporal McCoy," he said, and pointed to it. "You will get in your machine and follow me."

"Where we going?"

"Wherever the hell I decide to take you," Stecker said.

McCoy followed him six blocks, ending up at the rear of the red-brick single-story building that housed the provost marshal's office. Next to it was an area enclosed by an eight-foot-high cyclone fence, topped with barbed wire. Every ten feet along its length was a red sign reading, MILITARY POLICE IMPOUNDING AREA OFF LIMITS. Inside a fence were a dozen vehicles, mostly civilian, but with several Marine Corps trucks mingled among them.

There was no one near the gate to the fenced-in area, so Stecker blew his horn, a steady ten-second blast, and then another. He saw that he had attracted the attention of the people in the provost marshal's building. His Packard was as well known as his pickup truck.

He motioned for Corporal McCoy to get out of his LaSalle and come to the Packard.

A minute later, the provost sergeant came out of the building and walked quickly over to him.

"What can I do for you, Gunny?" he asked.

"This is Corporal McCoy," Stecker said. "After you register his car and issue him a sticker for it, he will place his vehicle in the Impound Yard. From time to time, he will require access to his vehicle, to run the engine, for example. Therefore, you will put him on the list of people who are authorized access to the Impound Yard. Any questions?"

"Whatever you say, Gunny," the provost sergeant said. "Can he take the car out if wants?"

"It's his car," Stecker said. He turned to McCoy. "I think that's all the business we have, McCoy," he said.

"Thanks, Gunny," McCoy said.

"In the future, McCoy, be very careful when you tell somebody you don't think much of officers or that you have doubts about being one yourself. You just might run into some chickenshit sonofabitch with bars on his collar who will take offense."

"I will," McCoy said. "Thanks again, Gunny."

"It would be a damned shame to have a good-looking machine like your LaSalle fucked up," Stecker said, and got behind the wheel of his Packard and drove home.

(Three)

Elly was home. Her Ford was in the drive. He wondered why she asked him to come home early. Probably because she knew him well enough to worry that otherwise he would head for the NCO Club, establish himself at the bar reserved for senior noncoms, and start drinking hard liquor. She knew him well enough, too, not to call the office and order him home, or call the office and start whining and begging for him to come home. What she'd said was that "if he could come that would be nice."

So he was home. That was nice.

The sign (MASTER GUNNERY SERGEANT J. STECKER, USMC) was still on the lawn, equidistant between the driveway and the walkway, as housing regulations required, a precise four feet off the sidewalk. He wouldn't need that sign anymore; there'd be a new sign on the new quarters. He would have to remember to take this one down first thing in the morning. Or maybe, so that he wouldn't forget it, after dark tonight.

He entered the small brick house (the new quarters would

be just a little bigger, now that the boys were gone and they didn't need the room) by the kitchen door, opened the icebox and helped himself to a beer.

"I'm home," he called.

"I'm in the bedroom," Elly called.

He went into the living room and turned on the radio.

Jesus Christ, it's been a long time since I came home and she made that kind of announcement. But all she meant by it, obviously, was that she happened to be in the bedroom. That was all.

She came into the living room.

"Where were you, Jack?" Elly asked.

"What do you mean, 'where was I?'" he asked.

"Doan came by," she said. "He said you walked off without your orders, and he thought you might need them. He said you told him you were going home."

She had the orders in her hand. She extended them to him.

"I've read them," he said. "I know what they say."

She shrugged.

"It was nice of Doan, I thought," Elly said. "He told me you got him sergeant's stripes. That was nice of you, Jack."

"So you called the NCO Club and asked for me, and I wasn't there, right?" he said, unpleasantly.

"You know better than that, Jack," Elly said, and he knew he'd hurt her.

"A kid came into the office," Jack Stecker said. "A China Marine, a corporal."

"Oh?"

"He worked for Ed Banning over there," Stecker went on. "Banning got him sent to the Platoon Leader's Course."

"And he came in to say hello for Ed Banning?"

"He came in because he's got a LaSalle convertible machine, and the kids in the Platoon Leader Program aren't supposed to have cars with them, and the provost marshal wouldn't give him a post sticker for it."

"Oh," she said.

"At first, I thought he reminded me of Jack," Stecker said. "Nice kid. Good-looking. Smart. But then I realized that he reminded me of me."

"Good looking and smart?" she teased.

"Like I was when I was a corporal," he said.

"I remember when you were a corporal," she said.

"He doesn't want to be an officer," Stecker said. "At least not very much."

"Neither did you," she said. "They would have sent you to Annapolis, if you had wanted to go."

"I wanted to get married," he said.

"You didn't want to be an officer," she said.

"I still don't, Elly," he said.

She started to say something, then changed her mind.

"Could you help him about his car?" she asked.

"I fixed it so he could leave it in the MP impounding area," he said. "That's where I was."

"I knew if you could come home early, you would," Elly said.

"Why did you want me to?" he asked.

"I bought you a present," she said. "I was afraid it wouldn't come in time, but it did, and I wanted to give it to you."

"What kind of a present?" he asked. "You keep this up, there won't be anything left in the retirement fund."

"Come in the bedroom, and I'll give it to you," Elly said.

"You give me a present in the bedroom, and I'll come home early all the time," he said.

Elly ignored him and walked toward the bedroom.

He got up, put his beer bottle down, turned the radio off, and walked into their bedroom.

There was a complete uniform on the bed.

"What the hell is this?" he said. "What did you do, go by the clothing store?"

"This comes from Brooks Brothers in New York City," she said. "I asked Doris Means where I should buy them, and that's where Doris said to go."

"You're now calling the colonel's wife by her first name?"

"I've known her for twenty years, Jack," Elly said. "She said I was to call her by her first name."

He looked down at the uniform. Good-looking uniform, he thought. First-class material. It had certainly cost an arm and a leg.

"Well?" she said. "Nothing to say?"

"Looks a little bare," he said. "No chevrons, no hash marks."

"Attention to orders," Elly said. Stecker looked at her in surprise. She had the orders in her hand, and was reading from them:

"Headquarters, United States Marine Corps, Washington, D.C., General Orders Number 145, dated 15 August 1941. Paragraph 6. Master Gunnery Sergeant Jack NMI Stecker 38883, Hq Company, USMC Schools, Quantico, Virginia, is Honorably Discharged from the Naval Service for the convenience of the government effective 31 August 1941. Paragraph 7. Captain Jack NMI Stecker, 44003 USMC Reserve is ordered to active duty for a period of not less than three years with duty station USMC Schools, Quantico, Virginia, effective 1 September 1941. General Officer commanding Quantico is directed to insure compliance with applicable regulations involved with the discharge of an enlisted man for the purpose of accepting a commission as an officer. For the Commandant, USMC, James B. McArne, Brigadier General, USMC."

"Well," Stecker said, "now that you've read it out loud, I suppose that makes it official?"

"Aren't you going to try it on?" Elly asked, ignoring him.

"I'm not sure I'm supposed to," he said. "I'm not an officer yet."

"Put it on, Jack," Elly said. "You can't put it off any longer."

He reached for the blouse and started to put his arm in a sleeve.

"No!" Elly stopped him. "Do it right, Jack."

He stripped to his underwear, then put on the shirt and the trousers, and then tied the necktie. Then he put on the tunic, and the Sam Browne belt, and the sword, and even the hat.

"You look just fine, Jack," Elly said. She sounded funny, and when he looked at her, she was dabbing at her eyes with a handkerchief.

"What the hell are you crying about?" Stecker asked.

She shrugged and blew her nose, loudly.

He examined his reflection in the mirror. He looked very strange, he thought. Very strange indeed. He saw for the first time that there was something new in his array of medal and campaign ribbons, an inch-long blue one dotted with silver stars, the one he never wore, the ribbon representing the Medal of Honor.

"What did you do that for?" he challenged.

"Colonel Means said to," she said. "And he said when you asked about it, I should tell you that he said that he expects his officers to wear all of their decorations, and that includes you, too."

"You really like this, don't you? Me being an officer?"

"All these years, Jack," Elly said, "I wondered if I did right, marrying you."

"Thanks a lot," he said, purposefully misunderstanding her.

"Otherwise, you would have gone to Annapolis," she went on. "And you would have been a major, maybe a lieutenant colonel, by now."

"Or I would have bilged out of Annapolis and taken up with a bar girl in Diego," he said. "I don't have any regrets, Elly."

"I don't have any regrets, either," she said. "But you deserve those bars, Jack. You should have been an officer a long time ago."

He turned to look at his reflection again.

"Maybe," Elly said, "you should take it off now, so it'll be fresh when you get sworn in."

He looked at her again. She was unbuttoning her dress.

"Don't look so surprised," she said softly. "I probably shouldn't tell you this, but I've always wanted to go to bed with a Marine officer."

"I'm not a Marine officer yet," he said. "Not until oh-eight-thirty day after tomorrow."

"Then I guess you want to wait till then?" she asked.

"No, what the hell," Captain-designate Jack NMI Stecker, USMC, Reserve, said. "Take what you can whenever you can get it, I always say."

X

(One)
Quantico, Virginia
1 September 1941

The U.S. Rifle, Caliber .30, M1, was known as the Garand, after its inventor, John B. Garand, a civilian employee of the U.S. Army's Springfield Arsenal. The Garand fired the same cartridge as the U.S. Rifle, Model 1903, the U.S. Rifle, Model 1903A3, and the Browning light machine guns. This cartridge was known as the .30-06.

The 1903-series rifles, known as "Springfields," were five-shot rifles, operated by a bolt. This bolt was a variation of the action designed by the Mauserwerke in Germany in the late 1800s and had been adapted by the United States after the Spanish-American war. The Spanish Army's Mausers were clearly superior to the American rifles. And when Theodore Roosevelt, who had faced the Spanish Mausers on his march up Kettle and San Juan Hills in Cuba, became President, pretty nearly his first order as Commander in Chief was to provide the military services with a Mauser-type weapon. A royalty was paid to the Mauser Company, and the Springfield Arsenal began manufacture of a near-copy of the Mauser Model 1898, differing from it in caliber and some minor details.

The Spanish Mausers had 7-mm bores, and the German 7.92. The Springfield Rifles had .30-caliber (7.62-mm) bores. In 1906, an improved .30 caliber was developed, which became known as the .30-06. The Springfield rifles served in World War I, where they proved reliable, efficient, and extremely accurate.

Development of the Garand began in the early 1930's,

when General Douglas MacArthur was Army Chief of Staff. It was accepted for service, and production began in 1937.

It had a magazine capacity of eight rounds, as opposed to the Springfield's five. Far more important, it was semiautomatic. Once a spring clip of eight rounds was loaded into the weapon and the bolt permitted to move forward, it would fire the eight rounds as rapidly as the marksman could pull the trigger. When the last shot was fired, the clip was ejected, the bolt remained in its rearward position, and another eight-round clip could be quickly loaded.

The Ordnance Corps of the United States Army (which is charged with providing every sort of weaponry, from pistols to artillery, to the United States Marine Corps) was convinced that it was the best infantry rifle in the world. In the opinion of most Marines, the U.S. Rifle Caliber .30, M1 "Garand" was a Buck Rogers piece of shit with which only the lucky could hit a barn door at ten paces.

Experience had taught the Corps that skilled marksmen were very often the key to victory in a battle. Experience had further taught the Corps that the key to skilled marksmanship—in addition to the basics of trigger squeeze sight picture, and the rest of the technique crap—was joining together a Marine and his rifle so that they became one. A Marine was thus taught that first he cleaned and oiled his piece, then he could think of maybe getting something to eat and a place out of the rain to sleep. The Marine Corps further believed that an officer should not order his men to do anything he could not do himself.

There were two schools of thought concerning the issue of the U.S. Rifle, Caliber .30, M1 to the students of the Platoon Leader's Course. The official reason was that nothing was too good for the young men who possibly would soon be leading Marines in a war. It therefore followed that the young gentlemen be issued the newest, finest item in the Marine Corps' small weapons inventory. In the opinion of most Marines, however, the reason it was being issued to the young gentlemen of the Platoon Leader's Course was that real rifles were needed for real Marines.

It was therefore not surprising that Item #2 on the Training Schedule for Day #1 of Platoon Leader's Course 23-41 (right after "#1 Welcoming Remarks, Major J.J. Hollenbeck,

USMC'') was the issuance of rifles—Garand rifles—to the young gentlemen.

Some of the young gentlemen were wearing Marine Corps dungarees (sometimes called "utilities") and work shoes. They had been issued these uniforms during previous summer training periods. It was the prescribed uniform of the day.

But some of the young gentlemen, including Malcolm Pickering, were still in civilian clothing. It was not that they didn't have dungarees, but that they had not considered that day #1 would begin at 0345 hours and that they would be given ninety seconds to get out of bed, dress, and fall in outside the barracks. They presumed that they would have a couple of minutes to take their dungarees from their luggage before they stood the first formation and were marched to breakfast. There were 112 members of Platoon Leader's Course 23-41, and about a dozen of them were in civilian clothing. Most were in shirts and slacks, but there were two, including Malcolm Pickering, who had at the last second grabbed their jackets. Pickering had even managed to grab his necktie.

He was standing in the rear rank tying his necktie when he came to the attention of the Assistant Drill Instructor, a barrel-chested corporal of twenty-nine years with a nearly shaven head and a voice made harsh by frequent vocal exertion. His name was Pleasant, which later became the subject of wry observation by the young gentlemen.

On seeing movement in the rear rank, Corporal Pleasant walked quickly and erectly between the ranks until he was standing before Pickering. He then put his hands on his hips and inclined his head forward, so that the stiff brim of his campaign hat just about touched Pickering's forehead, and so that Pickering could smell Corporal Pleasant's toothpaste when he shouted,

"What the fuck are you doing, asshole?"

"I was tying my tie, sir," Pickering said, coming to attention. He was not entirely a rookie. He had been to two previous summer training encampments and knew that as a trainee, he was expected to come at attention when addressed by an assistant drill instructor, and to call him "sir," although in the real Marine Corps only commissioned officers were entitled to such courtesy.

"Why are you wearing a tie, asshole?" Corporal Pleasant inquired.

Pickering could think of no good answer to that.

"I asked you a question, asshole!" Corporal Pleasant reminded him.

"No excuse, sir," Pickering said, another remembered lesson from previous summers. One did not offer excuses. There was no excuse for not doing what you were supposed to do, or for doing what you were not supposed to do. The proper response in a situation like that was the one he had just given.

Corporal Pleasant was more than a little disappointed. He had hoped to have the opportunity to make an example of this candy-ass would-be officer, not because he disliked him personally, but because it would get the others in the right frame of mind. But there was nothing to do now but return to the front of the formation, which he did.

The young gentlemen were marched from the company to battalion headquarters, where Major J.J. Hollenbeck, USMC, on behalf of the Commanding General, U.S. Marine Schools, welcomed them to Quantico and wished them well during their course of instruction.

They were next marched to the company supply room. There they were issued a U.S. Rifle, Caliber .30, M1; a Sling, leather; and a Kit, Individual, for U.S. Rifle, Caliber .30, M1. This consisted of a chamber brush and a folding screwdriver (all of one piece); a waxed cord and a patch holder that could be used (by dropping it down the bore) if a Rod, Cleaning, for U.S. Rifles, Model 1903 and M1 was not available; and a small plastic vial of a yellow grease, known as Lubricant, solid, for U.S. Rifle, Caliber .30, M1.

The rifles came in individual heavy wrapping paper, which appeared greasy. The reason it was greasy was that the rifles themselves were thickly coated with Cosmoline to protect them from rust while in storage.

Corporal Pleasant gave the young gentlemen rudimentary instruction in the assembly of the Sling, leather, and its attachment to the U.S. Rifle, caliber .30, M1, and then informed them that by 0345 the next morning, he expected the rifles to be cleaned, and that each individual would be expected, by 1300 that very day, to be as familiar with the serial number of the weapon as he was with his beloved mother's face.

"Where's the serial number?" one baffled young gentleman asked. "This fucking thing's covered with grease!"

It was the opportunity Corporal Pleasant had been waiting for.

The first thing the baffled young gentleman was required to do, while double-timing in place with the rifle held above his head, was shout "This is not my fucking thing. My fucking thing is between my legs. This is my rifle. I will not forget the difference." When he had recited this litany ten times, he was ordered to run around the arms-room building, with his rifle at port arms, accompanied by two other young gentlemen who had the erroneous idea that his calling his rifle his fucking thing was amusing and had smiled.

The young gentlemen were then double-timed to the mess hall for breakfast.

And it was there that Platoon Leader Candidate Pickering first saw Platoon Leader Candidate McCoy. At first he didn't place him. The face looked familiar, but he thought it was a face from other summer training camps. Then he remembered who he was.

His first reaction was distaste. Breakfast was scrambled eggs and bacon and home-fried potatoes, two pieces of bread and a lump of butter. The only thing that Pickering considered safe to put in his mouth were the home-fried potatoes. The eggs were cold and lumpy, the bacon half-raw, and the bread dried-out. McCoy was wolfing down this garbage as if he hadn't had a decent meal in a week.

Pickering watched, fascinated, as McCoy ate everything on his stainless steel tray, even wiping it clean with a piece of the stale bread.

When he had finished, McCoy picked up his tray and walked toward the mess hall exit. Pickering picked up his near-full tray and followed him.

Corporal Pleasant was there, standing before garbage cans under signs reading "Edible Garbage" and "Non-Edible Garbage."

Corporal Pleasant examined McCoy's tray, and with a curt nod of his head, passed him outside.

When Pick Pickering reached Corporal Pleasant, Corporal

Pleasant said, "Over there, asshole," indicating with a nod of his head a group of perhaps a dozen young gentlemen holding their trays, U.S. Rifles, Caliber .30, M1 slung over their shoulders, standing against the concrete-block wall.

Eventually there were nearly thirty young gentlemen who had not found their breakfast appetizing and had left much, in some cases most, of it on their trays.

Corporal Pleasant stood before them.

"Gentlemen," he said. "The Marine Corps loves you. Because the Marine Corps loves you, it has gone to considerable effort and expense to provide you with a healthy, nutritious breakfast. The Marine Corps expects you to eat the healthy, nutritious breakfast it has provided for you."

The young gentlemen looked at him in some confusion for a moment. Then one of them, delicately holding his stainless steel tray in one hand, tried to fork a lump of scrambled egg with the other hand while simultaneously going into contortions trying to keep his U.S. Rifle, Caliber .30, M1 from slipping off his shoulder.

Corporal Pleasant immediately stepped in front of him, put his hands on his hips, and inclined his head so that the stiff brim of his campaign cap almost touched the young gentleman's forehead.

"What the fuck are you doing, asshole?" Corporal Pleasant inquired.

"Sir," the young gentleman bellowed, "eating my breakfast, sir!"

"With a fork! Did you hear me say anything, asshole, about eating with a fork?"

"No, sir!"

The young gentleman looked at him in absolute confusion, not quite able to accept what Corporal Pleasant seemed to be suggesting.

Corporal Pleasant nodded his head.

"Eat, asshole!" he said. "Every last fucking crumb!"

The young gentleman raised the tray, and then lowered his face and began to gulp and lick the tray.

Corporal Pleasant looked at the others.

"On my command," he said, "slurp it up. Ready, slurp!"

Nearly thirty young gentlemen raised their stainless steel trays to their faces and slurped.

When Pickering went outside the mess hall, McCoy was waiting where the trainees would be formed in ranks. There was a barely perceptible smile on his face. Pickering went and stood beside him.

"Now I know why you ate everything on your tray," he said.

"I've been through this sort of shit before," McCoy said.

"What are you doing here?"

"What does it look like?"

"I thought you were going to get out of the Marine Corps?"

"You were right, there's a freeze on discharges," McCoy said.

"Well, we can buddy around," Pickering said. "That'll be nice."

"It would be a bad idea," McCoy said.

"Why?" Pickering asked, surprised, wondering why McCoy was rejecting him. "Why do you say that?"

"I know about Pleasant," McCoy said. "Or people like him. If there's one thing he hates more than a college boy who wants to be an officer, it's another corporal who wants to be an officer. As soon as he finds out that I'm a Marine, he'll start in on me."

"So we'll be even," Pickering said. "He's already started on me."

"Take my word for it, Pickering," McCoy said. "It would be worse if he knew we were buddies. For both of us."

"I don't understand," Pickering said.

"You don't have to understand," McCoy said. "Just take my word for it. Stay away from me."

"Well, fuck you," Pickering said, his feelings hurt.

McCoy smiled at him.

"That's the spirit," he said. "Pick, honest to God, I know what I'm talking about," McCoy said. "Sooner or later, they'll have to give us some time off. Then we can see if there are any fourteen-year-old virgins in Virginia. But what you have to do until we can get away from that prick, especially if you plan to get through the course, is make yourself invisible."

Pickering still didn't understand. But he realized he was enormously relieved that McCoy was not rejecting his friendship. Then he wondered why he was so relieved.

(Two)
Company "C" Marine Corps School Battalion
Quantico, Virginia
1805 Hours 1 September 1941

Corporal Pleasant placed the platoon "at ease" and then announced that it was now his intention to show them how to disassemble the Cosmoline-covered rifles they had been carrying around all day.

When they had them apart, they would clean them, Corporal Pleasant said. He would return at 2100 hours and inspect the cleaned pieces, and then he would show them how to reassemble their rifles. He knew, he continued, that they all wished to begin Day #2 of their training with spotless rifles. Good Marines prided themselves on having clean pieces.

This was pure chickenshit, Platoon Leader Candidate McCoy decided. A little chickenshit was to be expected, and was probably even a good thing: Pleasant had to make it absolutely clear to these college boys that they were under his absolute control. The college boys who had slurped their breakfast from their trays would never again take more chow than they could eat from the mess line. There had been a point to that.

But there was no point to this rifle-cleaning idea except to make everybody miserable. Except, of course, that Pleasant wanted something on every last one of them that would give him an excuse to jump their ass. There was absolutely no way to remove all the Cosmoline from a rifle with rags. Cosmoline did what it was intended to do, preventing rust by filling every last nook, crevice, and pore in both the action and the stock. You could wipe for fucking ever, and there would still be Cosmoline oozing out someplace.

There were two good ways to clean Cosmoline from a weapon. The best (and most dangerous) was with five gallons of gasoline in the bottom of a garbage can. If you didn't strike a spark and blow your ass up, the gasoline would dissolve the Cosmoline.

The second way was with boiling water. You took a field mess water heater[1] and filled it with rifle actions and let the sonsofbitches boil like lobsters.

---

[1] A gasoline-fired water-heating device inserted into a fifty-five gallon garbage can. Mess kits are sterilized by dipping them into the boiling water.

Pleasant was offering neither alternative. He was just being a prick, and McCoy decided there was a limit to the chickenshit he would take. He had promised himself he would keep his nose clean, stay out of sight, and do whatever was demanded of him. But that did not go so far as spending the next three hours in a futile attempt to rub a rifle free of Cosmoline.

He was standing one rank behind and three files to the left of Pick Pickering as Corporal Pleasant delivered his lecture on the disassembly of the U.S. Rifle Caliber .30, M1. He considered for a moment taking Pickering with him, but decided against it. For one thing, cleaning an uncleanable rifle was probably an essential part of training for a college boy. For another, Platoon Leader Candidate McCoy was about to go AWOL, which (as Corporal Pleasant had with some relish informed them during one of the lectures during the day) was frowned upon. Anyone caught AWOL (defined as not being in the proper place, at the proper place, at the proper time, in the properly appointed uniform) would instantly have his ass shipped to a rifle company and could forget pinning the gold bars of a second lieutenant on his shoulders.

When they were dismissed and double-timed into the barracks, McCoy went directly to the latrine and washed his hands as well as he could with GI soap. Then he grabbed his Garand with a rag, and went out the back door of the barracks.

As he made his way toward the provost marshal's Impound Yard, he considered that after successfully evading every Jap sentry in Shantung Province, it was entirely possible that he'd be nailed cold by some eager college boy guarding a barracks with an unloaded Garand.

But he wasn't challenged. He hid the Garand in a ditch, and then went into the provost marshal's office. Master Gunnery Sergeant Stecker's order was on file, and an MP corporal went and unlocked the compound for him.

McCoy drove to where he had hidden the Garand and reclaimed it. Then he opened the trunk, took out a dungaree shirt with corporal's stripes painted on the sleeves, put it on, and then took his campaign hat from the hat press and set it on his head at the approved jaunty angle.

The MP at the gate, spotting the enlisted man's sticker on

the windshield and the stiff-brimmed campaign hat on the driver, waved the LaSalle convertible through, but McCoy slowed and stopped anyway.

The MP walked up to the car.

"Where's the nearest gas station, garage, whatever, with a steam cleaner?" McCoy asked.

The MP thought it over.

"There's a Sunoco station's got one," he said. "Turn left when you hit U.S. 1."

"Much obliged," McCoy said, and let the clutch out as he rolled up the window.

The Sunoco station's steam cleaner wasn't working, but they had something even better, a machine McCoy had never seen before. It was designed to clean dirt- and grease-encrusted parts. A nonexplosive solvent poured out of a flexible spout, like water from a faucet, over a sort of sink. Thirty minutes' work with a bristle brush and there was no Cosmoline left on either the action or the stock of the Garand, period.

An hour after he had gone out of the Main Gate, McCoy drove the LaSalle back through it and stopped.

"Found it," he called to the MP. "Thanks."

"Anytime," the MP said.

There was time before Corporal Pleasant reappeared in the barracks to take a shower. The water was cold. The college boys, McCoy decided, had tried hot water. All it had done was leave a layer of Cosmoline on the shower floor. Everyone was still furiously rubbing rifle parts with rags.

McCoy tied rags around his feet, showered, removed the rags, threw them in the pile, and put on clean dungarees.

Then he disassembled the Garand, laid the parts on his bunk, then crawled under the bunk and lay down to await Corporal Pleasant.

Five minutes later, someone called "attention," and McCoy started to roll out from under the bunk. He was halfway to his feet when Pleasant, storming purposefully down the aisle, spotted him getting up.

As he came to attention, Pleasant leaned the brim of his campaign hat into his face.

"Anyone tell you to get in the sack, asshole?" Corporal Pleasant inquired.

"No, sir!" McCoy said.

"Then what were you doing in the sack, asshole!"

"Sir, I wasn't in the sack, sir!"

Corporal Pleasant, seeing the disassembled Garand on the bunk, was forced to face the fact that there was not room for the asshole to have been in the bunk, too.

He leaned over the bunk and picked up the first part he touched, which happened to be the magazine follower.

"You call this clean, asshole?" he demanded, before he had chance to examine it at all.

"Yes, sir," McCoy said. "I believe that's clean, sir!"

Corporal Pleasant shoved the magazine follower under McCoy's nose, and in the very moment he demanded, "You call that clean, asshole?" he thought: *I'll be a sonofabitch, it's clean!*

"Yes, sir!" McCoy shouted.

"What's the serial number of your piece, asshole?"

"Sir, 156331, sir!"

Corporal Pleasant stood eyeball to eyeball with Platoon Leader Candidate McCoy for a moment.

"Assemble your piece, and then get your ass outside, asshole!" he ordered. "There is a light on a pole outside the orderly room. Guard it until I relieve you!"

"Yes, sir!" McCoy said.

Ten minutes later, Corporal Pleasant marched up to the light pole outside the orderly room.

McCoy came to port arms.

"Halt! Who goes there?" he demanded.

"Who the fuck do you think?" Corporal Pleasant replied, and then ordered: "Follow me."

He walked to the rear of the building, and opened the door of a 1939 Ford coupe.

"Get in," he said.

McCoy got in the seat beside him. Pleasant reached over the back of the seat and came up with two beer cans.

"Church key's in the ashtray," he said.

"Thank you," McCoy said, and opened his beer.

"You're McCoy, right? 'Killer' McCoy?"

"I'm McCoy."

"There's three Marines in there with the assholes," Pleasant said. "I wasn't sure which was who."

McCoy didn't reply.

"You going to give me trouble, McCoy?" Pleasant asked.

Strange question. Why should he think I might give him trouble? And why the beer? This sonofabitch doesn't have the balls to be a universal prick. He's only going to be a prick to those he's sure won't fight back. And for some reason, he's a little bit afraid of me. He called me "Killer." Does this dumb sonofabitch think I'm going to stick a knife in him?

"No," McCoy said. "Why should I?"

"How did you get that rifle clean?" Pleasant asked.

There was a time for truth, McCoy decided, but this wasn't it.

"Lighter fluid," he said.

"You must have used a quart of it," Pleasant said. "What you really need is gasoline."

"Lighter fluid works better than a rag," McCoy said.

"It also made you stand out from the others," Pleasant said. "That's not smart."

"I wasn't trying to be smart," McCoy said.

Corporal Pleasant looked at him for a long moment, and then nodded his head, accepting that.

"That wasn't the first Cosmolined rifle you ever cleaned, was it?" he asked rhetorically. "I guess I would have done the same thing."

McCoy didn't reply.

"There's two stories going around about you, McCoy," Pleasant said. "The first is that you killed a bunch of Chinamen in China. The second is that you have friends in high places who got you into this course. Anything to them?"

"There was some shooting in China," McCoy said. "It was in the line of duty."

"And have you got a rabbi?"

"Have I got a what?"

"Somebody important, taking care of you?"

"Not that I know about," McCoy said. "I applied for this, and I got accepted."

Pleasant snorted, as if he didn't believe him.

"Let me spell things out for you, McCoy," he said. "You stay out of my hair, and I'll stay out of yours. But there's two things you better understand: I don't give a shit about any rabbi. And there's people who think you belong in Portsmouth, not here."

"I don't know what you're talking about, Pleasant," McCoy said.

"The hell you don't," Pleasant said.

He put his beer to his mouth, draining the can, and then squeezed it.

"Finish your beer, McCoy," he said. "And go back to the barracks." He got out of the Ford coupe and walked away.

McCoy finished his beer slowly. He was sorry, but not surprised, that what had happened in China was apparently common knowledge. The Corps was small, and Marines gossiped as bad as women, especially when it was interesting, like a Marine shooting a bunch of Chinese. He figured that some other China Marines had come home and gone to see Gunny Stecker, another old China Marine, and told him what had happened at the ferry. And Gunny Stecker had connected it with him, and that was how Pleasant had heard about it.

But he couldn't figure out who his "rabbi" was supposed to be, or who the people were who thought he belonged in Portsmouth, instead of in the Platoon Leader's Program.

Ten minutes after Corporal Pleasant left him, McCoy got out of the Ford, put the U.S. Rifle, Caliber .30, M1 in the position of right shoulder arms, and in a military fashion marched back to the barrack, took off his utilities and climbed in the sack.

(Three)
Marine Corps Schools
Quantico, Virginia
12 October 1941

The six weeks passed quickly. As McCoy suspected, the training was a repeat of Parris Island boot camp. It was necessary to turn the college boys into Marines, before they could be turned into Marine officers. That meant they had to be taught immediate, unquestioning obedience in such a way that it would become a conditioned reflex.

Thus: If a Platoon Leader Candidate did not immediately and unquestioningly respond to whatever order Corporal Pleasant or another of the Drill Instructors issued, there was immediate punishment.

If, for example, the young gentlemen did not respond to an order to fall out on the company street with the proper speed and enthusiasm, they were required to fall out again and again and again until Corporal Pleasant was satisfied.

And Pleasant was a man of some imagination: He might suggest that the young gentlemen were slow to fall out because they were unduly burdened by their accoutrements. Instead of falling out in helmets, full marching pack and rifles, they could try it again wearing only undershorts, skivvy shirts, leggings, and steel helmets. Plus of course, their rifles.

This required that they remove their leggings and their utilities. The utilities were then folded in the proper manner and placed in the proper place in their footlockers, and the leggings laced back on over bare calves.

If this increased their speed, Corporal Pleasant then experimented. They would next fall out in only raincoats, utility trousers, skivvy shirts, and cartridge belts. This required unlacing the leggings, storing them as prescribed, then detaching the canteen, first aid packet, and web harness from the web cartridge belt, and storing these items in their appointed places.

Next, perhaps, Corporal Pleasant would order that they again try falling out with the proper speed and enthusiasm in full marching gear. This meant of course reattaching the canteen, the first aid packet, and the harness to the cartridge belt; folding the raincoat and placing it in its prescribed location in the footlocker; and then relacing the leggings.

The possible variations were almost limitless, and Corporal Pleasant experimented with as many as he could think of.

Then there was punishment for sin:

The greatest sin of all was dropping the U.S. Rifle, Caliber .30, M1. Anyone who did this could expect to double-time around the parade ground with the rifle held at arm's length above his head, while shouting in a loud voice, "My rifle is my best friend, and I am a miserable sonofabitch because I abused it. God have mercy on my miserable soul."

Another sin was laughter, or giggling, or even a detected snicker. These sinners would double-time around the parade ground with their rifles at arm's length above their heads, while shouting at the top of their lungs, "I am a hyena. A hyena is an animal who laughs when there is nothing funny to laugh at. This is the sound a hyena makes. Ha Ha Ha Ha Ha Ha."

Another means of instilling discipline was calisthenics and close-order drill. This also served to cause the young gentlemen to shed civilian fat and tone their musculature. There were thirty minutes of calisthenics (later forty-five minutes and then an hour) before breakfast. And there was at least an hour of close-order drill every day.

Individual young gentlemen who came to Corporal Pleasant's attention during the duty day (which ran from 0345 until whenever Pleasant decided the day was over) were often required to perform additional calisthenics. Normally, this was in the form of pushups, but sometimes, when one of the young gentlemen displayed what Pleasant thought was ungainly, awkward movement (such as being out of step) it took the form of the "duck walk."

When one did the duck walk, one first squatted, then one placed the U.S. Rifle, Caliber .30, M1 in a horizontal position against the small of the neck, and then one waddled, while shouting, "This is the way a duck walks. Quack! Quack! Quack! I will try very hard to try to walk like a Marine in the future!"

McCoy had been through all this before in boot camp at Parris Island, but that didn't make things any easier. He had been genuinely surprised to learn (his feet became raw and blistered and his muscles ached) how badly out of shape he had become. In fact, the only real advantages he (and the other two Marine noncoms) had over the college boys was that responding to commands had already been drilled into them and was a reflex action. Similarly, they had experience in giving close-order drill, had already learned how to bark out commands from the pits of their stomachs, and, more importantly, had learned the cadence so that it too was automatic.

All three of the Marines in the platoon learned something else: Taking close-order drill from someone who doesn't know what he is doing, someone who doesn't understand the cadence and the timing, could turn the Marine Corps Drum and Bugle Corps at the Marine Barracks in Washington into a mob of blind men stumbling over their own feet.

In addition to the inspections Pleasant called whenever the whim struck him (and sometimes, if he woke early, the whim struck before the official rising hour of 0345), there was a regularly scheduled inspection each Saturday morning. The official inspection was conducted by the gunnery sergeant of the company and the company commander.

In order that he not be embarrassed by slovenly young gentlemen or equipment, Corporal Pleasant conducted both a preinspection and a pre-preinspection of the platoon. The latter was held on Friday evening after the barracks had been scrubbed and polished. It was necessary that the platoon pass the pre-preinspection before they were permitted to retire for the evening. Sometimes the pre-preinspection did not meet Corporal Pleasant's high standards until very late at night.

The preinspection was conducted the next morning, half an hour before first call. It was to determine if the assholes had fucked anything up in the three or four hours while they'd been in the sack after the pre-preinspection. If they had, it could be corrected in the time officially set aside for breakfast.

Scuttlebutt had it that today's inspection was going to be a real bitch. The company commander, who was rough enough, was not on the base. Thus the inspection would be conducted for him by another officer, the battalion mess officer; and the scuttlebutt on him was that he had a corn cob up his ass and was a really a chickenshit sonofabitch.

McCoy was not particularly concerned. He knew that once you had prepared your gear and arranged it, the situation was out of your hands. If an inspecting officer decided to jump your ass, he would. He would find something wrong, even if he had to step on the toes of the boots under your bunk so that he could get you for unshined shoes. If you couldn't control the situation, there was no point in worrying about it.

When Pleasant barked, "Ten-hut on the deck!" McCoy came to attention, his toes at a forty-five-degree angle, the fingers of his left hand against the seam of his trousers, his right hand holding the Garand just below the bayonet lug.

He stared straight ahead and heard the clatter of the rifles as one by one the young gentlemen came from attention to inspection arms. While this was going on, he had speculated—a little unkindly—that with just a little bit of luck, one of the young gentlemen would catch his thumb in the M1 action during the inspection. That produced a condition known as M1 thumb.

If he howled in pain, that just might bring the inspection to a quick end.

But there was no such fortuitous happenstance. The sound of clattering rifles moved closer to him. Out of the corner of his eye, he saw the inspection party approaching.

He shifted the Garand to a diagonal position in front of him, slammed the action open, bobbed his head over the action to insure that it was unloaded, and then looked ahead, waiting for it to be snatched from his hand.

He found himself looking into the face of First Lieutenant John R. Macklin, USMC.

There was no smile on Macklin's face, not even a flicker of recognition.

"This man is unshaven," Lieutenant Macklin said.

The gunny trailing him dutifully wrote this down on his clipboard.

Macklin snatched the Garand from McCoy's hand, looked into the open action, and then raised the butt high in the air, so that he could look into the barrel.

"And this weapon is filthy," Lieutenant Macklin said, before he threw the Garand back at McCoy so hard that it stung his hands and he almost dropped it.

The gunny dutifully wrote "filthy weapon" on his clipboard.

Lieutenant Macklin moved down the aisle to the next man. McCoy closed the action of the Garand and returned it to his side.

The Garand had been clean before McCoy had disassembled it and cleaned it, and he had shaved no more than two hours before.

There didn't seem to be much question any longer who believed that Killer McCoy belonged in the U.S. Naval Prison, Portsmouth, rather than in the Platoon Leader's Course at U.S. Marine Corps Schools, Quantico.

Captain Banning, McCoy concluded, had probably eaten Macklin's ass out for letting the Japs catch him at Yenchi'eng.

McCoy was summoned to the orderly room half an hour later.

The gunny was there, and Pleasant.

"Mr. McCoy," the gunny said, "there is no excuse in the Marine Corps for a filthy weapon."

McCoy brought the Garand from the position of attention—

that is to say, with its butt resting on the deck beside his right boot—to the position of port arms. And then he threw it, like a basketball, to the gunny.

"What the fuck do you think you're doing?" the gunny said, furiously. He had been so surprised he had almost failed to catch it.

"Look at it, Gunny," McCoy said.

"Who the fuck do you think you are, telling me what to do?" the gunny snapped, but he slammed the action open and looked into it, and then raised the butt so that he could look down the barrel.

"You want to feel my chin, Gunny?" McCoy asked.

"This weapon is filthy, Mr. McCoy," the gunny said, throwing the Garand back to him, "and you need a shave. Because Lieutenant Macklin says so. You get the picture?"

"I got the picture."

"Corporal Pleasant will now escort you to the barracks, where he will supervise your shave. Then he will supervise you while you clean your filthy weapon. When you have shaved, and your rifle is clean, he will bring you back here, and I will check the closeness of your shave, and the cleanliness of your rifle. That means I will have to stay here, instead of going to my quarters. That pisses me off, McCoy. My wife has plans for the weekend, and you have fucked them up."

McCoy knew enough to keep his mouth shut.

"And I'll tell you something else I agree with Lieutenant Macklin about, McCoy. I don't know how in the fuck a China Marine motor transport corporal with a reputation like yours got it in his head he should be an officer. Or how you managed to get yourself in here. Except that you had your nose so far up some officer's ass that your ears didn't show. I don't like brown noses, McCoy, and I especially don't like people with rabbis. You get the picture?"

"Yes, sir," McCoy said.

"Finally, Mr. McCoy, I would like to make sure you understand that participation in the Platoon Leader's Course is purely voluntary. You may resign at any time, and keep your stripes."

"I'm not about to quit, Gunny," McCoy said.

"If you bust out of here," the gunny said, "for misbehavior, or malingering, something like that, they ship your ass to some rifle company. It's something to think about, McCoy."

"Yes, sir," McCoy said.

"Corporal Pleasant," the gunny said. "I think the deck in the barrack could stand a sanding. Do you think it might help Mr. McCoy to remember to shave and to keep his piece clean if he spent the weekend doing that?"

Pleasant nodded his agreement. He looked a little embarrassed, McCoy thought, but he was going to go along with the gunny. He had no choice.

(Four)
Headquarters, 4th Marines
Shanghai, China
19 October 1941

Only a few people were made privy to all the details, actual and projected, of the removal from China of United States Military and Naval Forces. Among these was Captain Edward Banning, S-2 of the 4th Marines.

The Yangtze River Patrol, its gunboats and personnel, was to sail as soon as possible for the U.S. Naval Base at Cavite, on the tip of a narrow, four-mile-long peninsula sticking into Manila Bay. It was intended that the Yangtze River Patrol reinforce U.S. Naval Forces, Philippines. How much value the old, narrow-draft, lightly armed riverboats would be was open to question. There was even concern that should there be severe weather en route to Manila Bay the gunboats would founder and sink. They were designed to navigate a river, not the high seas in a typhoon.

Likewise, the small, old pigboats of SUBFORCHINA were as soon as possible to sail for Cavite, though they were subject to similar fears as to their seaworthiness, for they were old and small and designed primarily for coastal, rather than deep-sea operations. But unlike the riverboats, if it came to it, the pigboats could submerge for maybe five, six hours at a time, and ride out a storm.

The two battalions making up the 4th Marines were something else. They were Marines, which was to say they were trained and equipped to fight anywhere. But what they would be in fact, if war broke out, was infantry. The official role of the Marines was to make amphibious assaults on hostile shores. Two battalions of Marines without landing craft and without larger forces to reinforce them once a landing was made weren't going to make much of an amphibious assault force.

The advance party of the 4th Marines would sail from Shanghai aboard the U.S.S. *Henderson,* a Navy transport, on 28 October. The *Henderson* would then continue on to the United States, to on-load Army reinforcements for the Philippines. The U.S.S. *Shaumont,* the other U.S. Navy transport that normally served China, would similarly be involved in moving U.S. Army troops from the West Coast of the United States to reinforce the Philippines. The Navy had also chartered space aboard two civilian passenger liners. On 28 November, the *President Madison* would embark the First Battalion and the *President Harrison* the Second Battalion. If nothing went wrong, the 4th Marines would arrive in Manila during the first week of December. Then, either the *Henderson* or the *Shaumont* would be free to sail to Tientsin and pick up the Peking and Tientsin Marine detachments.

U.S. Navy Forces, Philippines, was sending to Shanghai a Consolidated Catalina, a long-range amphibious reconnaissance aircraft, to pick up senior officers of the Yangtze River Patrol and SUBFORCHINA and carry them to Cavite to prepare for the arrival of their vessels.

At the last moment, the colonel learned of this, and prevailed upon his Naval counterpart to make space available for one of his officers.

The colonel did not anticipate any logistical problems when the regiment arrived in the Philippines. The Cavite Navy Base was enormous—capable of supporting the Far East Fleet. It would be able to house and feed two battalions of Marines without difficulty.

But the colonel *did* want to know how Douglas MacArthur, former Chief of Staff of the U.S. Army and most recently Marshal of the Philippine Army, intended to employ the 4th Marines. The obvious officer to find that out was his S-2, and Captain Edward Banning was given twenty-two hours' notice to pack his things, make arrangements for the personal property he would necessarily have to leave behind, and be aboard the Catalina when it took off for Manila.

The first thing Captain Ed Banning did when he heard that

was get in his Pontiac and drive to the headquarters of the
Shanghai Municipal Police Department. He found Sergeant
Chatworth there and told him he needed a big favor.

"Like what?" Chatworth asked, suspicious.

"I want to marry a stateless person," Banning said. "To
do that, I need a certificate from the Municipal Police stating
there is no record of criminal activity."

Chatworth's bushy eyebrows rose.

"Or moral turpitude," Chatworth added.

Banning nodded.

"That isn't all you'll need," he said. "You better figure
on two weeks, at least, pulling in all the favors anybody owes
you."

Banning looked at his watch.

"I have nineteen hours and thirty minutes," he said.

"What's her name?" Chatworth asked.

When he got back to his apartment, Milla told him she
didn't want to marry him: She knew what it would do to his
career, and she understood how things were when they'd
started, and she didn't want him to marry her out of pity.
"I'll be all right," she said finally, obviously not meaning it.

Two hours later, she held his hand tightly during the brief
ceremony at the Anglican cathedral, and when she kissed him
afterward, her cheeks were wet with tears.

"Sir, I ask permission to discuss a personal matter," Banning, standing at attention, said to the colonel.

"Just as long as you get on that plane, Ed, you have my
permission to discuss anything you want with me."

"Sir, I was married this afternoon," Banning said.

"I don't think I want to hear this, Ed," the colonel said.

"Sir, my wife is a stateless person, with a Nansen travel
document."

"Jesus Christ, Ed! You know the regulations."

"Yes, sir, I know the regulations."

"I didn't hear a word you said, Captain Banning," the
colonel said. "I don't wish to believe that an officer of your
rank and experience would deliberately disobey regulations
concerning marriage and get married without permission."

"If I asked for permission, sir, it would have been denied."

"Or make a gesture like this, throwing a fine career down the goddamned toilet," the colonel said, angrily. "Jesus Christ!"

Banning didn't reply.

"Do you realize what a spot you've put me on, Ed?" the colonel asked in exasperation.

"I regret any embarrassment this may cause you, sir," Banning said. "I am, of course, prepared to resign my commission."

The colonel stared at him coldly for a long moment.

"It's a good goddamned thing I know you well enough, Captain Banning, to understand that was an offer to pay the price, rather than an attempt to avoid your duty," he said, finally. "Mrs. Banning must be quite a lady."

Again, Banning could think of nothing to reply.

"Sergeant-Major!" the colonel bellowed.

The sergeant-major appeared. The colonel told him to close the door.

"Captain Banning," he said, "was today married to a stateless person. Captain Banning did not have permission to marry."

The sergeant-major looked at Banning in surprise.

"It will therefore be necessary for you, Sergeant-Major, to prepare—suitably back-dated—the application to marry, and whatever other documentation is necessary. That includes, I believe, a letter to the Assistant Chief of Staff for Intelligence, Headquarters, USMC, explaining my reasons for not pulling Captain Banning's security clearance once it came to my attention that he is emotionally involved with a foreign national."

"Aye, aye, sir," the sergeant-major said.

"My reasons are that I believe the Corps cannot at this time afford to lose Captain Banning's services, despite his actions in this matter, and that I believe the disciplinary action I have taken closes the matter."

"The disciplinary action, sir?" the sergeant-major asked.

"You will prepare a letter of reprimand as follows," the colonel said. "Quote. It has come to my attention that you have married without due attention to the applicable regulations. You will consider yourself reprimanded. Unquote."

"Aye, aye, sir," the sergeant-major said.

"Thank you, sir," Banning said.

"If that's all you have on your mind, Captain Banning," the colonel said, "I'm sure you have a number of things to do before you board the aircraft."

Despite the sergeant-major's claims about his busting his butt to get the Consulate to issue Milla a "non-quota, married to an American citizen" visa, when Banning turned over the keys to his Pontiac to her, he had a strange feeling that he would never see her again.

They both pretended, though, that everything was now coming up roses: She would promptly get her visa. His (now *their*) furniture and other belongings (including, ultimately, the Pontiac) would be turned in for shipment to the Philippines. If it proved impossible for Milla to get her visa in time for her to ship to the Philippines with the other dependents, she would travel on the first available transportation once the visa was issued.

What was more likely to happen was that his car and household goods were going to be placed in a godown (warehouse) on the docks and more than likely disappear forever. And that when the dependents sailed, Milla would be left behind with no visa.

And he could tell from the look in her eyes that she knew.

On the Catalina he forced Milla and the future from his mind. There was no sense bleeding to death over something he had no control over.

It occurred to him that nice guys, indeed, do finish last.

Macklin, that despicable sonofabitch, had had three weeks to arrange for the shipment of his car and household goods. They had gone on the ship with him. And he was in the States, not headed for the Philippines.

He was, he realized, of two minds about Macklin. On one hand, it was goddamned unfair that the sonofabitch should be safe in the States. On the other hand, if there was to be war, it was better that the sonofabitch should be someplace else.

There was no question in Banning's mind that the officer corps of the United States Marine Corps was about to start earning its pay, and in that case, a slimy sonofabitch like Macklin would do more harm than good.

And finally, before the roar of the engine put him to sleep, his thoughts turned to Corporal "Killer" McCoy. Poor McCoy, hating every minute of it, was probably greasing trucks and keeping his nose clean in Philadelphia, waiting for him to come home from China and arrange for his transfer. McCoy, the poor sonofabitch, was going to have a long wait.

XI

(One)
Known Distance Range #2
U.S. Marine Corps Schools
Quantico, Virginia
19 November 1941

Because he'd participated, back in '38, in the troop test of the Garand rifle at Fort Benning, Captain Jack NMI Stecker, USMCR, Assistant S-3 of the School Battalion, U.S. Marine Corps Schools, Quantico, did not share the generally held opinion that the Garand was a piece of shit. The Corps had sent to the Army's infantry school a platoon of Marines, under Master Gunnery Sergeant Jack NMI Stecker, to find out for themselves what this new rifle was all about.

He hadn't liked it at first. It was bulky and heavy, and didn't have the lean lines of the Springfield. And he had found it difficult to accept that as soon as the slam of the butt into the socket of the shoulder was over, the fired cartridge was ejected, another cartridge was chambered, the action was cocked, and the Garand was prepared to fire again.

As a young Marine, Stecker had spent long hours endlessly working his Springfield until the action was as smooth as butter. And he had learned to fire and work the bolt so fast and so smoothly that the Springfield seemed like a machine gun with a slow rate of fire.

He and the other Marines involved in the troop test had been proud of that skill. *Most of them.* So that the test would not be conducted by forty expert marksmen, the Corps had detailed a dozen kids fresh from Parris Island to the platoon. They weren't experts. It took years to really become an expert with a Springfield.

241

Stecker went to the infantry school at Benning prepared to dislike the Garand.

But that changed. For one thing, even if this came close to heresy, there was no question that the sights on the Garand were better than the sights on the Springfield. On the other hand, the trigger pull started out really godawful, must have been ten pounds when they gave him the new Garand. But he was able to fix that with a little careful stoning of the sear. And the action was stiff as hell too, but that wore itself in after a couple of hundred rounds. And it actually got pretty slick once he learned, by trial and error, just how much of the yellow lubricant to use, and where.

And then the Doggie armorer loaned him his own Garand. What the hell, even if he was a Doggie, they had things in common. The Doggie armorer was a master sergeant, the same rank as Stecker, and he'd done a hitch with the 15th "Can Do" U.S. Infantry in Tientsin, 1935–38. And they knew about rifles. Stecker and the Doggie armorer had more in common with each other than Stecker had with the kids fresh from Parris Island involved in the troop test.

So first they had a couple of beers together at the NCO Club, and then the Doggie invited him to his quarters for supper, and the next morning, the Doggie armorer handed him a Garand and told him he'd "done a little work on it." What he'd done was a really good job on the trigger, and the action was really smooth, and he'd taken chisels to the stock and cut away all the wood, so the barrel was free floating, and (he wasn't sure if Stecker would like this) he'd replaced the rear sight with one he'd rigged up with an aperture about half as big as issue.

The first time Stecker fired the Doggie's Garand—at two hundred yards—when they marked the target and hauled it up again, there was only one spotter[1] on it, a white one, but only one.

"Have them re-mark that goddamned target!" Stecker demanded, angry and embarrassed. He had fired two loose

---

[1]Bullet holes in rifle targets are marked with circular cardboard disks, white if the hole is in the black of the bull's-eye, and black for holes elsewhere on the target. A peg in the center of the disk is inserted in the bullet hole. The bullet strike is thus visible from the firing line.

rounds and an eight-round clip at that target, and apparently hit it only once.

The Doggie corporal on the field phone to the pits ordered the target re-marked, and it disappeared into the pits. It came back up a minute later with just the one white spotter, and Stecker felt humiliation sweep through him.

"Two and a quarter," the Doggie corporal sang out.

"What the hell does that mean?" Stecker asked. There was no such terminology in the Corps.

"That means, Sarge," the corporal said tolerantly, "that you put them all into just over two inches. Not bad!"

Stecker was so pleased (and to tell the truth of it, so relieved) that he'd put ten rounds into an area smaller than a spotter—which was damned near minute of angle[2]—that he didn't even jump the Doggie corporal's ass for calling him "Sarge."

That would have been good shooting even with Stecker's own personal Springfield, which he privately believed was as accurate as any Springfield in the Corps.

That was when he began to change his evaluation of the Garand. Obviously, when properly tuned, the ugly sonofabitch would shoot. Which was the important thing. And being absolutely fair and objective about it, which is what he was supposed to be as the NCOIC of the Marine Troop Test, you could get back on target after the recoil faster than you could with a Springfield. Like it or not, the gas-operated mechanism of the Garand ejected a round and chambered another faster than even a master gunnery sergeant of the Marine Corps could work the bolt of a Springfield.

And there was more to think about. Not only were the Marine marksmen doing well with the Garand—the sergeants and corporals who knew something about shooting — but the kids from Parris Island, too. They didn't, he realized, have a hell of a lot to unlearn. They just took the Garand and learned how to use it.

He didn't easily give in to admitting that the Garand was actually a fine weapon, though. For instance, he surprised hell out of a squad of the kids by ordering them not to detail strip their pieces when the day's firing was over.

[2]One inch at 100 yards. Two inches at 200 yards, etc.

"Just run a couple of patches, first bore cleaner, then oil down the bore. Don't brush the bore. I want to see how much it will take to jam it."

It was three days of firing before the first Garand jammed.

That night, he ordered the squad to detail strip and clean their Garands but not to reassemble them. When all the parts were clean, he ordered the kids to put them all together in a pile on the deck of the barrack.

The kids thought he was really nuts then, and even more so when he stepped up to the pile and stirred the parts around with his toe. One of the claimed merits of the Garand was interchangeability of parts. This was a good way to find out.

"Now put them together," he ordered. He stood watching as the kids assembled rifles.

"I don't want anybody exchanging parts after I'm gone," he said. "I'm trying something."

There was only one malfunction of the squad's Garands the next day, a stovepipe[3] he suspected was a freak. He proved this by firing three clips through the rifle as quickly as he could and without further failure to eject.

Master Gunnery Sergeant Stecker returned from Fort Benning one of the few people in the Corps who believed the Garand was the best infantry rifle to come down the pike in a long time. He was worried then not about whether the Garand would be good for the Corps, but when—or even whether—the Corps would get it. The Army would take care of itself first, of course. The Corps would probably wind up with the Army's worn-out Springfields rather than new Garands.

Captain Jack NMI Stecker, USMCR, was therefore pleased when the first Garands were issued to the Corps. There were not enough of them to go around, of course, but the door was open. For the moment, unfortunately, there were only enough of them to equip a few detached units, and for instructional purposes.

Captain Stecker read with interest the reports of scores fired with the new rifle by the students of the battalion; and he was not happy with the results from either the commis-

---

[3]When the action fails to eject a fired cartridge case properly and jams it in place with the open end erect, it is known as a "stovepipe."

sioned officers at their annual qualification at Quantico or of
the kids in the Platoon Leader's Course. He decided first to
see what was wrong with the training of the Platoon Leader
candidates and fix that, and then he'd see that the same fix
was applied to the abbreviated training course given the officers before they fired their annual qualification.

At 0805, which was late enough for the firing on the
known distance range to be well under way, he got up from
his desk and walked out of his office.

"Come with me, son," he said to the S-3's jeep driver, a
small, very neat PFC trying to make himself inconspicuous
on a chair in the outer office.

As he invariably did when he went for a ride in the jeep
with a PFC at the wheel, he thought about how much he'd
liked it better when he'd been a master gunnery sergeant with
the pickup and didn't have to sit like a statue on an uncomfortable pad in the jeep.

In the center of the line of Known Distance Rifle Range #2
(where the Platoon Leader Candidates were firing for record),
there was a small clutter of buildings surrounding the range
master's tower. Next to the buildings, several vehicles were
parked with their front wheels against yellow-painted logs
half-buried in the sand. There were two jeeps (one assigned to
range NCO and the other to the range officer), two pickups,
and a three-quarter-ton Dodge weapons carrier, which had
brought the ammo from the dump. Two ambulances (new
ones, built on the Dodge three-quarter-ton weapons carrier
chassis) were backed up against the logs.

Stecker told the driver to park the jeep beside the weapons
carrier. When he stopped, Stecker removed his campaign hat
and took from the crown a small glass bottle, which once
contained Bayer Aspirin. He took from it four globs of what
looked like wax at the end of short pieces of string and
handed two of them to the PFC.

"Here," he said to the driver. "Stick these in your ears."

"What is it, sir?" the PFC asked doubtfully.

"Genuine Haiti Marine earplugs," Stecker said. "Do what
I tell you."

"Aye, aye, sir," the PFC said, and after he watched
Stecker carefully push with his index finger one of the wax

globs into each ear, he somewhat uneasily put the plugs into his own ears.

Unless someone looked very carefully at his ears (which was highly unlikely) the earplugs would go unnoticed.

The night before, when Stecker checked the jar where he kept his earplugs, he found only one pair left, so he decided he had to make some more.

So Captain Stecker spent an hour at his kitchen sink making six pairs of the earplugs. He knew that he would be spending several hours on the known distance range, and he had long ago learned that ear damage from the muzzle blast of rifle fire was permanent and cumulative. There were a lot of deaf gunnery sergeants in the Marine Corps as proof of that.

From the time he had been a PFC, Stecker had understood that the Boy Scouts were right. "Be Prepared" said it all. He didn't really need any more earplugs than the pair he had in the Bayer Aspirin bottle, not for tomorrow. But the day after tomorrow was something else. He had no spares, and therefore it was time to make some.

The Haiti Marine earplugs were a good deal more complicated than they looked: He first carefully cut the erasers from a dozen pencils. Then with an awl heated red on the stove, he burned a hole through the center of the eraser. He then knotted a length of strong thread through the holes of a small button, just a bit larger than the diameter of the eraser. The loose end of the thread was then fed through the hole in the eraser.

One at a time, the dozen erasers were carefully placed in holes bored through a piece of wood. Then, in a small pot reserved for this specific purpose, he melted paraffin and beef tallow and carefully poured it into the holes in the wood. When it had time to cool, he pushed each earplug out with a pencil. While the beef tallow/paraffin mixture would remain flexible enough to seal his ear canal, it would neither run from the heat of his body, nor harden to the point where removal would be difficult.

It was a trick Captain Stecker had learned when he was a corporal in Haiti in 1922. A staff sergeant named Jim Finch had taken a shine to him, shown him how to make the plugs, and warned him that if he was going to spend any time around ranges, he had goddamned well better get in the habit of using them.

Stecker put the Bayer Aspirin bottle back in the crown of his stiff-brimmed campaign hat, and then with a quick, smooth movement to keep the bottle from falling out flipped it onto his head.

Aside from his field shoes, the campaign hat was about the only part of his enlisted man's uniforms that he had been able to use as an officer. He had to change the insignia on the campaign hat, but it hadn't been necessary to put it up for sale in the thrift shop along with just about everything else.

When he was ten feet away, the range officer spotted him and saluted, raising his arm crisply until the fingers touched the stiff brim of his campaign hat.

"Good morning, sir," he barked.

"Good morning," Stecker said.

"Is there something special, sir?" the range officer asked.

"Just checking," Stecker said. "But how are the young gentlemen doing?"

"Not bad, sir," the range officer said. "I think we have two who are going to shoot High Expert."

"And the low end?"

"I think they're all going to qualify, sir," the range officer said.

"You think, Lieutenant?" Stecker asked. Out of the corner of his eye, he had just seen Maggie's Drawers[4].

"Yes, sir," the range officer said.

"Think won't cut it, Lieutenant," Stecker said. "If one of the young gentlemen fails to qualify first time out, that means his instructors haven't been doing their job."

"Aye, aye, sir," the range officer said.

"I'm going to have a look around," Stecker said. "I won't need any company, and I don't want the pit officer to know I'm here."

"Aye, aye, sir," the range officer repeated.

Stecker walked erectly to the end of the firing line. There were twenty firing points, each occupied by two platoon leader candidates, one firing and one serving as coach. For

[4]A red flag waved before a target to show a complete miss.

each two firing points, there was a training NCO, so-called even though most of them were PFCs and not noncommissioned officers. A half dozen NCOs, all three stripe buck sergeants, moved up and down the line keeping an eye on the training NCOs and the firers.

The firing was near the end of the prescribed course. The young gentlemen were about to fire slow fire prone at bull's-eye targets five hundred yards down range. The course of fire would be twenty shots, with sixty seconds allotted for each one. The targets would be pulled and marked after each string of ten shots.

What they were doing now was firing "sighters." They had changed range and were permitted trial shots to see how they had done changing their sights.

The target before which Maggie's Drawers had flown was down in the pits. As Stecker watched, it came up. There was a black marker high on the right side of the target outside the scoring rings.

This young gentleman, Stecker thought wryly, had probably never held a gun in his hands before he became associated with the Marine Corps. Some people learned easily, and some didn't.

"Bullshit!" the firer said when he saw the marker, more in anger than embarrassment.

"Watch your mouth, Mister!" the training NCO snapped.

The firer turned his head in annoyance. And then he recognized Stecker as an officer and looked down the range again.

He didn't recognize me. Except as an officer. But I recognize him. That's the China Marine with the LaSalle convertible. That's surprising. A Marine noncom ought to be at least able to get them inside the scoring rings.

He watched as McCoy single-loaded another round.

At least he knows enough not to mess with the sights, Stecker thought. That was probably a flier.

He watched as McCoy slapped the stock of the Garand into the socket of his arm and wiggled his feet to get in the correct position. And he thought he could detect the expelling of half a breath just before the Garand went off again.

The target dropped from sight. When it appeared again, there was another black marker, this time low and left—in other words on the opposite side of the target from the last spotter disk.

"Oh, bullshit!" McCoy said, furious.

His coach, another young gentleman, jabbed him with his elbow to remind him that he was being watched by an officer.

Stecker gave in to the impulse. He reached out and kicked the sole of the coach's boot. When the coach looked up at him in surprise, he gestured for him to get up.

Stecker lay down beside McCoy.

When McCoy looked at him, there was recognition in his eyes.

"All sorts of people get to be officers these days," Stecker said softly. "What seems to be your trouble?"

"Beats the shit out of me," McCoy said, still so angry— and perhaps surprised to see Stecker—that it was a moment before he appended, "Sir."

Stecker reached up and tried to wiggle the rear sight. Sometimes they came loose. But not there. And neither was the front sight when he tried it.

"Try it again," Stecker ordered, turning and holding his hand out for another loose round.

When McCoy reached for it, Stecker saw his hands. They were unhealthy white, and covered with open blisters.

"What did you do to your hands?"

"I've sanded a couple of decks[5] lately, Captain," McCoy said.

Stecker wondered what McCoy had done to deserve punishment. The boy probably had an automatic mouth.

Stecker watched carefully as McCoy fired another round. There was nothing in his firing technique that he could fault. And while they were waiting for the target to be marked, he saw that McCoy had wads of chewed-up paper in his ears. It wasn't as good as Haiti earplugs, but it was a hell of a lot better than nothing. And it reminded Stecker that this boy had been around a rifle range enough to know what he was doing. There was no explanation for his shooting all over the target, much less missing it completely, except that there was something really wrong with the rifle.

---

[5]Sanding decks (cleaning them with sand and a brick) went back to the days of wooden-decked sailing ships. Now it was used as a punishment.

When the target appeared, the marker was black, just outside the bull's-eye.

"That's a little better," Stecker said.

"I should have split the peg with that one," McCoy said, furiously.

By that he meant that he was confident of his shot, knew where it had gone.

That's either bravado, or he means it. And there's only one way to find out.

"Get out of your sling," Stecker ordered. "And hand me the rifle."

As McCoy pulled the leather sling off his arm, Stecker turned to the training NCO and signaled that he wanted a clip of ammunition. When McCoy handed him the Garand, Stecker put the strap on his own arm and squirmed into the correct position.

"Call my shot," he said to McCoy. "I'm going to take out your two-hundred-yard target number."

McCoy looked at him in surprise. So there would be no confusion about which was the correct target, there were markers at each distance with four-inch-high numbers painted on short, flat pieces of wood. They were not designed as targets.

Stecker himself wondered why he was going to fire at the target number, then realized that he thought somebody might be fucking around with McCoy's target in the pits. If that was the case, which now seemed likely, he would have the ass of the pit officer.

You just don't fuck around in the pits. The Marine Corps does not think rifle marksmanship is an area for practical jokes.

Stecker lined up his sights and squeezed one off.

"You took a chip out of the upper-right corner, Captain," McCoy reported.

Maggie's Drawers flew in front of McCoy's target.

Stecker fired again.

"You blew it away, Captain," McCoy reported.

Stecker snapped the safety in front of the trigger guard on, then slipped out of the sling.

"The piece is loaded," he said. "Be careful. Have a shot at the target marker. Number eighteen."

"Aye, aye, sir," McCoy said.

The target number disappeared with McCoy's first shot.

"Nineteen," Stecker ordered.

McCoy fired again. Half of the target number disappeared when the bullet split it.

"Do you think you can hit what's left?" Stecker asked.

He saw Maggie's Drawers being waved furiously in front of the target.

McCoy fired again, and the narrow half remaining of the target number disappeared.

"At targets of opportunity, fire at will," Stecker ordered. softly.

McCoy fired the remaining two rounds in the eight-round en bloc clip at other target numbers. He did not miss.

"Insure that your weapon is empty, and leave the firing line, bringing your weapon with you," Stecker said calmly, reciting the prescribed litany.

By the time they were both on their feet, the range officer and the range NCO were standing beside the training NCO. Having witnessed not only a captain blowing away the target numbers, but apparently encouraging a trainee to do likewise, they were more than a little uneasy.

"This young man has a faulty weapon," Captain Stecker announced. "I think he should be given the opportunity to refire for record."

"Aye, aye, sir," the range officer said.

The range sergeant took the Garand from McCoy and started to examine it.

"Don't you think I know a faulty weapon when I see one, Gunny?" Captain Stecker asked.

"Yes, sir, no offense, sir."

"I realize that tomorrow is the first day of Thanksgiving liberty," Captain Stecker said, "but as we want to give this young man every opportunity to make a decent score, I think we should have the pit officer back, too. Who is he?"

Stecker had decided that the pit officer, whoever he might be, would never forget that Marines don't fuck around the pits after he had spent the first day of Thanksgiving liberty personally hauling, marking, and pasting targets for a Platoon Leader Candidate. That made more sense than in writing him an official letter of reprimand, or even turning him in to the battalion commander.

"Lieutenant Macklin, sir," the range officer said.

"I don't think I know him," Stecker said.

"He's the mess officer, Sir. He volunteered to help out in the pits," the range officer said.

And then Stecker saw understanding and then bitterness in McCoy's eyes.

"Do you know Lieutenant Macklin, McCoy?" Stecker asked.

"Yes, sir, I know him."

Stecker made a come-on motion of his hands.

"We were in the Fourth Marines together, sir," McCoy said.

"I see," Stecker said. *I'll find out what the hell that is all about.* "I think you can get on with the firing, Lieutenant." Stecker said.

"Aye, aye, sir," the lieutenant said. And then when Stecker was obviously going to walk away, he called attention and saluted.

Stecker went back to his jeep and was driven off.

Since there was no point in his firing anymore with a faulty weapon, Platoon Leader Candidate McCoy and Platoon Leader Candidate Pickering were put to work policing brass from the firing line until that relay had finished. Then Platoon Leader Candidate McCoy served as coach for Platoon Leader Candidate Pickering while he fired for record. Platoon Leader Candidate Pickering qualified as "Expert."

(Two)

After leaving McCoy, Captain Stecker went to Battalion Headquarters, where he examined the personal record jacket of First Lieutenant John R. Macklin, USMC. The personnel sergeant was a little uneasy about that—personal records were supposed to be personal—but he wouldn't have dreamed of telling Master Gunnery Sergeant Stecker to mind his own business, and Gunny Stecker was now wearing the silver railroad tracks of a captain.

Then Captain Stecker got back in the jeep and had himself carried to the Platoon Leader Course orderly room.

Word had already gotten back that Captain Stecker had

been out on the range, and that he had ordered the re-firing for record of one of the candidates. And that the pit officer be in the pits when he did so. The sergeant-major had been sort of a pal before Stecker took a commission, and he knew there was more to it than he had been told.

He came to his feet and stood at attention when Stecker walked in.

"Good morning, sir," he said.

"As you were," Stecker said.

"How may I help the captain, sir?" the sergeant-major said.

"You wouldn't happen to have a cup of coffee, Sergeant-Major?"

"Yes, sir," the sergeant-major said.

"And if you have a minute, Sergeant-Major, I'd like a word with you in private."

"We can use the commanding officer's office, sir," the sergeant-major said. "He went out to check on the range, sir."

A corporal followed the two of them into the commanding officer's office with two china mugs of coffee, and then left, closing the door behind him.

"Tell me about a kid named McCoy, Charley," Stecker said.

"That's the one was a China Marine?" Stecker nodded. "What do you want to know, Jack?"

"How come he's been sanding decks?"

"I don't know," the sergeant-major said. "He fucked up, I guess."

"What do you know about Lieutenant Macklin?"

"Not much, Jack," the sergeant-major said, after thinking it over. "The cooks hate his ass. But that always happens when there's a new broom. And he's an eager sonofabitch. The scuttlebutt is he's got a lousy efficiency report and is trying to make up for it."

"So he volunteered to be pit officer?"

"And he takes Saturday inspections for the officers. That kind of stuff."

"I want a look at McCoy's records," Stecker said.

"Anything in particular?"

"Just say I'm nosy," Stecker said.

The sergeant-major went into the outer office and returned with a handful of manila files.

"He's more of a fuck-up than I thought," the sergeant-major said. "Jesus, he's been on report at every fucking inspection. He's given lip to the DIs. Even Macklin wrote him up twice for failure to salute. He'll be scrubbing decks again over the Thanksgiving liberty. He's right on the edge of getting his ass shipped out of here. He's going before the elimination board[6] on Friday."

Stecker grunted.

He took McCoy's records from the sergeant-major and read them carefully.

"Very odd," he said. "His last efficiency report says his 'personal deportment and military bearing serves as an example to the command.' I wonder what turned him into a fuck-up here?"

The sergeant-major raised his eyebrows but said nothing.

"It says here that he's an Expert with the Springfield and the .45, and the light and water-cooled Brownings. I was on the range before . . ."

"So I heard," the sergeant-major said.

"He could barely get a round on the target, much less in the black," Stecker said. "I found out he had a faulty weapon. He could hit target numbers with it. It was just that he was all over the target when he fired at a bull's-eye."

"Jesus, was he fucking around on the rifle range, too?" the sergeant-major asked.

"He wasn't fucking around on the rifle range, Charley," Stecker said.

"And Macklin was the pit officer, right?" the sergeant-major said, finally putting things together.

"Was he?" Stecker asked, innocently.

"Jesus Christ!" the sergeant-major said.

"I'm sure you know as well as I do, sergeant-major," Stecker said, "that no Marine officer is capable of using his office and authority to settle personal grudges."

"Yes, sir," the sergeant-major said.

---

[6] A board of officers charged with determining whether or not a platoon leader candidate had proved himself unfit or unworthy of being commissioned.

"And under the circumstances, Sergeant-Major, I can see no reason for Platoon Leader Candidate McCoy to refire for record. It would be an unnecessary expenditure of time and ammunition. If he had a properly functioning rifle, I'm sure that he would—since he has been drawing Expert marksman's pay since boot camp—qualify with the Garand."

"Got you," the sergeant-major said.

"Further, it would interefere with his Thanksgiving liberty. Platoon Leader Candidate McCoy is shortly going to be commissioned . . ."

"He'll have to get past the elimination board," the sergeant-major said. "With this record, he has to go before it."

"What record do you mean, Sergeant-Major?" Captain Stecker said, as calmly and deliberately he tore from the manila folder all the official records of misbehavior and unsatisfactory performance Platoon Leader Candidate McCoy had acquired since beginning the course. He shredded them and dropped them into the wastebasket.

"What do I tell the old man, Jack?" the sergeant-major asked.

"Three things, Charley," Stecker said. "First, that if there is some reason McCoy can't have Thanksgiving liberty, I want to hear about it. Second, that the colonel has taken two evening meals in the mess and found them unsatisfactory. And third, that I politely and unofficially suggest that maybe the chow would be better if the mess officer stayed where he belongs, in the kitchen."

The sergeant-major nodded.

"I'm sorry about this, Jack," he said. "I feel like a damned fool."

Stecker did not let him off the hook.

"When I was the gunny, Charley," he said, "the colonel expected me to know what was going on in the ranks. I found the best way to do that was get off my ass and have a look at things."

And then he walked out of the office.

(Three)

Inasmuch as ceremonies are an integral part of the life and duties of young officers, and because the Marine Corps Schools believed that "doing is the best means of learning," ceremonies of one kind or another were frequently on the training program of the Platoon Leader's Course.

One such ceremony was scheduled for 1700 hours, 19 November 1941. It was a formal retreat. The platoon leader candidates would be returned from the Known Distance Firing Range in plenty of time to clean their rifles, shave and wash, and change into greens. The training schedule allocated all of thirty-five minutes for this purpose.

Waiting for Corporal Pleasant to blow his whistle, McCoy was pretty well down in the dumps. At first, he had been almost thrilled that Macklin had been caught sticking it to him. He'd thought that luck was finally falling his way. It hadn't taken long for the old-gunny-now-a-captain to figure out that somebody was fucking him in the pits, or even that the sonofabitch sticking it in him was Lieutenant Macklin.

But the good feeling soon dissipated. For one thing, officers took care of one another, and the captain, if he said anything at all to Macklin, wasn't going to jump his ass. Stecker believed that Macklin was either sloppy in the pits, or that he thought what he was doing was funny. Stecker had no reason to think that Macklin was personally doing his best to get him booted out of the Platoon Leader's Course.

All the whole incident had meant was that he was going to get a chance to fire for record again. That was all. And Macklin was being taught not to "fool around" when he was pit officer by having to spend Thanksgiving morning on the range. It was possible that he would pull the same shit all over again. Why not? There would be nobody there to watch him.

When he came off the rifle range, the sand and the bricks would be waiting for him, and he would spend Thanksgiving afternoon on his knees scrubbing the decks. For "disrespectful attitude."

And, on Friday morning, he would go before the elimination board. Pleasant had told him about that. He could get out of it, Pleasant said, and probably get the whole Thanksgiving weekend as liberty, if he would just face the fact that they weren't going to make him an officer and resign.

He had told Pleasant to go fuck himself. Which is why he would be sanding the deck.

McCoy didn't believe he was ever going to get a gold bar

to put on his shoulder. Not really. Not inside. But he was going to take the one chance he saw: Sometimes the elimination board wouldn't bust people out, but would instead "drop them back," which meant that you went through part of the course again with a class that started later. That happened when somebody bilged academics. He had never heard of somebody being dropped back for "attitude" or "unsuitability," which is what they called it when they sent you before the elimination board for fucking up.

But that's what he was going to ask for. He had come this far, and he wasn't just going to belly up for the bastards. He probably wouldn't get it, and next Monday he would probably be on his way as Pvt McCoy to Camp LeJeune, or maybe Diego, as a machine-gunner.

And it was a real pain in the ass to get all shined up for a retreat parade knowing that they were going to read your name off on two lists, one for "extra training" which is what they called the deck sanding, and the other to go before the elimination board. And when they had done that, knowing that while everybody else was off getting beered up at the slop chute, he would be on his fucking hands and knees sanding the deck.

"If I helped you with the deck," Pick Pickering said, as if he was reading his mind, "maybe we could get done quicker."

"Pleasant would get you your own deck," McCoy said. "But thanks, Pick."

"Let's give it a shot," Pickering said.

"When they hold formation," McCoy said, "they're going to read off names of people going before the elimination board. Mine is on it."

"You don't believe that," Pickering said, loyally.

"I know," McCoy said. "It's not scuttlebutt."

"That's not right," Pickering said. "Christ, it's goddamned unfair."

"It's an unfair world," McCoy said. "This is the Marine Corps."

"There ought to be some way to register a complaint," Pickering said.

McCoy laughed at him, but then, touched by Pickering's loyalty, punched him affectionately on the arm.

Pickering was a good guy. Dumb, but a good guy. Even

after McCoy had told him that he was on everybody's shit list, and that if he kept hanging around, some of the shit they were throwing was bound to splatter on him, he'd hung around anyway. Pickering was going to be a good officer.

"Turn around, asshole," McCoy said. "Let me check you out."

There was nothing wrong with Pickering's uniform or equipment. But a pin on one of McCoy's collar point "oxes"[7] had come off, and the ox was hanging loose. Pickering fixed it.

What the fuck difference does it make? McCoy thought bitterly. *This is the last time I'll wear it anyway. I'll go before the elimination board in dungarees.*

Corporal Pleasant blew his whistle and all the freshly bathed and shaved young gentlemen rushed out onto the company street, where they formed ranks. Corporal Pleasant then issued the appropriate order causing the young gentlemen to open ranks so that he could more conveniently inspect their shaves, the press of their green uniforms, and the cleanliness of their Garand rifles.

They would be inspected again, a few minutes later, by the company commander and gunnery sergeant, but Corporal Pleasant wanted to make sure they were all shipshape before that happened.

To McCoy's surprise, Pleasant not only found nothing wrong with his appearance, shave, or shine, he didn't even inspect his rifle when he stepped in front of him.

He probably figures he doesn't have to bother anymore.

The company commander and the gunnery sergeant made their appearance at the end of the company street, and one by one, the drill instructors of the four platoons of platoon leader candidates called their troops to order.

McCoy's company commander, a lieutenant, spoke to him as he inspected his rifle.

"I understand you had some trouble with this today, McCoy?"

"Yes, sir."

---

[7]Platoon Leader Candidates wore brass insignia, the letters OC (hence "Ox"), standing for Officer Candidate, on shirt collar points and fore-and-aft hats in lieu of insignia of rank.

"And I also understand the stoppage has been cleared?"

What the fuck is he talking about? Stoppage?

"Yes, sir."

The company commander moved on. The sergeant-major looked right into McCoy's face, but said nothing, and there was no particular expression on his face.

When the four platoons had been inspected, the officers took their positions, and the gunny read the orders of the day.

The next day was Thanksgiving[8], the Gunny announced, as if no one had figured that out for himself. Liberty for all hands, with the exception of those individuals requiring extra training, would commence when the formation was dismissed. The next duty day, Friday, would be given over to the purchase of uniforms. Those individuals who were to appear before the elimination board would not, repeat, not, order any officer-type uniforms until the decisions of the elimination board were announced. Liberty would begin on Friday, until 0330 hours the following Monday, as soon as the platoon leader candidates had arranged for the purchase of officer-type uniforms. There would be no, repeat, no, liberty for anyone called before the elimination board.

The gunny then read the list of those who required extra training, and then the list of those to face the elimination board.

And then he did an about-face and saluted the company commander, who returned the salute, ordered him to dismiss the formation, and walked off.

The gunny barked, "Dis-miss!"

Pick Pickering punched McCoy's arm.

"See? I told you you weren't gonna get boarded!"

And neither, McCoy thought, *did I hear my name called for extra training. And they didn't say anything about refiring for record, either.*

What the fuck is going on?

He thought it was entirely likely that the gunny had "forgotten" to read his name, so that when he failed to show up to sand the deck, or to refire for record, or for the elimination board itself, they could add AWOL to everything else.

[8]Until December 1941, Thanksgiving was celebrated on the third Thursday of November.

He saw Pleasant going behind the building to get into his Ford. He ran after him.

Pleasant rolled down the window.

"Something I can do for you, Mr. McCoy?"

"What the fuck is going on, Pleasant? Why wasn't my name called for extra training and for the elimination board?"

"Because you're not on extra training, Mr. McCoy, and because you're not going before the elimination board. You are on liberty, Mr. McCoy.

"You going to tell me what's going on?"

"Very well, Mr. McCoy. It's very simple. In ten days they are going to pin a gold bar on your shoulder. Between now and then, the gunny and I will do whatever we can to make things as painless as possible for you."

"I thought you wanted to bust me out of here."

"Oh, we do," Pleasant said. "Nothing would give us greater pleasure. But then, we know better than to fuck with a rabbi."

"What rabbi?"

"Is there anything else, Mr. McCoy?" Pleasant said. "If not, with your permission, sir, I would like to start my Thanksgiving liberty."

"Fuck you, Pleasant," McCoy said.

Pleasant rolled up the window and drove off.

Pick Pickering was waiting for McCoy in the barracks.

"Well?"

"I'm on liberty like everybody else," McCoy said. "And no elimination board."

"Great!" Pickering said, and punched his arm. "Let's go find a cab and get the hell out of here."

"Out of here, where?"

"In compliance with orders from the United States Marine Corps, I am going to buy some officer-type uniforms."

"What the hell are you talking about? We're not supposed to buy uniforms until Friday."

"Right," Pickering said.

"Well?"

"I'm learning," Pickering said. "You will recall that they didn't say anything about where we were to buy the uniforms. Just that we buy them on Friday."

"So?"

"On Friday, I am going to buy uniforms. In Brooks Brothers in New York."

"What's Brooks Brothers?"

"It's a place where they sell clothing, including uniforms."

"Jesus!" McCoy said.

"And when we're not buying our uniforms, we can be lifting some skirts," Pickering said. "The only problem is finding a cab to get us off this fucking base to someplace we can catch a train to New York."

"We don't need a cab," McCoy said. "I've got a car."

"You have a car? Here?" Pickering asked, surprised.

McCoy nodded.

"Mr. McCoy," Pickering said. "The first time I laid eyes on you, I said, 'Now, there is a man of many talents, the sort of chap it would be wise to cultivate in the furtherance of my military career.' "

McCoy smiled.

"And will this car of yours make it to New York? Without what I have recently learned to call 'mechanical breakdown'?"

"It's a LaSalle," McCoy said.

"In that case, if you pay for the gas," Pickering said, "I will take care of the room. Fair?"

"Fair," McCoy agreed.

XII

(One)
The Foster Park Hotel
Central Park South
New York City, New York
2320 Hours 19 November 1941

Pick Pickering was at the wheel of the LaSalle when it pulled up in front of the marquee of the Foster Park Hotel. They had gassed up just past Baltimore and changed places there.

McCoy had gone to sleep thinking about Ellen Feller, about her probably being somewhere in Baltimore, and about what had happened between them in China—memories that reminded him of the very long time since he'd had his ashes hauled.

The doorman stepped off the curb, walked out to the driver's side, opened the door, and said, "Welcome to the Foster Park Hotel, sir," before he realized that the driver was some kind of a soldier, a Marine, and an enlisted man, not even an officer.

"May I help you, sir?"

Pickering got out of the car.

"Take care of the car, please," he said. "We'll need it sometime Sunday afternoon."

"You'll be checking in, sir?"

The question seemed to amuse the Marine.

"I hope so," he said. "The luggage is in the trunk."

He turned back to the car.

"Off your ass and on your feet, McCoy," he said. "We're here."

262

McCoy sat up, startled, looked around, and as almost a reflex action, opened his door and got out.

"Where are we?" he asked, groggily.

"My grandfather calls it Sodom-on-Hudson," Pickering said, and took McCoy's arm and propelled him toward the revolving door.

The desk clerk was busy with someone else as Pickering and McCoy approached registration. Pickering pulled the Register in front of him, took the pen, and filled out one of the cards.

When the desk clerk turned his attention toward Pickering, he thrust the Registration card at him.

"We'd like a small suite," he said.

"I'm not sure that we'll be able to accommodate you, sir," the clerk said.

The clerk didn't know what the OC insignia on the collar points of the uniforms meant, but he knew a Marine private when he saw one, and Marine privates couldn't afford the prices of the Foster Park Hotel.

"House is full, is it?" the Marine asked.

"What I mean to suggest, sir," the desk clerk said, as tactfully as he could, "is that our prices are, well, a little stiff."

"That's all right," the Marine said. "I won't be paying for it anyway. Something with a view of the park, if one is available."

The desk clerk looked down at the card in his hand.

He didn't recognize the name, but in the block "Special billing Instructions" the Marine had written: "Andrew Foster, S/F, Attn: Mrs. Delahanty."

"Just one moment, please, sir, I'll check," the desk clerk said.

He disappeared behind the rack of mail-and-key slots and handed the card to the night resident manager, who was having a cup of coffee and a Danish pastry at his desk. He handed him the registration card. The night resident manager glanced at it casually, and then jumped to his feet.

He approached the Marines standing at the desk with his hand extended.

"Welcome to the Park, Mr. Pickering," he said. "It's a pleasure to have you in the house."

"Thank you," Pick Pickering said, shaking his hand. "Is there some problem?"

"Absolutely no problem. Would Penthouse C be all right with you?"

"If you're sure we can't rent it," Pickering said.

"Not at this hour, Mr. Pickering," the night resident manager said, laughing appreciatively.

"Well, if somebody wants it, move us," Pickering said. "But otherwise, that's fine. We'll be here until Sunday afternoon."

The night resident manager took a key from the rack and came from behind the marble counter.

"If we had only known you were coming, Mr. Pickering . . ." he said. "I'm afraid there's not even a basket of fruit in the penthouse."

"At half-past four this afternoon, it was even money that we would be spending the weekend with a brick and a pile of sand," Pick Pickering said. "I don't much care about fruit, but I wish you would send up some liquor, peanuts, that sort of thing."

"Immediately, Mr. Pickering," the night resident manager said, as he bowed them onto the elevator.

Penthouse C of the Foster Park Hotel consisted of a large sitting room opening onto a patio overlooking Fifty-ninth Street and Central Park. To the right and left were bedrooms, and there was a butler's pantry and a bar with four stools.

When he went directly to answer nature's call, McCoy found himself in the largest bathroom he had ever seen.

By the time he came out, there were two room service waiters and a bellboy in the room. The bellboy was arranging cut flowers in vases. One waiter was organizing on the rack behind the bar enough liquor bottles to stock a saloon, and the other was moving through the room filling silver bowls from a two-pound can of cashews.

Pick Pickering was sitting on a couch talking on the telephone. He saw McCoy and made a gesture indicating he was thirsty.

"Scotch," he called, putting his hand over the mouthpiece.

By the time McCoy had crossed to the bar, the night resident manager had two drinks made.

"We're glad to have you with us, sir," the night resident

manager said, as he put one drink in McCoy's hand and scurried across the room to deliver the other to Pickering.

When they were all finally gone and Pickering finished his telephone call, McCoy sat down beside him.

"What the hell is all this?" he asked.

Pickering leaned back against the couch and took a swallow of his drink.

"Christ, that tastes good," he said. "Incidentally, I have located the quarry."

"What quarry?"

"The females with liftable skirts," Pickering said. "There's a covey of them in a saloon called El Borracho . . . which, appropriately, means 'The Kiss,' I think."

"I asked you what's going on around here," McCoy said.

"We all have our dark secrets," Pickering said. "I, for example, know far more than I really want to about your lady missionary."

"Come on, Pick," McCoy said.

"This is the Foster Park Hotel," Pickering said. "Along with forty-one others, it is owned by a man named Andrew Foster. Andrew Foster has one child, a daughter. She married a man who owns ships. A lot of ships, Ken. They have one child. Me."

"Jesus Christ!" McCoy said.

"It is not the sort of thing I would wish our beloved Corporal Pleasant, or our sainted gunny, to know. So keep your fucking mouth shut about it, McCoy."

"Jesus Christ!" McCoy repeated.

"Yes?" Pickering asked, benignly, as befitting the Saviour. "What is it you wish, my son?"

(Two)

They did not get laid. All the girls at the first night club had escorts. They smiled, especially at Pick Pickering, but it proved impossible to separate them from the young men they were with. The candy-asses were worried about leaving their girls alone with Pickering, McCoy thought, approvingly. He was sure they had learned from painful experience that if they blinked their eyes, Pickering and their girls would be gone.

Most of the time McCoy didn't know what the hell anyone was talking about. Only one of the girls showed any interest

at all in him. She asked him if he had been at Harvard with
"Malcolm." When he said no, she asked him where he had
gone to school. When he said "Saint Rose of Lima," she
gave him a funny smile and ignored him thereafter.

In the second place, which was called the "21" Club,
McCoy thought they probably could have gotten laid: There
were enough women around, but the son of the proprietor
fucked that up. He wanted to hear all about the Platoon
Leader's Course because he'd joined the Corps and was
about to report for active duty.

Pick kept him fascinated with tales of Corporal Pleasant
and slurping food from trays and doing the duck walk. When
they left, he insisted on paying for their drinks and told
McCoy that he was welcome any time. But that didn't get
them laid either.

The third place McCoy remembered hearing about somewhere. It was called the "Stork Club." When they got there,
he didn't think they were going to get in because there was a
line of people waiting on the sidewalk. But Pick just walked
to the head of the line, and a bouncer or whatever lowered a
rope and called Pick "Mr. Pickering," and they walked in.

There was a table against the wall with a "reserved" sign
on it, but a headwaiter snatched that away and sat them down
there. Moments later a waiter with a bottle of champagne
showed up, soon followed by the proprietor of the Stork
Club. The proprietor asked about "Mr. Foster" and told Pick
to make sure he carried his best regards to his parents.

Like the guy at "21," he picked up the bill. That meant
they got a decent load on without spending a dime.

"Tomorrow, Ken, we will get laid," Pickering said as they
got in a cab to return to the hotel. "Look on tonight as
reconnaissance. The key to a successful assault, you will
recall, is a good reconnaissance."

As they were having breakfast the next morning, Pick had
an idea.

He called the Harvard Club and had the steward put a
notice on the bulletin board: "Mr. Malcolm Pickering will
entertain his friends and acquaintances at post–Thanksgiving
Dinner cocktails from 2:30 P.M., Penthouse C, the Foster Park
Hotel. Friends and acquaintances are expected to bring two
girls."

McCoy had a good time in the morning. He made some remark about what a nice hotel it was, and Pickering then took him on a tour. This was fascinating to McCoy; and it was a complete tour, kitchens, laundry, even the little building up above the penthouses where the elevator machinery was.

McCoy saw that there was more to the tour than showing him around. Pickering looked inside garbage cans, even went into rooms with open doors. He was inspecting the place, looking for things that weren't as they were supposed to be. The other side of that was that he knew how things were supposed to be. He might be rich as shit, but he understood the hotel business.

He wondered if Pickering had learned that in school, and asked him. Pick laughed and told him that the first job he'd had in a Foster hotel was as a twelve-year-old busboy, cleaning tables.

"I can do anything in the hotel except French pastry," Pickering said. "I've never been able to handle egg white properly."

About one o'clock, as they sat in the sitting room in their shirts and trousers drinking Feigenspann XXX Ale from the necks of the bottles, the hotel started setting up for the cocktail party. There was an enormous turkey, and a whole ham, and a piece of roast beef. And all kinds of other stuff. Thinking of how much it was costing made McCoy uncomfortable. No matter how nice Pick was being, McCoy was beginning to feel like a mooch.

It got worse when the people started showing up for the party: It wasn't hard to figure that if all the guests weren't as rich as Pick, they were still rich. And he had nothing in common with them. The only thing he had in common with Pick was the Marine Corps. And then there was one particular girl. She really made him uncomfortable.

He had never seen a more beautiful girl in his life. She was fucking near-perfect. She had black hair, in a pageboy, with dark, glowing eyes that made her skin seem pure white.

She wasn't dressed as fancy as the others, just a sweater and a skirt, with a string of pearls hanging down around her neck.

His first thought was that he would happily swap his left nut to get her in the sack, and his second thought was that she wasn't that kind of female at all. She wasn't going to give any away until she had the gold ring on her finger—not because she was careful, but because that was the kind of woman she was. Once, when she caught him looking at her, she looked right back at him, as if she was asking, "What's a scumbag like you doing looking at me? I'm not like the rest of these people."

And for some reason, she kept him from putting the make on anybody else. Not all of Pick's "friends and acquaintances" had shown up with two girls, but a lot of them had. And a bunch of women had come by themselves. One of them, a sharp-featured woman with blond hair down to her shoulders, had even come on to him, smiling at him and touching his arm when she asked him if he was in the Marines with Pick.

But he saw the girl in the pageboy looking at them with her dark eyes and didn't do anything about the blonde. After a moment, she went away.

Ten or fifteen minutes later, the smoke in the place (there must have been a hundred people, and they were all smoking) got to him; and he realized he'd had more Scotch than he should have. He didn't want to get shit-faced and make an ass of himself and embarrass Pick in front of his friends. So he took another bottle of ale from the refrigerator, walked into "his" bedroom, where he interrupted a couple kissing and feeling each other up, and went out on the patio for a breath of cold, fresh air.

The sun had come up, there wasn't much wind, and it wasn't as cold as he thought it would be. It was nippy, but that's what he wanted anyhow. He sat on the wall, carefully, because they were twenty-two floors up, and looked down at Fifty-ninth Street. When that started to make him feel a little dizzy, he looked into Central Park.

He was pretty far gone from where he thought he would be on Thanksgiving afternoon, he thought, sanding the fucking deck. Then he remembered he was really far from where he had been last Thanksgiving, a PFC machine-gunner in Dog Company, First Battalion, 4th Marines, in Shanghai. He'd taken the noon meal in the mess hall. They always sent in frozen turkeys on Thanksgiving and Christmas, and that was the only time there was turkey in China. They even bent the rules for Thanksgiving and Christmas, and you could bring guests who weren't European. He remembered that Zimmerman had brought his Chinese wife and all their half-white kids to the mess.

"Don't go to sleep," a female voice said to him. "That's a long step if you walk in your sleep."

Startled, he stood up and then looked to see who was talking to him.

It was the perfect fucking female in the pageboy haircut.

"I wasn't about to go to sleep," he said.

"You could have fooled me," she said. "You looked like you were bored to death and about to doze off."

"I was thinking," McCoy said.

The string of pearls around her neck had looped around one of her breasts. It wasn't sexy. It was feminine.

"About what?"

"What?"

"What were you thinking about?" she pursued.

She sat down on the wall, and looked up at him.

Jesus Christ! Up close she's even more beautiful!

"Where I was last Thanksgiving," he said.

"And where you might be next Thanksgiving?"

"No," he said. "I wasn't thinking about that."

"I thought you might be," she said, and she smiled.

"Why?"

"Well, you're a Marine," she said. "Don't they wonder where they'll be moved next?"

"I don't," he replied without thinking. "Not any further than the Corps, I mean. I know I'm going to be in the Corps. It doesn't matter where I'll be. It'll still be the Corps."

She looked as if she didn't understand him, but the question she asked was perfectly normal: "Where were you last Thanksgiving?" she asked.

"Shanghai," he said. And added, "China."

"So that's where Shanghai is," she said brightly. "I knew it was either there or in Australia."

I knew fucking well that I would show my ass if I tried to talk to somebody like this. What a dumb fucking thing to say!

She saw the hurt in his eyes.

"Sorry," she said.

"It's all right," McCoy said.

"No, it's not," she said. "There are extenuating circumstances, but I shouldn't have jumped on you."

"What are the extenuating circumstances?" McCoy asked.

"I'm an advertising copywriter," she said.

"I don't know what that is," McCoy confessed.

"I write the words in advertisements," she explained.

"Oh," he said.

"Our motto is brevity," she said.

"Oh," McCoy repeated.

"We try not to say anything redundant," she said. "It's okay to jump on somebody who does."

"Okay," he said.

"I had no right to do that to you," she said.

"I didn't mind," McCoy said.

"Yes, you did," she said, matter-of-factly.

When she looks into my eyes, my knees get weak.

"What did you do in China, last Thanksgiving?"

"I was in a water-cooled Browning .30 crew," he said.

"Browning machine gun, you mean?" she asked.

He was surprised that she knew. He nodded.

"I somehow didn't think you were up in Cambridge with our host," she said.

"I guess that's pretty obvious, isn't it?"

She understood his meaning.

"Different means different," she said. "Not better or worse."

The door to the sitting room opened, and six or seven people came onto the patio and headed for them.

They sure as hell don't know me, which means they're headed for her. Probably to take her out of here. And if she goes, that's the last I'll ever see of her.

"Prove it," McCoy said.

"Huh?"

"Go somewhere else with me," McCoy said.

"Where?" she asked, warily.

"I don't know," McCoy said. "Anywhere you want."

She was still looking at him thoughtfully when Pickering's friends came over to her.

"We wondered what had happened to you," one of the girls said. "We're going over to Marcy's. You about ready?"

"You go along," the most beautiful female McCoy had ever seen said. "I've other plans."

She looked into his eyes and smiled.

He realized that his heart was throbbing. Like the water hose on a Browning .30.

(Three)

"Where are you taking me?" she asked, as they walked through the lobby of the Foster Park.

"I don't know anyplace to take you," he said. "I've never been in New York before."

"I have sort of a strange idea," she said. "Chinese food."

"Huh?"

"I guess your 'Thanksgiving in Shanghai' speech triggered it," she said. "Or maybe I'm over my ears in turkey."

"You'll have to show me," he said. "I don't know anything about this town," he said.

"I think we could find a Chinese restaurant in Chinatown," she said.

"Let's get a cab," he said.

"Let's take the subway," she said.

"I can afford a cab," McCoy said.

Which means, of course, that you can't.

"I like to watch the people on the subway," she said, took his arm, and headed him toward Sixth Avenue.

"Why?" he asked.

"You ever been . . . No, of course, you haven't," she said. "You'll see."

His eyes widened at the variations of the species *homo sapiens* displayed on the subway. And they smiled at each other, and somehow she wanted to touch him, and did, and put her arm in his, her hand against the rough fabric of his overcoat.

Maybe it is the uniform, she thought. *Men in uniform are supposed to get the girls.*

She let herself think about that. It was not her style to leave parties with men she had met there. Especially friends of people like Malcolm Pickering. What was there about this young man that made him different?

A drunk, a young one in a leather jacket and a knitted hat with a pom-pom, walked past them and examined her with approval.

And something happened to the eyes of the young man

whose arm she was holding. *And, my God, whose name I don't even know!* His eyes narrowed, just a little, but visibly. And they brightened and turned alert. And menacing.

She was more than a little frightened.

My God, he is a Marine! And all I need is to have him get in a fist fight with a drunk on the subway.

She watched, fascinated, as the drunk sensed the menace, put on a smile, and walked further down the car. McCoy's eyes followed him until he was sure the threat had passed. Then his eyes moved to her, and they changed again. The menace disappeared and was replaced by something much softer. It was almost as if he was now frightened.

My God, he's afraid of me!

"I don't know your name," she said.

"McCoy," he said.

"McCoy Smith? McCoy Jones?" she asked.

"Kenneth McCoy," he said.

She took her arm from under his and gave him her hand.

"Ernestine Sage," she said. "My parents obviously hoped for a boy. Please don't call me either 'Ernestine' or 'Ernie.' "

"What can I call you?" Kenneth McCoy asked.

Not "what do I call you," she thought, *but, "what can I call you." He's asking permission. He doesn't want to offend me. I don't have to be afraid of him.*

"Most people call me 'Sage,' " she said. "Sage means wise."

"I know," he said.

She slipped her hand back under his arm. And she saw the skin of his neck deepen in color.

They walked down Mott Street with her hand very much aware of the warmth of his body, even through the overcoat.

"There is a legend that young white women should not come here alone," Sage said. "That they will be snatched by white slavers."

He did not sense that she was teasing him.

"You'll be all right," he said.

When she looked into his face, he averted his eyes.

"They say the best food is in little places in the alleys," Sage said. "That the places on Mott Street are for tourists. The trouble is that they speak only Chinese in the little places."

"I speak Chinese," he said, and while she was still wondering whether or not he was trying to pull her leg, he led her into one of the alleys. Fifty feet down it, he stopped in front of a glass-covered sign and started to read it.

He's really very clever. If I didn't know better I'd almost believe he knew what he was looking at.

"See anything you think I'd like?" she asked, innocently.

"No," he said. "This is a Szechuan restaurant. Most Szechuan food is hotter than hell."

An old Chinese woman scampered toward them.

McCoy spoke to her. In Chinese. Sage looked at him in astonishment. But there was no question he was really speaking Chinese, because, chattering back at McCoy, the old woman reversed direction and led them farther down the street.

"Her nephew," McCoy explained, "runs a Cantonese restaurant. You'll like that better, I think."

The restaurant was on the fourth floor of an old building. There were no other white people inside, and the initial response to the two of them, Sage thought, was resentment, even hostility.

But then McCoy spoke to the man who walked up to them, and smiles appeared. They were bowed to a table, tea was produced, and a moment later an egg roll rich with shrimp.

"This is to give us an appetite," McCoy said. "Hell, I can make a meal of egg rolls." Then he heard what he had said. "Sorry," he said. "You have to remember, I'm a Marine. We get in the habit, without being around women, of talking a little rough."

"Hell," Sage said. "I don't give a damn. If it makes you feel any better, cuss as much as you goddamn well please."

He looked at her without comprehension, then he smiled. When he smiled like that, he looked like a little boy.

Their knees touched under the table. He withdrew his as if the contact had burned. With a mind of its own, seemingly, Sage's foot searched for his. When they touched, he withdrew again. She finally managed to pin his ankle against the table leg.

Now they didn't seem to be able to look at each other.

There was a steady stream of food. Very small portions.

"I told him to bring us one of everything," he said. "If you don't like something, give it to me."

"What does that OC mean on your collar?"

"They call it the oxes," he said. "I suppose it stands for officer candidate."

"You're going to be an officer?"

He nodded, wondering if that would surprise her, and then hoping it might impress her a little.

"When?"

"End of the month," he said.

"Then what?"

"What do you mean, 'then what'?"

"Where will you be stationed?"

"I don't know," he said.

"I remember. It's all the Corps, and therefore it doesn't make any difference, right?"

"Something like that."

We are both pretending, Sage thought. *He is pretending that I am not playing anklesy with him, and I am pretending that I am not doing it.*

"I can't eat another bite," she said, after a while.

"I don't even know what I've eaten," McCoy said.

"To hell with turkey anyway," Sage said. "This is what I'm going to do from now on on Thanksgiving."

For some reason, when they got to the street, Sage felt a little dizzy.

"This time a cab," she said.

"Where are we going?"

"West Third Street," she said.

"What's there?"

"Another Chinese restaurant I heard about, what else?"

She motioned him into her apartment and then closed the door and locked it.

He roamed the apartment, and when he came back, she was still leaning on the door.

"I like your apartment," he said.

"I'm glad," she said. "My father calls it my hovel."

"I was afraid you were going to turn out rich, like Pick."

"Would that have bothered you?"

"Yes," he said, simply.

They looked at each other, their eyes locking for a long moment.

"I don't know what the hell I'm doing," McCoy said. "All I know is that I don't want to fuck this up."

He's so upset that he didn't hear himself. Otherwise I'd have got an apology for the "fuck," and he would have blushed like a tomato.

"Neither do I," Sage said. "I don't expect you to believe this under the circumstances, but neither do I."

"I think maybe I had better go."

She pushed herself off the door and walked so close to him that she could smell the wet wool odor of his overcoat.

"There's a time and a place for everything," she said. "And this is the time and place where I think you should kiss me. If that goes the way I think it will, then I think you should pick me up and carry me into the bedroom."

"Pick you up?" he asked, incredulously.

"I could crawl, I suppose," she said.

He laughed, and scooped her up, and carried her into the bedroom. He lowered her onto the bed and then stood up.

He still hasn't kissed me. All we've done is play anklesy. And the way he's standing there with that dumb look on his face, nothing is going to happen.

Very deliberately, she reached for the hem of her sweater and pulled it over her head. He stared at her in marvel. She reached behind her back and unhooked her brassiere, so that he could look at her, naked to the waist.

"Now you," she said, very softly.

She looked at him then as he ripped the uniform off.

He's good at that. Very fast. He's probably had a lot of experience taking his clothes off in a hurry in situations like this.

And then he was naked.

"You're the most beautiful thing I have ever seen," he said.

"So are you," Sage said.

As McCoy came to the bed and put his arms around her and with a great deal more tenderness than she expected held her tight against him, Sage thought, *I wonder if it's going to hurt as much as they say it hurts, and if there will be a lot of blood, and if that will embarrass him.*

(Four)

Pick was sitting in his underwear having breakfast in the sitting room of Penthouse C when McCoy returned.

"Been out spreading pollen, have you?" Pick said.

McCoy didn't reply.

"I wondered what the hell had happened to you," Pickering said. "I took a chance and ordered breakfast for both of us."

"I'm not hungry," McCoy said.

But he sat down for a cup of coffee and wound up eating a breakfast steak and a couple of eggs and the half dozen remaining rolls.

"I thought you might take just a little bite," Pickering said, "for restorative purposes."

"Fuck you," McCoy said.

"Then you didn't get any," Pickering said. "With your well-known incredible good luck, you fell into the clutches of one of our famous cockteasers."

"I got a goddamned cherry," McCoy said.

"I didn't know there were any left," Pickering said without thinking, before realizing that McCoy wasn't boasting; that quite to the contrary, he was ashamed.

"Who was she?" he asked.

"There were two poor people in here yesterday," McCoy said. "I found the other one."

"What has being poor got to do with getting laid?" Pickering asked. "Just looking around, I get the idea that poor people spend a lot of time screwing."

"She's a nice girl, Pick," McCoy said. "And I copped her cherry."

"Death," Pickering said, mocking the sonorous tones of the announcer in the March of Time newsreels, "and losing cherries comes inexorably in due time to all men. And virgins."

"Screw you," McCoy said, but he was smiling.

"Which one was it?" Pickering asked.

McCoy didn't want to tell Pickering her name.

"We're going to have lunch," he said.

"I will, of course, vacate the premises," Pickering said.

"Nothing like that, goddamn it," McCoy said. "She has to work this morning. She said she would meet me for a sandwich. Someplace called the Grand Central Oyster Bar. You know where it is?''

"Oddly enough, I do. The Grand Central Oyster Bar, despite the misleading name, is in Grand Central Station.'' He stopped himself from saying what popped into his mind, that McCoy's deflowered virgin had apparently heard of the aphrodisiacal virtues of oysters. "It's right around the corner from Brooks Brothers.''

"She said twelve-thirty,'' McCoy asked. "Is that going to give us enough time?''

"Sure,'' Pickering said.

Platoon Leader Candidates Pickering and McCoy were not the first about-to-be commissioned Marine officers the salesman at Brooks Brothers had seen. More than that, he was pleased to see them. Not only was it a sale of several hundred dollars (more if the customer wanted his uniforms custom made rather than off the rack), it was a quick sale. None of the saleman's time had to be spent smiling approval as the customer tried on one item after another. There were no choices to be made. The style was set.

"Uniforms, gentlemen?'' the salesman said.

"Sure,'' one of the Marines said. "I thought it would be a good idea if you remeasured me. I have just gone through a rather interesting physical training course, and I think I ain't what I used to be.''

"Oh, you have an account with us, sir?''

"Yes,'' Pickering said. "But I'm glad you brought that up. This is Mr. McCoy. He's just come from the Orient, and he doesn't have an account. I don't think he's even had time to open a bank account, have you, Ken?''

"I've got a bank account,'' McCoy said.

"In any event, you'll have to open an account for him,'' Pickering said.

"I'm sure that won't be a problem, sir,'' the salesman said. "I didn't catch the name?''

"Pickering, Malcolm Pickering.''

"One moment, sir, and I'll get your measurements,'' the salesman said.

Pickering's measurements were filed together with his account. There were coded notations that payment was slow, but was always eventually made in full.

Brooks Brothers preferred to be paid promptly, but they were just as happy to have very large accounts (the last order from young Mr. Pickering had been for two dinner jackets, three lounge suits, one morning coat, a dozen shirts, a dozen sets of underwear, a dozen dress shirts and two pairs of patent leather evening slippers) paid whenever it was convenient for the affluent.

The fitter was summoned. Mr. Pickering was an inch and a half larger around the chest than he had been at his last fitting, and his across-the-shoulder measurement had increased by an inch.

"You know what we're supposed to have?" Mr. Pickering asked.

"Yes, sir."

"Well, measure him, then, and we can get out of here. Mr. McCoy has a pressing social engagement."

When McCoy signed the bill, he couldn't quite believe the amount. They were to be paid a $150 uniform allowance. The uniforms he had just ordered (Brooks Brothers guaranteed their delivery, if necessary by special messenger, in time for their commissioning) were going to cost him just under $900.

He had the money in the account at the Philadelphia Savings Fund Society, but it was absolutely unreal that he was going to pay nearly twice as much for uniforms as he had paid for the LaSalle.

When they were on the street, Pickering said: "I debated you getting your uniforms there," he said. "They're expensive, but you're going to need good uniforms. In the long run, they're just as cheap. If you don't have the dough, I'll lend it to you."

"I don't need your money."

"Hey, get off my back. Get two things straight. First, that you're my buddy. And second, that being rich is better than being poor, and I have no intention of apologizing to you because I was smart enough to get born to rich people."

"The last shirts I bought cost me sixty-five cents," McCoy said. "I just bought a dozen at six-ninety-five apiece. That's what they call 'unexpected.' "

"Then you had better be careful with them, hadn't you?" Pickering said. "Make a real effort not to spill mustard on them when you're eating a hot dog?"

McCoy smiled at him. He found it very difficult to stay sore at Pickering for very long.

"It's five minutes after twelve," McCoy said. "Where's Grand Central Station?"

"Yonder," Pickering said, pointing at it. "Do I get to meet your deflowered virgin?"

"That's going too fucking far!" McCoy flared.

Pickering saw icy fury in McCoy's eyes.

"For that I apologize," he said.

The ice in McCoy's eyes did not go away.

"I'm sorry, Ken," Pickering said. "You know my mouth."

"Well, lay off this subject!"

"Okay, okay," Pickering said. "I said I was sorry and I meant it. If you're free, I'll be either in the room, or '21.' Call me. If you're not otherwise occupied."

McCoy nodded and then turned and walked toward Grand Central Station. Pickering watched him. Halfway down the block, he looked over his shoulder as if to check if Pickering was following him.

Pickering pretended to be looking for a cab.

The poor sonofabitch has really got it bad for this broad. I wonder who she is?

A cab stopped, and Pickering got in.

"Grand Central," he said.

"It's right down the street, for Christ's sake!"

Pickering handed him five dollars.

"Take the long way around," he said. "I'm in no hurry."

Feeling something like a private detective shadowing a cheating husband, he stationed himself in the Oyster Bar where he felt sure he could see McCoy and the deflowered virgin, but they could not see him.

Pickering was twice surprised when the deflowered virgin showed up five minutes early, and after a moment's hesitation kissed McCoy, first impersonally and distantly, and then again on the lips, looking into his eyes, as a woman kisses her lover.

Pick Pickering had known Ernie Sage most of her life. He was surprised that she had been a virgin. And he was surprised that McCoy thought she was poor. There were some people who thought Ernie Sage had gotten her job with J. Walter Thompson, Advertising, Inc., because she had graduated summa cum laude from Sarah Lawrence. And there were those who thought it just might be because J. Walter Thompson had the account of American Personal Pharmaceutical, Inc., which spent fifteen or twenty million a year advertising its wide array of toothpastes, mouthwashes, and hair lotions. The chairman of the board of American Personal Pharmaceuticals (and supposedly, its largest stockholder) was Ernest Sage.

XIII

They stopped for gas and a hamburger, and when they started off again, Pickering took the wheel.

"What did you think of the Met?" Pickering asked.

"What?"

"Since I didn't see you from the time we walked out of Brooks Brothers until five-thirty this afternoon, I naturally presumed that you had been enriching your mind by visiting the cultural attractions of New York City. Like the Metropolitan Museum of Art."

McCoy snorted.

"We did take the Staten Island Ferry," he said. "She said it was the longest ride for a nickel in the world."

"It must have been thrilling!" Pickering said.

"Fuck you," McCoy said, cheerfully. "Since you're so fucking nosy, we spent most of the time in her apartment."

"We are now going sixty-eight miles per hour," Pickering said.

"So what? You're driving. You'll get the ticket, not me." Then he added, "But maybe you had better slow down a little. The Corps goes apeshit when people get speeding tickets. Especially in cars they're not supposed to have in the first place."

"If you were to slug me, I would probably lose control, and we would be killed in a flaming crash," Pickering said.

McCoy looked at him curiously.

"I mention that because I have something to say to you.

281

Some things—plural, two; and I want you to understand the risk you would be running by taking a poke at me.''

''You can say anything you want,'' McCoy said. ''God is in his heaven, and all is right with the world.''

''Ernie Sage really got to you, huh?''

''How do you know her name?'' McCoy demanded, suspiciously.

''I followed you,'' Pickering said. ''When you met her in Grand Central, I was lurking behind a pillar.''

''You sonofabitch!'' McCoy said. But he wasn't angry. ''I hope you got an eyeful.''

''Very touching,'' Pickering said. ''Romeo and Juliet.''

''She's really something,'' McCoy said.

''I realize this is none of my business—''

''Then don't say it,'' McCoy interrupted.

''—but since you seem to put such weight on such things, I feel obliged to tell you something about her.''

''Be careful, Pick,'' McCoy said, and there was menace in his voice.

''Ernie is named after her father,'' Pickering said. ''Ernest Sage. Ernest Sage is chairman of the board of American Personal Pharmaceutical.''

''So what?'' McCoy said. ''I never even heard of it.''

Pickering recited a dozen brand names of American Personal Pharmaceutical products.

''In other words,'' McCoy said, finally catching on, ''she's like you. Rich.''

''The rich say 'comfortable,' Ken,'' Pickering said.

''I don't care what they say,'' McCoy flared. ''Rich is rich.'' There was a moment's silence, and then McCoy said, ''Oh, goddamn!''

It was a wail of anguish.

''As I have tried to point out, being rich is not quite as bad as having leprosy,'' Pickering said. ''I'm sure that if you put your heart in it, you could learn to like it.''

''She lied to me, goddamnit. Why did she do that?'' McCoy asked. Pickering knew he hadn't heard what he had told him.

''There is a remote possibility that the lady finds you attractive,'' Pickering said. ''Marines have that reputation, I'm told.''

"She made a fucking fool out of me!" McCoy said. "God-damnit, she got me to tell her all about Norristown."

"Norristown?"

"About why I went in the Corps. About my father. Even about my slob of a sister."

"If she wanted to hear about that, then that means she's interested in everything you are. What's wrong with that?"

"Just butt out of this, all right?"

"Now I'm sorry I told you," Pickering said.

"If you hadn't, I would have made an even bigger fucking fool of myself!" McCoy said, adding a moment later, "Jesus!"

"As I said," Pickering said, "there is a remote possibility that Ernie likes you—"

"She doesn't like to be called Ernie" McCoy said.

"—for what you are. Warts and all," Pickering continued.

"Jesus, you just don't understand, do you? this isn't the first time this has happened to me. All she wanted was a stiff prick. Marines have a reputation for having stiff pricks."

"I think you're dead wrong," Pickering said.

"Fuck what you think, I know," McCoy said.

"You told me that you"—Pickering paused and then went on—"were the first."

"So what?"

"That means something to women, from what I've seen. They can only give it away once. Ernie chose to give it away to you."

"She decided to get it over with, and I was available."

"That's bullshit and you know it."

"She lied to me, you dumb fuck! A whole line of bullshit, about this being her first job, right out of school, and I thought she meant high school, and how they were paying her eighteen fifty a week, and that's why her apartment was such a dump."

"That's all true," Pickering said.

"You know what I mean," McCoy said.

"She had to lie to you, you dumb fuck," Pickering said. "You have this well-developed inferiority complex, and she was afraid you'd crawl back in your hole."

"Do me a favor, Pickering," McCoy said. "Just shut your fucking mouth!"

"Ken, I want to keep you from—"

"Shut your fucking mouth, I said! The subject is closed."

Pick Pickering decided that under the circumstances, the only thing to do was shut his fucking mouth.

(Two)

The last week of training in Platoon Leader's Course 23–41 went just as rapidly as the previous weeks had, but far more pleasantly.

In the words of Pick Pickering: "It's as if the Corps, having spent all that time and effort turning us into savages, has considered the risks they'd run if they turned us loose on an unsuspecting civilian population and is now engaged in recivilizing us."

There were several lectures on the manners and deportment expected of Marine Corps officers, and lectures on "personal finance management" and the importance of preparing a last will and testament. There was a lecture on insurance, and another on the regulations involved in the travel and transfers of officers.

They were even taken to the Officers' Club, where the intricacies of officer club membership were explained in a hands-on demonstration. They were ushered into the dining room, allowed to order whatever struck their fancy from the menu (which Pickering and McCoy found somewhat disappointing), and then shown how to sign the chit. Commissioned officers and gentlemen do not pay cash in officers' clubs.

Afterward, before they marched back to the company area, a lance corporal at a table outside the dining room permitted them to redeem the chits for cash.

But they got the idea. And they had their first meal as gentlemen—if not quite yet officers-and-gentlemen—and were thus free, since they had paid for it, not to eat it if they didn't like it. Corporal Pleasant had not even marched them over to the officers' club (Platoon Leader Candidate McCoy had been ordered to do that) and there was thus no risk that any of them would be ordered to slurp it up.

And they were given liberty at night during the last few days, from retreat to last call. Pickering and McCoy went to the slop chute, where a pitcher of beer and paper cups were available for a quarter. McCoy put away a lot of beer; but neither he nor Pick Pickering got drunk or reopened the subject of Miss Ernestine Sage.

On Wednesday afternoon, in time for the retreat formation, most of the officer uniforms were delivered. The uniform prescribed for the retreat formation was a mixture of officer and enlisted uniforms. They could not be permitted to wear officer's brimmed caps, of course, because they were not yet officers. But they wore officer's blouses and trousers, without officer-type insignia, because the primary purpose of the formation was really to see if the uniforms would fit on Friday, when they would be sworn in.

Platoon Leader Candidates Pickering and McCoy did not have their officer's uniforms on Wednesday afternoon. When this was discovered by Corporal Pleasant, it afforded him one last opportunity to offer his opinion of the intelligence, responsibility, and parentage of two of his charges. But even after that, they were not restricted to the barracks for the evening. They got the LaSalle one last time from the provost marshal's impounding lot and went off the base so that Platoon Leader Candidate Pickering could make inquiries of Brooks Brothers.

It was a lot of trouble to make a lousy phone call, but there were few pay phones available on the base, and these generally had long lines waiting to use them. And they had to get the car from the Impounding Compound rather than take a bus, because the MPs checked passes on buses. McCoy's properly stickered car and campaign hat got them past the MP at the gate without inspection.

On Thursday morning, as the platoon was preparing to march off to rehearse the graduation and swearing-in ceremony, a blue Ford station wagon drove into the company area. A large black man emerged from it, and addressed Corporal Pleasant.

"Hey, Mac!" he called out. "Brooks Brothers. I'm looking for Mr. Pickering and Mr. McCoy."

Even Pleasant seemed amused.

"The asshole with the guidon," he said, "is Mr. McCoy, and Mr. Pickering is the tall asshole in the rear rank. Wave at the nice man, Mr. Pickering."

The man from Brooks Brothers cheerfully waved back at Mr. Pickering, and then began to unload bag-wrapped uniforms, cartons of shirts, and oblong hat boxes from his station wagon. He stacked everything on the ground, and then sought out Mr. Pickering and Mr. McCoy to get his receipt signed.

After the rehearsal, as they were unpacking their uniforms and preparing their enlisted men's uniforms to be turned in, Corporal Pleasant entered the barracks.

"Attention on deck!" someone bellowed.

"Stand at ease," Corporal Pleasant said. And then he went to each man and handed him a quarter-inch-thick stack of mimeograph paper. It was their orders.

There were three different orders, or more precisely, three different paragraphs of the same general order. The first sent about half of Platoon Leader Class 23–41 to Camp LeJeune, North Carolina, "for such duty in the field as may be assigned." The second sent just about the rest of 23–41 to San Diego, California, "for such duty in the field as may be assigned."

There were only two names on the third paragraph of the General Order. It said that the following officers, having entered upon active duty at Quantico, Virginia for a period of three years, unless further extended by competent authority, were further assigned and would proceed to Headquarters, U.S. Marine Corps, Washington, D.C., "for such administrative duty as may be assigned."

"What the hell does this mean?" Pickering asked, when Pleasant had left.

McCoy had a very good idea what it meant so far as he was concerned, but he had no idea what the Corps had planned for Pickering.

"It means while the rest of these clowns are running around in the boondocks, you and I will be sitting behind desks," he said.

At 1245 hours, Friday, 28 November 1941, Platoon Leader Candidate Class 23–41 fell in for the last time. They were wearing the uniforms of second lieutenants, U.S. Marine Corps, but Corporal Pleasant took his customary position and marched them to the parade field.

The first order of business was to give them the legal right to wear the gold bars on their shoulders. They raised their right hands and swore to defend the Constitution of the United States against all enemies, foreign and domestic, and to obey the orders of such officers who were appointed over them, and that they would discharge the duties of the office upon which they were about to enter to the best of their ability, so help them God.

"Detail commander, front and center, harch!" Corporal Pleasant barked.

McCoy, to his surprise, had been appointed to this role. He marched from his position at the left of the rear rank up to Corporal Pleasant.

Pleasant saluted.

"Take the detail, sir," Pleasant said.

"Take your post, Corporal," McCoy ordered.

They exchanged salutes again. Pleasant did a right-face and marched off to take a position beside the gunny and the first sergeant, just to the right of the reviewing stand.

McCoy did an about-face.

"Right-face!" he ordered, and then, "Fow-ward, harch!"

He gave them a column right, and then another, and when they got to the proper position relative to the reviewing stand, bellowed, "Eyes, right!" and raised his hand to the brim of his new Brooks Brothers $38.75 Cap, Marine Officers, with the cord loops sewn to its crown.

At the moment he issued the command, the Quantico Band, which had been silent except for the tick-tick beat of its drummers to give them the proper marching cadence, burst into the Marine Corps Hymn.

And the moment Second Lieutenant Pickering, USMCR, snapped his head to the right, he saw two familiar faces on the reviewing stand. His father and his mother.

On the goddamned reviewing stand; not with the other parents and wives and whoever had showed up for the graduation parade. On the goddamned reviewing stand!

The officers on the reviewing stand returned McCoy's hand salute.

"Eyes, front!" McCoy ordered when he judged the last file of the formation had passed the reviewing stand. He marched them back to where they had originally been.

The officers marched off the reviewing stand, in order of rank. When the colonel got to McCoy, McCoy saluted.

"Put your detail at rest, Lieutenant," the colonel ordered.

"Puh-rade, rest!"

They moved their feet the prescribed distance apart, and put their hands and arms rigidly in the small of their backs.

"Congratulations," the colonel said to McCoy. "Welcome to the officer corps of the U.S. Marine Corps."

He shook his hand and simultaneously handed him a rolled-up tube of paper, which contained his diploma and his commission. Then, leaving McCoy at parade rest, the colonel, trailed by his entourage, went down the ranks and repeated the process, exactly, for each man.

Finally, the entourage returned to the reviewing stand.

"Lieutenant," the colonel called. "You may dismiss these gentlemen."

McCoy saluted, did an about-face, and barked, "Atten-hut. Dis-missed."

23–41 just stood there for a moment, as if unwilling to believe that it was actually over and that they were now in law and fact commissioned officers and gentlemen of the United States Marine Corps.

And then one of them yelped, probably, McCoy thought, that flat-faced asshole from Texas A&M who was always making strange noises. That broke the trance, and they started shaking hands and pounding each other on the back.

Captain Jack NMI Stecker walked off the reviewing stand, and then across the field to McCoy. As he approached McCoy, Pickering started for the reviewing stand. McCoy wondered where the hell he was going, but with Stecker advancing on him, there was no chance to ask.

He saluted Stecker, who offered his hand.

"Despite what some people think of China Marines, Lieutenant," Stecker said, "every once in a while some of them make pretty good officers. I think you will."

"Thank you, sir," McCoy said.

"I thought you might need a ride to the Impounding Compound," Stecker said.

"I got the car last night, sir," he said.

"Then in that case, McCoy, just 'good luck.' "

He offered his hand, they exchanged salutes, and Stecker walked away.

McCoy saw that most of 23–41 had formed a line by the reviewing stand. Corporal Pleasant was saluting each one of them. They then handed him a dollar. It was a tradition.

Fuck him, McCoy decided. Pleasant had been entirely too willing to kick him when he was down. And he wasn't even that good a corporal.

I'm not going to give the sonofabitch a dollar to have him salute me. He'll head right for the NCO Club with it and sit around making everybody laugh with stories about the incompetent assholes the Corps had just made officers.

And then he saw that Pick Pickering was not in the line. He was standing with a couple, the man well dressed, the woman in a full-length fur coat. Obviously, Pick's folks had come to see their son graduate. McCoy started to walk back to the company area.

Pickering ran after him and caught up with him.

"I want you to meet my mother and dad," Pick said.

"Wouldn't I be in the way?"

"Don't be an asshole, asshole," Pick said, and grabbed McCoy's arm and propelled him in the direction of the reviewing stand.

"I didn't see you giving Pleasant his dollar," Pickering said.

"I didn't," McCoy said. "Just because we're now wearing bars doesn't make him any less of a vicious asshole."

"My, you do hold a grudge, don't you, Lieutenant?" Pickering said.

"You bet your ass, I do," McCoy said.

Fleming Pickering smiled and put his hand out as they walked up.

"I knew who you were, of course," he said.

"Sir?" McCoy asked, confused.

"One Marine corporal can always spot another, even in a sea of clowns," Fleming Pickering said, pleased with himself.

"Flem!" Mrs. Pickering protested. She smiled at McCoy and gave him her hand. "You'll have to excuse my husband, his being a Marine corporal was the one big thrill of his life. I'm pleased to finally meet you, Ken . . . I can call you 'Ken,' mayn't I? . . . Malcolm's written so much about you."

"Yes, ma'am," McCoy said.

"I would like nothing better," Fleming Pickering said, "than to sit over a long lunch and have you tell me how you shepherded the lieutenant here around the boondocks, but we have a plane to catch.''

"I'd forgotten about that," Pick said.

"This time tomorrow, we will be high above the blue Pacific," Fleming Pickering said. "Bound for sunny Hawaii. I was originally going by myself, but then some scoundrel told my wife about the girls in the grass skirts.''

"I wasn't worried about the hula-hula girls," Pick's mother replied. "What concerned me was the way you behave on a ship. If they serve eight meals a day—and Pacific-Orient does—and I wasn't along, you'd eat all eight of them, and they'd have to take you off the ship in a wheelbarrow.''

"You're coming back by ship?" Pick asked. "I thought you were flying both ways.''

"No," Pick's father said. "I put off the meeting in San Francisco until the twentieth. That way, we can board ship in Honolulu on the tenth and still make it back in plenty of time.''

Pick nodded his understanding.

McCoy finally figured out what they were talking about. He had been a little impressed that Pick's parents would come all the way to Virginia just to see him get sworn in. But, so far as they were concerned, that was like a trip to the corner drugstore for cigarettes. They were about to fly to Hawaii. The only thing that had surprised Pick about that was they weren't going to fly both ways.

Pick and his family were people from a different world.

A world like Ernestine Sage's. A world where I don't belong, even with a gold bar on my collar.

(Three)
Washington, D.C.
1600 Hours, 28 November 1941

Before Pickering's parents had showed up, it had been understood between McCoy and Pickering that immediately after they were sworn in, they would drive to Washington. The LaSalle was already loaded with their luggage.

He had been sure that would change because of his parents. But that hadn't happened. Pick shook hands with his father, allowed himself to be kissed by his mother, and then the Pickerings left. Taking trips halfway around the world was obviously routine stuff for them.

Pick and McCoy, as originally planned, then simply backed from the parade field to where McCoy had parked the LaSalle by the barracks, got in, and drove off.

There were no farewell handshakes with the others in 23–41. Because he had been on Pleasant's and the gunny's shit list, the others had most of the time avoided McCoy as if he were a leper. And they had avoided Pickering, too, because he was McCoy's buddy. And there had been whispers at the end about the two of them getting "administrative duty" in Washington rather than "in the field" at LeJeune and San Diego.

Pickering thought about this as they got in the LaSalle: If somewhere down the pike, Class 23–41 sent him an invitation to its twentieth reunion, he would send his regrets.

This time, they were stopped by the MP at the gate. First the MP waved them through, then he saw the bars and saluted, and finally he stepped into the road in front of them with his hand up.

He saluted as McCoy rolled down the window.

"Excuse me, sir, is this your car?"

"Yes, it is," McCoy said.

"It's got an enlisted decal, sir."

"That's because, until about twenty minutes ago, I was enlisted," McCoy said.

The MP smiled broadly. "I thought that was you," he said, admiringly. "You been sneaking in and out of here all the time you was in the Platoon Leader Course, haven't you?"

"How could you even suspect such a thing?" McCoy asked.

The MP came to attention and saluted.

"You may pass out, sir," he said. "Thank you, sir."

A minute later, after they had left the base, McCoy said, "I guess I better stop someplace and scrape that sticker off."

"And then what?"

"What do you mean, then what?"

"What are we going to do when we get to Washington?"

"I thought you'd be taking some leave," McCoy said.

"No," Pickering said. "I'd rather report in. I want to find out what's planned for me. How, exactly, do we do that?"

"Today is a day of duty," McCoy explained, patiently. "We get a day's travel time to Washington. That carries us up through midnight tomorrow. So long as we report in by midnight on Sunday, that makes Sunday a day of duty. So about eleven o'clock Sunday night, we'll find out where it is."

"You're not going home?" Pickering asked, and when McCoy shook his head, went on, "Or to New York?"

"No," McCoy said, stiffly.

"I thought maybe you'd come to your senses about going to New York," Pickering said.

"You miss the point," McCoy said. "I have come to my senses. And that's the end of that particular subject."

"Okay, so we'll go to the Lafayette," Pickering said. "It's a little stuffy, but it has a very nice French restaurant."

"Another hotel you own?"

"Grandpa owns it, actually," Pickering said. "It's right across from the White House. Do you suppose you can find the White House without a map, Lieutenant?"

"No, I've never been in Washington before, and I don't have a map, and I'm not going to sponge again off you or your 'Grandpa,' " McCoy said.

"Very well," Pickering said. "I will stay in the Lafayette, and you can stay in whatever flea-bag with hot-and-cold running cockroaches strikes your fancy, just so long as I know where to find you when it is time for us to go to the Marine Barracks and sign in. I hate to tell you this, Lieutenant, you being an officer and a gentleman and all, but you have a great talent for being a horse's ass."

McCoy laughed.

"You're sure you want to sign in early?" he asked. "It may be a long time until they offer you any leave again."

"I need to know what this 'administrative' duty is all about," Pickering said. "I don't like the sound of it."

"What's the difference?" McCoy asked. "Whatever it is, they're not offering you a choice."

"Indulge me," Pickering said. "Take me along with you, so that you can explain things to me. And for Christ's sake, stop being an ass about being comped in one of our hotels."

"Being what?"

" 'Comped,' " Pickering explained. " 'Complimentary accommodations.' It's part of the business. If you work for Foster Hotels, you're entitled to stay in Foster Hotels when you're away from home.''

"I don't work for Foster Hotels," McCoy argued.

"That's all right, you're with me," Pickering said. "And I am the apple of Grandpa's eye. Will you stop being an ass?"

"It makes me uncomfortable," McCoy said.

"So do you, when you pick your nose," Pickering said. "But if you agree to stay in Grandpa's hotel, you can pick your nose all you want, and I won't say a thing.''

The doorman at the Lafayette knew Pickering by sight. He rushed around and opened the door with all the pomp shown a respected guest. But what he said, was, "Jesus, Pick, are you for real? Or is there a costume party?"

"You are speaking, sir, to an officer and a gentleman of the U.S. Marine Corps," Pickering said. "You will not have to prostrate yourself; kneeling will suffice." He turned to McCoy. "Ken, say hello to Jerry Toltz, another old pal of mine. We bellhopped here all through one hot, long, miserable summer.''

"How long are you going to be here?" the doorman asked.

"I don't know. Probably some time."

"They know you're coming?"

"I don't think so," Pickering said.

"I thought I would have heard," Jerry Toltz said. "The house is full, Pick.''

"We need someplace to stay," Pickering said.

"Well, if they don't have anything for you, you and your pal can stay with me. There's a convertible couch."

"Thank you," Pickering said.

"Will you be needing the car?"

"Yeah," Pickering said. "I'm glad you asked. Don't bury it. We have to go out.''

"That's presuming you can get in," the doorman said, and motioned for a bellboy and told him to park the car in the alley.

The man behind the reception desk also knew Malcolm Pickering.

He gave him his hand.

"You will be professionally delighted to hear the house is full," he said. "Personally, that may not be such good news.

How are you? It's good to see you. Your grand-dad told me you were in the Marines.''

"Good to see you," Pickering said. "This is my friend Ken McCoy."

They shook hands.

"How long have you been an officer?" the manager asked.

"It must be, four, five hours now," Pickering said.

"And I don't have a bed for you! All I can do is call around. The Sheraton owes me a couple of big favors."

"What about maid's room in the bridal suite?"

"There's only a single in there," the manager protested.

"Put in a cot, then," Pickering said. "I'll sleep on that."

"I'll probably be able to find something for you tomorrow," the manager said.

"Lieutenant McCoy and I are going to be here for some time," Pickering said. "What about one of the residential hotels? I really hate to comp if we can rent it."

"There's a waiting list for every residential room in Washington," the manager said. "If you don't want to sleep on a park bench, you'll have to stay here. I'll come up with a bed-sitter for you in a day or two. Unless you need two bedrooms?"

"Lieutenant McCoy and I will not know how to handle the luxury of a bed-sitter. We have been sharing one room with thirty others."

"You want to go up now?"

"No, what we want to do now is locate the Marine Barracks."

The manager drew them a map.

They arrived at the Marine Barracks, coincidentally, just as the regularly scheduled Friday evening formal retreat parade was beginning. The music was provided by the Marine Corps Band, in dress blues.

It's like a well-choreographed ballet, Pickering thought as he watched the ceremony (the intricacies of which were now familiar) progress with incredible precision.

I'll be damned, McCoy thought, *these guys are really as good as they're supposed to be.*

There were Marines in dress blues stationed at intervals around the manicured grass of the parade ground. Their primary purpose, McCoy saw, was more practical than decora-

tive. From time to time, one or more of them had to restrain
eager tourists from rushing out onto the field to take a snap-
shot of the marching and drilling troops, or just to get a better
look.

When the Marine Band had finally marched off, the perimeter guard near them, a lance corporal, left his post.

When he came to Pickering and McCoy, he saluted snappily.

"Good evening, sir!" he barked.

"Good evening," McCoy heard himself say.

Something bothered him. After a moment, he realized what
it was. When the kid had tossed him the highball, he had
done so automatically. The kid had seen a couple of officers,
and he had saluted them. There had been nothing in his eyes
that suggested he suspected he was saluting a China Marine
corporal in a lieutenant's uniform.

I really am an officer, McCoy thought. *Until right now, it
was sort of play-acting. But now it's real. When that kid
saluted me, I felt like an officer.*

Well, this is the place to have it happen, he thought. *At the
Marine Barracks in Washington after a formal retreat parade, with the smell of the smoke from the retreat cannon still
in my nose, and the tick-tick of the drums of the Marine Band
fading as it marches away.*

(Four)

On Saturday, Pickering and McCoy drove around Washington. Pickering was at first amused at the notion of playing
tourist, but then he realized it wasn't so bad after all. He saw
more of Washington with McCoy than he'd seen during the
entire summer he'd spent bellhopping at the Lafayette.

And he came to understand that McCoy was doing more
than satisfying an idle curiosity: He was reconnoitering the
terrain. He wasn't sure if it was intentional, but there was no
question that's what it was. It occurred to him again, as it had
several times at Quantico, that McCoy was really an odd
duck in society, as for example a Jesuit priest is an odd
duck. They weren't really like the other ducks swimming
around on the lake. They swam with a purpose, answering
commands not heard by other people. A Jesuit's course through
the waters of life was guided by God; McCoy's by what he

believed—consciously or subconsciously—was expected of
him by the Marine Corps.

They spent most of Sunday at the Smithsonian Institution.
And again, Pickering was pleased that they had come. He
was surprised at the emotion he felt when he saw the tiny
little airplane Charles Lindbergh had flown to Paris and when
he was standing before the faded and torn flag that had flown
"in the rockets' red glare" over Fort McHenry.

At half-past ten on Sunday night (Pickering was still not
fully accustomed to thinking in military time and had to do
the arithmetic in his head to come up with 2230), Second
Lieutenants M. Pickering and K.J. McCoy presented their
orders to the duty officer at the Marine Barracks and held
themselves ready for duty.

"Your reporting in early is probably going to screw things
up with personnel," the officer of the day said. "I'll send
word over there that you're here, and they'll call you at the
BOQ [Bachelor Officers' Quarters]."

"We're in a hotel in town," Pickering said.

"Okay. Probably even better. As you'll find out, the Corps
is scattered all over town. What hotel?"

"The Lafayette," Pickering said.

"Very nice," the officer of the day said. "What's the
room number?"

"I don't know," Pickering said and started to smile.

"Then how do you know where to sleep when you get
there?" the officer of the day asked, sarcastically.

"Actually, we're in the bridal suite," Pickering said. And
then, quickly, he added: "In the maid's room off the bridal
suite."

At 0915 the next morning, the telephone in the maid's
room of the bridal suite rang. It was a captain from personnel.
Lieutenant Pickering was ordered to report, as soon as he
could get there, to Brigadier General D.G. McInerny, whose
office was in Building F at the Anacostia Naval Air Station.
Before McCoy's reconnoitering over the weekend, Pickering
had only a vague idea where Anacostia Naval Air Station
was. Now he knew. He even knew where to find Building F.
He had seen the building numbers—or rather building letters—in
front of the office buildings there.

Lieutenant McCoy was to report to a Major Almond, in

Room 26, Building T-2032, one of the temporary buildings in front of the Smithsonian. They knew where that was, too, as a result of McCoy's day-long scoping of the terrain.

"You drop me there," McCoy said. "I can walk back here. Anacostia's to hell and gone."

Pickering found Building F without difficulty. It was one of several buildings immediately behind the row of hangars. Three minutes later, to his considerable surprise, he was standing at attention before the desk of Brigadier General D.G. McInerney, USMC. Unable to believe that a brigadier general of Marines would have thirty seconds to spare for a second lieutenant, he had simply presumed that whatever they were going to have him do here, his orders would come from a first lieutenant.

General McInerney looked like a general. There were three rows of ribbons on his tunic below the gold wings of a Naval Aviator. He didn't have much hair, and what there was of it was cut so close to the skull that the bumps and the freckles on the skin were clearly visible.

The general, Pickering decided as he stood at attention, was not very friendly, and he was unabashedly studying him with interest.

"So you're Malcolm Pickering," General McInerney said finally. "You must take after your mother. You don't look at all like your dad."

Pickering was so startled that for a moment his eyes flickered from their prescribed focus six inches over the general's head.

"You may sit, Mr. Pickering," General McInerney said. "Would you like some coffee?"

"Yes, sir," Pick Pickering said. "Thank you, sir."

A sergeant appeared, apparently in reply to the pushing of an unseen buzzer button.

"This is Lieutenant Pickering, Sergeant Wallace," General McInerney said. "He will probably be around here for a while."

The sergeant offered his hand.

"How do you do, sir?" he said.

"Lieutenant Pickering's father and I were in the war to end all wars together," General McInerney said, dryly.

"Is that so?" the sergeant said.

"And the lieutenant's father called me and, for auld lang

syne, Sergeant Wallace, asked me to take care of his boy. And of course, I said I would.''

''I understand, sir.''

Pickering felt sick and furious.

''I think we can start off by getting the lieutenant a cup of coffee.''

''Aye, aye, sir,'' Sergeant Wallace said. ''How would you like your coffee, Lieutenant?''

''Black, please,'' Pickering said.

''Aye, aye, sir.''

''You get fixed up all right with a BOQ?'' General McInerney inquired. ''Or are you perhaps staying in a hotel? A Foster hotel?''

''I'm in the Lafayette, sir.''

''I thought you might be,'' General McInerney said. ''I mean, what the hell, if your family owns hotels . . . how many hotels does your family own, Lieutenant?''

''There are forty-two, sir,'' Pick said.

''What the hell, if your family owns forty-two hotels, why not stay in one of them, right? There's certainly no room service in the BOQ, is there?''

''No, sir.''

The coffee was delivered.

''Thank you, Sergeant,'' Pickering said.

''Certainly, sir,'' Sergeant Wallace said.

''I guess it took a little getting used to, not having someone to fetch coffee for you. At Quantico, I mean?'' General McInerney asked.

''Yes, sir,'' Pickering said.

''Well, at least here, you'll have Sergeant Wallace and several other enlisted men around for that sort of thing. It won't be quite like home, but it will be a little better than running around in the boondocks with a rifle platoon.''

''Yes, sir,'' Pickering said.

''It's not quite what the Corps had in mind for you,'' General McInerney said, ''but I've arranged for you to be my junior aide-de-camp. How does that sound?''

''Permission to speak frankly, sir?'' Pickering asked.

''Of course,'' General McInerney said.

''My father had no right to ask you to do anything for me,'' Pickering said. ''I knew nothing about it. If I had any idea that he was even thinking about something like that, I would have told him to keep his nose out of my business."

"Is that so?" General McInerney said, doubtfully.

"Yes, Sir," Pickering said fervently, "that's so. And with respect, Sir, I do not want to be your aide-de-camp."

"I don't recall asking whether or not you wanted to be my aide. I presented that as a fact. I have gone to considerable trouble arranging for it."

"Sir, I feel that I would make you a lousy aide."

"You are now a Marine officer. When a Marine officer is told to do something, he is expected to reply 'Aye, aye, sir' and set about doing it to the best of his ability."

"I am aware of that, sir," Pick said. "But I didn't think it would ever be applied in a situation where the order was to pass canapés."

"You're telling me that you would prefer to be running around in the swamp at Camp LeJeune to being the aide of a general officer?" General McInerney asked, on the edge of indignation.

"Yes, sir, that's exactly my position," Pickering said. "I respectfully request that I not be assigned as your aide."

"I am sorry to tell you, Lieutenant," General McInerney said, "that I have no intention of going back to Headquarters, USMC, and tell them that I have now changed my mind and don't want you as my aide after all. As I said, arranging for your assignment as my aide wasn't easy." He waited until that had a moment to sink in, and then went on: "So where would you say that leaves us, Lieutenant?"

"It would appear, sir," Pick said, "that until I am able to convince the general that he has made an error, the general will have a very reluctant aide-de-camp."

General McInerney snorted, and then he chuckled.

"Lieutenant, you are a brand-new officer. Could you take a little advice from one who has been around the Corps a long time?"

"Yes, sir."

"Don't jump until you know where you're jumping from, and where you're going to land," General McInerney said. "In other words, until you have all the intelligence you can get your hands on, and have time to evaluate it carefully."

"Yes, sir," Pick said, annoyed that he was getting a lecture on top of everything else.

"In this case, the facts as I presented them to you seem to have misled you."

"Sir?"

"Your dad is indeed concerned about you, and he did in fact call me and ask me to look after you. But what he was concerned about was the possibility that some chairwarmer would review your records, see what you did as a civilian, and assign you appropriately. He said he didn't want you to spend your hitch in the Corps as a mess officer. Or a housing officer. And when I checked, that's exactly what those sonsofbitches had in mind for you. If I had not gone over there, Lieutenant, and had you assigned to me, you would have reported for duty this morning to the officers' club at the Barracks."

Pick's eyes widened.

"So, because your Dad and I are old buddies—we were corporals together at Belleau Wood—I am protecting your ass. I think you would make a lousy aide, too. You will be my junior aide only until such time as I decide what else the Corps can do with you."

"I seem to have made an ass of myself, sir," Pickering said.

"We sort of expect that from second lieutenants," General McInerney said, reasonably. "The only thing you really did wrong was underestimate your father. Did you really think he would try to grease the ways for you?"

"My father is married to my mother, sir," Pickering said.

"I take your point," General McInerney said. "I have the privilege of your mother's acquaintance."

"May I ask a question, sir?"

"Sure."

"Was my moving into the hotel a real blunder?"

"Not so far as I'm concerned," General McInerney said. "I understand your situation."

"I was thinking of . . . my best friend, I suppose is the best way to describe him. I sort of pressured him to move in with me."

"I see," McInerney said. "Another hotelier? Classmate at school?"

"No, sir. He was a China Marine, a corporal, before we went through the platoon leader's course."

McInerney thought that over a moment before he replied.

"I think it might be a good idea if he moved into the BOQ," he said. "There would certainly be curiosity. It could even turn into an Intelligence matter. Where would a second lieutenant, an ex–China Marine enlisted man, get the money to take a room in the Lafayette? It could be explained, of course, but the last thing a second lieutenant needs is to have it getting around that Intelligence is asking questions about his personal life."

"Thank you, sir," Pickering said. "I was afraid it might be something like that. May I ask another question?"

"Shoot."

"How long will I be assigned here? I mean, you said something about deciding what to do with me. How long will that take?"

"That depends on what you would like to do, and whether or not you're qualified to do it. Presumably, you learned at Quantico that leading a platoon of riflemen is not quite the fun and games the recruiter may have painted it."

"Yes, sir."

"Have you ever thought of going to flight school?" General McInerney asked.

"No, sir," Pickering confessed.

General McInerney was a little disappointed to hear that, but decided that Fleming Pickering's kid meant what he said: that he simply had not thought of going to flight school—not that he had considered the notion and discarded it because he didn't like the idea of flying.

"That's an option," General McInerney said. "But only if you could pass the flight physical. On your way out, have Sergeant Wallace set up an appointment for a flight physical. And then take the rest of the day off, son, and get yourself settled. I'm talking about your friend, too, of course."

"I'll check out of the hotel, too, of course," Pickering said.

"Don't do it on my account," General McInerney said. "So far as I'm concerned, I'd be delighted to have you in there, in case my wife and I wanted to make reservations for dinner."

General McInerney stood up and offered his hand.

"Welcome aboard," he said. "You're your father's son, and that's intended as a compliment."

XIV

McCoy had seen quite a few office doors during his time in
the Corps. Most of them had a sign announcing in some detail
not only what function was being carried out behind the door,
but by whom.

The door to room 26 didn't even have a room number.
McCoy had to find it by counting upward from room number
2, which had a sign: OFFICER'S HEAD.

He thought he'd gotten it wrong even then, for what he
thought was room 26 had two sturdy locks on it—a storeroom, in other words, full of mimeograph paper and quart
bottles of ink. But with no other option that he could think of,
he knocked on it.

As soon as he knocked, however, he heard movement
inside, then the sound of dead-bolt locks being operated, and
a moment later the door opened just wide enough to reveal
the face of a grim-looking man. He said nothing, but the
expression on his face asked McCoy to state his business.

"I'm looking for room 26," McCoy said.

The man nodded, waiting for McCoy to go on.

"I was ordered to report to room 26," McCoy said.

"What's your name, please?" the man asked.

"McCoy."

"May I see your identification, please?" the man asked.

McCoy handed over his brand-new officer's identification
card. The man looked at it carefully, then at McCoy's face,
and then opened the door wide enough for McCoy to enter.

Inside was a small area, just enough for a desk. On the other side of the room there was another door, again with double dead-bolt locks.

When the man walked to the telephone on the desk, McCoy saw that he had a .45 Colt 1911A1 on his hip. On his tail, really, and not in a GI holster, but in sort of a skeleton holster through which the front part of the pistol stuck out.

If he was wearing a jacket, McCoy thought, *you'd never know he had a pistol.*

"I have Lieutenant McCoy here," the man said to the telephone. "He's not due in until 15 December."

There was a pause.

"Well, shit, I suppose everybody's been told but us. What does he get?"

There was obviously a reply, but McCoy couldn't hear it. The man put the telephone down, and then reached into his desk and came out with a clipboard and a small plastic card affixed to an alligator clip.

"Sign here, please," he said. "Just your signature. Not your rank."

McCoy signed his name.

The man handed him the plastic card.

"You use this until we get you your own," he said. "Pin it on your blouse jacket."

McCoy looked at it before he pinned it on. It was a simple piece of plastic-covered cardboard. It said "VISITOR" and there was the insignia of the Navy Department. It was overprinted with purple stripes.

"That's good anywhere in the building," the man said. "Or almost everywhere. But it's not good for ONI [Office of Naval Intelligence]. Until you get your credentials, you'd better avoid going over to ONI."

"Okay," McCoy said. wondering what was going on.

The man stuck out his hand.

"I'm Sergeant Ruttman," he said. "We didn't expect you until the fifteenth."

"So I heard you say," McCoy said.

"You just went through that course at Quantico, right?"

"That's right," McCoy said.

"Pain in the ass?"

"Yes, it was," McCoy said.

"They want to send me," Sergeant Ruttman said. "But I've been putting off going. I figure if they really want me to take a commission, they can give it to me. I already know about chickenshit."

"Good luck," McCoy said, wondering if Ruttman was just running off at the mouth, or whether he was telling the truth.

Ruttman replaced the clipboard in his desk, and then took keys from his pocket and unlocked both of the locks in the door.

"Follow me," he said.

Beyond the door was a strange assortment of machinery. There were typewriters and other standard office equipment. But there were also cameras; what McCoy guessed was a blueprint machine; a large photograph print dryer, a stainless-steel-drum affair larger than a desk; and a good deal of other equipment that looked expensive and complicated. McCoy couldn't even guess the purpose of some of it.

The equipment was being manned by a strange-looking assortment of people, all in civilian clothes, and all of them armed. Most of them had standard web belts and issue flapped holsters for the .45 1911A1s they carried, but some carried the pistols the way Ruttman carried his, and others were armed with snub-nosed Smith & Wesson revolvers.

"What is this place, Sergeant?"

"The thing you're going to have to keep in mind, Lieutenant, is that it's just like boot camp at Parris Island. If they think you should know something, they'll tell you. Otherwise it's none of your business."

He turned his attention from McCoy to the drawer of a desk. He took a loose-leaf notebook from it and two blank forms, one of them a card with purple stripes like his "VISITOR" badge, and the other a Navy identification card of some sort.

"Before I fuck things up," he called out, raising his voice, "has anybody made out any of these and not logged them in the book?"

There was no response to the inquiry, and he put both identification cards in a typewriter and typed briefly and rapidly on them.

"I need an officer to sign these!" he called out again, and one of the civilians, a slight, tall man, walked to the desk.

Despite the Smith & Wesson .38 snub-nose revolver on his hip, he looked like a clerk. He waited until Ruttman finished typing, and then took the card from him and scrawled his name on it. Then he looked at McCoy.

"You're McCoy?" he asked.

"Yes, sir."

"Not that I'm not glad to see you, but you weren't due to report in until the fifteenth."

"I reported in early, sir."

"You'll regret that," the officer said. " 'Abandon hope, all ye who enter here!' "

He walked back where he had come from. McCoy saw that he was making notations on a large map. Next to the map were aerial photographs and a stack of teletype paper liberally stamped "SECRET" in large letters.

"You want to sign this, Lieutenant?" Sergeant Ruttman asked.

There was space for two signatures on the identification: the holder and the issuing officer. The tall skinny civilian had already signed it. According to the card, he was Lieutenant Colonel F.L. Rickabee, USMC. He sure as Christ didn't look like any lieutenant colonel McCoy had ever seen before. He didn't even look much like a Marine.

"Just your signature, again," Ruttman said. "No rank."

"You didn't give me back my ID card," McCoy said.

"You don't get it back," Ruttman said, and then apparently had doubts. He raised his voice. "Does he get his ID card back?"

"No," the tall thin man who looked like a clerk called back. "Not anymore. They changed the policy."

As if McCoy hadn't heard the exchange, Ruttman said, "You don't get it back, Lieutenant."

The tall skinny clerk-type had another thought and turned from his map and SECRET teletype messages.

"How long is it going to take to get him his credentials?"

"I'm just about to take his picture," Ruttman said.

"Today, you mean? He'll get his credentials today?"

"He'll have them by lunchtime," Ruttman said, confidently.

"Okay," the clerk-type said, and returned his attention to the map.

Based on the total absence of military courtesy (Ruttman

had not once said "sir," much less "aye, aye, sir," to him, and the clerk-type hadn't seemed to care) McCoy decided that the clerk-type was not Lieutenant Colonel F.L. Rickabee, USMC. It was common practice for junior officers to sign senior officers' names to routine forms, sometimes initialing the signature and sometimes not. He went further with his theory: The tall skinny clerk was probably a warrant officer. Warrant officers were old-time noncoms, generally with some special skill. They wore officer's uniforms, could go to the Officers' Club, and were entitled to a salute, but the most senior chief warrant officer ranked below the most junior second lieutenant. And a warrant officer, particularly a new one, would probably not get all excited if an old-time noncom like Ruttman didn't treat him as if he was a lieutenant or a captain.

Ruttman stood McCoy against a backdrop, at which was pointed a Speed Graphic four-by-five-inch plate camera.

"Take off your blouse and your field scarf, and the bars," Ruttman ordered, "and put this on."

He handed McCoy a soiled, well-worn, striped necktie.

McCoy looked at him in disbelief.

"The way I'll shoot this," Ruttman explained, "that shirt'll look just like an Arrow."

He took McCoy's picture twice, "to make sure I get it," then led him to a table where he inked his fingers. He put his thumb print on both of the ID cards, and then took another full set on a standard fingerprint card.

Ruttman handed him a towel and bottle of alcohol to clean his hands, and then said, "That's it, here, Lieutenant. Now you go see Major Almond. He's in the last office down the passageway."

There was no sign hanging on Major J.J. Almond's door, either; but aside from that, he was what McCoy expected a Marine major to be. He was a short man, but muscular, and so erect he seemed taller than he was. And he was in uniform. His desk was shipshape, and two flags were on poles behind his desk, the Marine flag and the national colors.

And to the left of Major Almond's desk was a door with another sign: LT. COL. F.L. RICKABEE, USMC, COMMANDING. It was clear to McCoy now that he'd just gone through some sort of administrative service office where they made out ID cards and did that sort of thing, and that he was now about to face his new commanding officer.

"Let me say, McCoy," Major J.J. Almond said, "that I appreciate your appearance. You look and conduct yourself as a Marine officer should. As you may have noticed, there is a lamentable tendency around here to let things slip. Because of what we do here, we can't run this place like a line company. But we go too far, I think, far too often. I am going to rely on you, Lieutenant, to both set an example for the men and to correct, on the spot, whomever you see failing to live up to the standards of the Corps."

"Aye, aye, sir," McCoy said.

"Now, before we get started, you reported in early."

"Yes, sir."

"You are entitled to a fourteen-day leave. If it is your intention to apply for that leave now that you have reported aboard, I would like to know that now."

"No, sir."

"You're in the BOQ at the Barracks, I presume?"

"No, sir."

"Where are you?"

"In a hotel, sir."

"I don't want to go through this, McCoy, pulling one fact after another from you."

"I'm in the Hotel Lafayette, sir. Sharing a room with another officer, sir. Lieutenant Malcolm Pickering, sir."

"Well, that is fortuitous," Major Almond announced. "It is the policy of this command that both officer and enlisted personnel live off the base. You will draw pay in lieu of quarters. Will that pay be enough to pay for your hotel room?"

"Yes, sir."

"What's your room number?" Almond asked. "And I'll need the hotel telephone number."

"I don't know the phone number, sir," McCoy said. "We're living in the maid's room of the bridal suite, sir."

Major Almond smiled and nodded approvingly.

"Very enterprising," he said. "I wondered how you could afford to live in the Lafayette."

He reached into his desk drawer and came out with a three-inch-thick manila folder. He saw his name lettered on it, and that it was stamped "SECRET—COMPLETE BACK-GROUND INVESTIGATION."

"This is the report of the FBI's investigation of you, Lieutenant," he said. "It is classified SECRET, and you are not authorized access to it. I show it to you to show how carefully they have gone into your background."

McCoy had no idea what was going on.

Major Almond then handed him a printed form.

"In normal circumstances, the procedure would have been for you to complete this form before the FBI did its complete background check. But the circumstances have not been normal. Time was important. The FBI had to, so to speak, start from scratch using existing records. So what has happened is that I have had our clerks prepare your background statement using existing records and the FBI report. Are you following me, Lieutenant?"

"Yes, sir," McCoy said. "I think so, sir."

"The standing operating procedure requires that your completed background statement be in the files," Major Almond said. "Now, while I am sure that the FBI has done their usual thorough job, I am nearly as sure that they have missed something. What I want you to do is take your background statement to the desk over there and go over it with great care. If there is anything on it that is not absolutely correct, I want you to mark it. We will then discuss it. More important, I want you to pay particular attention to omissions, particularly of a nonflattering nature."

"Sir?"

"I want you to make sure that all the blemishes on your record are visible," Major Almond said. "The next step in the administrative procedure is to evaluate your record and judge whether or not you are qualified to be granted a top secret, and other, security clearances. If it came out later that there are blemishes which do not appear on the record, that would cause trouble, do you understand?"

"Yes, sir."

"The sergeant will give you a lined pad and pencils," Major Almond said. "Make your notations on the lined pad, not on the form."

"Aye, aye, sir," McCoy said.

"Work steadily, but carefully," Major Almond said. "Time is of the essence."

"Aye, aye, sir."

McCoy wondered if they had found out that he'd been under charges in Shanghai about the Italian marines, and whether or not he should tell them if they weren't. The charges had been dropped. Did that mean they didn't count? Was getting charged with murder a "blemish" if they dropped the charges?

He sat down at the desk and looked at the form.

It was immediately apparent that they knew more about him than he knew himself. He didn't know his mother's date of birth, or his father's, but they were in the blocks on the form. And so were Anne-Marie's and Tommy's, and even Anne-Marie's husband's.

(Two)

An hour later, he had worked his way through the six-page form to a section headed, "Arrests, Detentions, Indictments, Charges, et cetera."

They knew about the charges in China. (Not Prosecuted, initial facts in error.) And they knew about the old man signing the warrant for his arrest (Nol prossed on condition enlistment, USMC.) And they knew about speeding tickets, reckless driving, and even two charges of malicious mischief and being found in possession of a Daisy Red Ryder BB Gun in violation of the city ordinances of Norristown, Pa. (Nol prossed. BB Gun confiscated. Released in custody of parents.)

It was absolutely incredible how much they knew about him. He wondered what was going to happen when whoever reviewed his records came to the business about the Marines in China. Was that going to keep him from getting a security clearance?

The door opened and the tall skinny clerk-type walked in.

Without knocking, McCoy saw. In the same moment Major Almond rose to his feet.

He is about to get his ass eaten out.

The clerk-type walked toward the door of Lieutenant Colonel F.L. Rickabee and put his hand on the knob. For all intents and purposes he looked as if he was going to barge in there, too, without knocking. Then he stopped, turned to McCoy, and smiled.

"Come on in, McCoy," he said. "Whatever that is, it'll wait." Then he looked at Major Almond. "What the hell is that?" he demanded.

"Sir, it's Lieutenant McCoy's background statement."

"Isn't that a waste of his time?" Rickabee demanded sharply. "And ours? When I read the FBI report I had the feeling they knew everything there is to know about him."

Major Almond seemed to have difficulty framing a reply.

"I know, Jake," Colonel Rickabee said, more kindly. "It's regulation."

"Yes, sir."

"Come on in, McCoy, and you, too, Jake. It'll save time."

"Aye, aye, sir," Major Almond said.

Rickabee sat down behind his desk.

"For openers, McCoy, despite that inexcusable outburst of mine, let me make it clear that Major Almond is what keeps this lash-up of ours functioning. Without him, it would be complete, rather than seventy-five percent, chaos. I didn't mean to jump your ass, Jake. I've had a bad morning."

"Yes, sir. I know, sir," Major Almond said. "No apology is necessary, sir."

Colonel Rickabee turned to McCoy.

"With a three-inch-thick FBI report on you in Major Almond's safe, McCoy, we won't have to waste much time asking and answering questions about your background. And in addition to the official report, I have two personal reports on you. You made one hell of an impression on the boss in Philadelphia."

"Sir?" McCoy asked.

"You apparently delivered quite a lecture on the high state of discipline in the Imperial Japanese Army and how they were going to be formidable foes. Since the one true test of an intelligent man is how much he agrees with you, the boss thinks you're a genius."

" 'The boss,' sir?"

"The chief of intelligence," Rickabee said. "You don't know what I'm talking about, do you?"

"No, sir."

"Let it pass, then," Rickabee said, smiling. "Newly commissioned second lieutenants should not be praised. It tends to swell their heads. I had another personal report on you just a week ago. Ed Banning wrote me from Manila . . . you knew that the fourth has been shipped to the Philippines?"

"No, sir, I didn't."

"Banning said that he thought I should have you transferred to this lash-up and that I should consider, somewhere down the line, even sending you to officer candidate school."

McCoy didn't know how to respond.

In Japanese, Colonel Rickabee said, "I understand you're reasonably fluent in Japanese and Chinese."

"I wouldn't say fluent, sir—"

"Say it in Japanese," Rickabee interrupted.

"I can't read very much Japanese, sir," McCoy said, in Japanese. "And my Chinese isn't much better."

Rickabee nodded approvingly. "That's good enough," he continued in Japanese, and then switched to English. "We can use that talent. But there's a question of priorities. When we knew you were coming here, McCoy, what we planned to do with you was to have you replace Sergeant Ruttman. I want to run him through Quantico, too. He thinks he's been successfully evading it. The truth is that I needed somebody to take his place while he was gone. You seemed ideal to do that. You're a hardnose, and it would give you a chance to see how things are done here. But the best-laid plans, as they say. There are higher priorities. Specifically, the boss has levied on us—and I mean the boss personally, not one of his staff—for three officer couriers. We're moving a lot of paper back and forth between here and Pearl and here and Manila, especially now that the Fourth is in the Philippines. You're elected as one of the three, McCoy."

"Sir, I don't know what an officer courier is."

"There are some highly classified documents, and sometimes material, that have to pass from hand to hand, from a specific officer here to a specific officer someplace else—as opposed to headquarters to headquarters. That material has to be transported by an officer."

"Yes, sir," McCoy said.

"There's one other factor in the equation," Rickabee said. "The Pacific—especially Pearl Harbor, but Cavite too—has been playing dirty pool. We have sent officer couriers out there with the understanding that they would make one trip and then return to their primary duty. What Pearl has done twice, and Cavite once, is to keep our couriers and send the homeward-bound mail in the company of an officer they didn't particularly need. We have lost two cryptographic officers and one very good intercept officer that way."

McCoy knew that a cryptographic officer dealt with secret codes, but he had no ideas what an "intercept" officer was.

"I've complained, of course, and eventually we'll get them back, after everything has moved, slowly, through channels. But I can't afford to lose people for sixty, ninety days. Not now. So there had to be a solution, and Major Almond found it."

McCoy said nothing.

"Aren't you even curious, McCoy?" Rickabee asked.

"Yes, sir."

"Every officer in the Marine Corps is required to obey the orders of any officer superior to him, right?"

"Yes, sir."

"If the orders conflict, he is required to obey the orders given him by the most senior officer, right?"

"Yes, sir."

"Wrong," Rickabee said. "Or at least, there is an interesting variation. There is a small, generally unknown group of people in the Corps who don't have to obey the orders of superior officers, unless that officer happens to be the chief of intelligence. Their ranks aren't even known. Just their name and photo and thumbprint is on their ID cards. And the ID cards say that the bearer is a Special Agent of the Assistant Chief of Staff, Intelligence, USMC, and subject only to his orders."

"Yes, sir."

"Congratulations, Lieutenant McCoy, you are now—or you will be when Ruttman finishes your credentials—a Special Agent of the Assistant Chief of Staff for Intelligence. If anybody at Pearl or Cavite knows, or finds out, that you speak Japanese and decides they just can't afford to lose you, you will show them your identification and tell them you are sorry, but you are not subject to their orders."

Rickabee saw the confusion on McCoy's face.

"Question, McCoy?"

"Am I going to Pearl Harbor, sir?"

"And Cavite," Rickabee said. "More important, I think you will be coming back from Pearl and Cavite."

"And you can get away with giving me one of these cards?"

"For the time being," Rickabee said. "When they catch us, I'm sure Major Almond will think of something else clever."

"Let me make it clear, Lieutenant McCoy," Major Almond said, "that the identification, and the authority that goes with it, is perfectly legitimate. The personnel engaged in courterespionage activity who are issued such credentials are under this office."

"Major Almond pointed out to me, McCoy, that I had the discretionary authority to issue as many of them as I saw fit."

"Yes, sir."

"We don't wish to call attention to the fact that people like you will have them," Rickabee said. "For obvious reasons. You will travel in uniform on regular travel orders, and you will not show the identification unless you have to. You understand that?"

"Yes, sir."

"I don't know how long we'll have to keep you doing this, McCoy," Colonel Rickabee said. "We have a certain priority for personnel, but so do other people. And that FBI background check takes time. And the FBI is overloaded with them. You'll just have to take my word for it that as soon as I can get you off messenger-boy duty and put you to work doing something useful to us, I will."

"Yes, sir."

"What's his schedule, Jake?" Rickabee asked.

"Well, today of course there are administrative things to do. Get him a pistol, get his orders cut. That may run into tomorrow morning. He'll need some time to get his personal affairs in order. But there's no reason he can't leave here on Wednesday night, Thursday morning at the latest. Presuming there's not fifty people ahead of him in San Francisco also with AAA priority, that should put him in Pearl no later than Monday, December eighth, and into Manila on the tenth."

"Is that cutting it too close for you, McCoy?" Colonel Rickabee asked.

"No, sir," McCoy said, immediately.

Rickabee nodded.

"Take him to lunch at the Army-Navy Club, Jake," Colonel Rickabee ordered. "Sign my name to the chit."

"Aye, aye, sir," Major Almond said.

"I like to do that myself," Rickabee said, turning to McCoy. "We don't have time for many customs of the service around here; but when I can, I like to have a newly reported-aboard officer to dinner. Or at least take him to lunch. But I just don't have the time today. Won't have it before you go to Pearl. I'm really sorry."

Then he stood up and offered his hand.

"Welcome aboard, McCoy," he said. "I'm sorry your first assignment is such a lousy one. But it happens sometimes that way in the Corps."

He headed out of his office, and then stopped at the door.

"Get him out of the BOQ before he goes," he said. "If there's no time to find a place for him, have his gear brought here, and we'll stow it while he's gone, until we can find something."

"He's got a room in the Lafayette, sir."

"I'll be damned," Colonel Rickabee said. "But then Ed Banning did say I would find you extraordinary."

For some reason, McCoy thought, it was no longer hard to think of F.L. Rickabee as a lieutenant colonel of Marines.

(Three)

Second Lieutenant Malcolm Pickering, USMCR, was sitting in the maid's room's sole armchair, his feet up on the cot. When Second Lieutenant Kenneth J. McCoy, USMCR, carrying a briefcase, entered the room, Pickering was in the act of replacing a bottle of ale in an ice-filled silver wine-cooler he had borrowed from the bridal suite.

"What the hell are you doing with a briefcase?" Pick asked.

"That's not all," McCoy said. "Wait till I tell—"

Pickering shut him off by holding up his hand.

"Wait a minute," he said. "I've got if not bad then discomfitting news."

"Discomfit me, then," McCoy mocked him. "Fuck up what otherwise has been a glorious day."

"My general thinks you should move into the BOQ," Pickering said.

"Oh, shit!" McCoy said. "What the fuck business is it of his, anyway?"

"He's a nice guy," Pickering said. "He and my father were corporals together, and he stayed in the Corps. He's trying to be nice."

"Sure," McCoy said. "Just a friendly word of advice, my boy. An officer is judged by the company he keeps. Disassociate yourself from that former enlisted man."

"Jesus Christ," Pick said without thinking. "You do have a runaway social inferiority complex, don't you?"

"Fuck you," McCoy said.

"It's not like that at all, goddamn your thick head. What he's worried about is getting you in trouble with Intelligence."

"What?" McCoy asked.

"I don't know if you know this or not," Pickering said. "But the Corps has intelligence agents, counterintelligence agents. What they do is look for security risks."

"No shit?" McCoy asked.

"Listen to me, goddamn you!" Pickering said. "What these guys do is look for something unusual. Like second lieutenants living in hotels like the Lafayette. Expensive hotels. They would start asking where you got the money to pay for the bill."

"Special agents of the Deputy Chief of Staff for Intelligence, USMC, you mean?" McCoy asked, smiling broadly.

"You know about them, then? Goddamn it, Ken, it's not funny."

"It's the funniest thing I heard of all day," McCoy said. He took off his jacket, and then opened the briefcase.

"What the hell are you doing?" Pickering asked.

McCoy took a leather-and-rubber strap arrangement that only after a moment Pickering recognized as a shoulder holster. He slipped his arms in it, and then took a Colt 1911A1 from the briefcase and put it in the holster. Then he put his tunic back on.

"Goddamn you, you haven't listened to a word I've said," Pickering said.

"Well, I may be dumb," McCoy said. "But you're a Japanese spy if I ever saw one. Come with me, young man. If you cooperate, it will go easier on you."

It was some kind of joke, obviously, but Pickering didn't have any idea where the humor lay.

McCoy took a small leather folder from his hip pocket, opened it, and shoved it in Pickering's face.

"Special Agent McCoy," he announced triumphantly. "You're a dead man, you filthy Jap spy!"

"What the hell is that?" Pickering asked, snatching it out of his hand, and then looking at it carefully. "Is this for real? What is it?"

"It's for real," McCoy said. "And it's my ticket to sunny Hawaii and other spots in the romantic Orient."

"It's for real?" Pickering repeated, in disbelief.

"Well, not really real," McCoy said. "I mean it's genuine, but I'm not in counterintelligence. I'm an officer courier. They gave me that so no one will fuck with me on the swift completion of my appointed rounds."

Pickering demanded a more detailed explanation of what had gone on.

"But how did you get involved in intelligence in the first place?"

"That's what I did in China," McCoy said.

It was the first time he had ever told anyone that. He remembered just before he'd boarded the *Charles E. Whaley*, Captain Banning ordering him not to tell anyone in or out of the Corps about it. But that order had been superceded by his most recent order, from Major J.J. Almond:

"You'll have to tell your roommate something, McCoy. You can say where you work, advising him that it is classified information. And what you do, because that in itself is not classified."

And with the 4th Marines gone from Shanghai, there didn't seem to be any point in pretending that he hadn't done what he had done. And it was nice to have an appreciative audience, an audience that had previously believed he had been a truck driver.

"The important thing," he said finally, when he realized that he was tooting his own horn too much, "is that my colonel doesn't want me in the BOQ. So where does that leave us?''

Pickering reached for the telephone.

"This is Malcolm Pickering," he said. "Will you get the resident manager on here, please?"

When the resident manager came on the line, Pickering told him there had been "another change in plans."

"I will need that suite," he said. "Lieutenant McCoy and I will be here for the indefinite future."

They went down to dinner. There Pickering talked about flight school.

"I'm going to take a flight physical Thursday afternoon," he said. "If I pass it, I think I'm going to go for it."

And then they began a lengthy, and ultimately futile, search for a couple of skirts to lift.

It did not dampen their spirits at all. There was always tomorrow, and the day after tomorrow, and the week after that. There were supposed to be twice as many women as men in Washington. . . .

Despite the legend, McCoy said, it had been his experience that a Marine uniform was a bar to getting laid. When he came back from Hawaii and Manila, they would do their pussy-chasing in civilian clothes.

(Four)
Security Intelligence Section
U.S. Naval Communications
Washington, D.C.
1540 Hours, Wednesday, 3 December 1941

The sign on the door said OP-20-G, and there was a little window in it, like a speak-easy. When McCoy rang the bell, a face appeared in it.

"Lieutenant McCoy to see Commander Kramer," McCoy announced

"I'll need to see your ID, Lieutenant," the face said.

McCoy held the little leather folder up to the window. The man took his sweet time examining it, but finally the door opened.

"The commander expected you five minutes ago," the face said. The face was now revealed as a chief radioman.

"The traffic was bad," McCoy said.

He followed the chief down a passageway, where the chief knocked at a door. When he announced who he was, there was the sound of a solenoid opening a bolt.

"Lieutenant McCoy, Commander," the chief said. "His ID checks."

"I'm sure he won't mind if I check it again," a somewhat nasal voice said.

Commander Kramer was a tall, thin officer with a pencil-line mustache. He looked at McCoy's credentials and then handed them back.

"I was about to say that we don't get many second lieutenants as couriers," Kramer said. "That is now changed to 'we don't get to see much identification like that.' "

"No, sir," McCoy said.

"Are you armed, Lieutenant?"

"Yes, sir."

"And you're leaving when?"

"At sixteen-thirty, sir."

"From Anacostia, you mean?"

"Yes, sir. Naval aircraft at least as far as San Francisco."

"You normally work for Colonel Rickabee, is that it?"

"Yes, sir."

"I heard that they had levied him for officer couriers," Kramer said. "I'm sorry you were caught in the net. But it wouldn't have been done if it wasn't necessary."

"I don't mind, sir," McCoy said, solemnly.

Instead of heading around the world by airplane, I would of course prefer to be here in Washington inventorying paper clips. Or better than that, at Camp LeJeune running around in the boondocks, practicing "the infantry platoon in the assault."

"Your briefcase is going to be stuffed," Kramer said. "She was sealing the envelopes just now. I'll have her bring them in."

He pushed a lever on an intercom.

"Mrs. Feller, the courier is here. Would you bring the material for Pearl Harbor in here, please?"

Mrs. Feller?

Ellen Feller backed into Commander Kramer's office with a ten-inch-thick stack of heavy manila envelopes held against her breast.

"Mrs. Feller, this is Lieutenant McCoy," Commander Kramer said.

"The lieutenant and I are old friends," Ellen said.

"Really?"

"We got to know one another rather well in China, didn't we, Ken?"

"You don't seem very surprised to see me," McCoy said.

"I knew you were here," she said. "I didn't expect to see you so soon, but I did hope to see you."

"May I suggest you get on with the document transfer?" Commander Kramer said, a tinge of annoyance in his voice. "Lieutenant McCoy has a sixteen-thirty plane to catch at Anacostia."

There were thirteen envelopes in the stack Ellen Feller laid on Commander Kramer's desk. There was a numbered receipt to be signed for each of them, and McCoy had to place his signature across the tape sealing the flap at the place where it would be broken if the envelope was opened.

It took some time to go through the paperwork and stuff the unyielding envelopes into the briefcase. Enough time for Commander Kramer to regret jumping on both of them.

"Ellen," he said. "If you wished to continue your reunion with the lieutenant, there's no reason you can't ride out to Anacostia with him."

"Oh, I'd like that," Ellen said.

McCoy took the handcuffs from his hip pocket and looped one cuff through the handle of the briefcase, then held out his wrist for Kramer to loop the other cuff around it.

"Have a good trip, Lieutenant," Commander Kramer said, offering his hand. He then held the door for both of them to pass through.

"My coat's just down the corridor," Ellen said.

A Navy gray Plymouth station wagon and a sailor driver waited for them at the entrance. McCoy had ridden over to OP-20-G in the front seat with him, but when the sailor saw Ellen Feller, he ran around and held the back door open for her. McCoy hesitated a moment before he got in beside her, holding the heavy briefcase on his lap.

"You were right," Ellen said, as they drove off.

"About what?"

"That I could probably find a job because I speak Chi-

nese.'' She switched to Chinese. ''The first place I applied
was to the Navy, and they hired me right on. As a translator.
But there's not that much to translate, so I've become sort of
office manager. I'm a GS-6.''

''I don't know what that means,'' McCoy said, relieved
that they could speak Chinese and the driver wouldn't understand them. ''Where's your husband?''

''He's in New York, busy with his work,'' she said.

''You manage to smuggle the vase in all right?'' McCoy
asked

She raised her eyebrows at the question, but didn't answer
it.

''I have a nice little apartment here,'' she said. ''You'll
have to come see it.''

''The last time I saw you, you seemed damned glad to be
getting rid of me.''

''Well, my God, you remember what happened the day
before,'' she said. ''That was quite a shock.''

''Yeah,'' he said, sarcastically. ''Sure.''

''I was upset, Ken,'' she said. ''I'm sorry.''

''Forget it,'' he said. ''Those things happen.''

''I understand why you're . . . angry,'' she said.

He didn't reply.

She turned on the seat and caught his hand in both of hers.

''I said, I'm sorry,'' she said.

''Nothing to be sorry about,'' he said.

''If you're still angry, then there is,'' she said.

''I'm not angry,'' he said.

She rubbed his hand against her cheek and then let him go.

''Not everything that happened the day before was unpleasant, of course,'' she said.

He didn't reply.

''Do you remember what happened just before?''

You were blowing me, that's what happened just before.

''No,'' he said.

''I often think about it,'' she said.

''I don't know what you're talking about,'' McCoy said.

*Fuck you, lady. You get to screw old McCoy just once. I'm
not about to start up anything with you again!*

''Don't you really?'' Ellen asked, and then sat forward on

the seat to give the driver instructions: "Stay on Pennsylvania," she ordered. "It's faster this time of day."

"Yes, ma'am," the driver said.

When she slid back against the seat, her hand went under the skirt of McCoy's tunic and closed around his erection.

"Liar," she said softly.

"For God's sake," he said, pushing her hand away.

"Pity there's not more time, isn't it? But you won't be gone all that long, will you?"

At least with her, I know what she's after. It's not like with Pick's rich-bitch friend.

And thirty minutes in the sack with the old vacuum cleaner, and I won't even be able to remember Miss Ernestine Sage's name, much less remember what she looked like.

"No," he said. "A couple of weeks, is all. No more than three."

"That'll give us both something to look forward to, won't it?" Ellen Feller said.

McCoy reached out for her hand and put it back under the skirt of his blouse.

XV

Until this week, airplanes for Second Lieutenant Malcolm Pickering, USMCR, had been something like taxi cabs. They were there. When you needed to go somewhere you got in one and it took you.

That changed. The Navy medico (more properly, flight surgeon, which Pickering thought had a nice aeronautical ring to it) told him that he met the physical standards laid down for Naval aviators. General McInerney's senior aide-de-camp, himself a dashing Naval aviator with wings of gold, then explained that while there might officially be, say, fifty would-be birdmen in any course of Primary Flight Instruction at the Pensacola Naval Air Station[1], that was something of a fiction. More than the prescribed number were routinely ordered to the shores of the Gulf of Mexico. Experience had taught that a number of students would quickly prove themselves incapable of learning how to fly. By sending extras, the Corps wound up with the desired number after the inept had bilged out.

General McInerney was in a position to have Pickering sent as a member of the supernumeraries. Pickering knew his mother would have a fit when she heard that he was to become an aviator, which was a problem that would be a bit difficult to handle. On the other hand, there was a positive

---

[1]Flight training for Marine aviators is conducted by the U.S. Navy. Marine aviators wear the same gold wings as Naval aviators.

appeal about the prospect of swapping the slush-filled streets of Washington for the white sandy beaches of Pensacola.

On the way home from Anacostia Naval Air Station in McCoy's LaSalle on Friday evening, he stopped at a bookstore, asked for books on aviation (starting with the theory of flight), and bought half a dozen that looked promising.

He was now reading one of them, one with a lot of drawings. The others, stacked up beside his chair, waited for his attention. A small table beside him held a silver pot of coffee. He was attired for a more primitive means of transportation than he was reading about: A tweed jacket with leather patches over the elbows; a plaid cotton shirt open at the collar; a pair of pink breeches; and a pair of Hailey & Smythe riding boots, which rested on a pillow (to preserve the furniture) on the coffee table before him.

He had spent the morning in Virginia aboard a horse. Sort of a fox hunt without either the fox or the ceremony that went with a hunt. Just half a dozen riders riding about the countryside, jumping fences of opportunity.

They were going to sit around in the afternoon and get smashed. Rather nobly, he thought, he had pleaded the press of duty and returned to the hotel to read the airplane books.

The telephone rang, and he looked around for it, a look of annoyance crossing his face as he spotted it, ten feet out of reach. It had taken him some effort to reach his present comfortable position, with his feet just so, and his back just so, and with *The Miracle of Flight* propped up just so on his belly.

He had just begun to grasp the notion that aircraft are lifted into the air because there is less pressure on the upper (curved, and thus longer) portion of a wing than there is on the bottom (flat, and thus shorter) portion of a wing. As the wing moves through the air, it simply follows the path of least resistance, upward, and hauls the airplane along with it. He wasn't entirely sure he fully understood this. He was sure, however, that he didn't want to chat just now with whomever was on the phone, especially since he had to get up to go answer it.

"Yes?" he snapped impatiently, "what is it?"

Oh, shit! It's probably General McInerney. And I was supposed to have answered that, "Lieutenant Pickering speaking."

"Pick?"

It was a female. And a half-second later, he knew which one.

"Hello, Ernie," he said.

"Are you alone? Can you talk?" Ernestine Sage said.

"You have interrupted a splendid orgy, but what's on your mind?"

"I want to talk to you," Ernie Sage said.

"Then talk," he said. "Just make it quick."

"I'll be right up," Ernie Sage said.

"You're here?" he asked, genuinely surprised. "In the hotel?"

"I just happened to be in the neighborhood and thought I'd just pop in," she said, and the phone went dead.

Between the time she hung up and the time he answered her knock at the door, he had considered the possibilities: Certainly this had to do with Ken McCoy. But what would bring Ernie all the way to Washington except true love? And the possibility, not as astonishing when there was time to think it over, that Ernie was in the family way. Could she be sure, so soon? To the best of his recollection, it took several months to be sure about that. It hadn't been that long since he had seen Juliet kissing Romeo in the Grand Central Oyster Bar.

"Hi," Ernie said, when he opened the door. "Don't you look horsey?"

For the first time in a long time, Pickering looked at her as a female, and not as part of the woodwork.

Damned good-looking, he judged. Marvelous knockers. They had obviously grown a good deal since (he now remembered with somewhat startling clarity) he had last seen them, looking down her bathing suit in Boca Raton. He and Ernie must have been thirteen or fourteen at the time.

"Come into my den, as the spider said to the fly."

"You're a hard man to find," she said. "I called your mother, or tried to, and they said she was in Hawaii. So I called your grandfather, and he told me where you were."

"Why do I suspect that you weren't suddenly overcome with an irresistible urge to see me?" Pickering asked.

She looked into his face.

"Where is he?" she asked.

"Where's who?"

"Come on, Pick," she said.

"Ken, you mean?"

"Where is he?"

"In Hawaii, too, come to think of it," Pick said.

"Oh, hell," she said.

"Not to worry," he said. "He will be back."

She looked at his face.

"That's important to you, isn't it?" Pickering asked.

"Don't be a shit about this, Pick, please," Ernie Sage said.

"Okay," he said. "It will be an effort, obviously."

"Do you have something I could have to drink?"

He gestured to the bar.

"Help yourself," he said.

She walked to the bar and made herself a Scotch.

"You want one?" she asked.

"I want one, but . . . oh, what the hell. Yes, please."

She made him a drink, handed it to him, and then sat down on a couch and stirred the ice cubes in her glass with her index finger.

"I never imagined myself doing this," she said, without looking at him.

"Doing what?"

"Running after a boy," she said, and corrected herself: "A man."

"I'm not surprised," Pick said.

She looked at him quickly.

"For one thing, McCoy's quite special," Pick said. "And for another, I saw the two of you in the Oyster Bar."

She did not seem at all embarrassed to hear that. Just curious.

"What were you doing there?"

"McCoy had led me safely through the wild jungles of Quantico," Pickering said, "protecting me from unfamiliar savage beasts. I thought it only fair that I return the favor."

"Protect him from me, you mean? Thanks a lot."

"I didn't know who it was until I saw you," Pickering said.

"Where did you meet him?"

"On a train from Boston," Pickering said. "He had just

escorted prisoners to the Naval Prison at Portsmouth. And then he showed up, wholly unexpected, at Quantico.''

"Why unexpected?"

"Because our peers were . . . our peers. McCoy was a noncom of the regular Marine Corps, just in from years in China.''

"He told me about China," she said. "He took me to a tiny little Chinese restaurant off Mott Street, where he talked Chinese to them.''

"As I say, he's something special.''

"Isn't he?" she said. Then she looked up at him. "Four hours after I met him, I took him to bed.''

"He told me," Pickering said.

"I don't know what you think of me, Pick," Ernie Sage said. "But that's not my style.''

"He told me that, too," Pickering said, gently.

That surprised her. She looked into his face until she was sure that she had not misunderstood him.

"Pretty close, are you? Or did he proudly report it as another cherry copped?''

"Actually, he was pretty upset about it," Pickering said.

"But not too upset to tell you all about it?''

"We are pretty close," Pickering said. "I don't know. It's something like having a brother, I guess.''

"You heard about his brother? The one who was offered the choice of the Marine Corps or jail?''

"I even know that was the choice they gave him, too," Pickering said. "Like I say, Ernie, we're close.''

"Okay, so tell me what happened? I have six letters, all marked 'REFUSED.' ''

"He found out you were rich," Pickering said.

"Oh, God!" she wailed. Then the accusation: "You told him. Why the hell did you have to do that?''

Pickering shrugged his shoulders helplessly and threw up his hands.

"Now I'm sorry that I did," he said.

She turned her face away from him. Then turned back, frowning.

"But I suppose I was thinking that the bad news better come gently, and from me. I didn't want that shocking revelation suddenly thrust upon him.''

"If you came from a background like his, it would upset you, too," Ernie Sage said, loyally. "He has pride, for God's sake. I know he's a fool, but—"

"Did he tell you about the lady missionary?"

"What lady missionary?"

"There was a lady missionary in China who apparently gave him a bad time. Strung him along. Hurt him pretty badly."

"I'd like to kill her," Ernie Sage said, matter-of-factly.

"You've really got it pretty bad for him, don't you?"

"As incredible as it sounds," she said, "I'm in love with him. Okay? Can we proceed from that point?"

"Love, as in 'forsaking all others, until death do you part'?"

"I was disappointed when I found out I wasn't pregnant," she said. "How's that?"

"I hope you know what you're getting into," Pickering said.

"It doesn't matter, Pick," she said. "I have absolutely no control over how I feel about him. I thought that only happened in romantic novels. Obviously, it doesn't only happen in fiction."

"I'm jealous," Pickering said.

"What have you got to be jealous about?" Ernie asked, and then she understood. "You should be," she said. "But that's your problem. What do we do about mine?"

"I don't know," Pickering said. "If you're really sure about this, Ernie, Big Brother will think of something."

"I have never been so sure of anything in my life," she said. "It's either him and me, hand in hand, or to hell with it."

"For what it's worth, with the caveat that I am relatively inexperienced in matters of this kind, I would not say it's hopeless."

Ernestine Sage brightened visibly.

"Really?" she asked.

"Really," Pickering said. "For reasons I cannot imagine, Lieutenant McCoy seemed to be more than a little taken with your many charms."

"God, I hope so," she said, and then asked, "what's he doing in Hawaii?"

"They made him an officer courier," Pickering said. "He carries secrets in a briefcase."

"I never heard of that," she said. "How long did you say he'll be gone?"

"He's going to Hawaii. He got there today. Or will get there today. There is something called the International Dateline, and I've never figured it out. And from there, he's going to Manila, and then back to Hawaii, and then back here."

"And what are we going to do when he gets back here?"

"We'll arrange for him to find you in a black negligee in his bed," Pickering said. "As a Marine officer, he would be duty-bound to do his duty. You can play the ball from there."

"If I thought that would work," she said, "I'd do it."

"I think, Ernie," Pick Pickering said seriously, "that all it would take would be for him to find you sitting there, just like you are now."

She looked at him and smiled. Then she got up and walked to him and kissed him on the cheek.

"And I was really afraid that you'd be a shit about this," she said.

"My God! Me? Pick Pickering? Cupid's right-hand man?"

She chuckled and looked at her watch.

"I was so sure of it, that I reserved a compartment on the three-fifteen to New York. I've still got time to make it."

"Maybe," Pickering said, "you should get some practice riding coach."

She looked at him curiously for a moment until she took his meaning.

"If that's what it takes, that's what I'll do," she said. "But the next time. Not today."

He smiled at her and walked with her to the door, where she kissed him impulsively again.

He had just rearranged himself in the chair with his feet on the pillow and *The Miracle of Flight* propped up on his belly when there was another knock on his door.

"Jesus H. Christ!" he fumed as he went to answer it.

It was Ernie Sage, and he could tell from the look in her eyes that something was terribly wrong.

"A radio," Ernie said. "Have you got a radio?"

"There's one in here," he said. She pushed past him into the sitting room.

She had the radio on by the time he got there.

"Repeating the bulletin," the voice of the radio announcer said, "the White House has just announced that the Navy Base at Pearl Harbor, Hawaii, has been attacked by Japanese aircraft and that there has been substantial loss of life and material."

"Jesus Christ!" Pickering said.

"If he's dead," Ernestine Sage said melodramatically, "I'll kill myself."

"You don't mean that," Pickering said.

"Oh, my God, Pick! Your mother and father are there!"

He hadn't thought of that.

Somehow, he wound up holding her in his arms.

"Everything is going to be all right, Ernie."

"Bullshit!" she said against his chest.

And then it occurred to him that he was a Marine officer and that what he should be doing now was getting into uniform and reporting for duty.

(Two)
Pearl Harbor, Hawaii
7 December 1941

The Japanese task force, which had sailed from Hitokappu Bay in the Kurile Islands, began to launch aircraft at 0600 hours. The task force was then approximately 305 nautical miles from Pearl Harbor. In relation to the task force, Pearl Harbor was on the far side of Oahu Island, the second largest island of the Hawaiian Chain.

Japanese Intelligence was aware that the attack could not be entirely as successful as was initially hoped. In the best possible scenario, essentially all of the United States Pacific Fleet would be in Pearl Harbor. The worst possible scenario was that essentially all of the Pacific Fleet would be at sea. The reality turned out to be between these extremes. All the battleships of the Pacific Fleet were in Pearl Harbor, as well as a number of other ships.

But the seven heavy cruisers and the two aircraft carriers the Japanese had also hoped to find at anchor were at sea. The Japanese knew the composition of the at-sea forces, but not their location.

Task Force 8—an aircraft carrier, three cruisers, and nine

destroyers and destroyer minesweepers—was approximately 200 nautical miles from Pearl. Task Force 3—one cruiser and five destroyers and destroyer minesweepers—was 40 nautical miles off Johnson Island, about 750 nautical miles from Pearl Harbor. Task force 12—one carrier, three cruisers, and five destroyers—was about as far from Pearl Harbor as Task Force 3, operating approximately 400 nautical miles north of Task Force 3.

The decision was made to attack anyway. There was always the chance of detection; the destruction of harbor facilities and airfields was of high priority, and the destruction of one or more battleships would severely limit the capability of the American fleet.

The code command for the attack was "Climb Mount Niitaka 1208."

Approximately 125 nautical miles from Pearl Harbor, the stream of aircraft from the Japanese task force split into two streams. Fifty miles from Oahu, what was now the left stream began to split again, this time into three streams. The first two turned right and made for Pearl Harbor across the island. The third stream continued on course until it was past the tip of Oahu, and then turned toward the center of the island and made an approach to Pearl Harbor from the sea.

Meanwhile, the right stream had broken into two, with one crossing the coastline and making for Pearl Harbor across the island, and the second continuing on course past the island, then turning back to attack Pearl Harbor from the open sea.

The first wave of Japanese bombers struck at 0755 hours and the second at 0900. By then the task force had changed course and was making for the Japanese Inland Sea, hoping to avoid any encounter with carrier-based aircraft from Task Forces 12 and 8 or with land-based aircraft on Oahu. Intelligence reported that at least one squadron of long-range, four-engine B-17 bomber aircraft was en route from the continental United States.

Despite the risk of detection by radio direction finders, shortly after 1030 hours, a priority message from the Japanese task force was radioed to headquarters of the Imperial Japanese Navy in Tokyo: "Tora[2], Tora, Tora." It was the prearranged code for the successful completion of the attack.

[2]Tiger.

(Three)

Although he tried to be very nonchalant about the whole thing, Second Lieutenant K.J. McCoy made his first aerial trip from Anacostia to the West Coast. All in all, once he got used to it, he found it very enjoyable. The airplane was a Navy transport, but so far as he could tell, identical to the Douglas DC-3s used by civilian airlines. The Navy called it an R4-D, yet it even had white napkins on the seats to keep your hair tonic from soiling the upholstery.

It was considerably more plush than the aircraft that carried him from California to Hawaii. As Major Almond had warned, there were a lot of people in California with an AAA priority waiting for air transportation to Hawaii. He could wait, the sergeant told him, until there was a space, but he should understand that when two people had an AAA priority, the one who was senior in rank got the seat. As a second lieutenant, he was liable to wait a long time.

There was another way to get to Hawaii. The Army Air Corps was flying a squadron of B-17 bombers to Hickam Field. They had excess weight capacity because they would not carry bombs, and they were carrying passengers.

"Well, if that's the only way to get there, Sergeant," McCoy said, with feigned reluctance, "I suppose that'll have to be it."

The truth of the matter was that he was a little excited about the idea of flying on a bomber. And the flight started off on an ego-pleasing note, too. When he got to the airbase and presented his orders, a thoroughly pissed-off Air Corps major had to get out of the airplane so that Second Lieutenant McCoy of the Marines with his briefcase and AAA priority could get on.

They were supposed to land at Hickam Field about noon. An hour before that, the radio operator established contact with Hawaii. Moments later the pilot came back in the fuselage and told the crew and the four supercargo passengers (two Air Corps lieutenant colonels, an Army master sergeant, and McCoy) what had happened in Hawaii.

It was all over when the B-17 appeared over Oahu, but some dumb sonsofbitches didn't get the word and shot at the B-17, not just once but twice, the second time as they made their approach to Hickam Field.

The airfield was all shot up. There were burning and burned-out airplanes everywhere, and not one hangar seemed to be intact. An enormous cloud of dense black smoke rose where the Japs had managed to set off an aviation fuel dump.

They had no sooner landed than an Air Corps major appeared in a jeep and told the pilot to take off again for a landing field on a pineapple plantation on one of the other islands. He seemed thoroughly pissed-off when the pilot said he didn't have enough fuel aboard to take off for anywhere.

McCoy very politely asked the Air Corps major about transportation to the Navy Base at Pearl Harbor.

"Good Christ, Lieutenant!" the Air Corps major said, jumping all over his ass. "Are you blind? Pearl Harbor isn't there anymore!"

There was no point arguing with him, so McCoy, the briefcase in one hand and his suitcase in the other, started walking.

There were a lot of other excited types at Hickam running around like chickens with their heads cut off, and even more who seemed to be moving around with strange blank looks in their eyes.

None of them were any help about getting him from Hickam to Pearl Harbor, even after he showed a couple of them his credentials. So McCoy decided that under the circumstances it would be all right to borrow transportation. He found a Ford pickup with nothing in the back and the keys in the ignition.

The MP at the gate held him at rifle point until an officer showed up. The officer took one look at the credentials and let him go.

As he approached the Navy Base, there was even more smoke than there'd been at Hickam Field. When he got to the gate, the Marine MP on duty wasn't any more impressed with the credentials than the Army MP at Hickam Field had been, and he had to wait for an officer to show up before he would let him inside.

While he was waiting for the officer to come to the gate, McCoy asked the MP if the Marine Barracks had been hit, and if so, how badly. The MP wouldn't tell him. That worried McCoy even more. Tommy was in the Marine Barracks, which meant in the middle of this shit. He didn't like to consider the possibility that Tommy had got himself blown up.

The officer who came to the gate passed him through and told him where he was supposed to go.

The Navy seemed a lot calmer than the Air Corps had been, but not a whole hell of a lot. Still, he found a classified-documents officer, a middle-aged, harassed-looking lieutenant commander, who relieved him of the contents of the briefcase. As McCoy was taking off the handcuff and the .45's shoulder holster so he could put them into the briefcase, he asked the lieutenant commander what he was expected to do now.

"Get yourself a couple of hours of sleep, Lieutenant," the lieutenant commander said. "And then report back here."

"Aye, aye, sir."

The lieutenant commander looked at him strangely.

"You got a wife, anything like that, Lieutenant," he said. "You might want to write a letter."

McCoy's eyebrows rose quizzically.

"You're going on to Cavite," he said. "With a little bit of luck, you might get there before the Japs do."

"The Japs hit Cavite, too?"

"And everything else in the Philippines," the lieutenant commander said. "But what I meant is 'before the Japs land in the Philippines.' "

"Is that what's going to happen?" McCoy asked.

The lieutenant commander nodded. Then he shrugged.

"There was a Secret Operational Immediate [the highest-priority communication] a couple of hours ago," the lieutenant commander said. "A Japanese invasion fleet was spotted headed for the Lingayen Gulf. Why the hell it was classified Secret, I don't know. The Japs must know where they are and where they're headed."

"And you think that once I get there, I'm stuck?" McCoy asked.

"I didn't say that," the lieutenant commander said. "But if I was going to fly into Cavite on a Catalina, I'd write my wife, or whatever, a letter."

"Thank you," McCoy said.

McCoy didn't even consider writing his sister. If anything happened to him, she would find out when they sent the insurance check to her kids. Briefly, the notion of writing Pick entered his mind, but he dismissed it. He wouldn't know what the hell to say. And he thought, for a moment, of writing Ernie.

Just for the hell of it, I thought you would like to know I love you.

Then he saw that for what it was, a damned-fool idea, and went looking for Tommy. It wouldn't be exactly what he had had in mind when he'd thought about seeing Tommy at Pearl Harbor. Tommy didn't even know he was an officer. He'd planned to surprise him with that, to see what he did when he saw him with the lieutenant's bars.

He got back in the borrowed pickup and drove to the Marine Barracks.

One of the barracks buildings had been set on fire, but the fire was out. There were bullet marks all over, and in the middle of the drill field was a huge unidentifiable, fire-scarred chunk of metal.

There weren't very many people around. A few noncoms, and some other people. But no troops. Nobody seemed to be running around looking for something to do.

He found the headquarters building and went inside. There was a guard in field gear and steel helmet at the door. He saluted.

And there was a first lieutenant and a PFC in the personnel office.

The lieutenant spotted him before the PFC, who belatedly jumped to his feet.

"Reporting in, Lieutenant?" the lieutenant asked.

"Passing through, sir," McCoy said. For a moment, he thought about dazzling the lieutenant with his special agent credentials, and then decided that wouldn't be right.

"What can I do for you?"

"My brother's assigned to the First Defense Battalion," McCoy said. "I've been wondering about him."

"No doubt," the lieutenant said. He handed McCoy a yellow lined pad.

"This is the first casualty report," he said. "My clerk's about to type it up. All the names on there are confirmed casualties, or KIA, but that's not saying all the casualties are on the list."

"Thank you, sir," McCoy said. He quickly scanned the names. Tommy's name wasn't on it.

"Well, he's not on it," McCoy said. "He's a private. McCoy, Thomas J."

The lieutenant started to consult a list, and then remembered just seeing that name. He consulted another list at the head of which he had penciled, "Cut orders transferring Wake Island."

One of the names on the list of those to be shipped out (as soon as transport could be found) as reinforcements for the small Marine force under Major James Devereux on Wake Island was McCoy, Thomas J.

"He's in the beach defense force," he said. "I don't know where the hell to tell you to look for him."

"I don't have the time, anyway," McCoy said.

"You said you were passing through?"

"On my way to Manila," McCoy explained.

"To the Fourth Marines?"

McCoy nodded. There was no point in telling this guy he was a courier.

"You're going to have a hell of a time finding transport," the lieutenant said.

"Maybe, with a little bit of luck, I won't be able to," McCoy said.

"I did a hitch with the Second Battalion until '39. As an enlisted man. Good outfit."

"I used to be on a water-cooled .30 in Dog Company, First Battalion," McCoy said.

"Look," the lieutenant said. "They're not going to ship you out of here for a couple of days, at least. The odds are, your brother will be back in here. If he gets in, I'll pass the word you're here and send him over to the transient BOQ."

"Thanks," McCoy said.

"What the hell, a couple of old China Marines have to take care of each other, right?"

"Absolutely," McCoy said. "Thanks again."

When McCoy had gone, the lieutenant looked over the list of names of people to be transferred to Wake Island as soon as possible, erased Private Thomas J. McCoy's name from it, and penciled in another. He had no doubt that Wake Island would fall. And besides, no matter where he was, there would be enough war left for Private McCoy. And for his brother. The Philippines were probably going to go under, too, if what happened this morning was any indication. Christ, Hawaii might fall.

This would give them a chance to say hello. Or good-bye.

When McCoy drove back to COMPACFLEET, he parked the borrowed truck where no one could see him get out of it, and then went in search of something to eat.

The lieutenant commander found him in the cafeteria eating a bologna sandwich.

"I just looked all over the goddamn BOQ for you," he said. "That's where I told you to go."

McCoy, his mouth full, held up the bologna sandwich.

The lieutenant commander handed McCoy a briefcase and a pad of receipt forms. Then he took him to Ford Island, where a Catalina was being fueled by hand.

The airbase was a shambles, and the dense cloud of black smoke rising from Battleship Row was visible for a long time after they had taken off.

(Four)
Headquarters, 4th Regiment, USMC
Cavite Naval Base
Manila Bay, Territory of the Philippines
1300 Hours, 9 December 1941

The 4th Marines was just about clear of the area when McCoy finally found it. They had apparently moved out in haste. There was a large pile of packaging material, rough-cut lumber, cardboard, and wood shavings, on what had been the neatly trimmed lawn in front of Regimental Headquarters.

The buildings were deserted. Completely deserted, McCoy thought, until he was nearly run down by the colonel, trailed by the sergeant-major, as he turned a corner.

They were in khakis, no field scarves, wearing web belts with .45s dangling from them, and tin hats. Both of them had '03 Springfields slung over their shoulders.

McCoy was in greens, with a leather-brimmed cap.

The colonel's eyebrows rose when he saw McCoy.

"I know you. Who are you?" the colonel demanded.

McCoy popped to attention.

"Corporal McCoy, sir!" he barked.

"Shit," the sergeant-major said, and laughed out loud.

"Lieutenant McCoy, sir," McCoy said.

"I'll be damned," the colonel said. "What the hell is
going on, McCoy? *Lieutenant*?"

"I just graduated from Platoon Leader's Course, sir."

"And they assigned you back here?" the colonel asked,
incredulously.

"No, sir," McCoy said. "I'm an officer courier. I just got
in. I thought I'd . . . come by and say hello to Captain
Banning."

"Jesus H. Christ!" the colonel said, and shook his head
and marched out of the building.

(Five)
Santos Bay, Lingayen Gulf
Luzon, Territory of the Philippines
0515 Hours, 10 December 1941

Captain Edward J. Banning lay behind a quickly erected
sandbag barrier at the crest of the hill leading down to the
beach.

The day was going to be cloudless. Cloudless and probably
hot.

It was entirely likely that he would die here today, possibly
even this morning. Behind a sandbag barrier on a hot, cloudless day.

The beach was being defended by two companies of Marines. They had not had time (or material) to mine the ap-
proaches to the beach. They had four water-cooled .30-caliber
Brownings, six air-cooled .30-caliber Brownings, and half a
dozen mortars. Somewhere en route, allegedly, were two
75-mm cannon from a Doggie-officered, Philippine Scout
Field Artillery Battery.

A mile offshore were two dozen Japanese ships, half mer-
chantmen converted to troop transports, half destroyers.

At first light, they were supposed to have been attacked by
Army Air Corps bombers. Banning was not surprised that
they had not been. The Japs had wiped out the Air Corps in
the Philippines after it had been conveniently lined up on
airfields for them. It had occurred to some Air Corps general
that since there was a chance of sabotage if the planes were in
widely dispersed revetments, they could be more "economi-
cally" guarded if they were gathered together in rows.

They had been all lined up for the Japs when they came in.

There would be no bombers to attack the Japanese invasion force, and the Japanese landing force would not be repelled by two companies of Marines and a handful of .30-caliber machine guns.

These two companies of the 4th Marines would die here today, in a futile defense of an indefensible beach.

And the rest of the regiment would die on other indefensible beaches.

He was resigned to it.

That's what he had been drawing all his pay for, for all those years, so he would be available for a situation like this.

He heard movement behind him and turned to see what it was, and had trouble believing what he saw.

It was Corporal "Killer" McCoy, without headgear, wearing a khaki shirt and green trousers, staggering under the load of a BAR (Browning Automatic Rifle, Caliber .30–06) and what looked like twenty or more magazines for it.

"What the hell are you doing here?" Banning asked.

With what looked like his last ounce of energy, McCoy set the BAR down carefully on the sandbags and then collapsed on his back, breathing heavily, still festooned with bandoliers of twenty-round magazines for the BAR.

It was only then that Banning saw the small gold bars pinned to McCoy's collar.

"I found the BAR and the Ammo at a checkpoint," McCoy breathed, still flat on his back. "Whoever was manning the checkpoint took off."

"What are you doing here?" Banning asked. "And wearing an officer's shirt?"

"I thought you knew," McCoy said. "I went to the Platoon Leader's Course."

"No, I didn't know," Banning said. "But what the hell are you doing here?"

"I came in as a courier," McCoy said. "Now that I am here, I guess I'm doing what you're doing."

He rolled onto his stomach and raised his head high enough to see over the sandbags.

"Jesus Christ, they're just sitting out there! Isn't there any artillery?"

"There's supposed to be, but there's not," Banning said. "There was also supposed to be bombers."

"Shit, we're going to get clobbered!"

"Did somebody order you up here, McCoy?" Banning asked.

"No," McCoy said simply. "But I figured this is where I belonged."

"Where are you supposed to be?"

"They told me to hang around the Navy Comm Center, in case there was a way to get me out of here. But that's not going to happen."

"You've got orders ordering you out of the Philippines?" Banning asked. McCoy nodded. "You goddamned fool! I'd give my left nut for orders like that."

McCoy looked at him curiously.

Perhaps even contemptuously, Banning thought.

"Get your ass out of here, McCoy," Banning said.

McCoy didn't respond. Instead he picked up Banning's binoculars and peered over the sandbags through them.

"Too late," he said. "They're putting boats over the side."

He handed Banning the binoculars.

Banning was looking through them when the tin cans started firing the preassault barrage. The first rounds were long, landing two, three hundred yards inland. The second rounds were short, setting up plumes of water fifty yards offshore.

The third rounds would be on target, he thought, as he saw the Japanese landing barges start for the beach.

The first rounds of the "fire for effect" barrage landed on the defense positions close to the beach.

The fucking Japs knew what they were doing!

When the first of the landing barges was five hundred yards off shore, maybe six hundred yards from where they were, McCoy brought it under fire.

The noise of the BAR going off so close to Banning's ear was painful as well as startling. He turned to look at McCoy. McCoy was firing, as he was supposed to, short three-, four-, five-round bursts, aimed bursts, giving the piece time to cool a little as he fired.

He's probably hitting what he's shooting at. But it's like trying to stamp out ants. There's just too many of them. And in a minute, some clever Jap is going to call in a couple of rounds on us. And that will be the end of us.

Captain Edward J. Banning's assessment of the tactical situation proved to be correct and precise. Two minutes later, the first round landed on their position, so close to him that the shock of the concussion caused him to lose control of his sphincter muscle. He didn't hear the sound of the round explode, although he heard it whistle on the way in.

It's true, he thought, surprised, just before he passed out, *you don't hear the one that gets you.*

Banning awoke in great pain, and in the dark, and he couldn't move his right arm. He sensed, rather than saw, that he was no longer on the crest overlooking the beach. Then he felt his body and learned that he was bandaged. He was chilled with panic at the thought that he was blind, but after a moment, he could make out vague shapes.

He lay immobile, wondering where he was and what he was expected to do. And then there was light.

One of the vague shapes moved to him and put a matter-of-fact hand on his neck to feel for a heartbeat.

"McCoy?"

"Yes, sir."

"Where the hell are we?"

"In the basement of some church," McCoy said.

"You brought me here?"

"The sonsofbitches dropped one right on us," McCoy said, without emotion. "I don't know what the hell happened to the BAR, but it was time we got the hell out of there."

"Did you get hit?"

"I took a little shrapnel in the side," he said. "They just pulled it out.."

"Where are the Japanese?" Banning asked.

"Christ only knows," McCoy said. "They went by here like shit through a goose."

"We're behind their lines?"

"Yes, sir."

"This may sound like a dumb question, but what kind of shape am I in?"

"We got you pretty well doped up." McCoy said. "The Filipino—she's a nurse, the one that took the shrapnel out of me—says you shouldn't be moved for a couple of days."

"Then what happens?" Banning asked.

"They say we probably can't make it back through the Jap lines. So when you can move, they're going to take us up in the mountains, and maybe off this island onto another one. Mindo something."

"Mindinao," Banning furnished.

"That's right."

"What happened to the Marines on the beach?"

"They were gone before we got hit," McCoy said.

God forgive me, I have absolutely no heroic regrets that I did not die with the regiment. I'm goddamned glad I'm alive, and that's all there is to it.

"Do you think you could make it through the Japanese lines?" Banning said.

"You can't go anywhere for a while," McCoy replied.

"That's not what I asked," Banning said.

"What the hell is the point?" McCoy asked. "I think I'd much rather go in the hills for a while and see how I could fuck them up. If I go back, they'll just give me a platoon, and the same thing will happen to me as happened to those poor bastards on the beach yesterday."

"The point, Lieutenant McCoy, is that you are a Marine officer, and Marine officers obey their orders. You have two that currently affect you. The first is to leave the Philippines."

McCoy chuckled.

"Who's going to enforce that one? They'd have to come get me."

"I am," Banning said. "This is an order. You will make your way through Japanese lines and report to the proper authorities so that you may comply with your basic orders to leave the Philippines."

"You're serious, aren't you?" McCoy asked, genuinely surprised.

"You bet your ass, I'm serious, Lieutenant. You better get it through your head that you'll fight this war the way the Corps tells you to fight it, not the way you think would be nicest."

"And what happens to you?"

"I am in compliance with my orders. I was ordered to resist the Japanese invasion. I'll continue to do that, as soon as I am physically able."

"This sounds like one of those dumb lectures at Quantico," McCoy said.

"Maybe you should have paid closer attention to those dumb lectures," Banning said.

"Shit," McCoy said.

"Has it ever occurred to you, goddamn you, that you can do a hell of a lot more for this war as an intelligence officer than you could running around in the boondocks ambushing an odd Jap here and there?"

"So could you, Captain."

"But I can't move, and you can."

McCoy, several minutes later, asked once more: "You really think I should go back and try to get back to the States?"

"Yes, goddamnit, I do."

"Aye, aye, sir," McCoy said. "As soon as it gets dark, I'll go."

(Six)
Quarters 3201
U.S. Marine Corps Base, Quantico, Virginia
14 December 1941

Elly Stecker knew what was happening when she saw Doris Means at her door with her husband, but she pretended she didn't. Even after she saw the staff car parked behind the Means's Lincoln on the street.

"Is Jack home, Elly?" Doris asked.

"Jack!" Elly called brightly. "It's Colonel and Mrs. Means!" Then she turned and said, "Excuse me. Please come in."

Jack came to the door to the living room in his shirt sleeves.

He seemed to know, too, right off, Elly thought. But he didn't say anything out of the ordinary.

"Good evening, sir," he said.

"We've got a telegram, Jack," Colonel Means said.

"Yes, sir?"

Colonel Means took it from the crown of his cap and extended it to Stecker.

"Would you read it, please, sir?"

Means cleared his throat.

"The Secretary of the Navy deeply regrets to inform you that your son, Ensign Jack NMI Stecker, Jr., USN, was killed in action aboard the U.S.S. *Arizona* at Pearl Harbor, Hawaii, 7 December 1941. Frank Knox, Jr. Secretary of the Navy."

Captain Jack NMI Stecker, USMCR, stood there at attention a moment, rigidly; then his body seemed to tremble, and then the sobs got away from him. Making a noise much like a wail, he fled into his living room.

"Jesus Christ, Elly," Colonel Means said. "I'm sorry."

(Seven)
The Madison Suite, the Lafayette Hotel
Washington, D.C.
2215 Hours, 17 January 1942

McCoy pushed open the door and threw his suitcase in ahead of him.

"Pick? You here?"

There was no response. He went to Pick's bedroom and pushed the door open. The bed was made.

He shrugged and went to the bar and poured two inches of Scotch in a glass and drank it down. And then poured another two inches into the glass. He was so fucking tired he could barely stand, which meant he would not be able to get to sleep. He didn't know why the hell it was, but that's the way it was.

They'd sent him out of the Philippines on a submarine. The sub had gone to Pearl. Stopping only for fuel, he had flown directly from Pearl, via San Francisco, here. His clothes had not come off for sixty hours. And he was so fucking tired he hadn't gone to see Ellen Feller, although he was convinced that was the only way he was going to get Miss Rich Bitch out of his mind.

"Welcome home," Ernie Sage said.

She was standing in the door to his bedroom, wearing a bathrobe.

Jesus Christ, she's beautiful!

"What are you doing here?"

"You can't get a hotel room in Washington," she said. "Pick's letting me stay here."

"Oh," he said.

"When did you come back?"

"About an hour ago," he said.

"Is it as bad as they say?"

"It's pretty fucking bad, lady, I'll tell you that."

"I was worried about you," she said. Then she raised her eyes to his: "Goddamn you, we thought you were dead!"

"No," he said. "Why did you think that?"

"Because there was a cable that said, 'Missing and presumed dead,' that's why."

"I was behind the lines for a while," he said. "They must have sent another cable when I got to Corregidor."

"And you think that makes it right? *Goddamn* you, Ken!"

"Why should you give a damn, one way or the other?"

"Because I love you, goddamn you!"

"You don't know what you're saying," he said.

"You'll get used to it in time," she said.

"I said, you don't know what you're saying," McCoy said. She ignored it. "What happens to you now?" she asked.

"I'll get sent back out there, sooner or later."

"So we have between now and sooner or later," she said. "That's better than nothing."

"Will you knock that off?"

"Meaning 'stop'?"

"You got it."

"You didn't feel a thing? I was just a piece of ass? One more cherry to hang on the wall?"

"Goddamnit, don't talk like that."

"I want to put my arms around you," she said.

"You wouldn't want to do that, I smell like a horse."

"Just as long as you don't smell of perfume," she said. "That I couldn't handle."

"I thought of you," he said. "I couldn't get you out of my mind."

"Me either," she said. "Then what the hell are we waiting for?"

"I don't know," he said. Then he said, "Jesus, when I saw you there I thought I was dreaming!"

She walked to him and took his hand and guided it inside her bathrobe.

"No dream," she said. "Flesh and blood."

After that he forgot that he smelled like a horse. And she didn't mind.

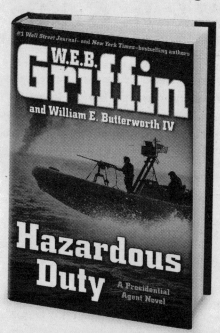

THE *NEW YORK TIMES*
BESTSELLING SERIES
THE CORPS
W.E.B. Griffin
Author of the bestselling BROTHERHOOD OF WAR series.

**THE CORPS chronicles the most determined branch of the
United States armed forces—the Marines. In the same gripping
style that has made the BROTHERHOOD OF WAR series so
powerful, THE CORPS digs deep into the hearts and souls of the
tough-as-nails men who are America's greatest fighting force.**

penguin.com